LATE AND SOON

Carroll & Graf Publishers
An Imprint of Avalon Publishing Group Inc.
245 West 17th Street
New York, NY 10011

AVALON
publishing group incorporated

Copyright © 2005 by Robert J. Hughes

First Carroll & Graf edition 2005

Library of Congress Cataloging-in-Publication Data is available.

ISBN: 0-7867-1588-X

Interior design by Jamie McNeely
Printed in the United States of America
Distributed by Publishers Group West

*To my mother*

# ACKNOWLEDGMENTS

I am grateful for all who helped me in the writing of my novel and the reading of my manuscript, including S. J. Rozan, Paul Gruber, Catherine McWeeney, Steven Blier, James Russell, Michael Carroll, David Ebershoff, Adriana Trigiani, Matt Murray, Heidi Rosenau, Todd Doughty, Ted Gideonse, and Don Weise. I should also like to thank Diana Phillips of Sotheby's, who vetted my take on the auction world, Alexandra Peers, who taught me so much about the business of art, and especially Edmund White, for his encouragement, extraordinary generosity, and unerring ear. For art-historical information, I relied on public sources and Sotheby's research, and I found *James Tissot: Victorian Life/Modern Love* by Nancy Marshall and Malcolm Warner to be particularly helpful on Tissot's paintings as they relate to my novel. Any mistakes are the author's.

*What is it now with me*
*And is it as I have become?*
*Is there no state free from the boundary lines*
*Of before and after?*

—John Ashbery

# AFTER LEONARDO

The noises bounced off the floor and the gleam of Empire busts, and mingled amid the Vivaldi, the clatter of glasses, the braying guffaws of the bankers, the cawing of society wraiths. Five more minutes. Then she'd go. But she was already too late: Claire spotted Tobias, ringed by votives at a candlelit table, trying to flag a waiter. Italianate canapés floated by, tidbits, morsels, mushrooms. She caught his eye, shrugged her eyebrows, thought she conspired with amusement. Her ex-husband, Peter, had left her for him.

She had been idling, if one could call it that, wondering whether to approach anyone else, her chattering acquaintances, flush with the crowd. These sameish museum openings could pale, but still, she was drawn to them, for the art, the sense of belonging, even the crowds, though she fluttered through them alone. And they were held at night, which she preferred. She detested the day at the museum, this one, anyway, the throngs were worse, if less soigné, than at this clamorous cocktail party, than any afternoon thick with school groups and wide tourists. After dark, even the haunted, artificial, not-ideal light did not matter. To her, anyway, as she preferred so often the artificial illumination, the manufactured glow, the flattering dimness. And for a drawing show, brightness mattered

1

less. The drawings here, tonight, were after da Vinci, and before him. Studies and drawings of his circle, the influenced, the guided, the admirable. The taut muscles of the facial studies, the stretch of a corpse's rictus, the gaping maw, ferocious musculature, detailed architectural renderings, architectonic physiognomy, in sepia ink, faded paper, tattered, even; they were sublime, though, moments of rendering. She had particularly admired a study of hands, in various curls or cupped positions. She was conscious of hands, her own being so unsatisfactory, rather plump. An ideal in another century, but now, well . . . plump. Claire often found herself studying hands in portraits. Ingres' Madame d'Haussonville, with her dimpled fingers. Now *those* were plump hands. But sensitive, with seductive innocence, if anyone were ever innocent in Ingres, his portraits probed so deeply that he elicited something that the sitter would probably have preferred unexamined. These "after Leonardo" hands, by whom she couldn't remember—a professional lapse— had a gestural evanescence that moved her, unexpectedly, like a remembered fleeting emotion, the tumult of her life a few years ago, perhaps. The curve of the fingers, something, recalled those faraway days.

The exhibition was large, cluttered by curatorial zeal, which happened when experts got their hands on so much good stuff that they couldn't let go of any. She caught up briefly with one of the show's organizers, who had nattered on in exhaustion and triumph about the tricky negotiations from all over, the wily Vatican, the possessive Louvre, the spinsterish National Gallery, a retinue of geopolitical clichés. The curator herself, blonde, willowy Anna de Los Angeles, hailed from Chile, and besides her native Spanish spoke Italian, German, and English with an annoying accented charm. Thin hands, too. Claire remembered thinking her own unkind cliché about her, and smiled.

"You look like a Leonardo face, caught in a private joke." It was Tobias. He gave her a wan grin.

"Toby," she said, kissing his cheek. "Is Peter here?"

"No," he said, drawing it out. He looked around, as if to check. "He won't be here."

The way he said this, with more ostinato to his sighing than usual, prompted her to ask if anything were wrong.

He looked at her, and held her eye. "He's left me." He gulped some wine, his glass holding a smear of fingerprints, glinting from the flickers.

"Toby, I'm so sorry. Is it true?"

"True as can be."

"When?"

"Yesterday. Well, he told me yesterday."

She flashed back to her own similar scene, when Peter had told her he was a) Gay and b) Leaving. c) Toby, was the third revelation. The kind of tableau vivant one always carries, like a fire, a catastrophe, a crash. Here, though, she felt the hint of well, not triumph exactly. Yes, actually, triumph. Hah. So now he's left you, too, she thought. What she said, though, was, "Has he moved out?"

"He hasn't moved out. It's . . . it's awkward." Toby and Peter lived together about ten blocks north of her, at 104th Street, an apartment of clashing interests in brokered taste. She wondered who was going to give up the place, or be forced out. He hailed a passing waiter, finally, and snared a fresh glass. "Kind of rough." He looked at her. "This. The situation. I'm sorry to spring it on you."

He looked around the room, and came back to her eyes. "I know it's weird," he said, "but I'd hoped to run into you."

Tobias hadn't stolen Peter away from her those years ago, as much as given him an out, the out. He'd already been gone. Mentally. Physically. Geographically, later. That was five years ago. A

3

world away and time. She'd minded less the abandonment than her own ignorant denial. Claire was easily duped; the self-deception that believes the lie, she knew. She innately trusted, despite her training on matters of provenance, research, authenticity, she wanted to believe people, if not their possessions or acquisitions. She had a perceptive sympathetic emotiveness that ran along with her speculative tendency, or maybe it was an appraising judgmentalism. She was unsure.

She and Peter had not had the happiest marriage. But happy enough when one person believed the lie the other lived. Thinking of it now, with Toby suddenly in dilemma here, she remembered how, even after finding out, she didn't want to lose what she did have, even that unhappiness. The moments counted, needed cherishing. In spite of his growing isolation, her dawning realization, their disintegrating relationship, what she hoped to maintain, in some way, was her sense of enchantment: illusory, feeble, wrongheaded. No, she really had been happy, for a time. What she wanted to remember, by being approachable, by staying in touch, by being civil, by being truly—she hoped—kind, was herself then, however deluded, and herself now, in a temporal coexistence. She'd hoped not to be bitter. She'd hoped not to be like so many couples who'd broken up, who never spoke, who swept aside what they had had in the acrimony of remorse at time wasted, love squandered. She kept reminding herself of this, still, as Toby relied on her shoulder, ex-to-ex, as if the threat of becoming bitter mattered. But it did; it might turn her into her sister, an angry educator for whom whimsy was sulfurous and bitterness fueled achievement. It had been hard enough to will herself to move forward without forgetting, than to let down her guard and submit to anger. She wanted to trust herself to be better than she thought she had the capacity for being.

And Toby. Stranded here like she had been. But differently, of course. He'd only had to learn of Peter's gadfly emotions, if that is what had happened, if that is what they were—she thought so, but she'd been wrong, of course, before. This was different than with her; she'd had to endure the awakening. She'd had to become forgiving, the picture of urbanity, so chic, the ex, so art world, kiss-kiss, change partners. She'd become quite blasé about it all, she was sure of it. But she wasn't sure of exactly how that delicacy of avoidance had played into her ongoing emotional life.

Claire had liked Tobias, despite herself, had admitted defeat, had moved on. She hadn't expected him to be what he was, she had envisioned a male version of herself. But his groundedness charmed her, it was actually based on reality—rather than her shaky cognizance of the world, not the work world, but the emotional world. Or to her, perhaps, his reality seemed like a reality that carried more weight than hers, so she succumbed, as it were, to it.

Following her divorce, she had kept up with Peter and Tobias, friendly first as in not crossing the street when seeing them together, friendly later as in awkward dinner, friendly recently as in meaning to call. They tended to meet often enough in their circles, anyway, at openings, previews, sales. Tobias, a video curator for PS1, Peter a dealer in antiques. She was an auction house specialist in nineteenth-century paintings, and Old Masters. They could have been *Design for Living* minus badinage and glamour, joy, insouciance.

In any event, Tobias was smart and, somehow, over the years, she became his occasional confidante, ex-to-ex, with the occasional Peter mishap or misfire or miscue or whatever. Peter often had to explain himself, and Toby sometimes needed the glossary. Claire sometimes provided the meanings, which was funny, now, since she couldn't for the life of her provide them when she was married to him. Toby was often easier to talk to than Peter had been, and Claire had the liberty of no past history to prompt her impatience.

He'd sought her advice, he'd shown her kindness. The kindness of the vanquisher, but still. She thought, too, that her confidante role was one she played throughout her life, her career, even—and she was a confidante who had so little actual regard, she thought, for the essential other humanness of those who chose her for verbal intimacies. She didn't know if her demeanor—a kind of hesitant acceptance of the suggestive other—led people to sense demureness that suggested depth of feeling.

She looked around for a place where they could speak. "Do you mind?" she asked him, leading him back toward the exhibition galleries, which had emptied, the remaining guests drifting toward the reception. She felt comfortable around the drawings, positioned stiffly in their plastic walls, in the quieting hall. The lights were low, the yammering gone.

"So," she said, sitting on one of the benches. "Tell me what's been going on."

"The same old humiliation. Somebody else."

She waited for him to speak. She would not sympathize with his humiliation, having suffered her own, even if only indirectly through him way back when. She'd been, what, twenty-seven? She'd been young, but too old to be so duped. She felt since then that she'd aged more than her peers, even the married ones—or especially them, with their children, and their husbands, underfoot.

"It's been going on a month. He says. Longer, I think." Tobias stood and walked on to a drawing, a gathering of instruments, various blades from different angles. He put his hands behind his back and peered, as if suddenly lost in contemplation of the weapons. Claire wondered if the new person would be as much of a surprise to Toby as Toby had been to her. He turned around to face her. A guard ambled by, a reminder that the gallery was soon to close. "He's a cop," he said.

6

"A cop?"

"I know. Actually a detective, I think. A fantasy. He lives with his mother in a brownstone, I think, in Brooklyn. I don't know how it can last. But I don't think Peter thinks of that. I don't know what he thinks of. Anyway, this cop was working crowd control way downtown." He clasped his hands again, behind his back, looked around the still gallery. "I wish I could say it was tragic, but it isn't. It's just unfortunate. A sordid commonplace."

"Not so much," Claire said. "Not for us. For him, maybe."

They fell into a silence, a momentary pause that became a quiet with the shimmer of reflected sounds from the hall beyond. They held from each other, from continuing to speak—the delicacy of his feelings for her, perhaps; or, she thought, her reticence in actually offering the bromides of the adviser. But people in the aftermath of a significant event fail to speak, often, as if what they'd borne witness to couldn't be expressed even in the pleasantries of conversational diversion. This was momentous enough for anyone—but, and she was cruel, she thought, these things happen. She felt that, having anguished through her own wasted romance, she should have somehow prepared those she knew so that they might learn from her stoicism.

"Who was thinking of you?" Tobias said. "Back then. I wasn't."

She hadn't expected him to speak just then, wandering through her own reverie. No one had thought of her then, either; she had thought little enough of herself.

Back at the reception, the crowd had thinned out a little. The musicians continued on, a baroque trifle undulating and introspective around them. "Things don't just blow over," he said. "They sort of fade, or you let them matter less. I'm waiting for when this will seem less painful."

It had taken her a long time even to think without anger. But it had actually been sorrow, or loss. She liked to think it was sorrow rather than rage at Peter's treachery. At what might have been, what she did not have. It was months before she was less preoccupied by various aspects of it. She realized now, here, it had preoccupied her to some extent for years, like the prospect of getting older, but obliquely. It was as if she expected the experience to have a receding, vanishing point, but it never did. It was always there, triggered by circumstance, a quotidian triviality. And for someone who remained in so many ways still so trusting, each new person had, at some level, the potential for undermining her trust. She knew her wariness hid behind her wish to believe.

"You know," Tobias said. "In the years I've known you, you've never had a long relationship, or any you've told me about."

"Should I have? No, I guess I haven't. I know I haven't. Someday. You'll know."

"Well."

"I've been . . . guarded. I know. Mr. Right . . ." she trailed off.

"Or Ms. Right."

"Or her. Unlikely. But no." She looked into the vague middle distance for a moment. "I could rely on saying the good ones are taken, but they're not. The good ones—I don't know where they are. The bad ones are taken."

"That's just the bitterness talking," he said.

"Oh, right. Everyone feels that a woman always looks for the relationship, the husband. And I don't know what I do want, exactly. I just see such odd people together and wonder. I do miss moments. For me it's so much about yearning, like the Wagner song, 'Träume.' Do you know it?"

"Unless it's been sung by Björk, no."

"It's just the most haunting song about dreaming, dreaming of love—building to a fantasy of it, all yearning and expectation.

There's a line about sinking to the grave after finding a dream. Kind of like Björk, actually—it's got that kind of loopy intensity. In the German, even in the German—I mean, even without knowing the German, it sounds sublime."

"Even better in Icelandic English."

"Sometimes, I feel the yearning is more real than the actual. Once you're in a relationship, it's different."

"No, no," he said. "You still yearn. For someone better, or someone else, or a different life."

"Well, we never get anywhere, then, do we?" she said.

They drifted toward the exit, their feet making satisfying clacks on the empty marble, and headed onto the street. It had rained and sleeted and frozen; the steps down to Fifth Avenue were puddled with gelled slushy footprints. They didn't want to part, not yet. Though Claire had hoped for her usual evening alone, she didn't want to leave Tobias. "Come over," she said, after they'd been debating about cabs. "We can talk about our ex."

That was unlikely, given how they had only talked about him when one of them was still involved with him. And less likely that once having broached the subject inside, Toby would talk again about being hurt, with her. She couldn't anticipate bonding over their loss, here.

"You know that Frank is coming for a few days," she said to Tobias.

"I didn't," he said.

Claire wasn't sure whether she'd told Peter or not, and if she had, Peter might have neglected to tell Toby. Or forgotten, or withheld information, which was more likely. She wasn't even sure Frank had told Peter. The brothers had a sometimes prickly relationship. During her marriage, though, Claire had become close to Frank—as close as one can get to a priest, which is pretty close without being intimate. He was a Franciscan, she recalled—or he had been, since he had left the order a couple of years ago. Frank had married them, and in the week leading up to the wedding she and he had chatted often. She learned more of Peter's childhood, his late parents, through him than her husband.

Though he expressed tolerance for Peter, he said, Frank seemed to Claire to hold his brother responsible for his desire—as if it were a choice rather than innate. Frank had an aloof hidden—well, not so hidden—judgmental nature that he pretended he suppressed or even got the better of, that suggested itself in his further distancing of himself from his only sibling. She didn't remember Frank's ever having spent a holiday with Peter and Tobias. She didn't know if he'd even been asked or even if it had been approached. But after Peter had come out and left her, Frank had called to sympathize.

"If I had known, I never would have married you," he had told her. Idiotically, she thought.

"You're not helping," she'd said, and the conversation had turned toward how she might find solace, in meditation. She'd prayed only that she might learn to cope. She'd been too mortified at her predicament to think beyond her present. Still, she had appreciated his call, but even in the cloud of her dismay she had been irritated by Frank, in his condemnation of not just the situation, but the reason—his brother—so tired an intolerance that she felt worthy enough herself to have overcome. She herself had been obtuse, but she had realized she didn't want to be married to unhappiness. She had wished it were different, but she'd accepted what had happened. Thinking back on it, she didn't ascribe any nobility of character to her behavior; it was more dignity through passivity. She'd seemed collected because she'd been too numb to react, and she'd come across as stoic when her mortification kept her silent. Later on, after the initial ugliness of unwanted emotional turmoil, she'd become used to the idea of the otherness of Peter's life, and after she had stopped wondering what he was doing at certain times of the day, when she'd inured herself to the prospect of someone else's romantic life, she considered the possibility of change. Even in bouts of self-righteousness—and she knew she was prone to thinking herself proudly benevolent—she couldn't sustain the energy needed for outrage. Scorn came more easily, but it frittered itself away, too, untended. So when Frank expressed his support through his own outrage, she had little patience. She even urged him to reach out to Tobias. But he'd kept his distance, wrapped in the discourse of the cosseted academic, the affect of clerical life, or the after-affect of one. Tobias had a strange respect for Frank, even suffering his slights. He'd accorded him respect that she couldn't comprehend. He, as fervent a nonbeliever as she knew, respected the vocation of a believer, and didn't react other than in sympathy when Frank left the order. Even when the very idea of priesthood had become risible or, worse, sinister, he tended not to mock the religious orders. She wondered whether his background—he was the son of actors who worshiped at the altar of more worldly superstitions—allowed him to be free of the blithe abuse many reared in religion felt later in life.

For herself, she felt the opposite. But for her awareness of it, she might have become one of Barbara Pym's excellent women, spinsterish, hovering around the parish hall, eager to help, anxious for the flakes of spirituality bestowed by grateful clergy like so much dandruff on black-suited shoulders, and the grudging thanks and catty envy of the parishioners. This tended to happen in cities other than New York, she felt, in villages, in England, but she'd seen aspects of it here. One woman in her neighborhood, not an excellent woman by any discerning but a solitary and devout churchgoer, Claire had seen at early Mass (when she'd had the wherewithal or had felt guilty enough to drag herself to it). She lived near her, at a residence for women, one of the few such places that seemed to remain in the city. The woman had the figure of the once-shapely, and dressed as if she either disregarded such earthly concerns or, more likely, lacked a sense of shame. She favored tightish blouses of the pink family that gave outline to her wattles as she waddled like a white Hottentot up the block, slowly, surely, serenely unobservant. On Sundays, she wore white gloves—gloves!—and carried her purse—a handbag, really, the kind favored by black Baptist grandmothers—draped over her crook'd arm. She must have been about forty-five, Claire thought, with a sense of style circa Selma 1965. Her head was topped by a tiny mantilla of white lace, and her stringy hair—at least it looked clean and at least she wasn't wearing a huge flowered hat—floated around her face like fiberglass insulation. She would pray with her arms held out, palms upward, as if to receive the grace that was denied Claire, who found herself observing the woman's worship with guilty disdain and a little regret at her own lack of concentration, her rambling divagations amid the tired discourse of the sermon. She had toyed, very briefly, with the idea of joining her local parish, if only because she admired the Guastavino arches within the church's mock Romanesque walls. But she had cured herself of any further action after spending a watery evening among the dingy cardigans and sensible black sneaker-shoes of the rosary ladies, who had met to decide how best to organize a fundraiser for the purchase of altar vestments. She was astonished at the outpouring of earnest spite, the clueless gazes of the timorous, anxious women, and at her own naïveté that it would be any different. She resolved over a manicure at a nearby Korean nail palace immediately following the meeting that her contribution to whatever parish life she considered worthwhile would be better served by throwing $10 bills into the collection plate instead of wasting her nights amid the dreary and depressive.

Having a priest for a brother-in-law had fed her atavistic clerical needs, to a point. She thought perhaps that this attraction for the religious life—not for herself, not for one second—was due to her mother's custom when Claire was a child: the dawn Lenten masses, the chilly rapture-free ceremony, the wheezing ancient crones who sawed through their rosaries like pagan postulants, the smoky aroma and pickle-nosed faces of the drunken old men. She equated childhood religion with dark, cold mornings in a dank church followed by a breakfast of cold bread and butter dunked in weak cocoa. As unpleasant as it all was, she was reminded of the scene from the *Aeneid*, when Aeneas is carrying his father on his back from burning Troy, and his father tells him, "Perhaps, at some future time, it will delight you to remember these things." She wasn't sure that she was delighted; but she was intrigued. Claire was just thirty-two; she had come of age as churchgoing faded, as the church itself became less imposing, more irrelevant, to her at least. But as an adult, she wanted perhaps to maintain a ceremony of remembrance through peripatetic attendance at services she no longer wholly believed, though with a belief that past beliefs may be believable in some distant necessary future. Having a devout family member, even by marriage, was maybe second best to being devout. It was like marrying into money, and hoping for a legacy.

Frank's devotion did not extend, she felt, to his brother's welfare. Nor to that of her brother's lover.

"I shouldn't stay long," Tobias said, walking around her living room, picking up a small blue vase she'd found at a flea market in Truro the summer before. He looked at its underside, replaced it on the bookshelf. He touched a framed photograph, running his finger along the top as if checking for dust. It was a picture of Claire and Peter, younger, smiling. "When was this from?"

Claire smiled with a wisp of guilt. "Before our wedding."

"Ignorant bliss," he said.

"I liked the picture. Does it bother you to see it?"

He didn't answer.

"I didn't want to throw out everything from the past, you know," she said a little quickly. "And I didn't want a wedding picture. Sad. Very Miss Havisham. I just wanted a keepsake."

"Don't you think this is a little sad, too?"

"No," she said. "I can't throw out everything."

"No current photos."

"What's the point, then? The point is to remember. The point in pictures, snapshots, is to flatter ourselves."

"You don't have any current photos, though," he repeated.

"It hasn't come up." she said. "Who's taken my photo lately? I just don't do it any more." She paused, looked at her hand, the marcasite ring she'd bought with Peter years ago, while they were foraging upstate for furniture and came across a barn-sized antiques emporium with shelves of jewelry from the Hoover and Coolidge years. She suddenly felt embarrassed to be wearing it and hoped—rather foolishly, since how could he know—that Tobias was unaware of its history.

"I used to drop people all the time," she said, looking up at Toby. "I let them disappear. I wanted not to do that. It doesn't hurt to remember, even the painful part."

He held the photograph, which showed Claire and Peter mid-laugh, she looking merrily away, he glancing after her. "It must be new; I don't remember ever seeing it. When did you exhume it?"

"Not too long ago," she admitted. "It was among some old boxes I'd found. I just liked it. It brought me back to a weekend we'd had out on the East End. I thought we looked good and so, why not?"

"We live so many lives," he said, replacing the frame. "I don't know if I can bear to keep photos around. Not for so long."

She thought of tomorrow's meeting, for some reason, an appointment with a consigner who was letting go a pair of Tissot paintings, that would help make her spring sale. Part of her job, a big part, was persuading people to part with things, the living and the dead. In her much younger days, she hadn't cared much for who she discarded; rather, she cared less for the people involved with the items than the items themselves. She had grown to be aware of her disregard as part of her cluelessness about the people with whom she'd come into contact. She was a person oddly sympathetic—at least others thought so—and yet inwardly rather callous regarding the effects of her actions or inaction on others. Her glancing regard for what others actually felt had changed, gradually, following her breakup with Peter, as she had been forced to realize her own blindness. She wondered if Tobias was blind, too, in some regards; we all are, to some extent, but she thought that he and Peter complemented each other—much more than she had Peter. Toby's watchful reticence married well the evasive jocularity of her ex-husband. Peter, she considered, could be rather a priapic Bertie Wooster, and Tobias his Jeeves.

"You know," Tobias said, "my parents' house is filled with photos— but not of me and my sister. They have headshots of themselves from various decades, and publicity stills from stock productions and movies and television. The headshots end in the 1980s, when they retired, as if they were frozen in another age. They have these black-and-white photos of themselves looking ridiculously like they're both in drag, and then the color snapshots of my niece and nephew. The photos skipped a generation, from summer stock to preschool."

"How odd."

"If you think about it—yes. But growing up with them, and their actor ways, it seemed normal. Actors aren't normal, my parents aren't normal, but this was normal to me, then."

"How are they?" She remembered the trouble Tobias had had a couple of years earlier, the intervention, getting them into rehab. They'd descended into a life of alcohol and Valium, their curtains closed, their house in disrepair, their finances a shambles. Toby had taken control of the mortgage, the money, and had been responsible for their getting sober. They were actually thriving now, in their eighties.

"Great, actually," he said. "They've even found an agent at an AA meeting, who's gotten them auditions. Apparently, older couples are easy to place. I even referred them to Jilly Fredericks, who was looking for 'types' for a video project, a kind of she-male 'Cremaster.' Mom plays that lesbian road-kill trucker, Aileen Wuornos. Dad plays one of her trucker victims. They're both about twenty years too old, but that's the point, apparently. She wants to savage the whole narcissistic hero-worship take on American killers. Having my four-foot-eleven mother pull out a gun should help her. So should a Vaseline-and-tapioca dildo. Who knows where it will lead?"

"What about your work?"

"It's all right." he said.

She was interested, if only because, in her field, the sale of video art at auction was so rare; it had little appreciating value beyond its installation use; stills, perhaps, sold, as in the Vanessa Beecroft post-happening photos, of attenuated models naked and European, stumbling around in high heels and "Victory of Samothrace" scarves or draped like figures in Parthenon processionals over the railing at the Guggenheim. But Tobias trafficked in curating the schemata of thematic posturing; it was a hard art for her to grasp, she knew—perhaps because she had never been asked to ascribe to it a value.

"But I am interested." She said. "You know that."

He looked at her, expecting mockery by eyebrow but, seeing

only what she hoped was her look of defenseless protestation, he relented.

"I've got a project going with an artist who makes a kind of Gerhard Richter video—watching a flower grow, we see her tending it; it reminds me of his candles and flames. It's about transience, nurturing, taking comfort in the act."

"It could sell—frames, anyway. Like stills."

"I don't know if that's the point," he said. "The point is watching it unfold. You certainly wouldn't want this in your house. This is intimate art on a grand scale. It's like a Gericault in scale if not subject matter; the antiheroic gesture, the 'Raft of the Medusa' as potting shed."

He walked toward the window, looking out onto the lights beyond, the apartments blocks away, the Hopper squares of yellow gleaming from the living rooms and bedrooms and other lives there. "A cop," he said.

Claire didn't answer. She looked up at him, silhouetted in the glare of reflected light; she couldn't see past him to the windows beyond, and the trellises of icicle lights people had swathed over their fire escapes and back windows. He looked to her just like Sargent's portrait of Dr. Pozzi at home, albeit a shade younger. Tobias was barely thirty, she recalled. But all he needed was the long red dressing gown and there he was, a late-Victorian dandy. Tobias had the same black hair, the beard—in his case, a goatee—and the sensitive, sensual face. "This is new, for you," she said.

"It's still not old for you," Tobias said.

"What do you mean?"

"Don't think that you've gotten over Peter, either. Look at the picture you keep. From before you were even married." He picked up the photograph again. "Look at how you excuse yourself, saying you like it because it looks good. Look at you trying to tell yourself

17

you're so generous and magnanimous." He put the photograph down, hitting the table with a hard knock. "Ridiculous," he said, as if to himself. "I don't know what I was thinking." She watched him look around the room, at her photographs, her eighteenth-century prints, her carefully chosen art, her demure, decorous home. "I'd better go."

"Toby, have I done something to offend you?"

"No, Claire." He managed a half-smile, and shook his head. "I just thought, wrongly, I could have a Lifetime TV moment, perhaps. Heart to heart, affirmation. But it's nothing that can be talked through, really. Or ignored. Just endured."

She saw him out, regretting her inability to connect in an essential way for an elemental need. She promised to call him tomorrow, but he didn't seem to respond to that. She watched him to the elevator, waving silently as he nodded a farewell, and she knew he was holding himself back from tears. She couldn't talk through; she presented the illusion of the capacity for reflection, for others. When does that illusion become reality, or at some point, does everyone realize it only goes so far? She looked up at the Greuze lithograph she'd bought the year before, at Swann. "The Ungrateful Son." Such an overwrought scene, flailing arms, pained expression, comic outrage. She had a fondness for such genre paintings, and while she was discouraged from collecting in her own field, this $2,000 lithograph was no problem. Greuze's little morality tales had a discreet charm; as bald as their dramaturgy could be, they were beautifully executed. One could argue that they were worthless since the intellect behind the execution was so feeble and uninteresting. But the heavy lines of such moral quandaries appealed to her, who shrank from expressions of morality, or of even outlining her own code of behavior, as if her actions needed a playbook.

Here, in this scene, a mother pleads speechlessly for the affection,

Claire assumed, of her wastrel progeny, who has either returned or is about to leave. His unrepentant raised hands, palms facing her, were semaphores of excuse, irritation. There had to be some human feeling here beyond the imaginative, the storybook; the mother's expression had to have had a real-world model. Greuze's harridan wife, Claire knew, was often his model—but idealized or, perhaps, denial-ized. Maybe he saw her as the gleaming beauty she used to be or that he wished she were. One portrait of her, her lips parted in postcoital rapture, her carefully disheveled hair hovering like a halo of tender lust around her face, was wholly at odds with her role as tormentor and savage muse. She could imagine the woman rising from her dreamy pose to hurl a prop at her useless husband, who had sadly rendered beauty out of her brutality. Portraying his wife as an eighteenth-century Vargas girl might have helped him bear her. Sketching a tumultuous family scene might suggest the happiness that once held them together, or the hope for it in a better world. She herself, with her pathetic photographs so carefully edited, curated even out of her unhappy past could create a nacreous memory, a pearl from the grains of revisionism.

She had preferred to think of her . . . revisions . . . as an acceptance of what she had lived through or, rather, her life as she remembered she had lived it. Claire had thought much about collating memories to suit a sense of order; the past—her past—deserved order. Why, she wondered, now? Toward what goal? She was torn between whether her thinking in this way was a gloss on the threat of pain or an avoidance of experience's blows. She thought her earnest appeal to what she'd hoped were her higher instincts would help her to live a nobler life, but what exactly was nobility of character now? Was it refraining from spite or retaining dignity through mortification? She realized, with some alarm, that she could not help ease the heartache of someone she cared about, perhaps because she couldn't relive her own, as she relived in some way only its less painful moments or, worse, retained only the promise of happiness that her relationship had never lived long enough to fulfill. She preferred cut flowers to houseplants, as well and for the same reason, perhaps, and the momentary bloom to the nurtured cutting, the petal to the frond.

# THE WIDOW

The next day, Claire chose her wardrobe with more care than usual. A sober suit, an Ann Taylor, nothing flashy—not that she owned anything flashy. She was well-dressed with a threat of dowdiness to her, sometimes too much like those women she would occasionally meet at some alumna event, those teachers for whom fashion-forward had no meaning, and A-line midcalf skirts were more-than-risqué enough. She couldn't imagine herself as a contemporary art specialist—to her, her clothes sense was far more vintage than avant-garde.

She chose with deliberation since her client, her consigner, was so sedate herself. Claire was to look at, in situ, two James Tissot paintings owned by Elizabeth Jane Driscoll, a wealthy widowed matron who divided her time between New York, Bridgehampton, and Palm Beach, and whom Claire had come to like a great deal. Claire had seen the Tissots before, of course, with her department head—she was second in the department—and they'd been appraised, verified, sanctioned, the works. She had been aware of them before, from the artist's catalogue raisonnée, but they weren't widely known. Mrs. Driscoll rarely loaned them—"My babies," she had called them. They'd been part of a retrospective in Buffalo,

New York, of all places, but rarely ventured beyond their Fifth Avenues digs. She was, though, about to part with them for, she hoped, a buyer who could provide a home. Preferably an institution. Mrs. Driscoll was getting on in years—she was eighty-three— and decided to let them go rather than bequeath them to her ungrateful children. Claire had heard of her intentions through an estate and planning lawyer she had briefly dated, Jamie Hindler, a stringbean of a man whom she'd liked but whose habit of chewing with his mouth open rather revolted her. She figured he didn't dine much with the elderly aristocrats who made up a sizable portion of his clientele, or if he did, they barely noticed his chewing through their cataract eyes or were too distracted by the clacking of their own false teeth to pay much heed to the dental grinding of their lawyer. He and Claire had dined together a few times—each time it becoming more difficult than the last for her to avoid staring at his mouth for signs of what he was chewing—before she had let him know it wouldn't go further. No dessert. He'd accepted graciously— she half expected him to say, "Was it my chewing?"—but then realized that, of course, estate attorneys were tactful in other regards, a necessity in the field, rather like being a kind of cultural oncologist. And savvy, too—he could point her toward business.

The Tissots complemented each other. All Tissots did, despite the subject matter. Tissot's oddness—for he *was* odd—gave each subject a similarity of mental texture, like the observations of a cultured roué who regretted only that his tastes weren't even broader. The market for Tissots varied. She sometimes thought he should have accepted Degas' offer to exhibit with the Impressionists. That name alone would have guaranteed another few million per picture, and to the eyes of this label-mad age would have validated him somewhat. Collectors, like theater audiences, need to be told what to like. Collectors like to categorize. Tissot, the contrarian, declined and became classified thereafter by category-defining auction houses and dealers as "nineteenth century," a term too vague to mean anything, too broad to help discern movements within the grand movement of Impressionism. He also committed the art-history crime of not advancing the art, which meant that he couldn't simply be good for himself, but that he should influence others, significantly, in ways that could be traced through artistic provenance. When painters became associated merely with an era—not even an epoch with a name—rather than a movement, they were taken less seriously by specialists, especially if the movement was taken seriously. Auction-house specialists, like certain academics, help determine a course for artists. Where musicians could keep certain composer's works alive based solely on the eagerness with which they played them, and, to a lesser extent, academics could help introduce students to writers whom they might have avoided or not known of, the art world had fewer opportunities for cultural validation. Auction houses helped create a market, too; more often, however, they relied on the validation of experts outside the auction house to bolster a case for the worth of the items they were selling, but also to justify the prices ascribed to them (although that was often a matter of market forces coupled with the greed of the consigner). If Tissot were at the center of a major museum show—a show at a major museum, not a provincial one—his work would appreciate considerably, given the reaction to the exhibition. It was unlikely, here. He was already appreciated for what he was. He was a significant but not a major painter. His oddness, the combination of tendresse and moral upbraiding—or rather tolerance for moral uncertainty—the balance between society and those just out of its censure, appealed. He'd never have a wide audience; his prettiness could become stultifying even when cleverly masking or even mocking the holy conventions of a bourgeois mise-en-scène. He undermined prettiness in a way that Renoir, more vibrant and less likely épater-le-bourgeois, did. Still, when Tissots found buyers, they could pull in up to $5 million. That was something. She didn't expect that in the current market—one driven by name recognition—he would sell for that much. And depending on the mood of a sale—each sale had a mood in the way a song had its own life—a good Tissot could be the star of a strong auction; if it didn't sell, it could be the centerpiece of a flop. And like other paintings on the auction circuit, some Tissots bore the taint of poor sales, associated with failure, the vagaries of the market, the weakness of an auction marked by minor works, the detritus of estates, family cast-offs. In Claire's business fiscal performance could signify artistic credibility. That kind of weighing-in could become entrenched. She often found herself, when at a museum, checking for price estimates alongside the identification plaques or scholarly snippets. And why not, really? The works didn't appear for free.

The Tissots for which she had negotiated were adding heft to the nineteenth-century sale she was in the middle of organizing, a sale that meant a lot to her rising career, to her next move, to her future in the field. She and her colleagues had persuaded Mrs. Driscoll to accept a reasonable price for them, had convinced her that at those prices these Tissots would most likely sell. A tricky negotiation, balancing a knowledge of the market against the expectations of the consigner. Some consigners had such an inflated sense of what their works were worth—or were so covetous and obtuse—that the only way to get the work was to promise too much, and then to have the paintings go unsold at auction, acquiring a reputation, lessening their value as a commodity, all because of addlepated avarice. The pictures could often be sold privately after a sale—indeed, many wily dealers (all dealers were wily) pounced on the specialist after a sale to make a grab for the unsold.

They would negotiate for a work and end up buying it for themselves or on behalf of a client, often for its published estimate or more. Although she was glad to complete the business, Claire was irritated that these same players hadn't raised their paddles during a sale, when it would have made a difference not only in the success of the auction, but the perception of the art's quality. It was so much about impressions and perceptions and face value.

But this was all part of the business, the manipulating, the underhanded trading to cut a deal, even at the expense of a work's reputation. She'd seen a work change hands, she could chart its history from owner to owner, from sale to sale—or sale to deal to deal to sale, and get a sense of its worth quite apart from its value. A specious, ultimately fraudulent exercise in competing justifications. But fascinating nonetheless, art as not only social indicator—a badge of wealth—but itself a social thing, rising and falling like a favored friend, a courtier, an acquaintance to be savored, a relationship to let dissolve into the nod of strangers, the half-forgotten face. Didn't I once own you? She doubted that serious—seriously wealthy—collectors forgot anything that took such effort to acquire or justify. Even for the grand rich, these were careful purchases. The rich were nothing if not careful. But the art world that served the moneyed was often careless. Not necessarily in the research, the deductive association that established attribution, clarified provenance, secured reputation: this was the province of passion, scholarship. No, the carelessness arose out of the pernicious bravado of the art buyers, the "personal curators," the swaggering shell game that dealers played. Art as investment meant art whose stock rose or fell according to the whim of the market. That didn't apply universally. Matisses may be overvalued from season to season, but they were still Matisses. The "name" had been earned. A Cézanne might sell for $6 million one year and five years later net $4 million or

$8 million for a similar work. But it was still a Cézanne, a work of a powerful and unique sensibility valued over others. Commodity, yes. Up to a point. But not really. Brokered, certainly. Valued inaccurately, and likely depending on the rating agency.

She was that agency often. Although less malleable than a freewheeling, needling dealer, she did nonetheless work for an auction house, which traded in perception and manufactured cachet. Claire had a sense of what the market might fairly bear, yet she felt that she had more at stake with both the art and the owner than others. She realized that, this, too, was often a naïve position—she often manned the phones at auctions, representing a potential buyer, trying to persuade him or her to proceed with the bidding. But she felt that since she herself cared so deeply for the artwork first, somehow she could protect the art as much as she could serve the consigner, and her employer. She could, she reasoned, preserve the reputation of the artist and help validate the work by helping it realize sums enough to have it taken seriously. She was to an extent aware of the tautology in her reasoning but looked beyond that. After all, she did get to handle beautiful things.

She knew she would not move Tissot beyond his station, that of a first-rate second-tier artist. But the thought of working toward a time, realistically, when a sale that contained one or, better, two Tissots was considered a major auction rather than merely a significant one because of those works, was appealing. She hoped, certainly, that this sale would have an impact. At best, she realized, owning a Tissot was what a connoisseur did, one who had already amassed a collection. Today's new and newish money often skipped the building, the steady accrual, and wanted highlights from the collections of others. That's why so many recently rich bought contemporary art; one could get a label for less, impress others easily. It was the perception of it.

Part of her role was in helping focus that perception. Worthy, lesser, older names needed to be explained both to the buyer and, by extension, to those whom the buyer sought to woo, cultivate, endear with the art. Rare collectors bought at this level, she found, solely for the love of an object: in antiquities, in certain other fields like snuff bottles that bordered on the fetishistic. She hoped to locate for these works the proper intellect behind the ample wallet. The slightly off and eccentric Tissot required an appreciation of absurdity. Exactly how much wealth enabled one to appreciate the absurd—or how much one brought a sense of the absurd to the acquiring of wealth—she did not know. One had to look beyond the surface mawkishness of Tissot's tableaux to grasp the sad futility, the very French elegance in the societal fray, the bitter longeurs between marginal acceptance and outright rejection that Tissot encapsulated. For herself, Claire realized that in many ways, she was deeply conventional, and this tension in the artist fascinated her. She hoped it would fascinate many another.

The painting that appealed more to her of the two she was getting for her sale was one of a widow—was, in fact, called "A Widow." It was a cluttered painting, its figures posed under a flowered trellis following or during a lull in a tea. At the center was a woman in black, the widow, young, fetching, needlework on her lap carelessly unattended, contemplating the needle poised aloft in her right hand, as if to strike or to sew. To the viewer's left, her right, a young girl with her chin resting upon her hand lounged in the carefree yet still somehow louche manner of the bored young. To the right of the picture sat an old woman, her body cut off by the wicker chair, intent on reading, her right hand resting, not quite in support, more as if in glancing suggestion, on her cheek, like the touch of a finger on a skein of silk, gentle and tentative. They were, rather unsubtly, three ages of woman. At the upper right in the middle distance, a statue of Cupid stringing his bow marked the scene with frozen romance or the possibility of *l'amour*. Cupid's body was obliquely turned, arms and hands holding a clothing, covering nakedness, the face looking toward an unseen figure, supplicant, modest, and suggestive of pleasurable future ravishment. The statue created a diagonal upward through the frame, from an overturned hyacinth-blue parasol at the bottom left, giving direction to the clutter, and suggestion to the viewer. The picture was a painting of clutter and unease. A beribboned wicker stand at the bottom right, adjacent to the widow, carried an effusive bouquet of mums, asters, daisies, its shelves filled with ribbons, pillows, cloth. The tea table behind the young girl, laden with sugar-water, tea, and even sherry, implied entertainment, a vanished guest. The attitudes of the three females differed. The girl, unrepentant and fidgety, short of childish querulousness, unconcerned about her attitude of feeble scorn and ennui. The old woman, her hand upraised, concentrates on her fiction, her fabled romance, so far from her life. The young widow, alluring in her gauzy gown, her hands half covered in sheer black fabric, only her come-hither fingers unsheathed. All three thinking of elsewhere, someone else, some other situation, scenario, time. The girl, anything of interest beyond her immediate tedium, the old woman of rapture far away, and the widow, focused on her needle, a gaze of remembrance, perhaps, or the possibility of longing for new excitement. The only figure looking at something directly, yet unseen, is the statue. A picture of restless illusion, then. The proprieties of widowhood are flouted—unseemly drinking at tea—and the widow's delicious cupid's-bow mouth invites carnality, not sedate repose and remembrance. An expression more of the possibility of desire—not the after-effects of grief. The widow's fetching ankles are also on display, her legs crossed, her pretty slippered feet visible, a flash of camisole, the lure of the underneath.

For all in this picture, a dream of romance—the girl, the widow, the old woman, the statue of Cupid. A longing, inchoate in youth, fictional in old age, just beyond reach in between. A painting of what might be, what was, what might have been, what can be only for others.

Claire didn't think she was over-reading the picture. If anything, she could be missing some Tissot-esque iconology, but she doubted it. Tissot's symbols were the everyday, the recognizable, not the sub-rosa symbols of a Poussin. She knew the evident social ideologies of the age and was certain that Tissot, a keen observer, placed his subjects well within them. He was a careful painter, the objects chosen just so, from the ribbon in the bored girl's hair that matched the table's festoonery and the chrysanthemums to the flowers descending the trellis. He was a careful painter, too, of the moments in between—after the visit, before the clearing up, after the mourning, after the chaste flirtation, before the palpable physicality. The fingers in the garments, after girlhood, before . . . well.

Claire glanced at the photographs of the painting she had with her, close-ups, details. She was meeting "the widow Driscoll," as she sometimes thought of her, for late-morning tea. Mrs. Driscoll's husband had been given the paintings early in their marriage, by his mother—an unsettling trousseau, certainly, from the in-law. But the works had been in the family and, as far as Claire could tell, not become omens of an unfinished life.

The other painting, a good one, "Waiting for the Ferry," was less eccentric in its charm, though Claire liked it. It showed a woman sitting at an embankment bridge, her daughter turned slightly toward her. A man, her husband maybe, his hands on a small boy's shoulders, looked just beyond the woman. The expressions were preoccupied by filling time. The little girl looked back toward her mother, imploring her to hurry the ferry to dock. The models,

Claire knew, were Tissot's mistress, Kathleen Newton, her son, her niece, and her brother, though a photo Claire saw showed Tissot in the brother's position, which he used as a study for the painting. Here again, he captured the waiting, the anxiousness of nothing.

Mrs. Driscoll herself occupied that position more clearly—she was old, wanting to settle things, aware of mortality. So few of us are aware of anything, Claire thought, as we spend our lives flitting thoughtlessly, directionless, onward.

Claire knew her interest in this painting, in their stylish drama, fed into her romantic view of herself—the chastened lover, the spurned woman, the tired spinster, the unalluring divorcée. She herself luxuriated sometimes in her apartness. She sometimes found herself daydreaming the scenarios of a painting; all wrong, terribly unprofessional, a girlish preoccupation with story and escape. And while she kept these random thoughts within herself—Claire Brogan *is* that seductive, preoccupied widow!—she still thought them, and rather belittled herself for her daydreams.

That other widow—the real one, who was decidedly no seductress—awaited her. The business end of things taken care of, Claire still cultivated her clients, her consigners—and Mrs. Driscoll liked Claire, her company. Mrs. Driscoll also had other works, Bérisot and Claudes, that might be included in this or future sales. Part of relationship building in her business involved just such get-togethers that she hoped weren't merely false friendships—although in money terms they were leagues apart—and she didn't fool herself that she was more than an outlet for one person's excess baggage. But Claire's business really necessitated the sororal chat, the quidnuncs, the face-to-face. Not that she minded. She felt that a good part of her rise at the auction house was because of her confidential manner—or her manner of a matter-of-fact confidante—that put consigners at ease and helped close the deal. This despite her still only-fair art-historical depth. And her admitted tendency to be rather blithe about the motives of other people, and her own gullibility. But she was doing well in business. She was a business person, not a scholar. A dreamy business person, but for all their savvy and perceived fustiness, auction houses sold dreams like any other merchant of the useless.

Mrs. Driscoll was not dreamy. She was of that well-to-do set, practical even in appreciating art, too sensible to go moony over baubles. But she had learned, through growing up with art, to appreciate it without the rapture of the grad student, or of the new-money millionaire acquiring his first Jeff Koons porcelain breast pump. She respected art, valued it, but didn't let it frighten. Like growing up with servants, and knowing how to deal with them. Claire had met her perhaps ten times over the past six months: alone, with her colleagues, with lawyers for both sides, with an independent art appraiser. Mrs. Driscoll was efficient, used to running things, holding both the prospect of becoming conspiratorial like a counsel in conference or girlishly intimate, as if they were giggling between stalls at a dance. She had some of what made Claire valuable in her field, the ability to imply an interest. It was a gift, confidentiality squared, the coquette's arsenal. This although neither Claire nor, now, Mrs. Driscoll, was coquettish. Claire suspected that Mrs. Driscoll had been, however, long ago, long ago. She was of the soi-disant debutante generation that learned to ingratiate and calculate, figuring the odds on effective maneuvers depending on the suitability of the suitor.

Mrs. Driscoll had that hale Anglo-Irish bearing that flirted now with the masculine, but in that Irish way, girlish—charm and hardness, flintlocked. Had she been brought up in Northern Ireland or England, she would probably have had the braying brutish bonhomie, horsy and harrumphing, that Claire occasionally heard in

Britain. Once on a ferry trip between Ireland and Scotland, Claire remembered the first class lounge awash with the shattering squalls of well-bred people shouting friendly idiocies at each other. Mrs. Driscoll's equally privileged but certainly more restrained upbringing did not foster the barking of the British upper class. She had a slight New York accent, but it was the accent of a long-ago New York, when cultured New Yorkers spoke with a slightly nasal, patrician gloss. Educated New Yorkers today had the neutrality of television newsreaders. Older New Yorkers bore the earmarks of a jumbled patois of privilege and density.

She had a full head of white-gray hair, not the wispy fronds of one's grandmother, but the steely locks of a girl's lacrosse coach. Dark eyebrows, like Mary McCarthy without ironic animadversion. It was a strong, smart face; cared for, not fussed over. Claire liked her for showing her the respect of an equal; a trick of confidence building, perhaps, but effective in seducing her.

For all her preparations, Claire met Mrs. Driscoll with less composure than she usually did. The previous evening had disturbed her more than she had wanted to admit, more perhaps for forcing her to admit how little she had admitted to herself. Beyond Tobias.

"My children are rather irritated," Mrs. Driscoll told her when they were seated, over coffee. "I think I'm a few paintings away from an assisted-living facility."

Claire smiled. "They realize they stand to make money, anyway," she said.

"Oh, of course. It isn't that. Well, not entirely. It's about the artifact. A family possession."

"They've had long enough to make up their minds—"

"And they could not decide. Why, they—I think it's Adelaide. Thom couldn't be bothered."

Claire had met Thom. Adelaide. Thom. They were in their early fifties. Adelaide lived in bitterness in Bridgehampton most of the year, and Thom and his wife—Jocelyn, wasn't it?—on Park. Board members. Jocelyn more so than he. He banked. Adelaide, divorced, rigidly bohemian—for her set, anyway—wrote on photography for small journals and maintained her own eccentric Web site. Adelaide was like Cosima Wagner without the diary. But like Wagner's wife, she too became the object of scorn for those around her who might have deserved it more. Adelaide probably would have sold her mother's paintings herself and resented having such a spiteful action taken out of her hands. She was always outraged at something, with the outrage of the entitled. It was so easy to be angry and daring when one had nothing to lose. Thom might not be as benign as his mother thought, though Mrs. Driscoll was certainly shrewd; he might have preferred at a later point to donate one of the Tissots to the Met, further securing Jocelyn's board tenure. In her spoken appraisals, Mrs. Driscoll probably underestimated the motives of one as laissez-faire and overlooked the clotted anger of the other. People tended to shift various denials according to the irritation they tried to avoid.

"How much longer have I got with these?"

"Six weeks," Claire said. Until the presale cataloging, the exhibition, the auction.

"I know you've told me several times," Mrs. Driscoll said. "I'm not forgetful, not really. It's just a reassurance. They've been dear to me, for so very long."

"I know that. I keep things out for that reason. Snapshots."

Mrs. Driscoll looked disappointed.

"Nothing as cherished as a painting. Only mementos. They don't have the same depth of interpretation, but then, I don't own great art. I only deal in it."

"You see how much things have meant to others. Or you see

great things stowed away. You see the relativity of the values we attribute to things. For some people, snapshots are more valuable than their heirlooms gathering cobwebs. But that's only because some of us know what things are worth, isn't it?" she said, looking away.

"Some of us need help with that."

"It took me a very long time to appreciate certain things about my life, my marriage," Mrs. Driscoll said. "I didn't even like my husband until we had been married for years."

Claire wasn't surprised; what surprised her was that she had liked him at all. People of Mrs. Driscoll's set, she had seen, maintained businesslike lives, very often carrying on almost separately, the wife doing wifely things socially and the husband being tended to and mollified as much as he needed with a proper home. A kind of arrangement that allowed a certain freedom. Not for affairs, though they could certainly enter into it, but for pursuing interests, or lack of them. It was these women, of course, for whom walkers existed. And, for the men, discreet mistresses. Mrs. Driscoll could have been one of those society hens who entertained a fashionable crowd, but whose husband barely popped his head into the room, obliging only then to retreat to an early bed and an earlier bank date, or who preferred to pop in and out en route to an assignation or misalliance of some sort. She hadn't been that kind of woman, but Mrs. Driscoll would have known women whose lives were ordered in that way, with that nonchalant rigor—rigor one was rather born to than educated in. It was a world far from Claire's, but she peeped in often enough. Through her position, she was accepted as some sort of predatory caregiver, like a governess with appraisal skills. Part of her job was building relationships to capitalize on people's needs to dispense their possessions or realign their wealth or stiff their families. Part of her skill was trying to suss out the nature of potential clients' areas of interest in either acquiring or disbursing: whether it was a blend of magnanimity and shrewd allotment or scattershot greed and spite.

With Mrs. Driscoll, she felt a twinge of oddly shaped nostalgia: as if the older woman had wanted somehow to preserve her own sense of what her relationship with her husband and his emotional legacy were, by divesting herself of his gifts in this regard, before they became tainted by the conflicting exigencies of her selfish children. They already had been, to a point—thus the sale. But lingering in Mrs. Driscoll's wandering gaze—Claire saw her turn to the paintings like a watch one checked too frequently at train stations—was the soft remembrance of an accrual, that is, the construction of a shared life. Claire knew little of that marriage and the patterns of its sustenance over the years. When, for instance, did love actually enter in? But what seemed to count for Mrs. Driscoll here were the pointillist distances that gave to the individual dots of experience the shimmer of a whole world, her past. She thought that past resonated because of the decisions she and her husband had made, their compact, as it were, to forge ahead, despite, Claire felt, the unfortunate limitations of their progeny, who were a clear sign that all was not right with the world. Claire wondered whether, and believed it might have been, their agreement to make a go of it had been the result of love or the beginning of an understanding that somehow led to love, as a forced smile sometimes begets an actual one.

"I shouldn't even be talking about it. It isn't proper," Claire said.

"Nothing is improper nowadays, Claire. Especially to me. You may think I'm a prim old woman, but that's just your idea of me. I suspect you suspect that, which is why you've allowed yourself to let down your guard."

Claire glanced at her with a mix of mild embarrassment and

some relief. She didn't want to unburden herself—she wouldn't—to a client, especially one such as Mrs. Driscoll. The widow Driscoll, though, had probably heard enough over the years that Claire's petty quandaries might be as insignificant a bother as a maid asking for a day off. But Claire had already so betrayed herself, her feelings, through her desire to connect that she figured she'd better plunge ahead. She mentioned meeting Toby the night before, and gave a précis of her whole marriage, the bad to worse of it, the mending, the amending, the forgetting or not.

"So just to get things straight," Mrs. Driscoll said. "This was your ex-husband's lover."

"Yes," she said, after a pause.

"And the problem is, of course, him being where you were, only different."

"Yes."

"It seems to me you worried far too much about your own feelings for him, and not enough for your own feelings for yourself. Didn't you just gloat?"

"Well, maybe a little."

"God, I know I would have." She stopped, and looked at Claire, with an expression of calculated amusement. "You're not the first one to run into the ex's ex," she said. "It's just that the little roundelay is a bit more gender-fluid than it had been in my circle. I usually had to worry about the secretaries. When he started fooling with the more educated floozies, then I put my foot down. I didn't want him involved with anyone he could actually hold a conversation with."

"Well, Toby was dumped for a cop. But I was dumped for Toby. And he's not exactly tongue-tied around me."

"You were dumped, as you put it, for different reasons. Though it is gratifying to see the scene unfold from a distance. Even a near distance. You're far too guileless, Claire," she said, brushing back her hair with her hand. Claire noticed an absence of age spots there. A privilege of wealth, to have blemish-free hands. "But I get the sense you dupe yourself into believing. You're rather old-fashioned, you know. I don't mean that in a patronizing way. Don't be startled. You know it yourself. I just think that somehow you're caught in the wrong time. Your points of reference are other than now. You don't quite fit in. Rather like that widow there," she said, glancing up at the painting. "Though you're not half so ready to be ravished, are you?"

"I frankly wish I were," she admitted.

"My advice is to get yourself out of whatever rut you're in. Don't stall. At least entertain the thought of romance, instead of trying to wait for someone who's some ideal. You're not getting any younger. There are thousands of women around like you, burned by men, meek as kittens, thinking they can bide their time. Well, you can't."

She said nothing.

"Claire. I'm glad your frustration somehow broke out," Mrs. Driscoll said. "You keep second-guessing yourself. Try not to. And," she said, rising, returning to her earlier efficiency of manner, "please come see me again. Or I'll call you. I much prefer your company to that of many others I know."

Claire promised she'd be back, to chat, to visit, even after the sale, perhaps before. She thought she'd arrange a little lunch for her and some dealers she knew, perhaps another specialist at the firm. Mrs. Driscoll had some lovely and very valuable Chinese export porcelain. Always thinking. Future sale. Connections. She'd help her let go of the past.

The air had the wintry New York brilliance it acquires after a storm, and shone shadowless on the sidewalks. She decided to walk to her friend Bernice's apartment, a few blocks south. Her cell phone rang. The number identified her ex.

"Peter," she said without intonation.

"Claire," he said, drawing it out. "Something wrong? You sound like you're in one of your moods."

She wasn't about to enter into their little baiting game. "I saw Toby last night," she said.

"So you know."

"Up to a point." She had a few tones, she realized, in speaking with Peter. Brusque, bravado, or bathetic. Brusque as in the conversation now. Bravado as in "Everything's fine," or bathetic as in "How could you?" Well, she had more tones than that, but those were the ones she remembered from various stages of their relationship. She was in the irritation-prone stage at the moment. Her tone had the ineffectual bark of a novice nun.

"You heard about Sean, then," he said.

"The cop?" So his name was Sean. So Toby had heard correctly, as of course he would. She remembered the first time she heard "Tobias," expecting an Etonian schoolboy. Of course Toby would remember who he was dumped for. "Yes, I'd heard about him. The cop you met. Near Ground Zero."

"You make it sound unseemly."

"I'm sorry. Perhaps I should have said tragedy brings people together."

"Claire, don't. It' s hard enough."

"And Tobias?"

"He came home rather late."

"You were there? Oh yes, I figured you wouldn't want to be with Sean. Sean, wasn't it? Three's a crowd."

"So we're taking sides. Claire. Jeez, I thought you'd moved on."

"Yes. And no," she said. "You've moved on. And on. Toby was

distraught." Well, just a little. And why should she care? She was getting herself angry over getting annoyed with her ex-husband for dumping the man he'd left her for. She wanted to ask Mrs. Driscoll's advice.

"I'm sorry you had to bear that. Don't let's do this, Claire. Listen. Not everything was perfect. I'm not perfect. Toby isn't perfect. I don't know what he told you."

"He told me enough." He told her nothing. She realized how much she regretted her own decorum. And his. She wished she had been the type people actually would break down and cry to. Instead of merely threatening to and then realizing they'd have to repeat themselves with an actual sympathetic person instead of a facsimile of compassion.

She was near her next appointment. "I can't talk about this now, Peter. I have to go."

"Claire," he said. "Can I see you? Tonight?"

She was free, she knew.

"I have opera tickets."

Her heart sank. Not at the opera. At the thought of his icky opera friends. "Not the Opera Club. Peter, I don't think I can spend an evening with those . . ."

"Those queens. No," he said. "It's not the Opera Club. No queens. Promise. Except me."

'What about Sean?"

"He's working. I'm not even sure he likes opera."

Not even sure. Well, it was early for them. But the length of a relationship didn't guarantee any real knowledge at all. "I see a long future for you together," she said.

"Ha. Look—I'd like to see you. Can we? *Fidelio*. It's short. We can have dinner afterward. At the Knickerbocker. It's ladies' night."

"Great. This keeps getting better. No queens, then dinner with the dinosaurs. What's Toby doing?"

"How am I supposed to know that? Do you have to know that to say yes?"

"No. Okay. I'll see you tonight."

"Lots to tell."

"No doubt. Tonight." It would be too late for dinner at his stuffy club, anyway. The club he'd finagled his way into somehow, en route to becoming a gay scion of a nonexistent old New York family. So what. Good for him. It would be too late for the club, and Pete probably remembered that but said it anyway. He often said whatever came to mind. He didn't consider it lying so much as padding, filling in the gaps between the few words of truth.

Her next appointment was with a friend—an acquaintance who could become a friend—Bernice Carton, whom she had met a couple of years earlier at a reception and with whom she liked to gossip. With Bernice, her sense of decorum vanished. Well, faded slightly. Claire was fascinated by her tales of treacherous amour with wastrels and lunkhead lotharios with too much money. They met at the occasional arty party—Bernice managed to appear on many invitation lists—and would have lunch on a weekend every other month or so when Bernice was in town. She had an apartment in the city but traveled frequently with her husband of the moment. Bernice looked as if she had been a swimmer; she had the broad shoulders and toned torso of an athlete, but one who had grown thicker with the years. That thickness—and her rather blasé exuberance—also gave her the air of a movie heroine's tough-talking best friend. In Claire's relationship with her, however, Claire was the one in the girlfriend role, while Bernice rushed into romance. Claire was the hapless girl next door unlucky in love, while Bernice was the sophisticated romantic gadabout.

Bernice had married and divorced on a continuing upward curve. Her first husband, who had invented a widget for cleaning aquariums, had left her for the wife of a client of his, a messy motel room ménage that netted her enough to live in comfort for life. Her second husband, an investment banker with a yen for landscape painting—acquiring, not creating—had skipped with a specialist in cloisonné he'd squired around town after meeting her over the Fabergé eggs at A La Vieille Russie on East Fifty-ninth Street. Dopey husband number two had left her the apartment across the street from the Frick. Dickie—the banker—had also left her a number of paintings; he'd taken the fetishistic Fabergé along with the specialist. The paintings included a decent Corot haystack and peasant pictures, a Delacroix tiger study, and some Dutch countryside scenes that Claire had hoped to convince Bernice at some point to give up for a sale. Depending on her romantic entanglement of the moment—she was on husband number four— Bernice was either adding to her collection or de-accessioning, depending on whether something she owned reminded her of one of her husbands in the wrong way, or if something she wanted did in the right way.

Bernice was about ten years older than Claire. She had a sharp intelligence and a man's man chumminess—savoir faire in a Bill Blass suit. Her feminine acuity and no-nonsense directness appealed to ambitious if wayward men, who inevitably tired of being with an equal and sought the company of what they hoped would be a more malleable kewpie doll. Even the cloisonné princess was a bit of a ditz. Cloisonné. Really. Like snuff bottles with shellacking. Bernice was in a de-accession phase at the moment, irritated by her current beau, a lawyer with a taste for photography, especially Nan Goldin and Diane Arbus. Bernice's own taste ran toward Marsden Hartley and Edward Hopper. Her Corots, for some reason, had begun to remind her of late twentieth-century photographers in their depiction of the downtrodden agricultural life. "I know they're supposed to fill us with regard for the salt of the earth," Bernice had told her. "But they sometimes make me want to shoot myself." Their slathered honesty reminded her too much of her handsome block-head lawyer's taste. So Claire had hoped she could be persuaded to part with them.

Bernice had no need to make money off her art, and she wasn't the kind of consigner who bought and sold as if to invest in art as a trader in stocks would. That was a shell game indeed. But Bernice wanted to keep her hand in the art world as an observer, and stay on the party list. She'd started out as a reporter for the *Times* Style section, but luckily broke free of that humiliation by meeting her husband at one of the vapid society soirees she was supposed to write about. After the nuptial freedom from journalistic squalor, Bernice began to move among the crowd she'd covered, and cer-tain New York crowds had a certain fluidity of entry. Her lack of pretense and her sure style opened many doors for her, as did her newly wedded wealth and her apparent lack of interest in becoming a society icon. So the icons accepted her for being Bernice. She had maintained her newspaper contacts and provided amusing anec-dotes of art world openings that helped fill in the blanks in Style section stories cobbled together by desperate editors whose élan had evaporated by their third paycheck. Bernice only went to open-ings where the art interested, or where the gallery owner was gen-uinely amusing, not merely with a vacuous grin behind a smarmy leer. Luckily, a lot interested her, and she maintained a string of art-dealer friends whose repellent avarice was offset by their penchant for tawdry gossip and good cocktails. She could afford to ignore the insulting fees newspapers paid, and she liked having press access without needing to either research or report in any substantial way.

"Should we go out for lunch or just sit here and gab?" she asked Claire.

"Let me take a little time actually going over the paintings," she said. "I've just had tea with Elizabeth Jane Driscoll."

"That tough old bird!" Bernice said.

"She's been very sweet to me."

"Of course. You're helping her unload those paintings."

"She loves them. I don't think her children do. She wants to find a nice home for them."

"Those ridiculous children of hers. You'd think someone as on the mark as Elizabeth Driscoll would have straightened them out. Adelaide, certainly. At least Thom keeps the cash coming in. Is Adelaide still doing nothing on daddy's money in Bridgehampton? Not that I should talk."

"We didn't talk about her. I think so. Probably. An angry woman."

"Angry and entitled. The worst kind. They think because they were born to money they can scorn with impunity."

"They pretty much can," Claire said.

"I know. Let's look at the Corot."

They did. It was a typical rain-swept landscape, gray and stark, with a hint of country lushness, but barren of tenderness, except in its realization of a quasi-idealized poverty.

"How much, do you think?" Bernice asked.

Claire considered. She'd thought of this, but part of her routine was in seeming to arrive at an estimate on the spot, as if she were seeing something new, or some flaw, in a work. Her training involved just such social ruse; it was like pretending to be thrilled at the sight of someone odious. "The market for Corot isn't bad now," she said, slowly, as if she'd just remembered the name of a possible buyer who might be talked into purchasing the painting. "Offhand, I'd say eight hundred thousand to one million."

"Is that all? I was hoping for more," Bernice said. A typical consigner response. But then, no one ever hoped for less.

"It wouldn't sell, Bernice. You know that. Don't tell me you're going to turn into one of those sellers who insist they know how much their paintings are worth."

"Don't tell me you're not toying with me," Bernice said. "I may have had a lot of husbands, but I'm no fool," she said, kindly.

"Honestly, Bernice. It's a tough market at this level. It's a specialized field. You know that. Besides, what do you want the money for, if I may be so unprofessional?"

"I don't need it. I just want the thing out of here. And money is always welcome. I suppose I could sell it back to Dickie, but I think I'd rather he discuss it with me when he sees it in the catalog."

"I thought you were selling it because it reminded you too much of Mitchell."

"Sometimes I get confused. They remind me of each other. Always a problem, but usually a pitfall for us serial marriers. We tend to fall for the same idiot again and again."

"I won't have that problem," Claire said.

"Don't count on it, dear."

"Toby told me last night that he's leaving Peter. Or that Peter's leaving him, actually," Claire said.

"Well, doesn't that serve them both right?"

"I feel sorry for Toby," Claire said.

"Oh, please," Bernice said.

"Really. Just a little. I admit I felt it was time someone did to him what he did to me. But he didn't do it to me. Peter did."

"Well, someone should do to Peter," Bernice said. "So who's the chump this time?"

"A cop."

"Typical. I bet he's good-looking and can use a nightstick."

"He's a detective, apparently."

"Which must make him, what? Easier to talk to?"

"I don't think talking is the issue."

"Men always think they can get around it. They're such idiots. Do you know how many men can actually carry on a conversation? That's one of the reasons Dick and Mitchell and every man I've ever gone out with has liked me. I can make them laugh."

"Men don't think that way until they are face to face with it, I think," Claire said. "The boredom."

"They don't care because they figure it isn't their problem. I give Peter and his detective friend two months."

"Peter's asked me to the opera with him tonight."

"And you're going, I hope?"

"Of course. I need to learn more about the new man in his life. And learn about what it was that Toby and I had that just didn't matter to Peter in the long run."

"What you and Toby had wasn't the same. Honey, you were a beard and Toby was the razor."

"Still," Claire said. "I'm curious." She looked around Bernice's apartment, similar in some respects to that of Mrs. Driscoll—the comfort of wealth and the sheen of furniture dusted by someone else. But it had a raffishness different from the Driscoll home; Bernice seemed to make a life as she went along, absorbing an experience, being amused or irritated with the same sense of blithe abandon as if she were choosing a blouse for a morning shopping excursion. She kept a photograph of her parents, a retouched wedding picture that showed them on the cusp of glamour, like so many newlyweds whom the camera captures exuberant with fear and the possibility of distant, continuing bliss. Her mother, whom Bernice resembled in the swagger of her eyebrows, had one of those lace burnooses covering her tightly curled hair, and she leaned into her new husband, a stolid yet smiling man with a sexy allure—Claire thought cigars, lingerie, and rough yet tender hands.

They looked carnal, she realized, and she recalled with a suggestion of dismay her own chaste wedding photos, the smiles, almost desperate in their toothy display, her grasping hands on her own new husband's arm, as if she could, Cassandra-like, foretell a future she herself refused to believe. Bernice's parents had had a long marriage, and her mother, now in her eighties, lived in a lair of Alzheimer's, in a home in Larchmont. Bernice also kept a picture of herself, a vibrant off-the-cuff portrait caught by a *Daily News* photographer at a fundraiser, a black-and-white testament to Bernice's photogenic flair. It was like that Weegee photo of transvestites from the 1940s, Claire thought, only Bernice, instead of camping it up in a floodlit paddy wagon, was emerging from the carapace of a limousine greeting the camera under the klieg lights, wholly at ease under a temporary flash, in the glare of false notoriety. She did not care if she was photographed, nor did she seek it, and she had a natural "up" quality that the camera devoured, ravenous and unforgiving. It was Bernice's life-philosophy in action—move on, have fun, take and disburse amusement.

"You look so marvelous here," Claire said, not for the first time, picking up the picture.

"I know," Bernice said. "So much better than any of my wedding photos. I'd just bought that gown, too. And I'd just dumped Dickie. Happy days."

Claire laughed. "I don't know how you just keep moving on," she said. "No regrets."

"Oh, I have them, Claire," she said. "I just don't dwell on them. I make a lot of mistakes, and don't necessarily learn. But I figure, what's next? At least I can have fun."

"You know," Claire said, "Peter's brother is coming to town. He's going to be staying in a building near me. I'd gotten him a sublet."

"Not the priest?"

"Ex."

"It's a family of exes, isn't it," she said, dryly. "I'd forgotten. Well, that was nice of you."

"He's taken a sabbatical, to write a business book he's gotten a good advance on. He's planning to meet with some executive types, or whatever—I'm not entirely sure—but he wanted to stay in the city, and my neighbor's away in Hong Kong for a few months. He just has to feed her cat. And pay the rent."

"Ideal. Except that he's a pill, as I recall."

"A bit angry, yes. But he's a good person. I like him. He has a hard time with his brother, which is a bit of a problem—"

"His, not yours," Bernice said.

"I know. Boundaries, as they say in self-help books. But I like him."

"You let everyone take advantage of you, Claire," Bernice said. "Once I divorce them, they stay divorced."

"I'm not trying to get back with Peter or anything ridiculous like that," she said. "I'm just being friendly."

"Too friendly," Bernice said. "Take the money and close the door. And sell the art."

Claire realized that she was fully complicit in how others used her, if they used her. Her good nature, her pliable and accommodating demeanor, her tendency toward delusive encouragement. Bernice had a toughness and humor that made her nobody's fool. Claire knew her marriage to Peter was based on her own enormous capacity for willful delusion, coupled with Peter's charming duplicity and, again, her desire to shape-shift like a sci-fi version of emotive responsiveness. Again, she thought of how these traits, which served her fairly well in her career, had let her to be, in relationships—what, exactly? Confidante? Shoulder? Her longing, her ineffable unhappiness, was seeping out into her work. Too intimate by far with Mrs. Driscoll, despite the older woman's obvious wish to become friendly—to go beyond her station, as it were. She regretted her visible agitation there.

I am so lonely, she thought, that even the tough old birds pity me. As if she were the delectable carrion of a rotting relationship. Claire despised that weakness in herself. She hated this tendency toward haplessness, hoping to be noticed. But still, she longed to be swept away, discovered. At the same time, she did not want to become one of those despised cultured women she encountered around New York, in line at Zabar's, overheard at the Metropolitan, spouting the cultural agitprop of the newspapers or mendacious magazines, one of the foodies, the fashionable, their repellent frenzy of scurrilous cultural awareness. Yet Claire wanted to be heard, to opine in a way that was both telling and pomposity-free, on matters of music and mores. She could see the ridiculousness of her oddly conflicting aspirations here, yet she couldn't see past them to being in any way able to realize them. She rather envied Bernice her rock-'em, sock-'em romantic life—moneyed and coolly passionate and discardable. Yet Bernice revered her parents' relationship, ultimately kept trying for the combination of malleable willfulness and determination that forged long-term love, if such were possible. Perhaps Bernice and Peter were right—keep trying, move on. Let the fallen clean up after themselves. Claire even saw the allure of the Driscoll way of life, a sturdy, intermittently steady marriage, even with children who became distant and seemed ungrateful. Claire knew she wanted something beyond what she had, yet was fascinated by her emotional dilemma, in a specious way something like Alphonse Daudet recording the testimony of his own syphilitic pain. She could not envision a life for herself beyond what she was living—her longing had an inchoate schoolgirl quality to it, as if her experience were read about rather than lived. She didn't envision this life, certainly, one in which she would be meeting her gay ex-husband the day after commiserating with the man he had left her for. And who knew the actualities of Peter and Tobias and their life together? Her chaste and straitened world, even amid the siroccos of art-world politicking and gossip, was less emotionally . . . dramatic . . . than she would have wished. She wasn't sure if drama were the answer or, rather, whether hers had been for too long a Ruth Draper monologue minus the fully realized supporting characters.

# THE FIDELIO QUARTET

C laire could not see herself pulling away from a domestic turmoil
that wasn't hers; she was too curious. Tobias had asked for her
help. Well, no he hadn't—he'd asked for her time and for momentary compassion, the first of which she'd reluctantly granted, the
second she'd been unable to provide. He had not called her, either
to thank her for whatever reason—a show of courtesy, maybe—or
to commiserate further, which she in all honesty did not expect.
Perhaps he had regretted leaving in a huff. She felt, however, a continuing longing to connect with him; their lives had been marked
by the machinations of the impossible man, the emotional ne'er-do-
well they'd shared. Claire thought to inch her way to a state where
she might, through a somewhat smug appraisal of what Tobias was
going through, learn to accept herself more. She knew how hard it
was ever really to know anyone, our perceptions refracted through
a prism of misunderstanding. But the talking cure, the chatty, nattering psychotherapy of the commiseration, the motes of insight
suggested by such, might help. Claire was selfish, she knew, and
realized that her usefulness extended here only in what she hoped
to take away.

Still, after being upbraided by Toby for lingering over a failed relationship, and one predicated on falsehood and willful ignorance, she was a little reluctant for further scornful truth-telling. And despite her real, if minimal, sympathy for his emotional distress (she could only hold so much energy for a grudge), she was truly shaken by how obvious to others her stagnant emotional life was. She was like a picture that had sat unclaimed too long, been shopped around so much that others no longer admired, but passed by.

Claire's afternoon had been busy enough to keep her from endlessly speculating on herself, a subject she had grown rather tired of. She was still assembling her sale, which, beside the Tissots, had some other promising lots, including an Alexandre Cabanel "Birth of Venus" she hoped to get a quarter of a million dollars for. She also needed to arrange the lot order, to help create a rhythm for the sale. It was like sequencing an album—what songs follow or lead into each other in the best way? Should she place the pair of French framed faïence roundels of birds by Creil & Montereau from 1875 near other similarly priced works—under $10,000—or should she place them as a respite from the ones she hoped to score more from? Should she intersperse the Belle Époque with the Barbizon or the Dutch romantics? She knew that one star, a Gérôme or a Bouguereau, would likely cause the gold to be lavished upon some lesser works, the kind that dealers and interior designers bought for clients and that made up the bread-and-butter of the business.

It was close to 7 P.M. when she left, and she didn't have time to change for the opera. She hoped Peter wouldn't be wearing a tux. That whole Opera Club thing—formal wear, private dining, bad sightlines—was so fraudulent to her. But it was a club she'd never been asked to join, anyway, not that she'd be eligible, since it mainly consisted of gay men. She appreciated like-minded souls sharing their cultural interests, but the whole fussiness of this endeavor seemed to make opera-going more removed than it should be from artistic experience. If that *is* what these people wanted out of it. She suspected they were the diva types, who swooned over tales of operatic excess or grew teary-eyed at the overwrought melodrama rather than the expression of psychological nuance through music. She also suspected she envied these people their fervor, since, while she loved vocal music, she only managed perhaps three operas a season, and then only as the guest of a more well-heeled acquaintance. Or ex-husband. Her own emotions were rather more confined to lieder than arias, she suspected, the small suggestion of a wayward heart rather than the blustering fury of the righteous and wronged.

She was grateful to find Peter in a business suit. He looked, typically, none the worse for the tumult of his romantic life. If he even considered it tumultuous rather than lively. When had she last seen him? A couple of months ago? She noticed a fringe of gray around his sideburns and the suggestion of it at his temples. Even though he was barely a year older than she, he was—prematurely?—letting himself show the first signs of middle age, she realized, which was something new. He'd been coloring his hair for years—professionally. His family tended to gray early—his brother, Frank, had black hair streaked with white—but Peter had resisted nature. He reminded her somehow of a Max Beckmann painting: angular and determined, but with more humor. He had the planar cheekbones of a German expressionist, but the merry gaze of a Watteau lover. Funny how she often thought of those she knew more often in terms of portraiture, rather than movie actors, as had become the common shorthand among most other people for description. It was her training, she knew. Too many people, she thought, described themselves in terms of some vapid film star, rather than, oh, what would she have preferred—a Bronzino? More of her living in a separate reality.

Peter smiled when he saw her, his sheepish grin softening his face. He always smiled as if he had been inches away from discovery, had just escaped detection.

"I'm glad you could come," he said, bending to kiss her cheek.

"It's as much for Beethoven as for curiosity," she said, but she gave him a kind look.

"I don't know what Toby told you," he said, handing the usher their tickets.

"Not much," she said. "But then, why should he?"

They made their way among the crowds, the doddering and determined who clogged the aisles. She saw a few tuxedoed types here and there, overgroomed and somehow, to her, desperate. But then, she noticed more than a few women with dresses, or gowns, even, which could be charitably called unfortunate. One woman who would never see sixty again, sheathed in silver satin, could have slithered out of *The Makropoulos Case,* her replacement hips swiveling as she stole down the aisle before Claire, looking to either side, anxious to catch the gaze of acquaintances, she so fiercely attired in evening finery, they so fiercely unobservant of her charms. Nobody but Claire looked at her, nobody but the seeing-eye dog that sniffed past her to the row of its owner's seat. She felt for her, a very little; she knew what it was to be unobserved.

"Where did Toby stay last night?" she asked Peter.

"Our place. On the pullout."

"And you?"

"The bedroom. Alone." He paused. "I should've had some champagne." He looked around them, at the gathering crowd. This was opening night, she realized, thus the starched glamour and bejeweled wattles. He looked at her, reading her mind. "No, you're not underdressed. You look fine."

"Thank you. But, Peter, tell me—what's been going on?"

"I'm not heartless, Claire, if that's what you're getting at."

"I didn't say you were."

"And this wasn't like us."

"I didn't say that, either. Except for the leaving someone for another man."

"Don't let's go there," he said. "Look," he said, as more people took their seats, "things weren't great between us. The sex—"

"I don't want to know," she said.

"Sure you do."

"I don't. Honestly," Claire said. "It's none of my business."

"I am trying to give you a sense of where we were."

"I know. I want to know what happened to you. Curiosity, of course. But you don't have to explain it all in detail to me. To me, of all people."

"I think I owe it to you, in a way. It's your business because of what had happened. Our lives have moved on, but thanks to you, we've kept in touch. But you still think I'm a cad and, I don't know, I feel I owe something to you. It's nothing sordid. Well, only a bit."

"You can leave that part out."

"You're so innocent. Look," he said, lowering his voice as a pressed businessman squeezed past them, "I wanted to make a go of it. I really did. I know you think I'm a gadfly. But I wanted Toby and me to go on. And everything I began to do just annoyed the hell out of him."

"I can see his point, frankly."

"Keep those resentments coming, Claire, and you won't be single for long."

"I'm sorry. Go on."

"I think Toby just wanted more than I had in me—he wanted something different. A depth of feeling for something he couldn't describe, that I couldn't understand. Maybe it was a seven-year itch. Maybe he was getting off on hand jobs in the steam room. I couldn't figure it out. I even asked him if he wanted children."

"God forbid."

"Exactly. But I thought he was turning into one of those, you know, family types. I even considered it for one ghastly moment. He said no. And certainly not with me. And when I asked him what he saw in me that he didn't have, he couldn't answer, just that he'd changed and I hadn't."

"Yet you found the cop."

"Detective. But that was something that happened, after this had been going on for a while."

"And you weren't fooling around yourself? Not that it mattered."

"The gym doesn't count," he said. "Believe me. Toby told me I'd gotten complacent. I know people grow tired of each other. Christ, my parents hated each other and each hoped the other would die first. But he didn't really want to talk. And this went on for months. Months. Then, when I was wandering around downtown, back where I used to bike on Sundays, down by City Hall, I started talking to Sean, who was giving directions. Things just happened. They do. When I finally told Toby—I did learn, Claire, the danger of living a lie, believe me—when I told Toby, he chose to be outraged. I was unspeakable. So I gave him an actual reason for unhappiness rather than his vague whatever. What he didn't know was that I had no conception of how I had made him unhappy before. It was as if he willed me into action so he could bust out."

"So you blame him."

"Claire. I'm not blaming anyone. You're not listening."

The lights began to fade in the hall and the chattering grew to an urgent hum. "You have this conception of me, Claire, that is entirely unfounded," he said with *sotto voce* irritation. "You'd think that after all these years you'd have learned."

She didn't reply, but regretted her sarcasm, if only a bit, since she had been rude and he was her host. But her temper unloosed too easily around Peter, she realized, which may have been a reason for her not having seen him in a few months, or for her never actually speaking to him about anything of interest. She was like a man in that regard, avoiding the speaking. But he had such a damned earnestness in his insouciance that she felt it always wanted puncturing. He believed in himself so much, that he was trying, trying, trying to do right when he seemed to be careless of how what he did affected others. But what was it to her? And here she was, in such a flurry of unease regarding her own emotional uncertainties, casting her lot, as it were, with Toby as victim, that she disregarded Peter. But that wasn't true. She found herself flippant in the face of Peter's sincerity. But hearing Peter, she could sympathize further with Tobias, his unease, his wanting more, and his vague dissatisfaction at a relationship under whose strictures he bridled—she didn't know what those strictures were, nor what Toby longed for, but she felt that frustration. At this point, it was with herself, since her most profound relationship at the moment was with herself, and she had realized that she'd not been exactly forthcoming with herself, either. She knew that vague dissatisfaction could express itself upon the particular, as Peter's confession had given Toby a reason to articulate something he couldn't quite before. She had to admit, too, that she enjoyed Peter's discomfiture, even as she reluctantly admired his embarking on yet another relationship, even one for which she saw trouble ahead.

As the overture was being played, she forced herself to give in to the score, the story. It wasn't that difficult, the production being one of the rare ones that seemed to understand not only dramaturgy but music. And she responded, as always—she was more like the opera queens than she cared to admit—to the tale of selfless love. The story, even in her naïve assessment of any underlying reasons for it, moved her unexpectedly, sitting as she was beside her exasperating ex-husband. The man in my life, she thought.

As the quartet floated from the stage, the "Mir ist so wunderbar," time stopped for her, and she was lost to the realm of rare feeling. Marcellina, Leonore, Rocco, Jacquino, singing thoughts of longing and despair. Marcellina her emotive urgent love for Fidelio, Leonore her dangerous anxiety, Jacquino's despair that Marcellina would ever love him, Rocco selfless for his daughter. It was as if, for a few minutes, a shaft of wisdom had illuminated her, and for her, it was the revelation of thought as pure contradiction, a sublimity of opposites, a duality of desire. She was ashamed of herself for her inanition, but felt as if this shame were a call to action rather than a mortification of the spirit. She noticed in the hall a hush of expectant attention as the singers revealed themselves canonically, as if there were a blanket of shared understanding at the possibility of some forceful change as layers of melody wrapped themselves around each other, the intertwined conflicts of duty, longing, destiny. There was a tense pause just as the quartet evanesced and ended; no one rushed in with the first "bravi" but waited, an intake of aural enchantment before the release of applause, an exhilaration of the moment. She turned her head slightly to see Peter, and their eyes met, differently than before, his with a touch of—for the first time—a sad appreciation of some feeling she could not express. She had underestimated him.

But she did not know how to change yet. And she wasn't sure that her behavior would reflect any new or fleeting understanding.

"Thank you," she said at intermission. "This is something special."

They went outside to get away from the crowd. It was a balmy February night, a warm interval between bitter snaps. She felt how lovely it was to have a date, even an ex for a date, wandering at the intermission, chatting with someone one knew intimately, even falsely. She wondered if others saw them as a couple, communing over Art. Or just relishing their weeknight date, away from their children and the nannies and the board meetings and the other necessities of well-to-do married life. A life that wasn't hers, she quickly reminded herself. A life that would not likely be hers anytime soon. And a life Peter wasn't interested in.

Smokers lingered by the signboards, sheltered from breezes; a poster for a new production of *The Magic Flute* had a "Sold Out" banner swathed across it, and Claire felt a pang of curiosity about seeing it, which was the point of such advertisement, she assumed. Standing by it was Nathan Gresham, an English expatriate whom Claire and Peter knew together from their earlier life together. He was clad, as usual, in a dark suit with a bold striped shirt and a too-large bow tie. He was one of those persons who had given himself a signature look, like a fashion editor who wears oversized glasses that look ridiculous but become an exclamation point in an appearance: he wrote articles for *The Collector,* and had been researching a book, she remembered, on the auction world. He was the kind of person who had a nodding acquaintance with the well-connected in the arts, but who rarely spoke with any degree of either enthusiasm or, indeed, knowledge about any one of them.

He had put on weight, Claire noticed, and his face had begun to assume the proportions of a Botero burgher with a greedy gaze. Perhaps he was eating for two; Nathan was a noted walker of socially prominent matrons—that breed of calcified clothes horse who never ate, and rarely even sipped water for fear of having to use a public restroom, and whose husbands absented themselves with mistresses, masseuses, nonstop moneymaking, or even background boyfriends while the wives bejeweled their parched throats for charity. She wondered if Mrs. Driscoll had ever resorted to walkers during the bygone years of her social outings. She certainly would have kept herself watered.

Because Nathan networked so relentlessly, and rarely displayed an actual emotion in his furtive eyes, Claire felt untouched by the contempt beneath his artificial amiability. He bored her and, she suspected, she probably did him as well. Claire didn't really care for him, but because she had gained entrée to the homes of the rich, and because she had begun to make a small name for herself in a field where the socially connected frolicked, Nathan usually feigned interest in her. He probably had an eye for Peter, too, she suspected, though such longings or even inclinations were safely hidden until the women were walked, the tuxedo removed, the day's mortification of the flesh and spirit one.

Tonight he was squiring Susanna Pauling, a brittle specimen of sixty shimmering in satin, whom Claire had often seen in the Sunday Style photo spreads that captured the latest fashions worn by the well-heeled. They were contemporary reinterpreters of bustled women in old horse-and-carriage days who on their morning calls would have their servants drop visiting cards at other well-bred homes, not in the hope of engaging in actual greeting with the residents, but merely to indicate that one was recognizing another equal in the social sphere, and hoping also to be recognized with similar *cartes de visite* to be displayed in a grateful array later in the foyer.

The smoke from Nathan's cigarette wafted up around him, and Susanna waved her ringed talon in a tiny sweep to disperse its faint, luminous fumes. It appeared to Claire that they had been having a little tiff.

"I never thought to see you here," Nathan said to her, showing his lopsided teeth, and exhaling behind him.

"Nathan *must* have his fix," Susanna said, a lacquered finger moving to her crisp fawn hair, to check whether an errant strand had unmoored itself. She gave a little shiver, and hugged her bony arms to her side.

"Susanna disapproves," he said, stubbing it out. "Peter—so lovely to see you. With the Opera Club tonight? Or slumming?"

"Darling, you know that I'd rather spend time with my beautiful ex-wife than a bunch of nattering opera prigs," Peter said smoothly. Claire noted the "darling," which implied both condescension and, in its way, some gay complicity that served to belittle—or reaffirm, Claire couldn't at first tell—Nathan's walker status. "Claire," he said, turning to her slightly, "do you know Susanna Pauling? You should—Susanna's got quite an exquisite Ingres at home."

Susanna greeted her with the warmth of an old friend who might be contagious, smiling broadly, touching her hand but keeping a distance—a perfect, enviable social maneuver.

"Claire's at Sotheby's," Peter added, at which Susanna seemed to brighten, since she could then place Claire within a hierarchy.

"It's my little jewel," Susanna said to her. "A Virgin Mother." Ingres painted quite a few Virgin portraits later in his career, which managed to show Mary as a demure haut monde saint with impeccable style. "I should love to show it to you." Claire envisioned a makeshift Marian devotional corner in a quiet morning room, a chintz-covered prie dieu, futile novenas muttered to fend off liver spots.

"I'd like that," she said.

"Peter," Susanna said, "do call me for lunch. It's been too long."

"I'll buzz tomorrow," he said, leaning over to buss her concave cheeks.

"We should get back in," Nathan said. "Susanna's indulged my addiction long enough."

Claire and Peter looked briefly after them, then back at each other. She realized how much she missed the united front, as it were, that deflected the casual, random pettiness one encountered. Peter had managed to put Nathan on his guard—Susanna might be looking for a new walker any day now—but also in his place and, also, in a way to affirm Claire's status as someone worth knowing. He may not have been responsible for her career advancement while they were married—she knew she was good at her job—but she realized how, then, she had relied upon him to smooth her social path. She had come, indeed, to take it for granted and had not, until recently, been aware that she'd learned lessons of her own in this arena; having Peter by her side, even figuratively, had given her a confidence and a shield that as a single woman she sometimes lacked.

They walked a few yards away from the warm glare of the Met, toward the fountain in the middle of the plaza; the dancing, lighted water making a misty scrim behind them as they sat perched on the marble rim.

"Thank you for that," Claire said.

"For Nathan? Or Susanna?"

"For both, I think. Can you see yourself as a society walker?"

"Like that twerp? Claire, darling, for one thing, I have a sex life, and for another, although I have taken women like Susanna out now and then for the occasional evening of glittering tedium, I don't have the stomach to do it night after night, talking about their hairstylist, being sympathetic to their marital problems, offering advice about the Pilates instructor they have a crush on. Nathan's good at it, because that's really all he cares about."

"He is dull."

"That's just it—he's an ear with an eye for what women wear, and women love to be complimented, especially if their husbands are absent. By the way, have I told you yet how good you look tonight?"

"If you did, I didn't believe you then, and don't now. But, anyway, I'm sorry I was so flippant before," Claire said.

"I usually like it."

"Tell me," she said. "To go from walker to walking out. If you don't mind. What do you think is going to happen? You know what I mean."

"With whom? Toby? Me? Us?"

"All of the above."

"Toby's staying until he can get a new place. Not a pleasant situation. That's all I know for now. We'll work out money details later."

"What about the detective?"

"We'll see," Peter said. "He's not moving in."

"His mother, right? He lives with his mother."

"You say that as if it were a bad thing."

"Really."

"It's tough for him. He's not out to her. It's hard in his line of work. I can understand. Look at me. It's difficult for some people. Still. I'm not going to push. Besides, I don't know where all of this is going."

"It all seems a little out of your circle."

"A detective? Maybe. But he's bright. He likes culture."

"What? *Riverdance?*"

"There you go. He may not have your acquired sense of the fineries in life, but he's a good guy. That's a lot more than most people can say. I'd take him over that tiresome fop Nathan Gresham any day."

She didn't respond to that, and didn't feel a need to apologize, either. Toby was a good person, too. Everyone was good. La-di-dah. She'd have to wait for Frank, the handsome ex-cleric—a world of exes—to inject some wickedness in her life. At least he could be caustic, as only the clergy or former clergy could. Unless, God help us, he'd reformed, too.

The rest of the performance did not for Claire equal the first act, even the jubilant, bracing finale. They had a quick bite at one of those indistinguishable Mediterranean-type restaurants on Amsterdam. Following the opera—indeed, following Act I—they were much more at ease with each other, and Claire even had some grudging momentary acceptance of Peter's point of view. She was less prone to finish his sentences with sarcasm, was aware, too, that she wanted that companionship again. Not necessarily his, but the duality of a relationship.

"You know how I've stayed in touch," Claire said, over indifferent tiramisù.

"I thought we'd become friends," Peter said.

"Well, yes. I've wanted that. I did want it. Sometimes, though, I think because I've—we've—done that, part of me has not moved on."

He put down his dessert spoon. "Being friendly, friends with someone doesn't stop you from growing, Claire. It helps. Even if you're friendly with your gay ex-husband."

"Toby said something to me last night that made me think twice about how I've been living my life," she said. "Just one of those little nudges you need now and then."

"It was probably out of anger," Peter said.

"It wasn't bitchy, it was frustration, I think. He said the picture I had of us together before we were married was a sign that I was deluding myself into not accepting the past, in pretending I was magnanimous. He told me I was kidding myself. I don't know if it was seeing a picture of you before he knew you or you knew him, or because it was of us in a life he didn't know, but he left shortly after."

"Christ, I don't even remember that picture," Peter said. "And besides, his parents are actors, you know."

"He was dramatic, but he had a point," she said.

"Mementos are one thing. Not changing is another. Maybe Toby knows you better than I do. I certainly don't think that way."

"But you've moved on."

"So have you," he said. "You just don't see it, because you haven't had another relationship that meant anything to you. You've had a career. You've built a different life, you're building a different one."

"You've built a life, too," she said, still unsatisfied.

"And you're still a part of it. I've learned from you, Claire. You're only stuck in a rut if you choose to believe it."

She chose to believe nothing. Perhaps, like Toby, she'd had a nebulous unease growing within her, a dissatisfaction she couldn't name, a phantom glimpsed in the eye's periphery, a shadow, the white birds a drinker sees hovering around his vision. She'd over-reacted in the past few days, a hyperemotional expectation, as if her feelings were weeping the false tears of a Catholic idol in some dusty South American country. She wanted to believe in the redemption of torment, the dreams of the poverty-stricken for release from care. But she did not know how.

Peter was too considerate, ultimately too kind, to her. He was never not kind, after all, now, but in the flesh he no longer fit with her picture of him, as he'd been to her, as he'd seemed to her memory. Even her meetings with him in the past few years had been colored through that memory, through her perception, and she had interpreted everything through that possible misperception. Perhaps because she had rarely seen him alone in such a long time, always with Toby, or others. She felt that her lingering memories of time, her expectations of being with people, the pleasure or tedium of company or the appraisal of behavior—before, during, later— shifted, depending on the memory, the remembrance, the denial, the absurdity of the day, or the time of the memory's recall. People were never wholly one thing to Claire, or they were for too long that one thing. They were shifting representations of her attitude toward them based on their actions, her moods, her building preconceptions. Some friends were better for her for their being known—or being maintained—through one form of communication only, through e-mail or telephone. Others were dear for being distant, with intense days of visiting and relief at parting. Others, fewer, were alive to her variously. Just as we know our family through the hectic formative years we have spent together, and carry those sensations, physical, mental, emotional, with us far into our adult lives, with those thoughts rarely changing an underlying disposition toward sister or brother or cousin, so, too, do we react only to an aspect of a person we love, or an incident that has charmed or flattered or repelled us, she thought. So few people existed for Claire as being beyond a function in her life; she rarely thought to consider that other people were fully as human as herself. To her—and she occasionally realized this—they existed only partially in the "now" of any encounter with her, and were judged according to that fixed idea. Rarely did she consider the action only a part of one's fullness as an individual.

So for her, Peter had for a very long time been the man who had deceived her by deceiving himself or who had deceived her by not admitting to himself the truth about himself before becoming tied up with her before she had had a chance to realize the breadth of her self-delusion about him and about herself. In other words, she blamed him for not knowing himself enough to spare her the mortification of reluctant self-discovery. For her, she realized, after meeting his eyes in the tender sublimity following the transcendent *Fidelio* quartet, she had thought of him for so long as a kind of idiot savant, managing to get ahead in life without thinking of its workings. She'd considered him through only a few images she'd carried with her; one of them, she realized, was that signified or made manifest to her by the snapshot of the two of them from years earlier. It wasn't so much a dwelling in the past—though it was that, too—as it was a reinforcement to her of the particular picture of Peter she wished to maintain, even nurture. What, perhaps, struck Tobias as so odd about it, beyond his distress at Peter and his relationship, was its meaning for her, something that Tobias, with parents who assumed identities like clothes and whose self-perception, outwardly, to a child, lay in portrayals of people other than themselves, whatever those selves might actually be, Tobias seemed to her to be a man who could grasp the momentary impression of people as they shifted or evolved, and accept that change. But if that were so, why had he come to such an impasse with Peter? Was Peter changing in ways that Tobias no longer liked, or did he realize his image of his partner was wrong, and that perhaps he was evolving in ways he himself did not care for?

She could not answer for him, but saw that she need not be ashamed of her need to be at ease, if ease it was, with an earlier life. She did, however, question her ability to interest—or even recognize—the different facets of people she knew beyond either what she chose to recognize, or what they opted to display to her, to the world at large, at any particular time. In that regard, she wondered how complicit Peter was in her perception of him. Did he play the hapless charmer only for her? What role did he assume for Tobias? Did it change? She did not think him guileless, but neither did she credit him with duplicity, beyond their history together. And yet he had helped her decide herself about him, and their relationship, until when? Until it became too difficult to maintain a deception, or until whatever opposing selves within him became reconciled, or conquered, so that his true nature, in this one regard, forced itself into the open, for both of them? We lied to our lies, but at what point did this vortex of exploitation resolve itself into truth, if it ever did?

In any event, while Claire had eased her mind a bit about Toby's criticism of her, she was unsettled by her budding understanding, or a glimmer of something approaching it, of the capacity for imaginative manipulation in something as simple as "hello."

# THE CEO OF ÁVILA

The bleak outdoors: the craggles of snow on the wizened fields streamed by in a slow current. The train, a rambling Amtrak, creaked and sagged on the tracks near Rhinebeck. Two hours or so, Frank thought. Time to get off and turn back. Still time to stop. But, no. His path was clear for the next few months. Go on. Plod. Get done.

He'd taken a sabbatical for the semester, shouldn't renege. His substitute was arranged for—starting tomorrow, actually—a jocular newswoman, ex-reporter, sure to have the class on her side, happy and helpful, eager and pleasant, buoyant and insightful. A far remove from his own style, which he thought of as atavistic clerical military, the priest as drill sergeant, the students sniveling rookies, the course a minefield of pablum, agitprop, and obfuscation. Obfuscation. Obfucsation. Oh, for fook's sake, the little fooker, as the ridiculous leprechaun *oirish* visiting student from Eire would say, twisting words, having a ball with the written swill in his class: "Writing for Communication," a primer on corporate doublespeak, how to compose it, how to deconstruct it, how to wield it. The essential—well, a must—for the business-bound students and a fun gut, they thought, for the English majors who would use its tenets, such as they were, after their literary dreams had come to naught and they ended up in the poky public affairs office of a godforsaken development fund dreaming of Dickens and doling out policy wonk crap for the doubting cynics at endowment agencies and the earnest eggheads at foundations. Yes. It was time for a break.

Christmas had been hard. But really, it was a culmination of a year spent cultivating solitude. Little refusals of social engagement— no, thank you, I'm working on a proposal—turned into a steady prelapsarian solipsism: Frank before the fall. He'd taken pains to break out of his shell of isolation. Every so often he needed to remind himself that his was a service profession, and that, although an ex-priest, he did not live in a trailer writing tracts about Giotto. He had neither the liberty nor the blessing of any church behind him to concentrate on studies. He was paid to engage. He was a professor of English and writing. He had students. He had office hours. He had little use for them, he realized, and wondered if he'd turned into the kind of drone researcher who peopled the science labs. All bio research, no biography.

He had done the minimum, taught the minimum caseload, tutored the fewest students. He was a hardass, but the gullible students lapped that up, guileless guppies whose parents never disciplined them. A few barks, a pungent sarcasm, victory. He'd been—he was—oddly popular. Students warmed to his aura of iconoclasm, the ex-priest, when actually to have stayed might have been more iconoclastic these days. He never discussed doctrine, motives, religion. His was a private vocation, if vocation at all remained, and his a private torment publicly touted as belligerent taskmaster before business-bound students. Religious talks led to assumptive a priori arguments and he hated having to explain himself; he preferred gnomic cynicism. So he'd rather impress on the impressionable the mutability of language, the lurid falsehoods of the memo, the gesticulating cant of the prospectus, the honeyed ignominies of the annual report. He'd never write a devotional prayer book, a rhapsodic meditation, a treatise on supplication, or a commentary on mystic significance amid the everyday. What he was writing was a guide to business through the work of a genuine mystic, a genuine hard-edged soul, a genuine saint. The publisher loved his idea of a managerial book based on the writings of Teresa of Ávila, how her work in founding an order, running a convent might apply to an entrepreneurial business world. He'd hoped that using her forceful, admonitory prose, combined with his own knack for uncovering the sleight-of-hand in corporate babble, he might actually create something of use to the dunderheads who sought such encomiums in glib bookstores. Why not use the writings of a mystic to reveal the workings of the management mystique? And perhaps he'd actually have little lessons of morality embedded like computer viruses within the business-speak, to wreak havoc with the weak-willed who could use a little guidance toward the great beyond through the hortatory how-to of the self-help book. To him, the idea of daring to find spiritual transcendence in an age when mysticism carried the jejune air of tarot cards and tea leaves had a cunning allure. Accidental transcendence.

He avoided, would avoid, what he felt were the uncomfortable sexualities of her mystical meditations—his own take on Bernini's sculptural rapture, maybe. Though they could, too, be a selling point. Not that his own life benefited from his realizations. He felt as chaste as a nun.

Christmas had been, he had to admit, and admit again, hard. He'd stayed at the school, willfully snowbound, declining the requests of friends to share the day, the season, the festivities, the friendly mental frolicking, the folderol of cheer, emotional sustenance, savories, sweets, and fellowship. He'd avoided having to deal with his brother, who had finally gotten it through his thick head that he did not want to spend the holidays with him and his mopey boyfriend. Excruciating. He did not want to think of Peter. A constant irritant, always had been, always would be, it seemed. Frank had never felt a fraternal fondness for his younger brother; it was as if they were not only from two different generations, though only seven years apart, but different families altogether. It was more than his own vocation, at the time, and such as it was, which proved to be nothing more than an insipid grasping toward a profession, most likely, rather than the spiritual working en route to an elevation of soul. His vocation. His meager seminary class had five students, from the entire country. A pathetic posse of postulants. He knew he was odd, different. His stupid brother claimed the same thing, but for his own selfish reasons.

He looked up from his unread book, out the hatch-marked glass, at the now-undistinguished scenery, the cold Hudson. He liked these limbo hours of travel, suspended between responsibilities. He increasingly appreciated the suspension of responsibility, and realized he had abrogated many of his, in pursuit of nothing other than such limbos, as if he were floating in a clarity of drunkenness, an inebriation without the alcohol, musing, wishing, wandering, a wayfarer in daydreams.

He'd squandered Christmas, a season whose excesses used to charm him. He felt a pang, the first real longing for something he couldn't identify, since he could remember. This year, his natural remoteness had begun to give way to hostile isolation, deliberate separateness, armed withdrawal. His anxiety had surfaced, through a lack of form to his day, an uncertainty about his work or, more likely, seeing again his brother's ex-wife, and having to see his brother. Peter had done a number on Claire, that was certain. Why hadn't she hooked up with someone else? Another single woman in a sea of them in New York. Another one burned by romance. Well.

Not his problem, as she had told him long ago. And it wasn't likely to be. He knew better than to try to spark anything in that direction. No *Thorn Birds* manqué, no former priest fling with fallen idols, no fake Faulknerian melodrama. "Bless me, Father Yoknapatawpha, for I have sinned. This is my first incestation in three years. . . ." He'd chosen a different life, had different regrets, burned that bridge. He realized he'd become a freak in a benighted secular age that paraded religion yet parodied its practitioners, its conservatives. He still bore like a trace element the taint of religious calling; its half-life was markedly long. He felt in some way still part of what he had shunned, through cowardice or the revelation of deep-seated truth about himself. He had become embarrassed by his own training, as if he had awoken from a blackout to realize he'd been parading around in lipstick drag on the clammy streets of the Meatpacking district. A horrible nightmare. An unsettling image. He'd felt he'd become a risible anachronism, reviled by a populace repulsed by his Church's predators and their protectors, by a public convulsed with prurient apprehension and desire.

He hadn't even told his brother about his decision. They did not share secrets. They did not talk intimately. They did not suffer the soul-baring of siblings. It came out, in its usual way between them, with an offhand joke by Peter and a curt response by Frank. Peter, as usual, had called to ask him down. Thanksgiving.

"We'd love to see you," Peter had said. "It's just Toby and me, and maybe another lost soul without a family to be brutalized by. So we were hoping Father Frank could be part of it. We'd even let you say grace."

"I'm not Father Frank any more," he had said.

"Are you a monsignor now or something? Do we call you Excellency?" Peter had asked with a lilt in his voice, a humorous edge that got under Frank's skin.

"I've left the priesthood," he said, wishing Peter would drop it. But really, who could?

"Wow," he had said. "I'm sorry." Suddenly so serious. A galling concern. "What led you to this?"

"I just couldn't—it wasn't right for me. That's all. I really don't want to talk about it."

"That's big news," Peter had said. "I hope you're happy with your decision."

"I'm working on it."

"So, can you come for Thanksgiving?"

He hadn't answered immediately. He knew he was being rude, ruder than usual with his brother. "I'm going to beg off," he had told him. "I need to be alone up here for a while."

"Whatever you need. You know you're always welcome. Toby says hi."

"Hi to him, too."

To think he'd ever considered a life of service. He loathed himself, his anger, his yellow streak. He didn't have the conviction of deep belief, or the courage of seeing through a crisis of faith, or the backbone to consider options. He'd run, devolved into angry professor. So here he was, trying to cobble together the corporate-appropriate mantras of the mystic, make some money, escape. He did not have a particularly difficult life, he knew. Just an unfulfilling one maturing toward a miserable one.

Whom did he know who was happy? His ridiculous brother, probably. He always seemed to land on his feet. Even after wreaking havoc with others. Claire's was the tortured soul in that wrecked marriage, despite Peter's revelations and screwing around. Sure, she wasn't the first to be bamboozled by a sad closet case, but she was too sensitive to recover from duplicity. But why was he even wondering about her? She was no longer his sister-in-law, no longer family, barely a friend, he'd avoided getting in touch with her for so long, afraid of his own reproachful anger as much as his guilty tenderness. After the annulment, he'd pontificated at her with the boilerplate of spiritual blather he'd had no problem convincing himself of for a while, but then he'd let her lapse into fretful memory. It was as if she had never been there, merely an angel of light in his daydreams, an acquaintance of memory, outside the fold, beyond his ken. He hoped they could—connect—in a way that might spur him onward. He felt a certain avuncular regret at having let her remain merely distant, a chimerical fantasy of what might have been. Fulfilled, maybe, in work. But was there anything else? For himself, he did not really know. He had a temporary project, he had work of his own. But where was he to find solace, if that was what he wanted? One could live on bitterness for a while, like a car coasting on desert fumes. He didn't know if he was seeking or making busywork as a means of trudging through emotional stasis. Perhaps this work, this take on the genuine fervor and mission of a mystic would succor him in his own stumbling toward devotional enlightenment, but he doubted that. Devotion was no longer his stock-in-trade, in any form, neither blinding, disabling abandonment of a pathetic *Diary of a Country Priest* nor amorous, Franco-fatalistic Stendhalian *Red and the Black* intrigues. His was a black-and-white despair at ever becoming anything where he would feel comfortable.

He was a good teacher. He was a bad brother. He knew that, too. He really should make more of an effort. He should be the older brother, the responsible one. Peter was so much the feckless younger brother, the stand-in, the one who doesn't inherit the estate, the supporting role in the family drama. Frank had rather given up that mantle when he'd entered the seminary. Not that he needed to reassume it, really. He had not wanted to turn into either of his parents, but now felt he had become both. His recent life was one of expedience. So many wasted years in training, so many younger opportunities slipped away, so many choices chosen wrongly. Ah, me, he thought, as Lady Laura Kennedy said to herself, too late, when she discovered to her shame that by marrying the austere, dogmatic, and rich Robert Kennedy she had not solved her problems, but augmented them, and fated herself to misery. Too late, too late, she had told the penniless Phineas Finn. Her choices, ultimately selfish, had betrayed any hope of happiness. Was it so for him? Was it so, always? Did expedience pave the way to failure?

His vocation had been a road to nothing, however. Thus Ávila to the rescue. The saint's no-nonsense guide to meditation and business building.

His motives for this sabbatical, this break, were, despite his inner protestation or a priori arguments, he knew, less benign than he had admitted to himself. But so what? It worked for Mr. Kennedy and Emma Wodehouse. Though he was no Kennedy and Claire no Emma. What made him most anxious, he realized, was that he had no idea of how to proceed. He had no control over anybody, he had no idea how he would even feel face to face with his brother's ex-, or more accurately, according to Church canon, after the annulment, never-was, wife. He wondered if he were seeking the solace of work with the promise of commitment or stumbling toward a synthesis of devotional enlightenment and rapture. He really should reach out to his brother, if through nothing other than the courtesy of family ties. The truth was, he was a little frightened of Peter. While Frank himself had lacked the courage of his vocation, his brother, after lying to himself and others, finally fought his way to some sort of truth about himself. They were alike in that they had both been wrong about themselves—desires, beliefs—but it seemed that Peter had become free. While Frank remained fettered by continuing regret. Harboring disappointments led, naturally, to bitterness, Frank knew, and he knew, too, that he had for a while been heading toward becoming, instead of the celebrated celibate professor priest, the sour spinster professor. He was husbanding his resentments like resources to be unleashed later: the barren life of peremptory negation. At least one goal within his grasp!

He didn't think his idiot brother had such deception—or any—left. Frank had always suspected there was something amiss in him before, up to, and during Peter's marriage. But he figured Peter was too infatuated with frippery to conceal. Or maybe his demeanor, his unfussy friendliness, had covered the tortured soul of an artist. He doubted that. As if we were all personae with hidden agendas.

The cramped comfort of academic circles, the petty passions of discourse and infra dig dogma that plagued university departments appealed to his belligerence. How he had been able to argue himself into clerical garb for so long still puzzled him. He was by no means doubting, but he was sluggish, he was reluctant, he was a step away from taking faith for granted. His vocation had become a job he could trade in. When he was younger, the Church had lost many clergy to the secular life, to marriage, to the professions. His high school headmaster had been among them, marrying a Hungarian beauty, assuming a teaching position at Harvard, resuming a normal life—privileged, still, but more normal than a priest's. He couldn't predict that for himself; at this point, despite the lingering fantasy, he didn't envision himself in any kind of relationship, in any kind of emotional intimacy. He had given up the structured parameters of his religion, which he discovered offered little involvement for him intellectually—though it should have—or emotionally, though he'd hoped for that. His attenuated spiritual life, his empty emotional one, fed off each other, a starvation diet. He had not wanted the life of a parish priest; he loathed the homey, spavined churches, the dingy parish halls, the doughty parishioners. He much preferred tatty academics, and the cuirass of ironic arguments that belied a fusty professorial demeanor. His skirmishing, he had come to realize, was suited to the schoolroom, the hallway, the journal; his truculence in religious life was only a desperate dissatisfaction.

Frank knew that his strength as a teacher—his entertaining slander, and his refusal to suffer the smug cant of callow students—fostered lively discussions, helped make his classes well-attended, lively, rewarding forums for ideas. His ideas on the whole, but ideas nonetheless. Outside, he'd paint the party line—not that he didn't believe it—and usher the spiritually needy through a host of crises, anniversaries, doubts, sorrows, bereavements, a swath of personal counsel and catechistic guidance he frankly had grown to abhor. He used to question the veracity of his own beliefs, his belief in beliefs, knowing as he did how little service to the greater good he could provide. The Church had always had a place for scholars, for historians, for those whose inclinations lay outside the so-called domestic sphere. But he couldn't find that place for himself. He was furious with himself, with his choices, for the sense that his vocation should have, somehow, abandoned him, and refused to help him believe more than he had.

He looked at the slow scenery through the window. The train appeared reluctant to make it to Grand Central Station on time. Like him. He hadn't been to New York in years. He should reach out to his brother. Yet he felt so irresponsible, always had, even with the righteousness of false fervor. Nowadays, with the Church a gelastic symbol of bureaucratic morass, unctuous, dithering, its communicants in shame, a man's vocation was more an aberration of spirit than a journey toward service or even redemption. For him, anyway. His cynicism had blinded him to the possibility of salvation.

Even when Frank had begun his studies he was an anomaly. He had been sure, or thought he'd been sure, had burned with desire of a sort, such desire as he thought he had, and had he known or comprehended what it was? He had been certain that his path lay before him, a clerical life. So many wasted months, inculcated into the rituals. He had realized—when? Barely into his training he had wavered within, but had plodded on to ordination, like a fateful first date that ends inexorably in mortification and marriage. Or vice versa.

Certainly his leaving the priesthood hadn't made him happy—relieved, yes—but not happy. His was not a life of simple goals, hadn't been yet, unless one could call avoidance a goal in itself. His was a life of angry deliberation, though he felt neither righteous nor vindicated by his opprobrium, however sparkling his wit shone in the classroom. He had not yet learned grace. He hadn't mastered or, frankly, attempted the rigorous self-examination that might lead to a release from his baffling preoccupation—love, romance, denial, advancement, ease from imagined penury. And he a former confessor, trained in clemency. He had meant to follow, to lead others through following a higher path, but instead of that sureness he was one of the so many once-devout, now-aimless souls, untethered by belief and without the solace of even a questionable faith. There was succor in doubt, surely? But for him, now with his mind lapsing toward the trivial, he doubted doubt. He felt better equipped to deal with the ornate equipage of corporate doublespeak than the ornery lacunae of his beliefs. The chilly mental caress of indecision.

His phone vibrated with a call.

"Frank!" He heard the familiar voice.

"Peter," he said.

"I heard you were coming to town for a while. Why didn't you let me know?"

He didn't want to have to explain. "I didn't want to put you out," he said.

"How could you put me out? You've never stayed with me. It would have been good to know, that's all."

Peter was insistently chipper, sometimes. Frank always thought it masked nervousness. He knew he should probably try to put his brother at ease, but why start? Either you did or did not get along. It was the nature of family.

"I figured you'd be busy with Toby," he said.

"Ah," Peter said. "The thing is, Toby and I are kind of over."

"Over?"

"It's a long story, but we're not together any more."

This was something new. Despite Frank's dismisiveness regarding Peter's relationship, he actually counted on a certain stability there. It was an odd bulwark of sorts for him, unchanging in its otherness, even if he were uncomfortable being in the presence of that otherness.

"I'm sorry to hear that," he said, after a pause.

"Thanks." Frank could hear the street noises around his brother's voice. "It was inevitable."

Inevitable how? In the nature of such relationships, or just this one?

"Well," Frank said. "I'm sorry."

"Listen," Peter said. "I'd like to get together, when you're settled."

"Sure. Anything serious?"

"Not really. I just want to ask you about Mom and Dad."

"Mom and Dad? What's to know?"

"I came across some papers, stuff I'd never looked at, stuff I'd had since you were away, being a priest."

"What in particular?"

"It'd take too long on the phone," Peter said. "Let's talk when you're caught up. Okay?"

"Sure, tomorrow. I'll call you. I have your number."

"You do? Maybe you *have* changed."

What could Peter have about their parents? They were a doomed couple, who had kept retying the frayed marriage knot to keep it from unraveling, but failed in the end. Unlikely spouses, their father a rather bookish man who tended to bore insensibly anyone he managed to lure into conversation. His opening salvo in conversation promised chatty literary conviviality, but ended up in the pursuit of some dreary academic printing statistic. He loved the minutiae of the printing process—he'd worked at a small press. Fine, if you were Balzac, but most people were bored out of their skulls. Their father generally preferred the dry past to any present, until he left, of course, and all presumption vanished, along with him. Then it was speculation. He had been a devout man, as far as Frank could remember—as far as he chose to remember—involved in various church groups, parish activities. He took comfort in the ceremony of lay religious life. No, that was not it. He hadn't been comforted by ritual, but a slave to it. It was as if the rite were law, and deviation damnable. His father had been outraged by the change in the Church over the years, and lamented the loss of strictures of the past. He probably would have appreciated today's new conservatism, and probably even sympathized with its hidebound secrecy and sexual concealment. The hetero kind, anyway.

His father had been proud when Frank had announced his intention of becoming a priest. It was probably a good thing he hadn't lived to see Frank's failure. But Frank had certainly lived to see his father's. The ordination had been a high point of his father's life. There, at least, a majestic pomp remained, as the men were elevated into a life of service and prayer. Even then, Frank knew something was amiss. His mentor had had sessions with him, their purposeful guidance contrasted with his own rather more willful determination, but he had yessed and answered and resolved on pursuing this particular goal, much as a minor-leaguer whose natural talent lies a hair below the big-league players will, with constant exercise and pluck, eventually gain a spot on the stadium roster, for however brief a time. That was Frank. In the words of Matthew 18:17, he thought: "If he will not bear the Church, let him be to thee as a heathen and a publican." So, heathen that he was, he was glad his face—beaming with implied reference those twenty years ago—so filled his often-disappointed father with joy. But the illusion of vocation did not serve in the end to foster an actual one. The Apostolic Succession stopped with him. And he was still glad, even though his nagging doubt at his ordination was ex post facto a lie. He did have the grace, if that was grace, to realize that, if he no longer had the capacity for imparting truth or even the hope of salvation to anyone, then he could perhaps gain by stepping down.

And his father had vanished, shortly after his ordination—it was as if he had been waiting for such an event to leap into a different void of his own. He had taken off with, of all things, a nun. As if his mother hadn't been the joyless penitent enough, he had to find a wimpled hussy to run away with.

It all seemed so long ago. He hadn't said Mass in years, he hadn't studied scripture. He had forgotten the gospels, he had forgotten the ablution rites, he had forgotten his father's shameless desertion. He'd lasted ten years as a priest. Not one of them was happy. His father had left his mother about six months after he'd been ordained. And he had left the Church about six months after Peter had left Claire. Not that there was anything related to timing in either event. His father, probably. He doubtless wanted to ensure that his priest son was embarked on a life of spiritual healing, so that he could with impunity mock it with his affair. He and his brother, even his father, were more alike than he had wanted to admit. At least he wasn't a cocksucker. Though at this point that didn't seem like a plus. They'd all been disgraced, somehow. Only Frank knew it. And Peter didn't care. And their father was dead.

Frank disembarked at Grand Central Station, half hoping someone would be there to greet him. Claire, maybe, though he knew she had no reason to be. They planned dinner that night, a get-reacquainted meal, a date between the ex-priest, the shaky Catholic and the shapely ex-wife, the ex–sister-in-law. The moving chaos of the station brought him back to the present. He found a cab and headed uptown.

The apartment was as promised—a roomy two-bedroom with an office. The cat was, as cats went, not too threateningly feline. Frank knew if he ignored it the cat would respect him. The décor was not overwhelmingly feminine, for which he was grateful, except for an unfortunate tendency here and there toward angel motifs on the coffee mugs. He'd expected a banker to be less pagan in worshipping the heavenly demigods that populated the tchotchke shops at malls, the tutti putti emporia. But a talent for making money didn't extend toward any sophistication of thought. Perhaps she worshipped Baal. Angels had overtaken all other images as acceptable signs of sweetness and an abjuration of responsibility, Frank thought. When people relied on angels to get them through their days, they released themselves from thinking things through. In an age of hyperstimulation, and short attention spans, and an intolerance of any pain—*Parsifal* this was not—why not rely on the blessings of some other being to absolve one from accepting the world as it was? Raphael's winged angel heads had done as much to foster the decline of rational thinking as the most pernicious pyramid scheme did to empty one's wallet. But, here: this apartment wasn't too bad. Frank had done some cursory drawer-pulling to put away his clothes, set up his computer—he was glad to see she'd installed high-speed cable—and lay on the bed to rest, staring up at the dusty ceiling fan, which was idle but rimed with traces of soot. Missed a spot, he thought.

The cat—its name was Getty—jumped onto the bed and sat at his feet. So much for the cold shoulder. Its green eyes stared at him with that catty blend of malevolence and boredom. It began to lick its orange paws, and occupy itself with ignoring him conspicuously. A little nap seemed like a good idea. For both of them.

He awoke to the half gloom of fading day. The cat had settled on his suitcase. He hoped it—he, she?—wasn't a shedder. Not that it mattered. He was hardly a fashion plate. Prickly, impatient, and sarcastic, yes. Fashion-forward, no. At least he didn't have to walk the creature. The cat stared up at him, like a seer, and blinked back toward a sound from the street. Like the sudden crosscut in a movie between the tense dialogue, the fraught emotion, and—whoosh!— the unblinking cat, as if somehow it heightened the tension when a director intercut between the human and the animal. He remembered that vivid, clichéd old Bergman movie, *Clown's Evening,* when the circus couple, the bitter married—just like Mom and Dad!—were entwined in their vicious, spewing brawl in the airless hole of their wagon, their vituperation underlined with a shot of a circus pussycat, his head turned away from the threat of violence, his ears pricked in danger, rendering the brawl, now unseen, but heard, a pathetic litany of acrid sorrow and loveless recrimination. Maybe it hadn't been so clichéd. Just like Mom and Dad, their horrid muffled screeching waking him frightened, waking him to a feeling of longing for escape, hoping they would die, leaving him and his baby brother parentless and free, free, free.

"Meow," he said. The cat remained unamused. Cats were never amused. The doorbell rang.

He stretched, shook off his fatigue, and went to the living room. Peering through the cautious eyehole, he saw, in wide-angle expectation, Claire. In that second, he noticed how different she appeared than his memory had rendered her—her hair was cut shorter, her lovely face haunted by a questioning intelligence, expectant, though still vital. He opened the door to her, more nervous than he had any right to be.

# THE INADVERTENT HEADSHOT

How long had he been sitting here, staring, playing the same songs over and over again, listening to the soundtrack to *Magnolia*? Peter had left quietly that morning, trying to be as unobtrusive as, well, as Peter could be. Staying out of each other's way. Toby did not want to prolong this; he would leave soon. Nestor and José, his crazy architect friend and his boyfriend, who for some reason seemed to know every drag queen in town, had a spare room. They had offered to put Toby up for as long as he needed until he got his own place. Toby knew he was the one to leave the apartment he and Peter had shared. It felt somehow more Peter's place, anyway. Even though they'd moved in together, it was Peter who'd first seen it. So, in the housing universe, he who made earliest contact with the broker got the apartment after the breakup. It was one of those relationship things—who keeps what, who visits the dog. Who starts a new life. They both would, of course. Toby's seemed less of an adventure at the moment than an unmooring. Perhaps he'd visit his parents in L.A.; he hadn't seen them in a couple of months. His parents would love to see him, as stifling as he surely would find them, it. But at least they were sober. And alive.

He shook himself. Moping. No wonder Peter was tired of him.
He'd become a pill, rarely laughing, petulant, impatient, humorless.
When had this alienating unease crept in? It was a gradual decline,
a descent into nelliness. He'd been startled to learn how he'd begun
to appear to others. He had a photo of his last trip back to see his
parents. One of their A.A. buddies had snapped it. It was their
agent, Betty, actually, who'd started getting them acting gigs.
They'd met her at one of those superfriendly meetings near their
house in Studio City. When they had shared to the group they
were former actors, she plunged, like any ravenous agent, and had
begun to find them work. She'd become a part of their lives—for
which he was grateful, even if she was grating. They did commer-
cials, the occasional music video, the walk-on or speaking role in
an independent or student flick. They had a purpose, beyond
drinking, even as part of a sober life. She had become their friend,
their den mother, their booster, their agent. Was she really an agent?
He had expected someone more feral, though equally brash.
Anyway. "Let's get a shot of you all smiling," she said—she'd probably noticed the conspicuous lack of family snapshots in his childhood home, or even of pictures of his parents when they weren't
decked out as the Ghost and Mrs. Muir or one of their pre-Tobias
regional theater roles. Pity his sister Regan wasn't there. He wondered why they hadn't gone whole hog and just named her Goneril.
They could've chosen Cordelia, but no, daffy drunk drama queens
at heart, they went with one of the evil sisters. His mother had
loved the name, the actor, the politician, the Shakespearean lilt. She
had chosen to ignore the subtext, which was typical of his parents'
lives together. Betty had driven Celia and Bill—her new dear
friends—and newer clients!—home from a meeting, and saw the
perfect opportunity to continue her aggressive goodwill by wielding
her new digital camera. "I'll send it to you, Toby," she'd said. "That

way you can finally have a family photo." He'd actually laughed when she took the picture, as he'd just, minutes before their return, come across boxes of brand-new headshots that Celia and Bill— Mom and Dad—had had done of themselves, with various expressions, changes of clothes, all for their newly relaunched careers. It was like the old days—minus the inebriated squabbling, the pushed-aside furniture that had been stumbled over, and the teary invective. It was like the days when their other drunken gasbag actor friends, those hams who'd chewed up summer stock scenery from Williamstown to La Jolla, would just "drop over" every Friday for cocktails and torment. Reliving *Our Town* in Paducah, or *Harvey* in Harrisburg, or *The Corn Is Green* in five cities in two weeks. God we had fun, they'd shriek, amid the clinks, the catarrhal coughing, the hiccupping, and the patchwork regret of middle-aged despair. Toby had seen those hopeful boxes of 8x10s, his mother's raised plucked eyebrow—her schoolmarm dominatrix expression, he'd called it—and his father's equally raised bushy one, the quizzical scientist child-molester look—and had been moved by their timeless optimism. Ever actors, always one step ahead of disappointment, swallowing the gall of rejection. Here they were, eighty and some and silly and stalwart. Betty had said, "Say cheese!" and his parents' faces assumed the position—the non-paying role of parents—and Toby had laughed. Later, at his office in New York, a colleague, Lisa Farrell, had seen the image on his computer screen—Betty had been true to her word—and told him, "You never look like that here."

"Like what?" he'd asked her.

"Happy."

He'd considered that. He didn't, hadn't, felt unhappy, as much as restive. Or less likely to be entertained, which perhaps amounted to unhappiness, perceived, maybe actual. He never really felt happy with his parents, although he certainly was happy *for* them. And they were always so sweet to Peter. Even the first disastrous time they'd gone out to visit, when Peter and Tobias had made the mistake of staying with Toby's parents, toward the end of their drinking. They'd tried. It was about a year before they'd got sober. What possessed Toby ever to say yes to staying with them—he'd envisioned what would later occur—were his mother's teary pleas. "Please," she'd mooned into the phone, in her most desperate *Sorry, Wrong Number* voice. "We're so alone here." After the twentieth such variation, he'd relented.

"How bad can it be?" Peter had asked. "It's just a couple of nights."

"Sartre bad," Toby had said. "*No Exit* bad."

And it was worse.

His childhood home was in such a sorry state, he would have driven by it if his parents hadn't been waiting at the window when the car had slowed down, and staggered out into the yard. It looked as though they had tried to make it seedier, not only through neglect, but malignant bluster. The paint was blistered off the trim, the lone cactus by the driveway, even next to the sere brown lawn, was a forlorn sentry, the whole effect one of Dust Bowl desuetude over midcentury modern snappiness, and sadder than he could bear. It looked like they hadn't left the house for any period of time. Within, the curtains were drawn not only against the heat of the sun, but the prying light, the insistent day. The gamboge shag carpet held the fumes of countless cigarettes, quarts of cocktails, the scuffles and falls of the inebriated obtuse. Toby had forgotten how much it looked like urine—what were they thinking when they had bought it so many years before? The house itself, in a blandly fabricated faux Neutra style, would have been chic had it been cared for, had Celia and Bill a flair for decorating rather than for the dramatic.

The furniture, a mélange of quaint, dated 1960s artifacts and dull colonial pieces, said not home, but maybe, and barely, shelter.

"Welcome home," his father had said. They had been drinking, so slurry were his words already. It was 11 A.M. It was a Thursday. It was probably their typical routine. "And this good-looking young man must be Peter," his father had gushed, to Toby's alarm, at both the intoxication and the barely concealed flirtation. He'd rather not have known that possible side of Dad. Peter had been his usual suave self, able to glide over the choppy waters of mixed drinks and self-medication carelessly. They'd declined the cocktail his father had tried to force on them, put off the tour of the house and promised to look through their clippings later that day. His parents then had retreated for a "siesta" around noon, arguing incoherently and suddenly in their blacked-out bedroom, the darkness sliced by cruel shafts of light where the drapes didn't join fully. Toby had closed the door on their incomprehensible but loud bickering—he thought it had something to do with either dinner or Peter—and felt ashamed for them, helpless, strangely isolated, but glad of Peter's presence, despite the mortification. "You were a big help," Toby had told him. "My parents could occasionally be like that," Peter had said. "Only younger and pushier. I learned to avoid confrontation, I guess, and not worry too much about making sense."

Somehow, they'd managed to get through a night. Toby stayed in his old room, a shrine to his boyhood—only because it hadn't been changed since he'd left for college twelve years earlier. Less an homage than neglect. Peter had slept in his sister's old room, which was not a shrine by any means. It was a research center; it was where Toby's parents stored the artifacts of their acting careers. Toby imagined—correctly, it turned out—that they'd hauled the boxes of albums, occasional papers, and programs from various sozzled show-and-tell nights with their other retired actor friends and hadn't bothered to return the boxes to the attic. Thus was a repository born.

The evening had been spent with Toby trying to get dinner together with his parents bumbling through the kitchen—"I'll just freshen that up, dear" was the refrain from the living room as one or the other parent returned to the refrigerator for ice and vodka—while Toby threw together a quick pasta that neither his mother nor his father ate much of. They were alternately glassy-eyed and morose or belligerent and manic, sometimes within minutes. Peter had been calm throughout, as if his astral self were far away, and his physical form a mute observer. By the end of dinner, his parents had become almost insensate, though they had once or twice begun to argue about some tidbit from Toby's childhood. By eight o'clock, they had staggered to their bedrooms once again, just to pick up some trinket, and within seconds their snoring could be heard through the half-closed door.

The next morning, Toby and Peter made their escape, pleading a full schedule for Peter as Bill and Celia made coffee, very early. It seemed to Toby that they had welcomed being left alone again, so that they could retreat to the empty solace of a bottle, and not have to sneak some morning pick-me-ups. Toby told them the evening had been fun, which seemed to reassure them, somewhat, that they hadn't behaved too badly, since it was obvious they couldn't remember a thing, and would never remember, and were grateful for the lie.

Peter's trip included a colloquium on furniture restoration at the Getty, and he and Toby met Bill and Celia only once more on this trip, timed so that the visit was early enough for the coffee to kick in and not too late in the morning for the first swallow of alcohol to numb the senses overmuch. The next time he and Peter had seen

Toby's parents, as a couple, Bill and Celia had been sober for almost a year. The house still had the time-warp feel of something that hadn't been fully transported between dimensions, caught in a wormhole between Pop Art and postmodernism—it could've been an exhibition at the Tate Modern—but it felt clean, which was something. And it smelled of fresh coffee instead of liquor and cough syrup. His parents had taken to guzzling coffee—percolated—as if it had been booze, as if it were more than a jolt of burnt caffeine before the onslaught of alcohol of their drinking days. They seemed to thrive on gallons of it daily, to stay jittery through their twilight years.

Bill and Celia had come to New York and stayed with Peter and Tobias for a week. His parents, so glad to be back in Manhattan, had run into several acquaintances of yore at A.A. meetings near Times Square, in the theater district. They'd become so enraptured by the cast reunions of now-nondrinking actors that Toby had felt a bit jealous, even resentful, of their independence. His mapped-out itinerary, a careful diagram of theaters, museum art-world openings—he wanted to show off his insider pull—had become incidental to their new plans. Peter had sympathized with them, which annoyed him. At the same time he was irritated by his petulance; after all, it was their trip. He hadn't expected to be less useful than he'd planned.

"You're so blasé about everything," Toby had said to Peter after his parents had foregone a cocktail reception in order to have coffee with a couple with whom they'd overacted eons earlier.

"I wouldn't say that," he'd replied. "But you have to see their point of view: they've embarked on a new life. They're grateful for your help. But what is it exactly that you want them to do?"

He wasn't sure. What rankled most was his parents' disregard for his evident annoyance. He'd been responsible for their getting sober in the first place, assuming control of their muddled finances, their chaotic living arrangements. He'd given them an ultimatum, which had worked: sober up or lose everything. They had changed—which was remarkable enough—and were now, actually, different from what he'd imagined. Independent. Bright. Opinionated. Funny. And their daffy actor friends laughed at their earlier excesses—much as they had done during those interminable blotto soirees in L.A., but without the shrieking and shattered glass. Here they had laughed and laughed, in relief and gratitude for having made it so far. But he'd neglected to think how his role would change; he was now an onlooker in a different sense. This sense of prickly otherness with Toby lingered through their visit. It had been a triumphant return for them. He was happy for them, but dissatisfied with himself; it wasn't enough that he had helped them. Now that they had become adults, he had less focus, despite his job, despite his relationship. With them he could exercise, at first, some palpable results. Instead of the triumph of self righteousness, he had begun to suffer selfish regret—his journey was hardly as dramatic as theirs, he had been responsible, he was now, he had thought, disposable as a result. It hadn't mattered at the time—or he hadn't actually measured its importance—that the steady accrual of minutes, hours, into career, life, romance, because they were things looked back on rather than felt immediately—held little reward for him. He realized this delayed sense of worth, if that's what it was, was keeping him from appreciating the gifts he had in life—or at least, he agreed to realize this with a nod when his shrink had mentioned it to him. He had also begun to sense that his growing unease had arisen out of his impatience. He preferred to organize rather than contemplate.

Now, he needed to get past the present. Now that Peter had set things in motion, Tobias didn't want to be swept away. He certainly didn't want to end up as Claire seemed to be—aimless, passive. He didn't want to be what he already was in danger of becoming as well—the humorless, thin-skinned gay man, the art fag, the prissy prude who trafficked in disdain as an exercise against losing control. What we can't control we scorn. We scorn, we rue, resent, and scorn again. Was it ever too late to wean oneself of contempt?

But he had to admit his tendency to self-pitying flippancy—the barbed inward-turning verbal projectile—held little allure for him now, had held less and less than in his sarcastic college years. Then, of course, arrogance and earnest self-regard mingled with raw disdain. Increasingly, it took energy to inject comments with bile, mainly because he no longer felt it, and life-as-hissy-fit had grown tiresome. Even for the child of self-dramatizing actors, the fungible persona—a different face for a different room—was not attractive. Yet Toby was now uncertain in his persona. He didn't know what, or how, to project. Without meaning to, he had become separate selves, or was it a progression toward one mature self? His parents, for so many years living as fictional others—even in their actual at-home parental child-rearing years—seemed now to have come into being as real, wearing their craft lightly yet avid in resuming it, clear-eyed, competent, actual. He did not want to be them—even their half-finished-sentence life was a life sentence for him—but he envied them their new dignity, born of experience, even the experience experienced through the fog of booze, the mortification of their tangled passionate lives. He had drifted into his career. He had fallen into his relationship. He had been, perhaps, best in the only role he was actually born to—that of the dutiful scolding son. It gave him some comfort still that he had been instrumental in his parents' recent lives, despite his dissatisfaction with the change in their relationship. He realized that, amid the various assistances he had rendered Celia and Bill, he had not seen what had so begun to unnerve him in his own relationship. He now saw that he had recoiled, at first mentally, then emotionally, then physically, from Peter because their relationship had begun to demand more than the intimacies of physical affection but the discourse of the shared experience, the growing simpatico that led to the finishing of sentences, the punctuating of phrases, the loss of independent thought. "What was the name of that book I'm reading, honey?" he once heard a couple—a young couple, one of two pushing strollers, happy in the deluded enchantment of parenthood. "What was that book I'm reading?" He had thought, hearing their enthusiastic nonsense, the patter-chatter of couples meeting to gush about their children to the only other people who cared, other couples waxing dithyrambic over offspring no one but they heeded, remembering a book that provided—what?—a pleasant diversion from the demands of couplehood? Maybe one of them could start the book and the other finish it, like conversations. Anyway, hearing that breezy, nonchalant, matter-of-fact couple speak rather horrified him. Is this what life holds for those who remain? Are the shared moments worth it? Certainly he and Peter had memories together, happy days, hours, nights, passages. But as they lived longer together, Tobias had felt more an onlooker in their relationship, appraising himself, rather, he thought, like the more career-minded people he knew who actually considered where they might be in five years, or at a certain age, and how they might get there. He, however, if he were to have asked himself where he saw himself at some point, would think not of career, but his life with Peter, and he would wonder if it would be worth it, if anyone were worth giving up oneself with such indifference to individuality. Well, his own five-year plan was over. What was the name of that book we were reading?

# SEPARATE CHECKS

If she weren't so sure of its address, Claire could've sworn this was the same restaurant she and Peter had eaten at the night before. But it only looked similar: a Tuscan commissary surely supplied many of these neighborhood joints, grilled whatever over air-cured something. The beginning of the evening had gone more easily than she'd thought. Frank had been strangely awkward at first, as if they had not been related at some point—or maybe because they had been. He was still as good-looking as she remembered, if somewhat careworn. Father What-a-Waste, she used to think of him back then, one of those priests too dreamy for the vocation. He was a different sort of handsome from his younger brother, with the direct gaze of one of those Roman-era Egyptian mummy portraits, where the sitter—actually the prone—scrutinized one with a false impression of living, but a real impression of a life. Those portraits had such a poignant immediacy and economy of line that they could've been modern. But for his coloring, Frank, with his big eyes and verging-on-mournful expression, could have graced a funerary lid, if he were lifeless, that is. But she had been relieved to see him regain his sardonic composure as he showed her around the apartment.

"The cat seems to like you," she'd said.

"They generally do. I ignore them."

"Her last one, Vanderbilt, was not so friendly."

"Vanderbilt. She names them after—"

"Robber barons. Her banking joke."

"Better than Fluffy. I once knew of a professor who named her Great Dane Gertrude Himmelfarb, after the social philosopher."

"Do you think she ever found out? Gertrude?"

"She had to have. She included it in every bio for every article and book. 'Elisa Staunton is the author of *The Analects of Theodosia* and the owner of Great Dane Gertrude Himmelfarb.' Academic wit. So to speak."

"Poor dog. She was clueless, of course. The dog, I mean."

"It was a he."

"Worse," she said.

And so they'd bonded again, but it was tentative, since they hadn't discussed Peter. Claire had not known what to say, or, indeed, how to approach the subject if and when it was brought up. He did, eventually. They'd been nursing drinks—hers a very light vodka tonic, his a double scotch on the rocks. She could detect the sweet repugnant aroma of his whiskey as he whirled the glass around to chill the scotch. She saw that his large hands made the glass seem smaller than it was. The cuticle of his middle finger was split.

"Cheers," he said. "To—what?"

"Just cheers," she said. "It's nice to see you, after so long." She put her drink down. She barely drank, and rarely finished one. Her father had died of alcoholism—parental alcohol abuse was something that she had shared with Toby, that had helped them when they had first become acquainted, after the awkwardness of the situation.

Frank smiled at her. "So" he said, "Peter's at it again."

"At it?" she said.

"Screwing around."

"Is that what you call it," she said. She knew the two weren't close, but had forgotten Frank's dismissive intolerance.

"Well, what else is it?"

"Frank. I'm surprised at you. Maybe if you actually tried to get to know your brother you wouldn't be so coarse. And what is it to you, anyway? How many times have you actually met Toby? Do you actually care if he got hurt? And why are you putting me in a position to defend your brother?"

"Sorry," he said.

"It's like you've been living in another country," Claire said.

"In a way I have been," he said. "You don't know what it's been like, feeling as if you've wasted years doing something you had no reason to be doing. . . ." He trailed off.

"Try me," she said.

"Of course," he said. "Of course—sorry. But, I've been so isolated. It's as if I've forgotten all social skills." He told her about his semester, his growing solitary ways. He described his Christmas, the obstinate refusal to take part in academic parties, year-end festivities. He'd holed up, avoiding anything but the work needing to be done, the papers, the paperwork, the paper trails of departmental bureaucracy.

"I read four Agatha Christie novels in one day," he told her. "Four Hercule Poirot. From the 1930s."

"You could've seen your brother," she'd said.

"I couldn't," he said. "I just couldn't."

"Tell me," she said. "How did you spend your days, then? Besides the murder mysteries. You could've been watching daytime television. You could've been working on your book."

"I wasted time. I was lonely."

"But you brought that on yourself," Claire said.

"That didn't make it any less real."

She knew that, certainly. Often, after a few dates, she'd sense that a new relationship probably held no future, and would end it. She had chosen private resentments, or determined withdrawal, over building relationships. After Peter, she had been wary of being hurt, a natural thing. Who wouldn't have been? Peter, for one. But she could hardly criticize Frank for neglecting his brother. Her own relationship with her sister was barely cordial these days. They were only a couple of years apart—Catherine was older—but their lives had grown further apart than that. Catherine's husband was an anesthesiologist in Cincinnati, and Catherine taught at Indiana.

Her sister's hauteur had been evident early on; holidays were not exactly warm. They were more the occasion to mark the end of negotiations, or the fulfillment of treaty obligations. Catherine would give her a Christmas list—she had a separate one for her parents—with what she wanted, its approximate cost, and where Claire could most likely find the items. For her part, Catherine gave the gifts she thought Claire needed, rather like a humor-free, well-meaning aunt. "I noticed Mrs. Mirro praised your museum school trip report," Catherine had said at one of Claire's birthdays. Catherine often looked through Claire's papers. "When you have a younger sister you can look through her things, too," she'd told her when Claire had complained, knowing full well that the possibility of another sibling was remote, as they'd often overheard their mother lament to some Rosary Society girlfriend over the telephone, "Two's plenty. I don't know what I'd do if I had another." So Catherine had looked at Claire's assignment. "She said you noticed things," Catherine told her. "So I got you this to study. It's your birthday and Christmas present this year. And don't think you can get a similar combo for me." It was a used copy of Janson's *History of Art,* and in a way it had started Claire toward her career. But such bossy acts of gruff didactic altruism had been rare. For one Christmas, Catherine had given Claire a long skirt, with a written card that said, "Your hips are going to be a problem area—this should help with nature's mistake." She had been too mortified to do anything but hide the card, and had resolved never to wear the skirt. Until her sister had confronted her. "Don't you like it?" It was a demand, not a question. "I'm only doing it to help you," she'd said. "Trust me on this." Claire had eventually worn it, and reluctantly had had to agree. But despite the good intentions on Catherine's part, Claire resented not only the note, but the critical eye. In return, however, Claire went to the trouble of procuring whatever it was Catherine had asked for, terrified lest she not fill her sister's list. The gifts ranged from pantyhose to perfume to tapes and books. She ended up spending more on her sister than her mother, but her mother, for all her faults, would have been happy with a Play-Doh ashtray or a crocheted potholder. In filling Catherine's list, she felt, however, an accomplishment—a grudging one, but an accomplishment nevertheless—having appeased the angry goddess. To be sure, Catherine took her young sister's straitened financial state into consideration—but only just. "These are the things a person saves for," her sister would announce. "You'll appreciate it later." And strangely enough, Claire had. Her domineering sister had managed to give her a sense of working toward something, where her mother, myopic in some community church group, would rather she grow up without much interference. At least her sister, so intent on bettering herself and those around her, took notice of Claire. Even if Claire didn't want her physical flaws so cruelly observed.

But after Catherine had gone off to college, the University of

Michigan, Claire was left more or less on her own. When Catherine returned for holidays, levitating on cheers of "Go Blue" and football, she seemed to have grown younger, but unapproachable somehow, even though she was visibly happier. When Claire had asked her what she had wanted for Christmas that first year—not having received the usual list—Catherine had said, "Surprise me," which astonished Claire. "You know what I like." Well, she did and she didn't. She'd known the particulars in any given season, but she'd missed the pith, and the reason. At that time, that first fall of her sister's college career, Claire had determined to know, to understand what lay behind the likes or dislikes of those among whom she lived. Except for her parents. No one could fathom them. She was so used, had become so inured, to having the specific spelled out for her, that she also continued to believe what she was told, misread what was meant, ignored the subtle circularities of innuendo, of ordinary conversation, even, the lies that make up the typical talk throughout the day. So, dupe that she was, she'd vowed to learn people. But she'd failed again and again until, after Peter, she'd made the effort to acquire the skills to interpret signals, signs, meanings—in art, anyway. Life, as she realized, had continued to surprise her with her own obtuseness, her willingness to be fooled again and again, by a dubious faith in the kindness of those around her.

It wasn't that she ignored life. She had studied people, she had read them, and felt that she could accurately size up clients or consigners, could discern aspects of character that could affect a sale. In business, she didn't believe anybody, yet trusted her instincts. Elsewhere, if someone told her something, she accepted it, ignoring doubt. Her optimism was a stubborn irritant, because the stakes were different, and she always lost.

And here she was, with her ex–brother-in-law, a sad and staunch pessimist. Defending her ex-husband, who certainly needed no help from her. No, any slur on Peter still irritated her. He may be your brother, she had wanted to tell Frank, but he's my mistake. And he's nobody's fool.

"I will be seeing Peter," Frank said. "Soon. He called me. He wants to talk about our parents."

"That's a good thing," Claire said. "He at least doesn't give up."

"Well, not here, anyway. Something about some papers he found," Frank said. "He didn't say."

"Maybe a hidden legacy," she suggested.

"I doubt that. Maybe a hidden relative."

Claire wondered. Peter hadn't talked much about his parents, except to say his father was dead. Frank had filled her in on the background, the shorthand—not suited, not happy, a marriage not. Peter and Frank's father had been older than their mother, and though they initially had seemed suited—religious and righteous— that alone wasn't enough to soothe the wounded egos and stay the wandering eye.

She had learned that one of the defining moments of Peter's life was when their father had left him. Frank had been ordained for just a little while. Peter was eleven or twelve. Once, right after they had separated, Peter gave her the particulars, apropos of nothing other than revealing that he had not meant to keep so much from her. What happened: with his mother standing at the front door, his father shook his hand. "I can't say goodbye to your brother—he's gone on to greater good. But this is goodbye, Peter, Peter John. Be a brave boy." Then he picked up his suitcase and walked slowly to the car, parked on the street, not, as it usually had been, in the driveway. Peter saw another woman waiting there, seated in the front passenger seat; he remembered an elegant rich red hat and coat; she seemed distant. His father put the suitcase into the back, walked around to the driver's side—all the while, the woman looked straight ahead, not turning to the house his father had just left—and got in. The engine started, and they drove off. He never saw him again. A year later, his mother told him that his father had died, in a car accident. They had never known the woman in the car, although they'd heard she had been a nun, of all things. They hadn't known the circumstances of the accident. They were ignorant of the remainder of his life, except when the police had told his mother of the death. They knew little of what had really happened.

Surely they must have speculated, Claire had thought. She certainly would have. Frank might not have—he tended to block things off, she felt. And Peter ignored them. But Peter, growing up without a father, with a distant and cold brother, with a shattered mother—wouldn't he have thought about what might have been, or what actually was, in that year without his father's presence in his life, that last year of his father's life, the year leading up to his disappearance, the year of his death, and the fate of the nun?

She wondered if Toby had known of that incident. Peter had told her, reluctantly, after they had parted, but as a way of rectifying their previous breach of understanding, maybe. He had kept so much to himself that he hesitated to reveal more than what he thought was needed to maintain a façade of marriage and commitment. Had Peter thought, when he finally left her, that he had done what his father had done? That is, if Peter had had children, and had left her for a mystery woman. No, probably not. For Peter, it was an act of self-discovery and release. But who could say that his father's hadn't been as well?

Frank's lingering resentment—for surely that was what it was— toward his brother could have been a like judgment on Peter walking out on a marriage, as their father had done. But the resentment could have been more the discovery of Peter's homosexuality.

She liked Frank too much to sense a deep intolerance in him. She thought him narrow-minded, but that was ignorance and a refusal to learn about his brother's life.

She didn't resent *her* sibling. Well, only a little. No, not the irritating precocious children, whom she actually loved, or her dull brother-in-law—he could anesthetize by talking his patients into unconsciousness. What she resented about her sister, now that Catherine no longer had power over her, was the long-distance smugness, as if her life in a bosky suburb were idyllic and that had she, Claire, been more receptive to the lessons that her sister had sought to instill in her, she, Claire, could have earned similar rewards. But Claire did not want those rewards, if that was what they were. Nor had she learned what her sister had hoped she would from her teaching. In the end, how could she apply the lesson of procuring the proper gift for one's older sister to a situational ethos concerning marital choice? She'd learned to save, she'd learned to please to avert anger, she'd learned to accept what she was told. She'd learned not to trust herself so much regarding her emotional needs.

And what had Frank learned, in his own deliberate misery?

"What would Saint Teresa say to you now?" she asked him. He had told her about his book. He had talked of his advance, his hope for some leisure money, through a project begun almost as a lark. She couldn't see it taking very long to cobble together such a work—after all, these business books seemed thought-out on Power-Point presentation software designed to be used for the slow-learning class. He had hoped to imbue his book with a solidity of thought, he'd said—taking St. Teresa seriously as both a business leader and spiritual icon.

"She would have given me a meditation and made me work with the poor," he said.

"She might have told you to stop fussing about and build a convent. Or she might have cajoled you into raising money for her."

"She was determined, as everyone who's heard of her knows."

"She was also a visionary. Or given to visions."

"Ha," he said. "But she was plagued by doubt—so she also probably understood what I have felt. She was consumed by what she called a 'dryness and darkness of soul.' She was brave enough to admit her feelings of emptiness, and not just in the privacy of her diary. She even wrote to her father about it—she trusted in strong men. She had a remarkable capacity for forthright self-examination. But she still, despite this, could not find happiness. How am I supposed to?"

"*Are* you supposed to?" she asked. "You're the priest. Or you were. Didn't you believe that we would not be happy until the next life?"

"I thought that working toward a higher good might lead to a sense of accomplishment in a way. I don't know what I really expected. Contentment, maybe." Frank had been looking at the window while he spoke, idly watching the couples amble by outside the restaurant. He turned his face to her, and gave her a half smile. "I was naïve."

"I don't expect to be happy," Claire said. "That is, I don't expect happiness, exactly. Maybe an absence of unhappiness. It's a negative capability."

"I expect neither," Frank said, glancing away, again at the street. A couple had stopped to look at the menu. She wore a striped scarf, wrapped up around her head. He held his arm around her shoulder, companionable and protective. They shrugged and moved on, nothing enticing them in.

Claire spoke, after a minute. "You really don't believe in anything any more, do you?"

"Do you?"

"You know I do. If anything, I believe in too many things and too many people. What I meant was—when you gave up the priesthood, did you give up faith, too? How come you're so involved with Saint Teresa? Just curious."

"Hardly get-reacquainted talk, is it?" He paused, shaking his wrist, where his watch had shifted down toward his hand. He glanced at the time, barely registering it. He brushed away a few crumbs from the tablecloth. "The thing is, I want to believe. Again," he said. "I just find it too much trouble. I can't be bothered. I gave up. And yet. Yet. Yet. I keep being drawn to lives of the saints—apocryphal, even—eager for something I have not felt in so long. Not eager. But longing, maybe."

"Maybe you weren't meant to be a saint."

"It's not that. I don't want that. Who would be a saint, or fanatic, by choice?"

"Saint Teresa, for one."

"Even a single-minded businesswoman with orgasmic visions of God. She probably didn't choose that, but worked with what she was handed. Who wants that? I don't. I want the normalcy of belief. I want the legitimacy of ritual. But I don't want to offer it up. I don't want to proffer it—"

"You want the sidelines, like rooting for a team and feeling you've won because the team did."

"If you put it that way. It's just that I want to believe. It's like rooting for the Yankees, but not believing they're worth rooting for. I don't know. Don't you still believe in the Church? You even had an annulment."

"I did. I do," she admitted. "But I'm not really rooting for it, to keep with the sports analogy. I find comfort in ritual. We all do, I suspect. Despite any misgivings about its teachings, I am glad to have been raised in the Church, in any church. It's like a neighbor-hood I've lived in, but have moved far away from, and still remember, and still occasionally visit."

"You're on the sidelines, too," he said.

"Of course," Claire said. "As anyone can see, if you choose to see it that way: the auctioneer close to talent, but not of it. Like a teacher. Like you."

"That's not quite what I meant."

"Sure it is. Drones like me keep the art world moving, keep it cir-culating. You don't have to be an artist to be of the art in a serious way."

"It's like being a fan, at some level."

"Well, of course. But it's closer to being in the front office. Being someone who makes the trades, scouts talent. You don't really have a sense of what I do, Frank, and I can't comprehend what you're about right now. You're naïve, I'm gullible. You're caught between the logistical genius of Saint Teresa and a middle-aged crisis of faith, unresolved brother issues, and who knows what else. I'm trying to figure out what I've been doing outside of my career for the past five years. Shall we get the check?"

# PUTTING IT TOGETHER

The next four weeks were crucial ones for Claire's sale; she still
had a lot of acquisitions—or consignments—to make, and was
perilously short of works at the middle and lower price levels. She
saw less of her former brother-in-law than she had anticipated, and
the workings, or unraveling, of the Peter and Toby ménage had
taken a back seat to her more pressing professional demands. She
needed to get stuff together to be photographed, to send art to a
printer for the catalog, a prime selling point for any sale. These
midlevel works were important. The majority of auctions, unlike
the high-pressure and big-visibility contemporary and Impressionist sales, which could have maybe forty lots, or works, had as
many as a hundred or more. So-called Part Two, or day sales—and
the Impressionist, contemporary, and modern art sales had day
components as well—were where the bargains could be had, where
the second-tier could find homes, where the steadiest money was,
in fact, made. An evening sale of Impressionist and modern art
might make a newsworthy $140 million—in a very good year—
but the regular accrual from auctions generating $5 million or $7
million throughout the season was what paid the bills. Evening
sales made news; day sales made money. The purely estate-driven

auction houses, such as Doyle, which were wholly unpretentious, usually family-run, rarely turned down solid, homely attic finds, from Sèvres servers to David Webb animal jewelry to Colonial portraits of grim, forgotten ancestors. The estate houses almost always made a profit, never courting headlines or claiming bragging rights—who was the biggest, who made the most. Doyle might be where Mrs. Driscoll would consider leaving her horticultural prints, her Richard Dadd drawings, her Tintoretto-school sketches. If Claire worked the sale right, though, Mrs. Driscoll would most likely let her estate be sold through Sotheby's, since even the minor works—the Richard Dadd, for example, a minor Victorian genre painter—could be grouped as "From the Estate of a Lady" and accorded a certain quaint cachet that would doubtless appeal to Mrs. Driscoll's sense of fun, and that would annoy her ungrateful daughter.

Claire had quite a few possibilities to fill out her sale, from simple works brought in by families, survivors, longtime companions, including placid landscapes by Norwegian artists, picked up on tours of the Stockholm archipelago on a long-remembered Baltic cruise, or staid scenes from the Canaletto school, bought over delightful haggling during some Italian sojourn of a sunny youthful romance. These various works were stored in the auction house vaults awaiting assignment to whatever sale category would be most appropriate for unloading them—and getting the best price. The auction houses didn't like to keep things in stock—it was important to move paintings and sculpture and furniture out and back onto the market—but every so often the number of artworks being held for future sales bloomed like daffodils after a spring rain. At the moment, the firm had a large number of Old Master paintings—annunciation scenes were very plentiful, for some reason—and contemporary art, especially LeRoy Neiman sports paintings. But the vaults did hold a few nineteenth-century landscapes and portraits, which would likely find a home if the sale did well.

One of these paintings—Claire figured it would be about $4,000—was called "View of the Königsee," by a Hungarian artist, Daniel Smogyi. It was like a postcard—lifelike, virtually lifeless— and ideal for that space in someone's hall, where the light wasn't quite right but whose expanse of blank wall demanded a visual relief, preferably a nondescript vista by a middling artist one didn't have to study up close to appreciate. She'd seen so many similar scenes from rustic Edens at houses she'd visited over the years across the U.S. and in Europe. The homes of the well-off, the once-wealthy, the settled, the impecunious of good breeding. Often, she'd find a real artwork amid the junk, but she'd end up arranging to take on all of the pieces, just to get that one.

This had happened recently, for this sale, with an English family who had worked with the London office yet who wanted their collection sold in New York—more buzz, better bucks. Fortunately for Claire, the Hodgsons, in Circester, Gloucestershire, possessed no paintings worthy enough to catch the eye of the government, which would have given a local, i.e., British, institution first crack at ponying up the money to keep the treasure within the scepter'd isle. The works in question were merely very good, not irreplaceable.

They included a painting of great charm, if less depth, by a Belgian artist, Frans Verhas. The painting, "The Bride's Bouquet," from 1875, would be a nice complement to the Tissots in her sale. It wasn't nearly as strangely good or compelling as Tissot, but it was lovely and, for about $100,000, a much more affordable piece of enchantment to grace a salon, or the grand living room of a town-house.

The painting was typical of Verhas, who specialized in elegant Belle Époque women. It showed a Second Empire interior, complete with a Japanese frieze on the back wall behind the central figures, two women who were examining a bridal bouquet of small white flowers. The woman on the left, a blonde swathed in sumptuous pink, was clutching a folded white fan to her bosom, over which strings of pearls dangled loosely. Her right hand held her shimmering gown up, so that the artist could capture its ripples in the light, and the viewer could glimpse the petticoat. Just a hint of the possibilities underneath the folds and crinoline. The woman to the right, a brunette in a baby-blue dressing gown, held a translucent veil above the bouquet, which rested on a table, as if to see how the two would complement each other when worn and carried down the aisle. The woman in blue was the bride, and already her face had the slightly superior air of one who has moved on to the next stage in life; she wore no jewelry—her goal had been achieved—and her high collar displayed only a hint of neck. That hidden cleavage was for the groom, now within her grasp. The frieze behind them showed two storks, a nice nod to the *japonisme* vogue of the time and to the iconographic-minded viewer, as storks were symbols of Hera, the Greco-Roman goddess of marriage and childbirth. So the moral tone was there; in Tissot, it would likely have been subverted somehow, an attitude Claire preferred. One note of caution was what looked like the head of a ghoul attached to a curtain pull at the left; a premonition, maybe, of the horrors of matrimony. Claire's own experience warmed to that. Still, this picture was sweet, stylish, and, despite the frippery gargoyle, sedate. And the skill here was impressive, the handling of fabric, the different textures of the shiny wooden floor, the white fur rug, the gleaming metal legs of the table, all expert; the painting would grace any room, indeed, could be the centerpiece of any society designer's show house.

Claire's own wedding was a much less high-flown affair, certainly, since she and Peter had not moved in heady circles—even now, despite the aspects of her job that permitted her entrée into wealthy strongholds—and since she, with stubborn—make that antisororal—independence, had insisted on a small ceremony. Claire's sister had begun to reassert herself, following her own happy marriage to her internist beau, and Catherine had been sending Claire lists of things to do, even dresses Catherine thought flattering to her. Claire had told her that she could be her maid—matron—of honor only if Catherine kept her suggestions to herself, and that the wedding would be for family only. As Peter's parents were dead, and their father gone, and their relatives few, Catherine had agreed, albeit reluctantly; even some involvement was better than none for Catherine, and surely, Claire had reasoned, Catherine probably felt she would still be able to control the event, or the bride, in some way. But Catherine hadn't reckoned on Frank, who wouldn't hear of any changes in the ceremony, or on Peter, who had wanted it as simple as possible. In the end, it was business attire, a small church ceremony, lunch at a restaurant, and honeymoon in Ravello. So she and her sister had no beforehand comparison of attire, no days of discussions of bouquet, décor, dining, certainly no intimate chitchat before a marriage frieze. All neatly done, all messily followed up on. The more appropriate backdrop to her wedding, Claire thought now, would have been a Lichtenstein painting showing a cartoon woman drowning with her hand raised, a lacquered fingernail curled like a question mark, a large tear falling from anguished eye, her voice balloon crying, "Oh, Brad, how your secrets have hurt me!" as she was about to sink beneath the graphic waves. Comic-book despair, Pop Art irony. Definitely not Belle Époque charm with an undercoating of mystery.

The other works Claire had acquired from the Hodgsons included a French realist painting, "The Laundress," by Désirée-Françoise Laugée, from the 1880s, showing just that, a laundry-woman hanging wash on a line, an emotion-free scene; and a Dutch piffle, "Dreaming of Love," by Jan Frederik Pieter Portielje, which showed a silly woman—the year might have been anywhere between 1870 and 1880—sitting in a room with a moony expression, mired in reverie. This painting irritated and somehow intrigued Claire; she wouldn't ever want to own it, but she had to admit that, bad as it was, if it were any better, it wouldn't be worth looking at. The painter seemed to marry French sentimentality with conventions of Dutch paintings of interiors; the woman's dress was satiny, light blues and gold, sheathed in shifting light; the table beside which she sat was covered with an oriental rug, as in a Vermeer, and the mullioned windows cast a soft glow onto the table, the flowers, the dress, and the woman's fatuous face. It was all so wrong, as if the painter wanted to channel Vermeer but somehow had gotten the spirit of Fragonard without understanding the essence of either. Claire figured this work would bring about $20,000 to some collector with a sense of humor, or maybe even a dealer whose clients had new money and wanted the appurtenances of old wealth without the inconvenience of acquired taste.

But "The Bride's Bouquet," which Claire had assumed would be the prime consignment from the Hodgsons, happened to be displayed in their tatty living room, next to a very fine Bouguereau. This had been a surprise to Claire, since the Hodgsons had not mentioned the work when they'd approached the firm to look over what they'd amassed over the years, through inheritance, marriage, potluck, and whim. This work could stand alone, and might net the couple a quarter of a million dollars.

Many people who owned them underestimated the market for Bouguereau. Bouguereau wasn't an Impressionist, his paintings did not have that studied evanescence, and his originality lay more within the subject than the treatment. He painted shepherdesses, fisherwomen, knitters, beggars, gypsies—an idealization of the feminine. His young girls, while not as disturbing and alluring as Lewis Carroll's Alice Liddell, had an indefinable sauciness and purity. Bouguereau managed to combine the sentimentality of the age with a growing sympathy for the downtrodden as well as the era's yearning for rusticity as release from industrialized cityscapes and, most important, had captured its sugary pedophilia. That seemed to play as well in the nineteenth century as it had begun to today, Claire felt, though for different reasons. Now, people were far more apt to idealize childhood and ignore the sexual inferences of the painting, at least overtly. Bouguereau's depictions of unsullied girlhood had found ready buyers in today's age of hypocritical moralizing.

This one, "La Révérence," from 1898 showed a beautiful barefoot girl, her simple linen frock smudged with toil, or with frolic. She holds her head to one side, gazing with inviting, warm delight at the viewer, holding each side of her dress up with her still-delicate, girlish hands, to show her dusty ankles and feet. She is standing in a field before a wood, a human sprite, a forest imp.

The work would likely find a ready buyer: portraits of young girls—even those works less expertly rendered—usually found homes quickly. The current age was even more sentimental than the Victorians were said to be, Claire knew, for at least the Victorians lived closer to the reality of life, its physical turmoil, its diseases, its dirt, its dementia, the inadvertent ribaldry of the farmhouse. Today's moral age was marked by an abhorrence of physicality, even as its sexuality seemed more overt. Nature was something for other people, and fetishism the secret idol of the masses.

The Hodgsons also had some decent watercolor and gouache works of the British school—what English home of a certain class did not? These were inoffensive and appealing, little country scenes or portraits of young women of the 1800s, the kind of works that lined the studies and halls of many grand old piles, amid the mildewing books and cobwebbed shelves. All in all, she'd acquired about $1.5 million worth of works from them, money the Hodgsons would put toward what they called a holiday home in Donegal, that remote section of Ireland that attracted many English retirees, drawn by its low costs, low density, and low profile.

Claire had liked the Hodgsons a great deal, and was taken by their companionability with her and affection for each other. They'd been married some thirty-five years. He had been a headmaster at a local boys' school, and she, the second daughter of a baronet, had had some family money. They were childless and, while comfortable, were not rich. Mrs. Hodgson, Judy, had been given the home by her mother; the couple were planning to sell it at a reasonable cost to their nephew, the son of her sister, after they retired. Their appreciation for art was that of other privileged people Claire had met, who grew up with paintings on the walls but were not too sentimental about them. Certain works had a nostalgic appeal for them, but others were to be dealt with as fortunes changed or times moved on. The Hodgsons would keep a few works for themselves, a Courbet portrait, for example, but simplify their holdings, and ensure the comfort of their retirement. Their attitude, strangely enough, was in line with an auctioneer's: appreciate the value, get the most for it, move on. Something Claire was beginning to think of for herself. And something, perhaps, more in line with what her ex-husband did. Peter had an unsentimental regard for sentiment, or was less battered by the untidy pull of emotion.

In their relationship, as he found he could not sustain the falsehood once he finally admitted to himself where his feelings lay, Peter moved on. The same must have happened with Toby. Claire had tried to make herself emotionally available to Peter—she hadn't had to try, she simply was, she thought; it only was later, in the constant reappraisals her life had become made of did she need to categorize an aspect of what had been—simply—love. But when the love on one side is one that longs to thrive on the intimate susurration of shared physicality in space and contact, it must seem to the other, for whom love was, or had become, one merely nourished by companionability, the whole lopsided nature of the relationship must have begun to seem more than confining, but suffocating. She never regretted her love—it was truly given—but she did feel that she should have recognized how often her passion was met with what she had characterized as indifferent, but that was really negation: no, this is not me. How she must have come across, as if she were shouting in church regardless of the stares and hushed admonishments of others.

Claire now realized, as she worked her way through the storeroom, that Peter had moved on because he had realized that the extent of his relationship with Toby had probably reached the stopping point. Their affair, their partnership, their, whatever, had led Peter to realize something essential about himself. With Toby, Peter had probably realized something essential about Toby's nature that made Peter break away. Peter was not one to linger once he realized he couldn't change whatever it was about himself or someone else. Maybe he no longer cared for Toby in the same way. It was important for Peter to have some sort of actual give and take. She didn't quite know what Toby felt, and she suddenly realized she was trying to see Peter's point of view, which was a change from a few weeks earlier.

Claire had pulled out a Courbet from the racks where the paintings were held. They were positioned on sliding vertical files, upright in frames—usually—in the climate-controlled vault. This room was such a comfort to her; rarely was there more than one other person here. She felt she could drift off into a sweet reverie, besotted by the masterworks and even the lesser pieces that surrounded her in the low, cool light. It reminded her of her college library, minus the dust, where she would place herself to study during the long winter evenings, and nod off over a textbook illuminated only by a single lamp at a desk at the end of a bookcase, soothed by the silence, the dark, and the surrounding volumes, bounded by a bindery of learning and unopened scholarship. Many a night would find her diligent and dutiful, in the soft-spoken recesses of the stacks, awakening from a slumber she hadn't remembered lapsing into, her forehead aching slightly from having rested on a textbook or the curve of her arm.

Here, though, she was unlikely to doze, so delightful the atmosphere of inspiration and centuries of creative expression were to her; indeed, the stimuli of genius sometimes left her exhausted. But she couldn't pause for those long-ago naps, right now.

This painting had been in the back of her mind for a while. She had been so concerned with acquiring works from living consigners that this marvelous work, from an estate, had been waiting, like a relief pitcher, for her to call it into the game. It was perfect for the sale. The heirs had requested that the various properties in the estate be disposed among different sales, wherever they might be most appropriate and realize the greatest amount of money. The late owner loved western art—the American west—and also had the odd out-of-character masterpiece. He had a stunning Old Master Virgin and Child in an enclosed garden, from the late fifteenth century, which had sold for half a million dollars the month before, to the Getty.

This work, "Le Moulin de Longeville," was a landscape, but more than that. It was a portrait of nature. It showed a rustic mill, a building of stone and wood, almost pushed out of the frame, at the far right of the canvas, by the land to its left, which was dominated by a surging stream, a low falls, that broke from the verdant hill, a tumble of eroded rocks worn by the water that foamed and churned over them. The mill wheel seemed inert, hidden partially by the greenery, almost powerless against the barely contained torrent. The theme, if any, was likely the old nature-versus-man debate, and the futility of harnessing the power of the earth ultimately. But what was so vital about the painting was its realization of the water's energy, the worn-away rock, the stubborn, implacable exuberance of the world, and the intractable will of man; if the mill were to fall, its propped-up timbers suggested it would rise again. Man could only manage nature to a degree, but an artist could capture it, as well as man's pathetic hubris. We're like that with each other, as well, she thought. What Claire loved was the unorthodox painting technique. Courbet had used a palette knife and spatula instead of a paintbrush in places to produce the layered textures that heightened the effect of depth and volume—the gushing water, the bosky bushes, the weight-worn rocks. Its composition, a shifting series of horizontal planes that created a **V** toward the center that was kept from numbing regularity by the stippled vertical of the square waterfall to the left, was masterly.

The painting was not well known. In fact, its authenticity had only been attested to by a Courbet expert the previous year after the owner's heirs had brought it in, and it was to be added to the catalogue raisonné. The owner, a Mrs. Popplecourt, had acquired it from her mother, who had bought it in 1923 from the dealer who had acquired it from the person who had first bought it—how was that for lineage? A Karl Bodmer had been the initial buyer; he was also among the first Europeans to give an accurate pictorial account of the grandeur of the American landscape, before he himself began to paint among the Barbizon group in France. He had visited America in 1832 as the head artist for Maximillian, Prince of

Wied-Nerwied's scientific expedition to some of the outposts of the American frontier. That this painting, which had an aura that almost equaled the lofty intensity of some Frederick Church works, should end up in the collection of a wealthy western woman, this painting once owned by a traveler-artist to these shores who helped vivify the later European landscapes through his own experiences in America, thrilled her. This was not one of those troubled works that had a history, that bounced around from sale to sale every couple of years. This painting *was* history. Claire hoped it would find a public home, and not reside in the privileged privacy of a Barbizon connoisseur's den. It was a bargain, too; she thought it could fetch between four hundred and six hundred thousand dollars. It could be the pride of a midsize regional museum. But those museums usually couldn't afford forty dollars, let alone four hundred thousand. She knew of some dealers who would be very interested in this work; they'd already been sniffing around. Unfortunately, a dealer would find, most likely, a private aficionado. The Upper East Side was the center of the kind of shop that specialized in these intelligent paintings that the public was unlikely to know firsthand. The painting would probably end up gracing the foyer of a maisonette.

Claire had about 100 works for her sale so far. She knew she could find another seventy-five or so to round it out. She needed a variety, and she was getting it, from luscious soft-porn pictures of Alexandre Cabanel, a fine Academic painter, to the Tissots and Courbets to many genre paintings in the ten- to fifteen-thousand-dollar range. She even had a few sculptures, including an earnest German ode to a forge that in its streamlined way echoed the Goya painting in the Frick, without the emotional drama, sense of place, and heart of that great work. Someone would buy this, though. Almost-kitsch artifacts had a wide audience, among those who got the point too well or missed the joke, or both. Enough iffy art was out there to satisfy anyone. And Claire, though much wasn't to her particular taste, didn't really judge. She was there to sell the stuff, not appraise the buyers for their connoisseurship vis-à-vis her own sense of what was good or bad art. This had taken her some time to figure out; like many art specialists, she had developed a sense of what was quality, had what was known as a good eye, and had strong opinions pro or con. But unlike many, she usually kept these opinions to herself. Her line of work was, after all, a kind of service industry, and someone might adore what she deemed within to be abominable. Little by little she had also begun to be less cavalier about her likes and dislikes—less like her sister, perhaps, always a good thing—and more open to the possibility that someone else's point of view was worth admitting. Her marriage, of course, had led her to consider this, but its outcome had forced her to confront it. In matters of art, where public utterance could conflate offhand remarks into obiter dicta, Claire had learned to be circumspect as well as open-minded. She would often meet people who had treasures she hadn't anticipated, despite her generally shrewd sense of business. Sometimes she was beguiled by her own cynicism.

By chance she had come across a woman who had a particular jewel of a painting to sell. It was called "A Visit to Grandfather's," by Arturo Ricci, an Italian painter who excelled at depicting the textures of fabrics, from carpets that held the light to dresses that effulged with it. This particular picture showed a seated patriarch in a rich room. The time, judging by the head of the younger man in the painting, was the eighteenth century. The patriarch—grandfather—was being seen by his son and daughter-in-law and grandchildren. It was a troubling little scene of misdirection, a family meeting that held more anguish than the glow of fabrics and realization of opulence.

The woman who owned the painting, Nanette Soderberg, was as

deceptive as the painting itself. Claire met her just before a dinner at the Knickerbocker Club at Sixty-second and Fifth a couple of months earlier. Claire was in a bright room on the second floor that overlooked Central Park. She was examining brochures that were spread on a table just outside the main reception. The cocktail party and dinner were for an early-music chorale, one of whose singers was also a contemporary-art specialist at the auction house, and also a member of the staid Knickerbocker.

"Would you like to hear one of my poems?" asked a rather chirrupy New York voice.

Claire had looked up from the brochures of the musical society—the Collegium Choristers—and taken in the speaker, a woman of about eighty, she supposed. The woman had a wide, oval face, like a water-soaked Modigliani portrait, and her hair ringed her head in the manner of nineteenth-century matrons, as if Marmee from *Little Women* had just stepped through a portal in time. Her light blue eyes were festive.

"Hello," Claire said.

"I just wrote it," the woman said. "I saw a penny on the sidewalk, and thought of a poem about the economy. Would you like to hear it?"

"Of course," Claire said, not knowing what else to say, and hoping her friend Roger would rescue her from this apparently disturbed old woman.

"I used to send them in to the Metropolitan Diary at the *Times*," the woman said. "They've printed three of mine over the years. Tell me what you think. It's a haiku. I don't rhyme so well, so here goes," she said, pulling out a scrap of paper from a pocket in her skirt. "Penny on the street. Lying there unclaimed by all. Are things looking up?" She looked at Claire with a grin; a bit of her lipstick had been smeared over the left part of her lower lip. "What do you think?"

"It's good," she said.

"You think so? I do, too. I'm so glad. I've just noticed that when you see a lot of change on the sidewalks, the economic conditions must be improving. When times are tough, there aren't a lot of coins down there. You can go and talk to your friends now. I'm just a biddy," she added, without rancor, as if accepting the inevitability of abandonment as a course of her day.

"But I'm speaking to you," Claire said, unsure of why she decided to jump in to conversation with this woman, but forging on anyway. "My name is Claire."

"I'm Nanette Soderberg. I live just up the block."

"Do you have an interest in early music?"

"Not particularly," Nanette said. "I usually stop by here on Tuesdays, since that's Ladies' Night. My late husband was a member here, and they let me stay on as a member after he died. I like to pop in and look around before having dinner. I look at the Sargent painting there. It's comforting. But you'll want to be getting back to your reception," she said.

"Oh, no," Claire said, suddenly wanting to keep the woman talking, sensing something. "I gather you're interested in art, then."

"I am. But though I like this portrait here, my taste is more modern. If you can still call German Expressionists modern. Though you would think I'd collect paintings of bunnies or something simpering like other old women do."

"Do you have any German art?"

"I have a Max Beckmann," Nanette said. "You know him?"

"I know his work well," she said. "I work for an auctioneer."

"Oh! How perfect! You're just the person I want to talk to."

Nanette—please call me Nanette, she'd said—told Claire about her late husband, a doctor whom she'd married fifty years earlier when she'd been a nurse in her husband's unit. He'd had a successful cardiology practice and she had raised their child, who was also now a doctor. Along the way, he and she had collected art, but it was more to the doctor's taste than hers. "I found it easier to indulge Blake," Nanette said. "If he was happy, I was, too." Dr. Blake's taste ran to Victorian family scenes—the visual easy-listening. After his death, Nanette had begun to sell off the collection—a purchase here and there—to dealers. She had kept this Ricci painting for sentiment. The subject matter had appealed to her late husband, who had coped with the stern affection of a father who had not expected his son to marry a nurse.

The picture, a fractured family grouping, was beautiful, and the more one looked at it, the more unsettling it became as one grew aware of the interplay of the participants. The seated father faced the left of the frame. Next to him was his standing son—though Claire suspected it was a son-in-law, since the expression on the young man's face had the cautious courtesy of an uncertain new relation. The daughter, the wife, had her back to the viewer, the better for Ricci to paint the folds of light on her handsome white gown. Her face was turned diagonally past her father to where the mother was standing holding a toy just out of reach of the grandson, who looked about seven, who himself was reaching up to his Nana. The grandmother clutched an array of toys, an arsenal of indulgence, while the boy's mother smiled behind a half-raised fan at the little scene. Her own daughter, attired in a miniature version of her resplendent dress, offered a bunch of flowers to her grandmother, whose attention was taken up with the boy—the future patriarch. The girl was secondary to the grandmother's affections, as the young man seemed to be to the grandfather's, as the wife may have been to both though she was placed in the forefront of the picture, albeit with back turned upon the viewer, who could infer the various tensions and fitful joys of the tableau variously, depending on whom the eye rested upon.

A winning scene nonetheless, beautifully executed, that afforded great pleasures. Ricci was sought after. His engrossing domestic dramas were especially felicitous, and the demand would enable her to price the painting between $200,000 and $300,000.

So Nanette had kept this painting, for sentiment. Or because it reminded her of what it reminded her husband of: the demands of parents, the expectations of children, the futility of searching for happiness, maybe. Apparently Nanette had withstood the family slights herself equably, as she seemed to have a sure sense of her worth, and had been loved in return by the person who most counted, her husband. A rare thing, not to bridle under the disapproval of others, especially that of the family into which one marries. Claire found Nanette hearty indeed—haikus and all—but by no means simple. After she had seen the painting the next day, Claire had realized its worth, and had gladly accepted it for her sale.

"I thought that for this painting I might get more by selling it at auction," Nanette had told her. "I don't have much experience with auction houses. My husband bought through dealers, and I worked with them after he died. But you're never too old to change."

Nanette didn't need the money but needed the change, she said. "I'm kind of a bald-face girl," she told Claire. "I was always one to speak my mind, except when I thought it wouldn't be proper—I mean, I didn't want to hurt anybody's feelings. While my husband was alive, I could look at these pictures of pretty rooms and little dramas and not be troubled at all; and I could sympathize with him. He loved this picture so. They just weren't to my taste, though he certainly was. I grew to tolerate them. After Blake died, I lost my tolerance for them, somehow, though not for him. I wanted something bolder."

"Didn't your husband want you to be happy with these paintings?" Claire had asked.

"Oh, of course," Nanette said. "But our tastes were just so different. I felt that I'd be able to handle his tastes in art much more than he would mine. You know men. My husband loved me, and we were very, very happy. But in some ways, he thought he knew best. He was a doctor, you know. Doctors always think that. I knew differently, but what was the use of trying to convince him? I didn't marry him for his taste so much. At least not his taste in art. And he didn't marry me because I was some rich society girl. We loved each other. It was just Darby and Joan."

"Don't the pictures remind you of him?" Claire asked, realizing that her job was to acquire the art, not argue against its being consigned for auction. Yet she couldn't help but wonder, since for her, objects, no matter the resale value, no matter their artistic worth, always carried the tincture of remembrance.

"Yes," Nanette said. "But I don't need them to remember him. And when I look at the paintings—the one or two that I intend to buy—I'll remember him, and our compromise, or mine, and his taste and our marriage and our life together. Even though he never set eyes on anything I plan to have in my living room, I will think of Blake."

That was a difference between them, Claire thought. She clung to relics of the past, desperate for a touchstone of meaning or emotive resonance and remained, somehow, static. Yet here, this gracious and gregarious woman, no-nonsense but with an absurd poetry, moved on, her memories present. Was it a difference of having loved fully, or of having lived that way? Claire's life was full, certainly, and she had loved. Not wisely. Perhaps not even too well. What she missed, and what she clung to, were the mementos that suggested the possibility of fulfillment. So, a stagy snapshot served as a reminder of what might have been rather than what actually was. And Nanette's forward-thinking embrace of art that her husband might have abhorred was not, now that she had the freedom to display it, the sad blossoming of a free soul late in life, but a second harvest. Nanette had chosen the compromise to accommodate her husband's particular—Claire couldn't call it narrow taste, but it was particular. Nanette's husband had surely compromised himself with her, too, or was marrying Nanette compromise enough? Or was living with a chatterbox compromise? Nanette said they'd had a happy union, and what successful marriage is not a result of compromise, or continued denial? The German Expressionists that Nanette appreciated seemed to Claire an act not of widowed defiance, but a logical step: See, darling, I know you would have hated these, but I loved you enough to wait so you wouldn't see them. And yet they remind me of you. And yet they remind me of us.

# ABOVE THE ESTIMATE

A ndre Karl and his family entourage finally settled in the second
row, having lingered up the aisle shaking hands with dealers,
pretending to be delighted at the sight of one or two, exchanging
air kisses, tepid hugs, and two-handed grasps of cordial greeting
with most others. His hirsute sons followed, shambling, mock-
blasé, tossing their heads to show off their glistening manes, having
soaked up the surface gesture of their father's crepuscular charm
but, less savvy, visibly bored by the business of the auction room,
not grasping the significance of appearance. They hadn't yet learned
how to drip charm while calculating risk as well as the couture-clad
competition, they hadn't learned to mask their contempt with an
oleaginous shrug of kindness. They had been born into the business
but were still unused to the slippery maneuvering necessary to survive in it. Andre Karl did much of his dealing in Europe, had an
office in Israel, one in Zurich, and one in New York, where he himself spent two months a year, for the big fall and spring auctions. He
was one of the prime movers on the Impressionist and modern art
scene, whose purchases created a demand for artists. He had been
one of the first to drive up the price of late Matisses, and his interest
in contemporary painters helped secure their reputation. His varied

clientele, everyone from Thyssen-Bornemisza to rock star, relied on his taste, his eye, and his bargaining power. His sons were being groomed to take over but as yet had mastered only the knack of procuring tables, maintaining mistresses, and hiding their drug abuse from their father, whose art-world savvy became indulgent denial when it came to his ungrateful offspring. They sat next to him looking around the room to see who noticed them, a little too manic not to have been perhaps a bit too free with the fairy dust earlier that evening. Their seated father now concentrated on his catalog. Others in the white and teeming room, the European experts, the connoisseurs, the American corporate art buyers, the personal curators to the moneyed CEOs with a taste for expensive daubs, milled about or found their numbered seats eagerly or with the air of having been to one too many such auction nights to be thrilled by the expectation of the moment, the tossing about of millions of dollars in a flash of calculated frenzy. They, all business, found their seats, nodded to one or two, assumed the position of poker-faced procurers.

Claire, from her perch at the telephone desks, where specialists handled bidding by potential buyers who couldn't attend the sale in person or who preferred to gamble their money unseen by the soigné in the auction room, had been eyeing the crowd, waiting to place her calls to the three clients she was assigned to that evening. The large room tonight was a tightly arranged space, with rows of chairs reaching back toward the escalators, where those with standing-only tickets hovered like fans at the back of a rock club, for the show to begin. Off to the other side of the gallery, opposite the dais of telephones, was the press, cordoned off like visitors to the White House, to look but not touch the glamorous bidders and their companions.

The usual suspects had filed in variously, in addition to Andre

Karl. Richard Beckmeister, a dashing lothario with a high-end gallery that specialized in Impressionist works, and with whom Claire had had a brief dalliance, threw her a cuticled kiss, his fingers pursed from his lips to the air. She caught it and smiled at him. He was charming, and handsome in a mountebank sort of way. Although she'd enjoyed their times together, and he'd lavished enough attention on her to last a couple of months of dateless solitude, she was reluctant to let it last beyond the fling stage. He already had mistresses in Paris and London, and while by all accounts each was satisfied with the arrangement, and especially the duplexes and the relative freedom—he traveled a lot—she did not want to become part of Richard's menagerie—not that he wanted her to, or had asked her to be. He'd taken her out, he'd taken her to his place, he'd taken her pulse, probably, and had most likely realized she was just a touch too staid to be mistress number three. Either that, or he preferred to keep his New York life unencumbered by kept women. Not that his transatlantic women were kept—they were granted the use of his apartments, and acted more as caretakers with bedroom duties than bombshell floozies with dreams of stardom. But after a few tosses and turns, he and she had, unspoken, agreed to maintain a more equable acquaintance, with affectionate greetings free of saliva and afterthought. It was just as well, since their professional lives would have been compromised by a continued intimacy; she did, after all, have access to many works that were likely to end up in his gallery, and she wouldn't want to be accused of any impropriety in that regard.

Richard stooped to embrace Francesca Kinderling, the partner in a struggling auction house started by her and a colleague at a gallery they ran in Zurich and kept afloat with help from her current beau, Ron Levitz, a billionaire with an idea that he could tame his vulgarity if he turned it toward being an arts patron. Francesca seemed to be onto something. How she managed to bamboozle financial sharpies such as Ron Levitz was beyond Claire. Her talons clung to Richard's wrists, as if they were a lifeline to some fountain of youth she could scratch her way to, though Richard was older than Francesca. Yet he wore his age well—aided undoubtedly by weekly facials. And she, surprisingly for one so shrewd, seemed to be making the mistake that a certain class of European—not the French—made, of dressing beyond her years. Claire, though no fashion plate, would have advised against the leather pants, especially with the saggy bottom. What was she, fifty? No. Maybe they'd look good on Cher, but auctioneers were not entertainers, and entertainers knew how to pull off the outré with aplomb.

But thoughts of Francesca faded as soon as Claire saw Peter move up the aisle with a beefy-looking man in a jacket that looked a little tight. That must be Sean. She hadn't expected Peter here, but they hadn't spoken for a couple of weeks, since her schedule had become so tight. She shouldn't have been surprised. He usually attended one or two of the auctions, just to network, even though he usually bought at the furniture sales only. So . . . Sean. He had a sweet, youthful face, and white-gray hair. He looked about thirty-five, a bit uncertain, but stoic, as Pete greeted people here and there in his affable way, introducing Sean, who shook hands like a schoolboy and nodded hello. She didn't know what to make of him—he was a far cry from Toby, in demeanor and detail. He was cuddly—was this man a detective?—he was cute, he was the next stage in Peter's life. He was a plump puzzle.

Jurgen Hofritz walked in from a side door near the front of the auction room, ready to begin. He was director of contemporary art at the auction house, and usually handled the evening sales of Impressionist and modern art, since he was a first-class auctioneer, able to keep the auction going, building a rhythm, not letting the

pace lag if a work failed to sell. It was important to have a sale
flow, both to build anticipation that might lead to higher bidding,
and to create a drama for the auction—excitement was the key to
breaking records. Usually, an auctioneer moved from lot to lot—
each work was referred to as a lot—in a minute or less. Sometimes, with spirited bidding, this was drawn out, and as each new
bid was announced, each multithousand-dollar increment placed,
the audience followed the raising ante like the crowd at a tennis
match, heads turning from bidder to bidder until the money
could go no higher. At that point, at some record or some particularly felicitous price for a work, people would begin to applaud:
thrilled at the money well spent (or squandered). An amusing two
minutes of time, a delicious million-dollar parlay, a frisson before
late-night dinner.

Jurgen's head was shaped like Dürer's in his self-portrait, glistening locks and all, but without the narcissistic beauty. He had
small, alert eyes, like a donor figure in a Renaissance painting, and
a large Cubist nose, yet he was attractive in an ungainly German
way, someone weaned on East Berlin porridge discovering Bavarian
bounty. That is, he had a zest for life in a body marked for asceticism. He was impossibly hip—Claire felt coarse around him—yet
kind and funny. He wore the customary tuxedo, as evening auctioneers usually did, and his bow tie was rather large, more like a
propeller than an accent to the shirt, but he had nevertheless a kind
of carefree elegance that warmed him to the gathering, despite the
asceticism of his skinny frame.

Claire put the call in to her first client, Seth Thomas, a Los
Angeles collector who was interested in a Paul Cézanne landscape
from the late 1870s. It was painted at the same time as a similar
landscape by Pissarro, yet couldn't be more distinct. Instead of Pissarro's almost pointillist treatment of the trees and garden beds,

puffs of white over mottles of blue, Cézanne's picture, "Le Potager de Pissarro à Pontoise," had a geometric molding and an earthy palette, an early indicator of his use of fields of color to indicate depth of field. The collector had amassed a fortune in Microsoft stock and bailed out of Internet speculation to focus on the demented world of filmmaking. He'd produced an offbeat horror-movie hit, *The Sill*, about a window to a parallel universe where adults became slaves to their childhood nemeses. He had moved on to the speculation of art-house films—his current project was an adaptation of a Knut Hamsun novel, *Hunger*, a doubtful flick about a poverty-stricken writer dying for his art, but Seth loved the challenge. He also collected widely, and had put together a very respectable collection of Old Masters, and Impressionist and modern art.

Seth wanted to be in on the sale from its inception, to get a sense of its progress. And unlike many well-to-do collectors, he did not use an intermediary at auction. As an autodidact and a wheeler-dealer, he preferred the tussle of the sale itself. He hadn't been able to fly to New York to take part in the auction, since he was putting the financing together for *Hunger*—no fool he, he rarely coughed up his own money for his projects—and would be speaking to Claire on his cell phone. She dialed.

"So, are we ready?" he asked.

She could hear the sound of traffic. "Are you in your car?"

"Yes. Is that a problem?"

"No, but you really should be concentrating."

"Don't worry, Claire. I can do lots of things while buying art. Like drive."

"I just want to make sure you can hear the sale. And consult your catalog."

"I can hear it. If I can hear you. My assistant can help me out." He paused. "So, what are you wearing?"

"Very funny. You know this call is being taped."

"I know. Security and all that. So, what are you wearing? For the record."

"A blue suit."

"Chanel?"

"Yes. Now—Jurgen's starting. It's the first lot."

"Good evening," said Jurgen. "Lot number one. 'Portrait d'Edmond Maitre (Le Liseur),'" he said. "The reader. I should add that this work will be in the catalogue raisonné of Pierre-August Renoir being prepared now by the Wildenstein Institute. I will start at five hundred thousand dollars. Do I have five hundred thousand dollars?"

"Do I want this?" Seth asked.

"You had decided against it. If you want to bid, let me know."

"What do you think?"

"Time's running out."

"Five-fifty," Jurgen said.

"It's quite beautiful," Claire said. "But you know that."

"Not Renoir enough," Seth said.

"That's what we said when we spoke two weeks ago."

"I remembered. Now, I remember. Not Renoir enough. What's the bid at?"

"Seven hundred," she said.

"That was fast."

"You know how it is. Now it's seven-fifty."

"Maybe I should have bid, if it's above the estimate."

"It looks like the sale is going well from the start. That's a good sign."

"For you maybe, but it means I may have to pay more for mine."

"We'll see."

"What was that?"

"It's at eight-fifty. No. Now it's at a million."

"Suckers."

"Not everyone needs an iconic painting, Mr. Thomas."

"Seth. No. I do. You know. Hollywood. But still. Suckers." Many current buyers only chose works that best epitomized an artist. So Warhol "Marilyn" silk screens, or Jasper Johns "Flags" or Renoir scenes of Parisian life were the kinds of works that sold the best because they defined the artist and vice versa, whereas others, such as this handsome one of a man sitting on a sofa reading, while rich and expert, didn't scream "Renoir" enough for new money to justify having spent so much on something not immediately recognizable.

"It sold for a million two," she said.

"That's a relief. What's next?"

"Are you asking me?"

"No, my assistant. Okay," he said to someone sitting next to him. She tried to recall. Becky, was it? "The Redon. Nice. Do I want this?"

"You decided against him. You said it reminded you of pot roast." It was a bouquet of mixed flowers, quite a tender study of the shimmering colors of the blooms, as if through a haze of sleep. He thought it was grandmotherly, she recalled, and thus the pot roast reference.

"Oh yes, now I remember. Too soft."

"But tender. The bidding's up to seven hundred thousand already," she said.

"Now I'm worried. If they're paying that for this, the Cézanne's gonna be hot. Hold on," Seth said. "I've got another call."

"In the middle of a sale?" she said, but he'd cut her off. There were a few paintings to go before his Cézanne came up.

"'Notre Dame,'" said Jurgen. "Maximilien Luce's Neo-Impressionist painting of the cathedral. Very suave. Say three hundred fifty thousand?"

She watched the turntable at the front of the auction room turn to reveal the painting, which was about a yard square. She couldn't make out the details, but its mauve and deep blue colors were beautiful even from a distance. She'd seen the painting several times over the past few days as she walked through the gallery and had admired its airy tactility. The bidding now had stopped at about $550,000. The top estimate was $600,000, and Jurgen was urging the crowd on to reach the top estimate.

"Am I getting six hundred thousand? Anyone. All right. Sold!" he said. "Five hundred fifty thousand, to number one-oh-seven. Thank you," he said, banging his gavel. "Next, 'Voiliers sur L'Escault.' I will take a first bid of eight hundred thousand dollars." He surveyed the room. A bidder raised a paddle. "Eight hundred thousand. What say eight-fifty? Anyone?" Theo Van Rysselberghe, the artist, was another practitioner of Neo-Impressionism. The painting, a view of piers, a sailboat, and a near shore, caught as if at a yellow and blue dusk, was a haunting study of fading light searing the water from the angle of descent, yet with a calm redolent of carefree summer—it captured the longing of peace and the passing of the hours with a sedate exuberance in its careful mosaic of colored dots. It used a pointillist technique that seemed to mimic the quivering ripples of water and the evanescent glow of sunset. It was beautiful, and rare—there weren't that many Van Rysselberghes on the market—and with so many Impressionist works already having found homes in museums, collectors had begun to drive up the price of Neo-Impressionist artists.

The man sitting next to Peter raised his paddle, for $850,000. Peter turned, caught her eye and smiled. Sean—it was surely Sean, right?—leaned over to him and then turned to look at her with a quizzical expression. He smiled shyly at Claire. They looked chummy enough, Claire reckoned. New love. Such bliss. But what was he doing here? Had Sean wanted to see Peter in action, or did he have an interest in the art world? Sean, if that's who it was, did have a certain set to his eyes; he seemed to be taking everything in, as a detective would, perhaps. A bidder to the far left of the room raised a paddle for $900,000, and Peter and Sean turned their attention that way. She didn't see Peter in action very often, and had taken him in from this vantage point at the telephone bank only once before. Usually, she and he met over dinner or drinks or had run into each other at art openings. She could see him on stage, as it were, performing his role as dealer-bidder, and new boyfriend. He discreetly pointed out people here and there—Claire could see him keep his hands below shoulder level while pointing, so that others at seat level wouldn't see him gesturing (or mistake his movement for a bid). He wore French cuffs, as usual, which Claire never liked much. One could never roll up one's sleeves, but then, Peter rarely did. He was rather old-fashioned and sedate in his wardrobe, just this side of foppish. Sean looked positively bohemian next to him. Maybe that was part of the attraction. She hadn't really noticed before the delicacy of Peter's gestures, so different, she now saw, from his older brother's. Not that Peter was effeminate, but he had a grace about him, while Frank was more lumbering, stolid, almost clumsy. The varieties of masculinity had never crossed Claire's mind until she began to notice the distinctions between the two brothers, and even between the two men who were new lovers sitting there before her at a near distance. Peter and Sean cut a funny couple, of sorts, with Peter in his pinstripe suit and Sean in his tweed jacket and khaki slacks. Toby wasn't a fashion plate, but he did dress in a rather defined manner—arty elegance, which usually translated into black flat-front trousers, black shirt, black shoes. At least Peter wasn't doing the clone thing, and going out with someone who looked like him. She wondered if he was comfortable with himself, despite the shyness. But then, why should she care at this point? Still, she was curious about the nature of Sean's appeal.

"What did I miss?" It was Seth.

"It looks like the Van Rysselberghe will make its high estimate," she said.

"Not my style."

"Not well known enough, you mean."

"Just not my style," he said. "That was my director. I told him not to call me until later, but he just learned our leading man was having second thoughts."

"First things first."

"Yeah, but this is important. We can always find another—"

"Now it's the Monet," she said. "Sorry to interrupt, but you wanted to know."

"How much did the other go for?"

"One point six."

"That's a gorgeous painting. The Monet. Looks like a Monet."

"Yes. Bidding has started at two million," Claire said. The painting, "Vetheuil, Les Pruniers en Fleurs," was a radiant scene of a blooming plum-tree grove, timeless and vibrant with sun. The flowers on the trees glowed with the radiance of summer, and the colors created an atmosphere of pulsating life, with aqua, soft yellows, whites, browns, and a touch of green blending into an encapsulation of rural bounty. "The bidding is at two million five already," she said. She noticed that Peter had raised a paddle. Peter! He must be acting as someone's agent for the sale. He hadn't done that in a long time. It wasn't unusual for a dealer to act as liaison for a client at auction. But Peter didn't usually do so at painting sales. She hoped he wouldn't be bidding on the Cézanne.

"What's it up to?" Seth asked.

"Three million."

"I think I'm going to go for the water lily one that's coming up soon."

"Are you sure?" Clients usually apprised the telephone staff of their intentions before the sale, so they could make sure they weren't carrying on conversations with competing buyers. Claire's other two clients were coming along a little bit further into the sale, so Seth's change of plans wouldn't cause any difficulty. "You know the estimate on that? It's up to twenty million," she said.

"I know, Claire. But why not? Let's see where we go."

Peter had only raised his paddle two more times, and lowered it at $3.5 million. This Monet sold for $4 million, not a record by any means for this beloved artist, but above the estimate, and a good sign for the energy of the sale.

"Now it's your painting," Claire told Seth.

"All set," he said. "Start bidding at two million."

"Now we have 'Le Potager de Pissarro à Pontoise,'" said Jurgen. "We'll start at one point seven five million."

"What's he starting at?" Seth asked. Claire told him.

"Do I hear one point seven five million?" Richard Beckmeister lifted his paddle slightly to indicate a bid. This would be fun, Claire thought. Seth was a determined buyer. Unless Richard was working for someone very well heeled or very eager for the painting, it was likely to go to Seth.

"Thank you," said Jurgen, as someone raised a paddle for that amount. "Do I hear two million?"

"Here we go," said Claire, raising her hand.

"Claire," said Jurgen. "Thank you. Two million. Do I hear two point one million? Two point one million? Yes," Jurgen said, "the gentleman standing in the back. How about two point four million?"

Richard Beckmeister raised a paddle. "What's it up to?" Seth asked.

"Two point four million."

"Bid up to three million," Seth said.

"Do I hear two point six?" Jurgen asked.

Claire raised her hand. "Thank you, Claire," Jurgen said. "Two point six million."

Richard Beckmeister held his paddle up. "Are you bidding? What? Two point eight million?" Jurgen asked. Richard nodded. "Two point eight million. Thank you. Anyone? Three million?"

Claire paused. "Anyone?"

Claire raised her hand. "Thank you. I have a telephone bid for three million." She could see the journalists craning to see her, Peter and Sean gazing at her, Richard appraising her with a curatorial eye. "Do I have three point three million? Next bid. Three point three million. Anyone?" Jurgen asked. He leaned over the podium, he cockeyed triangular head scanning the crowd. "Anyone?" Richard Beckmeister raised a paddle.

"It's three point three million," Claire told Seth. "Any higher?"

"No," Seth said. "I'm going for the water lily one."

"Are you sure?"

"Positive."

It sold to Richard Beckmeister, on behalf of some client she'd find out about later. Next up was another Monet, a still life, which Seth was not interested in. That was followed by a Pissarro drawing, and then the Monet water lily painting, from 1906, a signature work if ever any was.

Claire called in quick order her other two clients, conferencing them in. They had wanted to hear the progress of the sale from the "Nympheas" onward. The first client, beyond Seth—who seemed to be in rapid chatter with his assistant—was Mabel Grex, a personal curator to Ezekiel Bonner, the CEO of Solar Microsystems, whose collection was representative of the arc of twentieth-century art.

They would be bidding—or Mabel would—on a Matisse still life coming up in a few lots, as well as a great Cézanne standing nude that prefigured the modern abstract take on figurative art, such as Picasso's "Demoiselles d'Avignon." Claire had worked with Mabel before, when Zeke Bonner was selling some nineteenth-century French academic paintings he had acquired many years earlier. Mabel was about forty, wore her hair in a serious unfashionable manner—bangs and a blunt bob, like a 1930s lesbian—and was identifiable from afar by her large rectangular eyeglasses, which looked like doorframes, perched on the expanse of her broad nose. She was rumored to have been briefly Zeke Bonner's mistress, but Claire doubted that—surely it would have been like sleeping with a Picasso monkey sculpture. Claire liked her, though, and appreciated her gruff manner.

"How's it goin'?" she said as soon as she answered.

"So far, it's a good sale," Claire said quickly, anxious to move on to the next call.

"Is this thing on? The tape—"

"Of course," Claire said.

"Shit. Then I can't collude," Mabel said. She was referring to a lawsuit involving collusion between auction houses that had ended in sizable fines paid to the government and tremendous bad publicity. Claire ignored the comment.

"You can hear the sale all right?" Claire asked.

"Fine."

She placed a call to her third client, Robert Carbury, a dealer in Chicago who was representing the Taft, a small but wealthy regional museum. Its founder had been a railroad baron who left a sizable and well-invested endowment. The museum was looking to add a Balthus painting to its holdings. The mandate of the Taft was to build a collection of contemporary art and late medieval works—

Silvington Taft had a funny bifurcated passion for illuminated manuscripts and twentieth-century art. So its collection included one of the largest libraries of books of hours outside Europe and a sizable showing of modern and contemporary artists. Robert Carbury was a taciturn and formal man. Claire had met him several times and likened him to a hungover sentry.

"Mr. Carbury?"

"Claire."

"Can you hear?"

"Perfectly. And the sale?"

"So far, so good. The Picasso landscape just sold for a million. Above the estimate."

Jurgen announced the Monet.

"Now, 'Nympheas' from 1906, by, of course, Claude Monet." He pronounced it with a swirl to his voice. The painting was estimated at $16 million to $20 million. Here, horizontal patches of flowers floated amid shimmering blues. The way the green leaves lay on the blue led the eye upward and gave the canvas a sense of spun movement, as if the constantly shifting light had been caught like filaments of glass, to reflect the day, a solid representation of the transitory. Without a visible horizon the picture still created a depth of field that allowed the mind's eye to see the further ripples of the plane of water and infer the dancing light as day deepened into violet dusk. These water lily paintings had been a tremendous success for Monet, and they remained among his most popular. This one had not changed hands very often over the past hundred years, and had come onto the market following the death of a significant collector, Ashford James, whose New York apartment was a cathedral of Impressionist and Post-Impressionist art.

"I will start at fifteen million," Jurgen said.

"Hop in at sixteen five," Seth told Claire.

"I remember," she said.

"Do I have fifteen?" Jurgen said.

"Who's bidding?" Mabel asked.

"Is someone else here bidding?" Seth said.

"Not on the phone," Claire said. Then, to Mabel, "I didn't recognize the bidder."

"Thank you," Jurgen said. "The gentleman standing in the rear. Sixteen point one. Number three seventy four. Thank you. Next bid, sixteen five."

Claire raised her hand. As did Andre Karl.

"Claire? I think you were first. Sixteen five," said Jurgen.

"Now, sixteen eight?" he asked.

Andre Karl raised his hand.

"Sixteen eight," Jurgen said. "Thank you."

"Who's that?" Seth demanded.

"Andre Karl," Claire said.

"That fuck. Bid against him now. His fucking son fucked my second wife."

"Seventeen?" Jurgen asked.

Claire raised her hand. "How high?" she asked Seth.

"I don't care. I want that painting. Fuck Karl."

"Thank you, Claire," Jurgen said. "Seventeen five?"

Another bidder raised a paddle. "Number two-six-seven," Jurgen said. "Thank you." Claire tutted.

"Who's that?" Seth asked.

"My ex-husband," she said. She hadn't wanted to mention that connection.

"This is getting interesting," said Mabel Grex.

"Who's that?" Seth asked.

"Another phone bidder."

"Your ex-husband?" Seth said. "Fuck him, too."

"Eighteen two," said Jurgen looking at the bidders who had raised their hands or paddles. His eyes met Claire's.

"Bid," said Seth.

Claire raised her hand. Peter glanced at her, then raised his hand, as Jurgen asked, "Eighteen five?"

Andre Karl raised his hand. "Thank you," Jurgen said. "Nineteen?"

"Bid," Seth said.

Claire raised her hand. The room had grown silent but for Jurgen, and Claire's murmuring, unheard by anyone other than nearby colleagues.

"Nineteen million," Jurgen said. "Next bid will be nineteen five."

"Bid twenty," Seth told her. She raised her hand at Jurgen's expectant eye.

"Twenty million," Jurgen said. "The next bid will be twenty-one. Do I hear twenty-one?" The room was silent. Jurgen learned forward on the podium, his head moving back from Claire—who had bid—to Peter, to Andre Karl. The silent room held anticipation as one. The journalists and writers were mainly quiet, too, though Claire noticed Cynthia Deutsch whispering furiously to her friend and familiar, Josh, speculating no doubt on the identity of the phone bidder. Claire saw Bernice, too, for the first time, amid the throng. Slumming, Claire thought; she could have had a seat easily.

Jurgen said again, "Twenty-one?" No one moved. "All right, then, I am—" Andre Karl raised his hand. The crowd murmured. "Twenty-one," said Jurgen. "Thank you." He paused, expectant.

"Was that that fuck Karl?" Seth asked.

"Yes," Claire said. "Bid?"

"Twenty-two," Seth told her.

Jurgen had been looking at her. "Claire? Has your client decided?"

Claire held up her finger to Jurgen to pause. "Are you sure?" she asked Seth.

"Tell him I'll call him later," he snarled to his assistant. "Yes, I'm sure. Bid."

Claire nodded. Jurgen looked at Andre Karl, then at Peter. "Are you still interested, number two-four-seven?" Jurgen asked. Peter shrugged; people around the room laughed here and there, like nervous giggles at a horror movie. Peter was on a cell phone, he too holding up a finger. He nodded to Jurgen.

"Who bid?" Seth asked.

"My ex-husband," Claire said.

"Another fuck. Okay. Bid."

"Twenty-four?" she asked.

"Bid."

In the meantime, Andre Karl had raised his hand

"It's just been bid on by Andre Karl," Claire whispered to Seth.

"Shit! Okay—Hold on. Let me pull over."

Claire held her hand up. Jurgen had his eyebrows raised to her. "Seth?" she asked.

"I'm pulling into an In-n-Out Burger," he said. "I couldn't drive."

"Is your client still there?" Jurgen asked.

"Yes," she said. "Just one moment." All eyes were on her.

"Okay," Seth said, exhaling into the receiver. "There. Okay."

"Claire?" asked Jurgen.

"The auctioneer is waiting," Claire said.

"I know, I know," Seth said. "Tell me," he added, a little less brusquely. "How much is this painting really worth?"

"It's worth what the market will bear," she told him. "You know that."

"Tell me honestly," he said. "Is it worth the twenty-five million it might take to nab it?"

"Claire?" Jurgen asked "We do have other lots to sell tonight."

She held up a finger and smiled.

"Can I make a return on this?"

"If you're buying it as an investment, no," Claire said quickly. "You know you shouldn't buy art as speculation. But if you care for a painting and you have the money, buy it."

"So I probably won't see my twenty-five million back?"

"If you look at it that way, no," she said.

"We all have dinner reservations," Jurgen said.

"Then screw it," Seth said. "Let that fuck Karl try to unload it."

Claire shook her head to Jurgen. The crowd let out a sigh of disappointment, robbed of the chance to see someone else spent vast amounts of money. But this was short-lived disappointment; as Jurgen pounded the gavel, announcing, "Sold, twenty-four million dollars," and the room resounded with applause. Substantial multi-million-dollar purchases usually earned kudos for the moneyed, happy that someone else spent so much, and gratified that a masterpiece had proved its mettle in the marketplace, thus validating not only their presence at this and other sales, but also whatever they sold and their own professions.

Following the Monet triumph, the sale proceeded rapidly, although it was almost anticlimactic. Even the $20 million Cézanne, a great work, which sold for $21 million after fast, sure bidding to Mabel Grex, was exciting, but had lacked the heady drama of the "Nympheas," when the people in the room could sense the theatricality, the unseen phone bidder driven by some private urge, the back and forth between Claire's bidder, Andre Karl, and Peter, triangulating the suspense of the evening. Each auction had a play-like rhythm. The first scene, with a strong or heralded entrance by the warm-up work, the arrival of the stars—the "Nympheas" for example and a late so-called eleven o'clock number, in this case the Cézanne standing nude, and the finale, which here was not one but two Balthus paintings. The gloomy Robert Carbury actually bought for the Taft the "Odalisque à la Mandoline," which showed a naked young woman, very much still a girl, her legs splayed at the knee, half reclining, half perhaps getting out of a four-poster bed. She held a mandolin, resting it on the floor in the light grasp of her left hand. Her face lay on the pillow, eyes shut, hair draped along the sheets. An austere, erotic, eerie painting that seemed to be from a younger period than it actually was. The Taft bought it for $3.5 million. Robert did well. Claire could actually detect a muffled joy over the phone. Perhaps the painting's old-man's fantasy of chaste carnality appealed to him. Who knew what wayward Eros haunted Robert's dreams?

The sale was a success. It took in $140 million, above the high estimate of $115 million. Auctions were always judged by the percentage of lots sold and then whether the net had reached the top estimates. If more than 85 percent of works found buyers, the sale was very good. If, on top of that, the works made even more than the most optimistic projections, it was deemed a triumph. When appraising the sale value of paintings or sculpture, specialists and their staff calculated the rise or stasis of a painting's financial history, the artist's reputation on the market, the rarity of the kind of work among the artist's oeuvre, the popularity of that style, the condition of the painting, the economic climate, and the provenance. The history of who owned a painting had become even more important to potential buyers as a sign of not only a work's inherent value—if that could ever truly be calculated—but its legitimacy. The antiquities market was rife with frauds—goods illegally brought into the country, stolen from digs, arranged through a network of black-market dealers—but the painting world had been sensitive to impropriety as well. Following a decade of hand wringing, grudging

returns, financial retribution, resale, and ownership attribution surrounding looted Nazi-era art, buyers, everyone from private ones to
museums or trusts, were cautious and wary of giving even the
appearance of collusion on such matters. Claire had often wished
that people in relationships came with just such due diligence. It
would save later emotional reparation.

# PARTY FAVORS

The "Nympheas" leaned against the back of the turntable, still colorful but almost forlorn, a canvas covered with paint. They all look so small after the sales, Claire thought, no longer buffeted by the force of desire, financial impetus, provenance, or acclaim. She remembered a few years earlier seeing a Rothko color field painting, which had sold for a then-record $15 million, propped up against a wall following the auction. It had the drab allure of a painted work shed, minutes after being fought over as an icon of twentieth-century modernism. It was humbling; so much effort spent on a mere canvas. It was more than that, of course, but at art auctions, postpartum depression set in quickly.

The room had begun to clear out quickly, as dealers, buyers, onlookers, consorts, and acquaintances rushed to dinner reservations and assignations. The food and beverage service was setting up tables on which to lay a spread of sandwiches and such for the journalists, who were fed after being made to stand and watch the sale from the sidelines. The tables were placed where the reporters were herded; they, meanwhile, chatted in small groups or sought specialists for comment on the sale. A press conference would follow shortly, after the final results were tallied and the auctioneer's commission calculated into the sale price of each work.

She saw Cynthia Deutsch, the *Times* art reporter, limpid as a ferret, whispering with Danny Morris, the number two Impressionist expert at Sotheby's, digging for background scoops, holding her pen in one claw, her tatty notebook in the other. She was wearing her first-evening auction dress, Claire noticed. She always had on the same clothes, showed up with the same limp hair, the same unpleasant expression, a vague disgust at the world around her and the job she was doing. Maybe it was the outfit that made her seem as if she lived on a diet of gumdrops and vegetable peelings and slept on a bed of straw. But it had become her uniform, of sorts, and surely Claire wasn't the only one who noticed Cynthia's Grey Gardens fashion sense. She had a brownish 1970s pantsuit for the second-night auctions, something very substitute teacher at the middle school of a lower-income congressional district. And she wore an odd ensemble of a leather jacket and denim skirt for the contemporary art ones, the clothes of someone whose cruel friends advised her that this was just the outfit to impress the quarterback.

Cynthia had often been patronizing to Claire, for some reason, as if, Claire thought, had their fortunes been what they should have been, their roles would have been reversed. Or maybe she just didn't like her. Claire usually chose not to comment for her stories, so perhaps her uselessness as a source earned her Cynthia's enmity. But in her reporting Cynthia seemed to rely less on background sources for any original material than she did on press releases, doctoring up with a quote or two the official blather, like a cake mix to which she'd added her own special ingredient, canned peaches. Cynthia usually stood near the front of the auction room, just beyond the ropes, like a sickly but mean-spirited calf that had gone astray, mingling with the experts, scanning the crowd, looking for familiar faces she might be able to identify as buyers of certain works of art that would sell this evening. She was abetted in this by her customary auction-night companion, a greasy-haired scalawag Claire decided was her familiar, Josh Reynolds, who bounced from job to job and was at the moment publishing an Internet newsletter on contemporary art sales. He had the unwashed feral look of a ladies' man, but only if the ladies were drunk or decrepit: the Don Juan of the dive. He used to be a gallery owner and then a dealer and knew by sight many of the potential buyers. He had once hit on Claire at a cocktail reception, but she'd brushed him off, figuring that he must have been desperate to want to spend time with her, or that Cynthia had dispatched him to try to get dirt on some back-office maneuverings that had been going on at the time.

She saw some other journalists she knew, and many she didn't. Where did all of these people come from? When she gave walk-throughs of her shows she met writers; in the week before a sale, its major pictures were displayed, so that the public could see the works, and the press and art world could appraise the nature of the sale and the paintings and such to be offered. Some of the scribes were diligent, some restless, some eager, some diffident, most polite, all hungry. But she couldn't figure out what the majority of them actually did, since the constricting economy affected art reporting, too; many magazines had folded and newspapers devoted less space to the art world. Most of these people must be trolling for stories, hanging on to the invitations, still part of the universe of art, such as it was. They had begun to chomp on potato chips and focaccia, and swill whatever it was that passed for wine. Claire usually ignored the spread and dined later. The press conference would begin shortly.

"You looked so commanding up there, Claire." It was Peter.

"I didn't feel that way. It was nerve-racking," she said. "Hello," she added, stopping to touch his hand. She was still standing at the telephone bank. "And I'm guessing that you must be Sean, right?" She offered her hand to the man who had been sitting next to Peter throughout the sale.

"Sean Ryan," he said, offering her his bear paw. He looked much larger than when she'd seen him across the room.

"Let me come round and chat," she said. "I have a few minutes before I need to get the paperwork done for tonight."

She saw Cynthia Deutsch making a beeline for Peter. "Ferret coming up on your left," she whispered quickly to Peter, who turned around and said, "Cynthia! Darling! How *are* you?" He kissed her on both cheeks, Euro-style. Cynthia gave him a snaggletooth smile.

Claire was mortified. Did he actually like her? And here she was about to be her most sarcastic.

"Claire," Cynthia said. "Great sale."

"Cynthia," she said. "Nice to see you. Yes, it went well."

"So, who were you working for?"

"You know we don't name names," she said.

"How about you, Peter?" she said, turning to him, and flashing him a revolting grin.

"Well, Cynthia, I was just doing some bidding for a friend," Peter told her. "He wouldn't want it to be known."

"I didn't know you'd begun to be a bidder."

"I've started to branch out into art consulting," he said. "Beyond furniture."

"Any hints on your buyer?"

"I'll call him and let you know," he said. Peter had successfully bid on a mid-period Picasso portrait of Dora Maar, which sold for $3 million. He took out his cell phone, moved a little aside, and placed a call. How could he so easily bend to her odious simpering? Cynthia stayed close while he spoke softly into the phone.

Claire noticed that Peter hadn't introduced Sean to Cynthia, or reintroduced him to her. She said, "Let's just let them do business," to him and, touching his arm, drew him aside.

"Is this your first sale?" she asked him.

"My first evening sale," he said. He had a pleasant light baritone and the well-fed look of a Frans Hals burgher. "It's all new to me, though."

"Are you interested in the art world?"

"Well, I'm interested in a lot of things. So I guess I am." Evasive, perhaps, she thought, but no, unwilling to commit to a statement that might lead to opening himself up, perhaps.

"You know, we were married, he and I," she said.

"I know. Peter told me all about it."

He did, did he? She wondered what his version was.

"All lies, of course. Don't believe a word of it."

"But he said you were terrific."

"All lies. But enough about me. What do you think of this all?" she said, indicating with her hand the room, the crowd, the business.

"It's fascinating. It was like theater. I don't know the ins and outs of it all, and why you'd spend so much for something to hang on a wall, but that's just me."

"You're a detective, right?" she asked.

"Yeah. Yes," he said, adjusting his tie, which was a bit short over the modest curve of his belly. "Downtown."

"Homicide?" She assumed all detectives worked homicide cases.

"More open than that," he said.

"I don't know what else might call for detective work."

"You'd be surprised."

I bet I would, she thought.

"Tell me," she said. "I don't mean to be pushy. But what's it like working for the police department, when—"

He nodded. "I keep it private."

"I understand," she said.

"No," he said. "Really. I don't see how you can."

He didn't admit much, but Claire figured it was part of his manner, since his was a profession that drew people out, not one that exposed itself to interpretation. "Well, you know it took a lot for Peter to admit it to me."

"I can imagine," he said, and as he looked at her, she saw how warm his eyes became, like those in a Velázquez portrait, expressive of a sharp longing one couldn't quite discern. Her inward debate about his suitability as either a partner for the man who rejected her, or as a man himself—she was uncertain of her assessment here—gave her an expression of distant scrutiny, as if she were looking at something farther afield than his expectant face. His gaze met hers with an unaffected questioning, a mingled appraisal of his own with a tender and awkward realization, she thought, that she had been caught at her own game. He, too, had been creating an impression of her, of course, and she, in her self-absorbed myopia, had forgotten that. His intelligent eyes cautiously surveyed the room, half-expectant, and this was evident in his perceptive looks even if the auction house and the auction crowd, the entire hullabaloo of created excitement, were new to him. She shouldn't underestimate him because she tended to group police work and thus policemen into some vague blue-collar universe of beer and brawls and tumbledown bohemia.

"I live with my mother," he said, as if that explained a lot, as if that were a revelation he had chosen to withhold from general knowledge, and had given her a clue to his life, an unexpected gift to her of his private world. "But you know that." He smiled, and seemed ready for her to believe that he had given her the clues she needed to begin to sort him out, or that he had revealed all he intended to for now.

"I do," she said, smiling back, almost blushing at his attention, a glow of mingled undefined sensibilities forming a hesitant admiration and raising further questions in her about how we choose to reveal ourselves. What was it about men and their secrets? We are all so reluctant to divulge what we are about, and men, gay men, even more so, for who wants to be scorned? It was surely even more difficult for a policeman, living in a world of tough guys and posturing, not only to admit to himself what he was, but to allow others to know. Certainly it had been difficult for her ex-husband, and because of the nature of their particular universe of artists and auctioneers and, well, gay people, it should have been easier. But it wasn't. Peter had to contend not only with whatever he might have expected Claire to think about what he was (and she hadn't even made up her mind about that) but with the emotional depredation from his disapproving brother's further belittling of him. What must it be like for someone like Sean even to admit to his mother, who surely must have reason to believe that her thirty-something son would never marry, that he wasn't going to provide her with grandchildren, if indeed that was what she wanted? Ratiocination regarding sexuality was so often fraught with shame, regardless of society. "Have you ever been married?" she asked him.

"No," Sean said. "But I was engaged once."

So he knew, too, how to hurt women.

"But I broke it off."

Had he realized enough about himself? Most men don't, they just barge on unthinking. "How did she take it? Did you tell her the truth?"

"I didn't think it would work. I saved her." Did he mean from The Job or something else? She felt that he had opened himself up to her more than he probably did to others, and perhaps her being a woman, and Peter's ex-wife, had led him to grant himself permission to speak in this way which, Claire admitted, wasn't particularly enlightening, except in tantalizing tidbits. Claire suspected she was lucky to get this amount of information from him.

So the fiancée probably hadn't known. About Sean's inner life, as such. Though it was none of Claire's business, of course. Still, she wondered just how much the girl had realized, or speculated on, regarding the engagement, the house, the kids, the future. Just reel him in and it'll all take care of itself, she had probably thought. We're all so besotted with possibilities that we forget the present.

"I didn't mean to pry," she said, controlling herself with a tingling annoyance at wanting to learn more than she had a right to, so soon, so suddenly.

"So you've been getting acquainted," Peter said, having finished up with whatever Cynthia wanted.

"Did you let Cynthia know?" Claire asked.

"I did," he said. "It was the Abingdon, you know, in Maine." The Abingdon was a midsize modern art museum near Kennebunkport. "The curator told me it was all right. It couldn't hurt to let the public know that the place was strengthening its holdings."

"Or that you were working for them," Claire said.

"Or that," Peter said. "Sorry not to introduce you to Cynthia, Sean, but you seemed so wrapped up with Claire, I didn't want to interrupt."

"We were just talking about my past," Sean said. He was both confident and closed off. She couldn't put her finger on why he seemed to be at ease with Peter, in a way that Toby hadn't been. But she hadn't known Toby all that well, either, even after five years. Perhaps he was closed off to Peter in ways that the relationship didn't reveal to outsiders like herself. An outsider, again.

"Did you mention your future?"

"It never came up," he said.

"Sean's considering a career change. He's got almost twenty years. Well, in a few years."

"Really? You don't look that old."

He didn't respond to that. "Just looking at options."

"Like art?"

"Not sure. Possibilities."

"Not a store, not a dealership, not with me," Peter said, laughing. "Can you imagine? Another cliché of two men and a shop."

"I don't see why not," Claire said. "But then, I don't really know you," she added, looking at Sean.

"But she will," Peter said. "She's got a knack for people. That's why she's so good here."

"Professionally speaking, I have a knack," she said. "On the personal level—I'm still working on that."

"She's too modest," Peter said. "I threw her for a loop, but she gets art mavens to unload in a flash. See how you two started talking so quickly?"

"Well, you were doing the publicity thing with Cynthia."

"She's a horror, but you've got to deal with the press, Claire."

"I do, up to a point. Just not her, when I can avoid it." It irked her that he had been so carefree and obliging, even charming, with a person she found so distasteful. Another aspect of his disarming personality that she hadn't realized, or had chosen to forget. He certainly could be an operator. But courting the press, especially if you were an independent businessman, as Peter was, was prudent. He was still, indeed, building a business, and taking on clients in a different capacity. Becoming a consultant carried with it more responsibility and perhaps a greater need for publicity of some sort. Or maybe not; consultants often acted as public faces for clients, but the clients often remained anonymous. Nevertheless, she resented her own annoyance, especially as Peter seemed so easily to slip into various characters, while she remained herself, whatever that meant.

"The press usually get things wrong," Sean said.

"You've dealt with them on cases."

"And other things," Sean said. "But as little as possible, if I can."

"We're alike there," Claire said. "Only your cases are more life-and-death. Mine are more art-and-money."

"And mine are money and art," Peter said. "Would you care to join us for dinner?" he asked Claire.

"I'm meeting Bernice," she said, "after I wrap up my work here in a little bit." She would have liked to talk more with Sean.

"We should have dinner, the three of us," Peter said.

"I'd like that, too," Sean said. "Getting to know the ex."

"Do you mean Toby?"

"Not him. Not yet," he said, with a timid look she hadn't expected after their conversation, and she saw he blushed slightly, as if unexpectedly caught in a thought he hadn't wanted to disclose. "Maybe later."

"Much later," Peter said.

"I *would* like dinner," she said, realizing as she spoke that she was again trying to open up the possibility of continuing friendship with her ex-husband's lovers. Did that matter? Did she want to be the third wheel in a relationship that really she couldn't participate in? Or did she care so much for her ex that his love life meant so much to her? How much was this a part of her continuing mortification at not being the chosen one, and how much a genuine affection for a man who could no longer be as close to her as he once was, but who still mattered? And, in the end, did it actually mean something worthwhile to her, that is, was she remaining trapped in an idea of herself that she should have outgrown had she severed ties with him, or was this acceptance of her ex-husband's path toward romantic comfort a part of her own maturation by taking part in his life, a life that only included her as an observer? Was she genuinely interested, or morbidly involved?

"You know," she added, discarding those thoughts, "I have a sale coming up in a month. There's going to be a big cocktail party for it—we're trying to drum up more business for the nineteenth-century departments outside of Impressionism—and I'd love it if you showed up. We could go out afterward."

They agreed, and Claire watched them leave, moving relaxed through the thinning crowd.

Jurgen had returned from the offices, and the press conference announcing the official sale results began. Claire saw Bernice, who waved her over. Bernice was, as usual, chic, especially compared to the frump-on-a-stick look affected by Cynthia Deutsch. Bernice was wearing a red print dress with a flared skirt, and a smart solid jacket in a shade that picked up one of the reds of the dress's flower pattern. "You look like spring," Claire said.

"You look worn out. First the phone bidding, then the old husband. Was that the new beau with him?"

"Yes. Very nice. I'll tell you all about him later."

"So who were you trying to nab that Monet for?"

"You know it's a secret."

"Give me a hint."

"Think Hollywood."

"That's a big hint. They're all trying to prove how smart they are by buying art. Well, it doesn't matter. I'll find out somehow. I'm more interested in the new man, anyway. What's he got over Toby?"

"I don't know," Claire admitted. "But I think it may be love."

"Well, that's a start."

And that was something Claire hadn't even considered, even as she'd voiced the word. Sean had a presence that Toby did not—it was either because of his profession (apprehending criminals took a certain kind of nerve) or something more she'd have to discover. Toby was grounded, certainly, up to a point. He had helped his parents in their hours of need, he had seemed real. But Sean had seemed, if anything, more real. Maybe it was his size—he was large where Toby was slight, though both men had a palpable physicality. As did Frank, she realized. It was Peter who seemed to be the shape-shifter. But Claire was impressed with Sean, despite what she knew was her innate snobbery, the conflict within her that both abhorred the human dross around her and that examined everyone she met with the curiosity of something laid upon a specimen table, inferring, sometimes correctly, the motives for their actions, and their means of realizing them, desiring to be a part of a world that only touched hers, envious of its complexities, afraid of its influence. She'd sized Sean up beforehand, figured he was just another trick for Peter, someone he'd grow tired of and toss off. Though this was unfair, since Peter had been in two relationships she knew of that had lasted more than a year—with her and with Toby. Still, she couldn't count out countless unknown assignations. But who was she to know or judge, or comment on anyone he knew or chose to consort with, or even to build a relationship with? As if she should talk, a middle-class Long Island girl hobnobbing with the wealthy just because she knew a thing or two, or thought she did, about pictures and their worth.

She'd meant to ask Peter whether he'd seen his brother. But she could ask Frank himself. She hadn't spoken to him in a while, yet she'd found herself thinking of him in the past few days, even as her work had grown more demanding as her sale neared. She half expected Frank to bristle when she would approach matters of his family that she wouldn't dare ask Peter, knowing he'd dissemble, or fearing he would. She herself took unspoken exception to anyone asking about her and her sister, sensing in the interest a judgment of their differences or an appraisal of their separate accomplishments. She would affect the demeanor of one assessing a query from a lower order, something she had, in fact, learned from her sister, Catherine. She wondered if she shared other characteristics with her sister, and how often family members aped or modified each other's manner.

Was Frank, whom she really was only beginning to know, and differently—in her marriage to Peter she had, despite their friendliness, seen him only from afar, as it were, outside the realm of her and Peter's relationship, as she realized she had seen Peter, tonight, as if on a stage—in many ways similar to his younger brother, or had he, sensing this, tried for gruff bravado instead of Peter's suave hypocrisy? She felt that people whom one desired or even thought one knew well were, in different stages of their lives among others, after the manner of a recently purchased artwork that had been haggled and agonized over, rather like that helpless Rothko she'd recalled, shorn of glamour in the glare of having been won. She wondered if Frank was worth worrying over, or, indeed, whether intimacy were an enrichment or merely the possession of one more overpriced canvas.

# A SUITABLE VASE

S o the days he'd dreaded, the long hours staring at empty air before an unmarked page, had not come. He worked. He wandered new through the city, alive to the fading winter, the lengthening day, the possibilities. It was good he'd taken this time; less than a month ago he'd despaired of connecting and here he was, albeit still solitary, but surrounded in a new way by a bustle of industry. He'd for the moment dismissed, as Teresa had written, the serpents of vanity and greed. Well, vanity, certainly.

The air, the patchy gray and blue days, were similar to ones he'd remembered from years before, when he came home for the first time after his father had left. He was newly a priest. Easter had been early, and the cool spring held little promise of summer—it had been a winter resurrection. Frank's studies had occupied him to the extent of erasing doubt up to that point, and the novelty of his orders, as well as the fear of discovering his inner failure of spirit— it burned low like a pilot light he didn't want to ignite—had kept him from fully comprehending the enormity of what had befallen his family, especially his mother and brother. Mainly he thought, when he did think of others in that way, of his mother. His brother had Frank's rather unexamined sympathy; he'd known that he should have embraced, at least metaphorically, his younger brother in his plight. After all, his father had just left him. But Frank felt that that emotional and physical hollowness was his only due. His brother might have watched their father walk coolly out to a waiting car and patient mistress, but he still had a future open to him, even a fatherless one. Peter hadn't signed his life away to spiritual servitude, nor had he been betrayed by the foolish wastrel dreams of illicit romance and barely mortified escape. The two boys had surely expected different things from their father. Frank had chosen the path his father had wished for him, had wished for himself, actually. Peter hadn't yet been given the impossible burden of fulfilling parental yearning, as far as Frank knew, and he usually didn't care to speculate on what lay behind his brother's mask of determined good cheer. He would be spared his father's disapproval. Peter had seemed happy enough, considering, without having had the benefit of parental subjugation. Oh, Frank knew it was tragic but had, he knew, little sympathy, since his brother had still been spared the sense of being measured against whatever it was their father had wanted. As far as he could tell, or as much as he wanted to examine it, only one child usually bore the imprint of a parent's unfulfilled life. For Frank, their father had made certain things clear—how marvelous it was to be called to a vocation (if so, why hadn't he done it himself instead of creating a family only to abandon it?)—how much responsibility was placed in the propagation of the faith, how sacrifice was the hallmark of goodness (his father must have been very good, since he sacrificed them all to his whims). But who could really know what was expected of us, groomed for or nudged toward a profession or calling that seemed to answer the needs of someone else's preconception? When one fails at that, having tried to plod along a path that had been chosen or insisted upon, do we despise ourselves for having disappointed the person who so wrongly steered us, or do we despise ourselves for having faltered to begin with or even for having submitted to such emotional battery? We do aim to please, and become less than we ought.

That first visit home was also when Frank noticed that what would turn out to be cancer had begun to show in the smudges under his mother's mournful eyes, when it had begun to eat away even at the anger that had fired her for those first months of abandonment and bitter widowhood and desultory, preoccupied child-rearing. She was relieved of that now, with Peter off at college.

He had found his mother seated in the shabby little room that looked out onto the side yard. The window view, such as it was, was blocked by an ungainly azalea bush in bloom, its vibrant pink red blossoms throbbing with life even as the gray day loomed disapproving. It hadn't been pruned in years, and the branches hugged the house, scratching the windows, begging to be let in. Frank had taken a train home and at the station grabbed a premade bouquet, thinking at that moment that the flowers might cheer his mother up. He was not generally given to such tokens of affection, for Frank considered showing up to be duty enough, but the roses and baby's breath in the scalloped cellophane cone had caught his unguarded eye as he hunted for a train schedule, so he picked them up, an eight-dollar gesture of offhand remembrance.

"They're just like what your father used to buy," his mother had said as he had handed the bouquet to her. "Put them in the kitchen and I'll get a vase later."

Frank had wanted to throw them out instead, hearing the reference and recoiling from mention of his now-dead parent. But what should he have expected? He hadn't been used to his mother's full frontal bitterness, had only experienced the telephone sighing and weary impatience of their brief and intermittent chats. He had arrived at a point when he not only questioned the joy in obedience to any authority, but he asked himself whether his mother's bitter suffering had allowed her over the endless years of his early youth to watch as her solitary son, who she must have known was not given to quiet meditation, but angry seclusion, dutifully, ploddingly, resentfully did what his father had wanted him to do. Frank had been surprised, really, to consider that with his father's death, his mother looked upon him as someone who, because he had, up to a point, fulfilled his father's wishes, now wasn't an example of dutiful virtue but of her husband's venality. He began to think that she had been as much to blame for his spiritual inadequacy as she had for his father's adultery. False, but satisfying to think ill of her in her willful unhappiness, even as she began to fade from the earth in bits and pieces of mortified, decaying flesh. He knew too, of course, that she was still ultimately responsible for her own failure of spirit.

So be it, he had thought. He did what he thought he had to do—show up, physically if not mentally—and throughout the few days of his visit his halfhearted perfunctory flowers limp in their vase had signaled to him not only his galling choices but the curse of his lineage; he couldn't escape what he was, what in him was linked to his father, as much as he would have loved to eradicate every mark of what he had done to please that dissolute and now very dead god. And his aim to please had not worked, neither for his heartless father nor for his dying reproachful mother. Wormwood, then, was his to savor.

After that first visit, the temptation to avoid responsibilities was great, and he evaded whenever he could, until her illness began to consume her. His visits illuminated for them both their regrets at what they had done or chosen not to do. She looked at her dismal future as a relief from whatever wreckage had been cast upon her, so she told him, in one of her last confessions, which she had begged him to hear, much to his revulsion. He couldn't refuse, and couldn't even pretend not to hear her wish, so close had she been to his ears. She had begun to lapse into a serene dementia, broken by fitful anger. The whispered hiss of her words, the "I have sinned," the meaningless "I have sinned" (for who hasn't) that made up her pathetic confessions, was all the she could say. "Please, let me go," she said, as if his presence had kept her among the barely living. As if he had the power, when he himself, at so many points, had wished himself away. And he did, he did. Peter was with her when she died, and Frank was sure that Peter had made it seem as if it were the most natural thing in the world for her to slip away into what she surely believed was a better life.

But that was then. That was long ago. Now his mind was on other things. Spiritual things, spirituality with a purpose, so to speak, especially as it applied to the business world, for what was salvation but the culmination of an ongoing series of five-year plans well executed? He was immersed in Teresa of Ávila, and how her works applied to corporate life. His "Teresa CEO" would be a skillful meditation on business and moral reckoning. That was the beauty of his book, he thought—and the publisher agreed—since it combined the encomiums of the corporate how-to with the wisdom (if such it was) of the beatified and sainted. He'd just finished a chapter on what to learn from Teresa's founding of the convent of San José. Frank had compared it to a corporate restructuring following a hostile takeover, except that here were no downsized employees, but forthright nuns.

His social life throughout the weeks of work hadn't been active. Apart from dinner with Claire, he'd kept to himself. He had even managed to avoid his brother, who kept calling him. Frank had been afraid of what seeing his brother would do to him—he couldn't pin down his unease. But that afternoon, he was taken by surprise when Peter showed up unannounced.

"It's me!" Peter had sung out when Frank peered through the lens on the door and seen his brother, looking hale and handsome.

"You keep avoiding me," Peter said when Frank opened the door. "I don't know what the problem is, but I figured I'd just drop in."

"How did you get in?"

"The doorman knows me. I told him I wanted to surprise you. And I did. You look well. At least I think that's what you look like when you're looking well, since I have very little to compare it with."

"Peter, I meant to get back to you eventually."

"When? When you'd moved back upstate?"

Yes, he thought. But he was suddenly ashamed of his childishness.

"Well, you've seen Claire. The least you could have done was see me, too," Peter said. "But I'm not going to lecture you—me, of all people! I know we're not going to be close, but still, you could've given me the courtesy of seeing me. Didn't they teach you anything in bible school? Love thy neighbor and all. There's got to be something in there about brotherly love, too. Or is that too New Age for you?" Peter walked around the living room as he spoke, picking up items and examining them briefly. He held a cloisonné box that had been lying on a side table, and looked back at Frank, who was still standing near the vestibule. "I hear you're going through a rough patch."

"You've spoken to Claire."

"She's told me *everything*," Peter said, suddenly laughing. "No, really. She mentioned she'd seen you. And her words were, I think, 'cranky as ever.'"

"What is it you want?" Frank asked, not meaning to sound as hostile as he thought he did.

"I don't want anything, Frank. Just to see you. Is that too much? I know you're busy and all, but everyone is. I don't know why you feel you have to avoid me. I'm not going to do anything. We hardly know each other, anyway. But we're still related. I'd hate for us to be one of those families that are torn apart by rifts."

"There is no rift."

"What do you call not returning my calls or turning off your cell phone? A rift in the making. I don't expect compassion from you, Frank—you're not the only one going through a rough patch—but I did sort of expect some respect. I am your brother, after all."

"Sorry," he said. "It's just that I've been busy."

"I know. I said that. I knew that. Still, you can't be alone forever. Or you could be. But you don't have to be. Anyway, I don't want to overstay my welcome, which I think was the moment I walked in the door, but weren't you the least bit curious about the news I'd found out about Mom and Dad?"

"I was," he admitted, slowly, "but I wasn't. I'm trying not to think of Dad too much." Which was a lie.

"I can't blame you. But I don't really believe you. Don't give me that look. You used to look at me like that when we were kids. Well, when I was a kid. You were never a kid, as far as I could remember."

"Well, maybe not to you. Peter, is this the time to go over the past?"

"Frank, all we have is a past, and barely one at that. No, I'm not going to go there. I just wanted to let you know about what I'd found."

"Is it so important?"

"Apparently important enough for me to see you in person. But maybe not important to you." He paused. "Anyway, did you know that between when you and I were born, Mom had two babies who died at birth. Two girls. You probably didn't notice.

You never noticed if she was pregnant, did you? You might have been too young, or maybe she didn't mention it. But you also didn't notice much beyond yourself, did you? I mean, what kid does? Especially you. But they never told us about them, and it looks like you never knew."

"What does it mean?"

"It means that I was probably a mistake. I think they'd given up, and then whoosh, I come along. Probably after a drunken night with Mom in between Dad's girlfriends. It also means they were probably pretty frustrated, and not taking it well. Or maybe Mom had an affair and I was the result. Who knows. God knows we're different enough, you and me. It also means that our parents were a bit more troubled than I'd remembered—and I remembered a lot, even if you think everything was okay because I wasn't you, and didn't have your burdens. Yes, I could figure that one out, Frank. I may be slow, sometimes, but I'm not an idiot."

"I never said you were. I never thought that."

"Of course you did. You still do, otherwise you wouldn't keep avoiding me. Unless you're afraid that I'll sprinkle fairy dust on you and you'll go all gay or something. Maybe you should think about that. After all, you know what they say about forty-year-old men who've never married."

"Now you're just being unpleasant."

"I am, and I apologize. But I'm sorry to place you in the position of being the recipient of bad news, instead of the bearer. If it is bad news. To you. And if you care. At all. You are the oldest, but you've had your share of bad things, I'm sure. Whatever they may have been. But you know, there are two little graves for the two little corpses that would have been your two little sisters. There probably wouldn't have been a little me. I never noticed the graves, of course, since I never looked for then, next to the plot where Mom is buried. We just thought it was the plot for him, but he's buried somewhere out west, who knows where, and the little headstones we never paid attention to weren't just place keepers but bore the names of Kathleen and Isobel. Sweet, isn't it? Easy to ignore when you're not looking for them. Hard to forget once you know."

"But what does it mean to you now? Why do *you* care?" Frank had asked.

"You mean because I never knew them or knew about them? I don't know. *I* think you should care more—your life might have been different. I don't know. But in a lot of ways you've got to learn a little about your family to get a sense of yourself. I'm probably like you in some ways you aren't even aware of, and you're probably like Dad or Mom in ways you wish you weren't."

"Why are you laying all this on me now? I'm just not interested."

"Oh that's it, is it? Close the door on me, close the door on the past. You can't always do that, Frank. I've learned what happens when you try to keep things shut off. You may have this picture of me as some flighty nothing, but—"

"I know. I have a lot of preconceptions." He couldn't apologize. Frank looked at his brother, who had stopped pacing, but was still holding the cloisonné box. He hadn't expected that Peter would show so much spirit, that after having been kept at bay he would have admitted defeat, as if it were a battle of wits, or a fraternal skirmish. It was almost four o'clock, and since Frank preferred to turn on lamps as late as possible, the light had faded, the shadows deep in the room. Peter had a gravity about him at that moment that surprised Frank. There was deep stillness in the room, broken only by the clock ticking on his landlady's mantel, a light rattle, a small sweeping sound of seconds passing. The cat slept noiselessly on the sofa, ignorant of, or ignoring, the scene. Peter had his face turned toward the doorway, fixing on it the gaze of a child stationed too long at the stairs, looking down upon a party, wondering whether to return unseen to bed. He looked younger, young, but like a man, one whom Frank did not know. He thought of Peter's words, unwelcome as all unfavorable fortune-telling is, and he began to regret that he had been so unpleasant, even as he still resented the intrusion on his ever-resentful isolation. He began to think Peter might slip away without his apologizing to him. He began to hope he might. But every feeling he had was accompanied by a new determination to prove that he was right, that he did not want to know more about his past, his parents, his brother, his newly dis-covered dead, unmourned sisters. He had a certainty close enough to doubt and uneasiness to hurry on a confession that he had hoped to delay by Peter's exit.

"I didn't mean to be so rude," Frank said. He took the knick-knack from Peter and placed it back on the table. "It's not mine," he said. He looked back at his brother, and then away. "I have a problem doing what is right," he said, sorry to have revealed so much, as he knew it to be so little.

"You can't escape everything," Peter said. He ran his finger over the side of an empty picture frame propped against a table lamp, let his finger rest there a moment, as if considering what it might have contained, and turned to Frank. "You've got to have some sort of plan in life."

"I used to. But I don't. My plan is to do what pleases me. But I don't know what that might be."

"Can you manage to feel only what pleases you?" Peter said.

"Frankly, I don't know what I feel, except that I'm at a loss. I used to do what pleased others, I think, as much as I could figure that out. I don't know what you hope to have me learn by what you've told me. You've got me at a disadvantage. I didn't expect you here."

"If you'd bothered to respond to any of my calls, you might have had time to prepare."

"I'm never prepared, even if I know beforehand what to expect. One thing I've learned is that I know little about everything."

"I don't have to be a stranger, you know," Peter said, with a different tone of voice. "You did marry me. So to speak. We both have learned something in our lives, I hope, about ourselves."

Frank eyed his brother cautiously. Peter was slightly taller than himself, and their eyes seemed to be on a level; there was only the faintest smile on Peter's face as he looked at Frank. His seemed to be a face often animated by humor, unlike Frank's own, which bore the hallmarks of self-absorbed worry in the frown lines that marked his brow—even he could see them, and he barely spent a minute before the mirror each morning. There was no trace of self-consciousness or anxiety in Peter's bearing, but a warm concern, as if he had been able to feel something beyond himself, something Frank found foreign.

Under Frank's somewhat self-repressed exterior was a fervor that led him to believe that he could find some romance among the events of everyday life, at least he thought, through fiction, that he possessed an ability to do this, if he could free his mind to appreciate beauty in the quotidian dullness of it all. But his phlegmatic nature led him to question his ability to be informed by either a revelation of unexpected loveliness or the grace of sudden friendship. How could he find awe and tenderness in a world that he had turned away from, that repelled him as much as it beguiled, as much as he would have thrilled for the touch of enlightenment brought about by emotional responsiveness to his unspoken pleading? He did not want to have to make himself clear. Any desire to know his family, his brother, was constantly haunted by dread. Any hope for love was filled with horror.

Frank felt that his expression probably betrayed his horror, as if he were listening to the aftershocks of an explosion, wondering what would come of it. The changes in this situation were bewildering. A few minutes before, he had been self-satisfied with the work he had done, a muted triumph of, admittedly, modest accomplishment. But now, this knowledge of facts regarding his parents—who knew the force of their embattled love or whatever passed for it between them—this startling show of strength in a brother whose memory was an illusion of contempt, Frank's contempt for someone he hadn't condescended to know as he pursued the vitiating course of higher learning toward the redemption of spirit—hah—gave him new disbelief in the worth of his insight into human nature. Not that he ever thought along those lines. The more one knew, or thought one knew, the larger one's ignorance loomed. Yet what was the good of Peter's coming to him? What did he wish?

He thought to buy time by agreeing. "You're right. And I've been in a muddle," Frank said. "I feel that I've just lurched from bad decision to bad decision."

"I've made quite a few in my day," Peter said. "And I'm not nearly as old as you."

Frank realized that the very vividness of his impressions had often made him enigmatic to those he considered friends—few believed he thought as he did. He had no idea how his brother viewed him, and he had not considered how he might seem; he had thought merely of what was his now-incorrect impression of Peter. Frank's imagination had become accustomed to seeing things as they probably did not appear to others, he thought, and partisanship had become insincerity for him. His sympathy had turned into a reflective analysis that tends to neutralize sympathy. Frank suspected himself of loving too well the losing causes of the world. Martyrdom changes sides, and he was in danger of changing with it. And yet his fear of falling into narrow hatred checked him: he shrank from overarching bitterness and the denunciatory tone of the unaccepted innovator. He was beginning to care little for actual knowledge unless it could be tied to his emotions; and he dreaded, as if it were a dwelling-place of lost souls, that dead anatomy of culture that turns the universe into a ceaseless answer to queries, and the insipid into the accepted. What he longed to be, yet was unable to be right now, was an organic part of social life, instead of roaming in it like a yearning disembodied spirit. At the same time, he longed, as Emerson urged, to be wholly self-reliant, and non-conformist, yet the pull of connections, human connections, was strong. Still, as for his behavior, he found some of the fault with the way he had been brought up—which Peter seemed to understand better, or articulate in a way Frank had not dared—which had given him no fixed relationships except one of a doubtful kind—thank you, Jesus—but he knew, too, that he had fallen into a meditative numbness and was gliding further and further from a life of energy and compassion that he knew to be the best, and for himself the only life worth living. He wanted some way of keeping emotion substantial and strong in the face of the angry reflectiveness that threatened to nullify everything. He felt as if he were Daniel Deronda, but instead of discovering an outlet for a longing and spiritual nature, he was looking to recover in some way what he had abandoned, even if he didn't fully want to wrap himself again in any kind of strong belief, believer though he remained. Perhaps it was the fetters of his loneliness that, despite his past redemptive work, weighed upon his mood.

And, again, he had hardly expected his brother to storm in and confront him with old news and a demand for—what? understanding? No. He thought Peter was beyond calling for that.

"Look," Frank had said. "I'm sorry to have been so nonchalant about getting in touch, or even keeping in touch. Still, I don't understand why you feel you have to barge in and start haranguing me. We haven't really gotten to know each other."

"I couldn't help myself," Peter had said. "The frustration of being cast aside as if I were a telemarketer rather than your brother. You're very abrupt."

"I know." He walked over to the cat, and stroked its sleeping fur. "It's served me well in the classroom. Less well in real life."

"I felt as if I've been alone for the longest time," Peter said. "I've been trying to create for myself a family, since the one I was born into hasn't so far worked out, what's left of it. I just wanted to reconnect. Despite your evident disapproval of me. It's a strong tie nevertheless, and maybe I like being beaten, but even your scorn hasn't kept me from trying."

Frank didn't answer. He took his lingering hand off the cat, which had uncoiled with feline pleasure at his stroking, and he reached up to turn on a lamp beside the sofa. The muted yellow light cast a halo around him, reaching to where Peter stood, still in the soft darkening corner of the room. He seemed suddenly to Frank to be what he felt himself to be: solitary. He hadn't imagined Peter being lonely; he was too confident for that, too engaged, and he hadn't expected him to care too much about family, despite the phone calls to get together. Yet he was dragging back the corpse of memory, the past, the family bonds, as if to solder something that time and distance and temperament had severed.

"I don't expect us to be friends," Peter said. "I just thought that maybe we could know each other on some level."

"Don't expect much," Frank said, after a pause.

"You haven't led me to expect anything at all," Peter said.

"Look," Frank said, getting up, abandoning the cat—when had he grown so attached to the thing? "I've never been the brotherly type. You know that. I don't know what you want from me."

"I told you. Nothing much. Just, well, a connection of some sort. I don't even know if I can articulate it more than that."

"You're asking me to 'violate my nature,'" Frank said.

"Which means?"

"Become a nice person."

"I don't expect anything as radical as that. I told you, I don't expect anything. I'm just asking, for some stupid reason, for a little of your time. I'm sure you have some. I may be making a mistake here—"

"Probably," Frank said.

"—but then, I may be wrong about you, too. Do you remember what Dad used to say at dinner, those times he was there?"

"What?"

"He told us to stick together, that no one was stronger than us being true to each other, you and I. Do you remember that?"

"No. I just remember him asking me about Jesus."

"Well, in between the God talk and the sniping at Mom, he'd lecture us on family ties, on sticking together."

"And you believed him?"

"I feared him. I remembered him saying that, and thinking how funny it was that he would be so insistent on filial duty and then disappear into the night, leaving us and Mom alone. She'd pine in her bedroom and we'd do . . . whatever. Now I know what he was doing, probably, and his hypocrisy was rich, but I still remember that. It's one of those things that somehow sticks with you, despite knowing what a liar the person who said it was, it remains somehow true."

"And so?"

"So I'm wondering whether you're worth it at all, but still I had to try. It's one of those things on my list of life's goals—'get to know distant, cranky brother; see if he's worth the trouble.'"

"So you have a list."

"A mental one, of sorts. You don't?"

"If I had a list, I don't think I'd be here. I never thought that far ahead; even when I planned, it was secondhand. It was someone else. It was never me. Until now, I think," he'd said, wondering at the sudden turn in conversation, the ease with which he answered Peter, the naturalness of it, despite his reluctance even to speak of himself in a way that might reveal that he had inner thoughts, if that were possible: every shrug conveyed a tortured calculation. And yet here he was, engaged in something approximating a conversation with a man, his brother, whom he had neither cared for nor admired, speaking as if he were an equal. He was uncomfortable. He felt he could have been a displaced modern mendicant friar, surviving on emotional handouts.

He had spent a frustrating evening with Claire, opening himself slightly, trying to reach out, but rebuffed by her. He had withdrawn into work, as much as the demands of the work he had undertaken permitted—for it was not particularly onerous—and had until now closed himself off, again as much as thoughts of Claire permitted this. Now, his brother had confronted his preconceptions and irrational emotional abnegation by his very presence. Frank had come here to effect a change, he had embarked on a lucrative project for a change, he had left his increasingly moribund work for a change, and he was still so unwilling to change in deeper regards that it hurt him to think of the consequences of his actions, or of his inaction, for that matter.

"How *are* you getting on with Claire?" Peter asked, as if reading his thoughts.

"I haven't seen her much, actually," Frank said. "I know she's in the middle of a big sale."

"I thought you two might hit it off, seeing as how you were there for her before, you know—"

"Oh, I remember. Yes. Well, who knows?"

"Who, indeed?" Peter said. "We're still friends, you know. But you wouldn't know, since you never keep in touch. But she's asked about you. Often. I was just wondering."

"She has?" he said, brightening.

"Well, once or twice. Give her a call. You never know. You are the better-looking brother, you know. And I'm man enough to admit it. But call her. Claire sometimes likes to be interrupted in her work. She can get awfully wrapped up. Sort of like you."

"I guess I will."

"Listen," Peter said, "I must get going. I have to meet Sean. Sean is my new boyfriend—don't recoil. Maybe you'll meet him some day. Now *there's* another fractured family tale." He walked over to Frank, who had been standing near the window, and extended his hand. "Maybe we'll see each other again soon. I know I put a lot on you just now. I didn't mean to be so, I don't know, pushy. But we'll talk. Maybe. I won't wait for your call." He shook Frank's hand and turned to leave. "By the way," he added, almost over his shoulder. "I love what you've done with the place," and he left, laughing.

How Peter maintained equilibrium was beyond Frank, especially after dropping such a load of Faulknerian melodrama at his feet. He could just as easily have told him that his parents were actually half-brother and sister as that there were two little unexplained sisters lying in their dead father's unclaimed grave. Where had he been? Had he even suspected his mother was pregnant? Had the idea ever occurred to him? Was he too young? His mother's affection was of a distant nature; she was more, he felt, distracted by her husband's demands than by a quiet, determined child. Surely she would have mentioned something to a firstborn, the bearer of responsibility, the shoulderer of burdens, the avoider of confrontation? He remembered when Peter was born, though; his father had told him shortly before his mother went into delivery that he was going to have a new sibling. Frank had thought she was just getting fat. And she had brushed off his childish inquiries with little jokes—if she ever did joke, that is. She was never unkind to him, really—until he became an adult, he thought—but she lacked what he would have now described as maternal love. She wasn't Medea, by any means, but neither was she warm. He had never minded; his was a cool nature, and he did much of what he was told, learning resentment as he got older, as the duplicity of adulthood took hold. But he was such a naïve boy.

His parents had had little social life—or his mother had, considering what his father eventually did—outside of church. His father had joined the Holy Name Society, a kind of Masonic order manqué without the secret handshakes, and his mother the Rosary Altar Society, a band of women who channeled their otherwise bingo-directed energies into group novenas and charity work. The Holy Name Society met monthly for evenings fueled by smoke and beer wherein the members came up with various strategies to raise money for the parish, usually involving a raffle and a potluck dinner, while the Rosary Society ladies, as often as not relicts of too-soon-deceased Holy Namers felled by cigarettes and alcohol, got together more frequently to pray, gossip, mend vestments, and plot how to lure their husbands or brothers-in-law away from the tube and sedentary temptation and into more fruitful, and presumably accountable, work. His mother was less given to the group's social leanings than the flower arranging and general dusting and polishing in the church, the provenance of dutiful female penitents with awkward interpersonal skills. They rarely had visitors, he recalled, and then he was usually shuffled off to his room for schoolwork, which he liked, given that his own preference was for being alone.

But it was still strange to him, now that he knew of it, that he was never told by his parents that he might have had sisters. Perhaps their grief, or shame, at the loss of unborn life had persuaded them not to burden his young and brooding mind with the knowledge of someone he would never know. Maybe their frustration led to peremptory denial. Maybe their silence to him reflected their growing alienation from each other. The secrets of families. Does knowing them make us better off? For Peter, it seemed a wish. For Frank, conscious of an uneasy, transforming process shaking his nature to its depths, a wish to reassert himself regardless of his upbringing. Frank wanted to define himself in a way he hadn't yet begun to see; he knew so little of himself, finally, that he had thought that his misery arose not from ignorance, or knowledge, but frustration, because his honesty did not extend beyond what had made him unhappy to begin with. That is, he had the courage only to abandon a vocation he could no longer endure. And he still faced the difficulty of wanting more than he knew, which was torture, since he was afraid to name what it was he desired, for fear of committing himself to a feeling that could lead to subjugation to an emotion he had only glimpsed and feared. Losing control was not an option for him right now.

His brother's parting flippancy in the face of such morbid revelations actually forced Frank to rally. He found Getty's food, topped off the bowl, and checked on his water. He searched through his absent landlady's CD collection, and chose highlights from *Parsifal*. He realized the easy irony, an opera about the search for spiritual fulfillment, but he loved its power, if he no longer struggled along the same path as Wagner's hero. Who was he kidding?

Everyone tries to find meaning in life. Many only find it in the thought of a blameless afterlife, and he used to be among them, if fitfully. He wished that others could know about him without his telling him, without his revealing his essence, without his needing to suffer the delights and demands and companionship. He wished people knew he was not so contemptible as he thought they considered him. He wished they knew he was trying to be better, if only he knew how. He sat back, rather hoping the cat would make itself at home on his lap—when had this happened, this cat–person nonsense?—and thought that he might give Claire a call. It was time, perhaps, to try. Maybe after Kundry awoke from her first bad dream. What was it some poet wrote? Something about the odd bliss in the recurrence of absurdity amid the profound. "And Kundry wakes up screaming. . . ." He smiled and closed his eyes, taking in the swell of sound and the possibilities inherent in someone else's noble quest.

# THE LOW-BACKED CHAIR

S he looked just like his cousin, from across the room. Same name, too, though spelled differently. Sean often made physical comparisons among people he saw. It was part of his training, to remember attributes, recognize similarities, identify characteristics. Everyone always reminded him of someone else. Everyone except Peter. He looked like a lot of people, only a bit better, and seemed to be a different person for everyone, but when he spoke to you in that easygoing way of his, as if what you had to say was most important, you saw his individuality. He was all things to all people, but he still looked like himself. Sean saw him in action before, but at the auction it was a real performance. He was impressed. It didn't seem phony, exactly; it seemed like business. This was a new world to Sean, and while he didn't feel in over his head—he was too streetwise to be taken in by the grasping glamour of an art auction—he wasn't exactly at ease. But neither was he uncomfortable. He was witnessing a different kind of larceny, perhaps. These people were operators, that much seemed clear to him, even if the particulars of their little con games were not. Peter hadn't told him anything about the nature of the art world, except to say that the dealers were dealers and the experts were

dealers and everybody tried to outfox one another, especially if the art was any good.

Claire, when she finally spoke to Sean, was nothing like Clare, his cousin, who taught kindergarten. Up close, Claire little resembled her, except for the hair color—light brown—and the large oval eyes. Their noses were different. But they held themselves in the same way. Maybe Claire—Peter's Claire, as Sean had begun to think of her—had a bit of the teacher in her. She seemed authoritative up there at the phone bank, whispering into the receiver, scanning the room, keeping her eyes on the auctioneer. For some reason, he thought of that old ballad his mother used to sing to him, "When first I saw sweet Peggy, 'twas on a market day / A low-backed car she drove, and sat / Upon a truss of hay. . . ." She wasn't anything like that peasant farmer lass, but her graceful composure brought to mind the picture of the pretty girl in the song.

His mother was staying with her sister in Florida for the month, which was a relief. It had given him a chance to have Peter over. He lived with his mother or, rather, she lived with him. That situation was likely to change in the near future, Sean thought. It was time.

Until he had met Peter, his romantic life was confined mainly to Internet chat rooms, massage assignations, and bathhouse shenanigans. He did have one brief almost-relationship with an officer in the Twentieth Precinct, but Larry, the officer, had feared too much the reprisals of his peers, real or not. He couldn't blame him. Things were better than they'd been for gay officers, but not great. Still a class thing. Still touchy. It was still tough, still awkward, he himself was out, barely, and had been since making detective. He was still something of an anomaly. For some reason, telling his mother was harder than facing his captain. His mother surely knew, bless her heart, but she kept suggesting this or that unsuitable woman for him to date. Maybe next life, mom. Thanks anyway.

Someday. Soon. With Peter nearby. If it came to that. If it worked out, that is. He didn't hold out—that is, he didn't expect much. But so far. He'd take it as it came.

He had to admit, he found the whole evening entertaining. He didn't know much about art, or the art world, just had an idea of tuxedos, ball gowns, misplaced bids, and mystery buyers. The actual event was more theatrical than he'd expected, and the only tuxedo was on the German auctioneer, who enjoyed toying with the crowd. He looked like Sean's high school chemistry teacher. The one who quit when Sean was a senior. Some scandal involving another teacher. Sean never got to the bottom of it, but it involved an abortion, everyone speculated at the time. This guy seemed more savvy than Professor Schickler, that long-ago romantic loser. He wondered what became of him.

"You're not too cowed by all this hoopla, are you," Peter had asked him as they walked in, noticing Sean's glances here and there.

"I don't feel at home. A bit underdressed, " Sean said. "But no. These are just people to me." Ever since Sean had covered crowd control at movie premieres and Broadway openings, he preferred to see his stars from afar, when they weren't surrounded by morose bodyguards he used to know from the force or the sycophantic entourages of dummies who couldn't hold a real job. He'd rather pay his ten dollars and watch them perform where he wouldn't have to think of them as anything other than an illusion.

But he liked the art for sale here, he realized. He didn't know much, and didn't pretend to, but, as Peter said, many of those in the art world didn't know much either but pretended they did, so Sean's honesty was bound to be refreshing. Not that he intended to express an opinion on anything. He just wanted to see an auction in action, and Peter was happy to have him along for company.

"You can protect me from some of the harpies," he'd said, as if Peter really needed protection from anything.

"So," Peter said, as they were seated at a small restaurant near the auction house following the sale. "What did you think of my ex?"

"She's too good for you. But you already knew that."

"Everyone's too good for me," he said. "Except you."

"Don't be too sure," Sean said.

"I'm glad you were there, even if it might not have made sense."

"What's to make sense of? People bidding, people buying. It was fun."

"I just thought it might be odd for you."

"I'm a big boy. I haven't been around the arty types much. People are pretty much the same no matter how you dress them up."

"And what type am I?"

"I haven't figured that one out yet. But give me time. And you're not so much a type, I think."

"Good to know. What types did you see tonight?"

Sean thought for a second. Actually, Peter probably was a type, but he couldn't quite pin it down. In his experience, everyone fit into categories; it was the nature of his work to size up people, especially in terms of how they might act, how they might reveal themselves depending on the situation. Peter had an ability to make himself pleasant that many people didn't bother to cultivate; most people cared too much what others thought of them, but were unaware how their demeanor affected others' impressions of them. Despite their concern for being liked or looked up to or admired or whatever, most people lived in a bubble of self-absorption, lost in thought about some triviality that they considered so important, their faces were always screwed up in determined frowns. Sean didn't know what could weigh people down so heavily that they walked around as if on their way to a court appearance. Usually it was work they dreaded, he figured. Fresh-faced or at least freshly dressed in the mornings, they plodded, coffee in hand, cell phone on ear, thinking: let me get to my desk, let me sit down now, let me have this coffee, let me not be too put upon, let this be over. But on seeing people walk in the other direction at night, they appeared to him equally downtrodden, only more tired and wrinkled; rather than the A.M. fatigue of uneasy sleep and that day's installment in an unhappy career, they carried with them the preview of the evening's unpromising home life. He figured most people weren't as miserable as they looked, just unaware of being happy with what they had. Or unwilling to change what they hated. Or worse. Most didn't consider the possibility that they had choices. He knew that on many days he was as guilty as the next guy of going through the motions. He thought he was saved, somewhat, by being aware of this. Even if you didn't quite have the courage to make a change, if you recognized that you might need to, it was a start.

But the generalization of faces into a cosmos of unhappy families and unfulfilled lives was not what he meant exactly by type, but how he thought of types of people, categorized by perceived behavior— or behavior as perceived by expression. He had studied the meanings of how the forty-three facial muscles revealed fleeting emotions; he had worked with the Facial Action Coding System that the FBI and CIA used to read subtle emotional clues from the voices, gestures, reactions of potential assassins, terrorists, and even petty criminals. He wasn't sure at times whether this was all worth it—how much could you really tell by looking at a person? But he continued to try, analyzing facial muscles, reading body language, posture, gestures. In his work, he had scanned the faces of thousands of passersby downtown after the September 11th murders, looking for signs of minds fraught with destruction. What he mainly saw were the looks of, at first, raw grief, a determination to be present near the site of such wrenching devastation. This over the months and years had evolved into looks of more mundane curiosity. He could never really read the conflicting responses that made up people's motives; he wasn't that presumptuous, though he drew conclusions of a sort based on his own mood or the urgency of the day's activities. Faces revealed more than one sensation—the trick was being quick enough to gauge the shifts. For many of the downtown visitors—not the people who worked there and had become used to the gawkers, the few subtly grieving and the blasé—had worn expressions of blank determination under which floated both a real curiosity, to see the site, to see what had happened since the attacks, as well as a vague compassion for all of those victims, those people whom they would never know, but whose names they'd read in a newspaper or seen on souvenir flags or mementos, names that themselves carried in some way the force of an actual life torn apart. They did not want to meet these dead people, the visitors, at least he felt they did not; they did not want to commit to any palpable relationship with someone who, after all, might not have been very nice. But they embraced the idea of communing with a spirit of the dead embodied in a list on a plaque affixed to a fence that overlooked the site of carnage they would really only prefer to imagine but that, seeing its aftereffects close up somehow conveyed a horror that remained blessedly distant. Oh, those poor people.

Again, though, while he lapsed easily into varying generalizations of crowds, for individuals he discerned, he hoped, a more specific reason for how a face appeared. Anyway, he knew that everyone could surprise, despite his study of surfaces that could lead to presuppositions about personality. When it came to what people said, that was another area where someone could more easily deceive. Yet if you worked from the premise that everyone lied more or less to each other all the time, then you could maybe distinguish what passed for truth between people by somehow interpreting how unwitting facial movements might play off against what was being said. Confession was in the dark for a reason; people probably felt more inclined to admit even a portion of whatever it was that made them feel guilty when they didn't have to meet the potentially disapproving eyes of a confessor, and could devote more energy to an oral explanation of sin without having to worry about facial betrayal.

Though Peter seemed to say the right thing in all sorts of situations, Sean felt that he was more easygoing than facile. That is, his charm was a genuine attempt to put others at ease, rather than a maneuver to avoid any revelation of the person within. Though, of course, Peter had to have something of that quality, too, not only having kept himself married for years, but because his career carried with it a certain glibness. To be able to sell something for more than its inherent value involved a degree of deception that undoubtedly seeped into personal relationships.

And, as Sean would be the first to admit, mistakes of perception quickly helped a person realign his behavior, his expectations, his sense of arriving at an understanding, a point where two people reached a rapprochement that could then be called a relationship, when they could begin to refine the observations that from then on carried more emotional weight, and whose interpretation caused greater possible damage. But, he realized, he had a tendency to think something through to its disastrous finish rather than staying within a moment and savoring whatever it held. His life, though, was one where it was necessary for him to anticipate wrong, as if in a science fiction movie where a hero would be cursed with second sight. Yet in relationships, any foreboding was either a sign that the relationship wasn't working or, more likely, in his case, a fear that it might be.

This was Sean's first real, open relationship, one where he actually met his date in public rather than in a shaded apartment or mildewed sauna. He continually willed himself to appreciate the actuality of what was going on between him and Peter and not look ahead to its inevitable—well, maybe not so—decline.

"It's not a parlor trick, you know," Sean finally said to him. "Guessing what types people are is just judging based on superficial data."

"But isn't that part of what you do, in crowds? Judge, based on what you think this person, according to how he seems to be acting in subtle ways, how someone's going to act?"

"Yes, but that's a variety of potential criminal types based on patterns of behavior and situations near possible danger zones. How many criminal types are here in this restaurant?"

"It's an art-world crowd, Sean. Everyone is a criminal except the waiters."

"Okay, then. Just so I understand."

"Just look around," Peter said. "Give me your thoughts, say, on those two in that booth there." Peter nodded to where two middle-aged men were sitting. One looked about ten years older than the other. The older one was wearing a navy suit with a subtle, barely noticeable plaid pattern. He had a short haircut, almost military, but not as severe; a stylish buzz. A red pocket handkerchief poked from his breast pocket—Sean hated those—and monogrammed French cuffs peeked out of his jacket. His nose had been broken, but it gave his broad face a pugilistic appeal—he was both a wannabe dandy and a lout, it seemed to him. His darting eye, his livid scowl, reminded Sean of certain gangsters, actually, those who had a bit of education but were pulled back into crime. Between his reddened cheeks and white furrowed forehead shone two small black eyes, designed for frightening the bravest of men. The immense curve of the forehead was set off by a thick mop of straight hair, black as tar. He was the type of person who could talk about ethics but not actually live by any, rather like many corrupt but ultimately stupid businessmen whose luck had begun to give out. His tablemate, a business partner, maybe, or a lover, he couldn't tell at first glance, met his companion's gaze only briefly, and showed little interest in what the other man was so brutally saying. The man's voice was low but harsh. Surely he was a business colleague of some sort. A lover would have taken pains to appear more sympathetic. Unless they were longtime lovers, but then they most likely would have lapsed into bored silence, and the talker would have done his complaining with someone newer. The younger man, who was maybe fifty, Sean estimated, kept looking past the man to the handsome waiter serving a table just beyond them. The relatively younger man looked well fed, certainly. He wasn't fat, but he had the prosperous jowls of someone who always ordered from the dessert menu after dinner, and who didn't regret it. Yet he also had an animal edge; if that good-looking waiter had been a flourless chocolate cake he'd have been devoured already. But this was evident mainly in his narrow, probing eyes. The bordering-on-stout look was a result, probably, of his usually getting what he wanted. The gaze was that of someone who knew what it was he wanted. So he was at this table with this other man—Sean had begun to think of them as Ben and Jerry, with Jerry the older man—either through politeness, or because they still could do something for each other. It was about connections, not affection. Ben was dressed in a blue suit, not too dissimilar from what Jerry was wearing, only on Ben it looked better. Still, both had an intensity—they were just this side of shady, but each had a different shade of, what was it exactly? manipulative excitement? Beyond the physical difference was perhaps what Sean decided was a level of greed that marked each. Ben, it seemed to him, had either just scored or was more concerned with human prey, while Jerry's appetites were probably based more on actually having won, the act of acquisition itself becoming a tangible.

"They're both doing something they detest, but one takes pleasure in what he's been given for the sake of fighting and the other is biding his time," Sean said. "They're like criminal types, but they're not criminal. They're like suspects I've seen who've been pulled in for questioning and have nothing to do with the crime at hand, but who are still not above suspicion for something else, whatever it may be."

"So you know them," Peter said.

"No, but you do, don't you?"

"I'm impressed."

"Just the table dynamic. Anyone could do it," Sean said.

"Maybe, but you've sized up the characteristics of two art dealers pretty well."

"So this was a test?"

"No, honey, not at all. Really," Peter said. Sean wasn't sure if he liked that "honey" just yet. "I just wondered," Peter added. "I was just curious. Okay, it was a test. But it was impressive. Let me tell you who they are. The younger one is Arthur Kirson. The other one, who looks like he gets his hair dyed at a shoeshine place, is Gregory Bonner. Greg has a gallery on Madison and Sixty-fourth and likes to sprinkle modern masters among the up-and-comers he anoints as such. He's the kind of guy who likes to be seen with models on his arm, just so people know he's straight. He makes sure he's seen, but no one knows what he does. He's really a thug, but his gallery helps with the reputation of young artists. Arthur is a former colleague who now advises CEOs on their collections. It's less stressful and actually pays better and it leaves Arthur more time to pursue his career, his sideline career. He's got a cabaret act, where he sings standards, some little-known old songs, and his own original ones. You haven't lived until you've heard Arthur sing 'The Man That Got Away' in his trembling baritone at Don't Tell Mama."

"So he knows you, too."

"A little. Enough to say hello and be pressed into going to one of his shows. I'm on the mailing list. I get a postcard every two months. It's got his picture on it, as if it were drawn by one of those Times Square street artists, with everything exaggerated and nothing right; you'd think someone with his connections could've arranged for an actual suave portrait. But Arthur probably considers it a joke, and like found art. Anyway, I know him well enough for him to ask me to his shows and for me to go once a year or so. He's two people: a sophisticated dealer who has absolutely no clue about how ridiculous he sounds on stage, and a stage performer who has no idea how ridiculous he sounds on stage."

"But maybe he's enjoying himself," Sean said.

"I'm sure he is. But—and here you'll find out my horrible prejudice—I just don't associate Arthur with show tunes. At least I didn't until I was subjected to him and them. I should have expected him to corral somebody into hearing him sing German art songs or something more rarefied than piano bar standards. But then, you really can't belt out *Die schöne Müllerin*, and for Arthur it's all about belting. Well, belting as if it were a hoarse shout."

"I'd like to go."

"Really?"

"In a couple of months. Sure."

"If I take you, it means you really like me, and I really like you, because it's the kind of event that can put a strain on a relationship."

"What does it do for his business relationships?"

"I don't think many people actually notice, or care. In some arty circles, being outré is considered good form, and Arthur's so trusted in some respects that people forgive the lapses or don't even think of that part of his life. Most people manage to keep their lives separate, don't you think? Even if they go parading around in cabaret drag, who's likely to find out except other people who like that sort of thing, or go to those sorts of places? Anyway, it's not like he's undermining the noble profession of art adviser."

"I've never been much of a cabaret fan."

"I didn't think so. Which is one of your many strong points. Still, it's a big deal for Arthur, even if I mock it and hate going to his awful shows. He considers himself a survivor, like so many amateur cabaret people. It's the last refuge of the talent-free."

"Did you know that I sang?"

"No! Really? What?"

"Well, if you can believe it, Irish songs. Songs my mother and grandmother taught me. If I ever get drunk, I'll sing you one."

"I can't wait to get you somewhere on Irish karaoke night. There's got to be some dump somewhere that caters to the Irish boys with mother issues." Peter looked slightly abashed at him.

"Don't worry," Sean said. "It's not going to happen any time soon."

"Anyway, that whole 'survivor' thing sticks in my craw. It's just a code word."

"For?"

"For having made so many bad decisions that you're lucky to be up there singing terrible songs in a terrible voice to a pained crowd of your almost-friends to prove that, damn it, you're still worth something."

"And what might that something be?"

"A good rolodex of potential clients."

"I don't know what the world did to you. But I see it's all about connections, no matter what a person has been through."

"Of course. You see. I'm a survivor, too. I'll let you know when my first show is."

"I'll be there." Sean looked around the restaurant, at the late-supper, well-heeled crowd nibbling and swilling. He gave a little start.

Peter turned to see. "Oh! That's José and Nestor. Do you know them? Toby's staying with them."

Sean knew José, certainly, and also Nestor. He'd had several dates with José, if you could call Internet liaisons and quick morning blow jobs when the boyfriend's out of town a date.

"Well," Sean said, slowly.

"So you do," Peter said. "They must have slipped in after us. How do you know him? Wait! Of course, you probably met him online, knowing José. He's always screwing around on Nestor, though no one thinks Nestor knows."

"Well, you've got me," Sean said, a little abashed. He'd hesitated to tell Peter, figuring that denying a lot about relations, or relationships, before they'd got together was part of what being together meant. But Peter was so matter-of-fact about it that the guilt was moot, proving there was nothing to be guilty about in that regard and making Sean wonder why he would have denied knowing someone such as José. He had begun already to regret the lack of emotional structure to his casual encounters, though he couldn't deny the pleasures of their brevity and usual lack of remorse. It was as you became attached, or began to think of someone as a sort of extension of your own well-being that you started to question what you'd done before. This was new to him, who had studied so publicly modes of behavior—never the private faces people assume, except in the theater of the interrogation, and never really that of the bedroom night after night. Not that he didn't always try to calculate what others were thinking, not of him so much, but thinking in general, plotting, or planning. He figured that people did the same in relationships, up to a point, but he knew that private behavior, that the realm of the heart, was not a specialty of his, and that although his mindset had been one of calculating the possibility of risk, he would have to attempt to assume a level of trust, he would have also to think of himself as trusted, which made him uneasy, as well. Not that he considered himself dishonest, far from it, but that he thought himself, perhaps, untested.

The waiter brought their appetizers, and Sean looked over again at José and Nestor, who saw him. He waved, but didn't get up. He would say hello later. Wasn't this a nice little coincidence.

Sean knew that José was interested in art, so his being here should not have been a surprise, really. Yet he hadn't expected him to be among Peter's acquaintances. He wondered if Peter had done any online trolling and come across Mr. Pacheco over there. Oh, well. But probably not. As far as he could tell, Peter preferred the relationship to the hunt.

As it was, when Sean had known José, or when he had first known him, José had shown Sean his collection, small though it was, of Mexican paintings, as well as the pointy pottery thrown by the boyfriend of a big fashion muckety-muck José was delighted to know—delighted enough to keep referring to him as a friend of his and Nestor's, for whatever that was worth, and Sean suspected not much to the potter or his boyfriend unless it led to more sales of the boyfriend's ugly pottery. José loved his small collection—Sean was pretty much unacquainted with the very idea of art collection except in the abstract, and some vague notion of robber barons and gilt-framed Impressionists. But he'd listened, more than once, to José's descriptions of his acquisition history, especially two colorful large paintings, one in the living room and one in the dining room, that José had bought for a considerable sum in Mexico City. All of that display of product on the walls took place before José began begging to suck Sean's leathery balls, a term Sean found somewhat revolting, though of course he let him, who wouldn't. Yet he found it odd talk well as odd coming from someone who was a fund-raiser for People for the Ethical Treatment of Animals among other consciousness-raising nonprofit organizations, and who claimed to avoid all tannery products unless the skin could be traced to the backs of animals that had died of natural causes. Actually, José had all sorts of rules he always broke, flippant in his disregard for self-imposed modes of behavior, but very touchy when confronted with lapses in his internal logic. Sean had also been a bit amused by José's dirty talk, as if he'd somehow figured that that's what casual sex partners wanted, as if all learned to speak the language of porno flicks. Sean had often wanted to tell him to shut up, bend over, but didn't want to be cruel, since José had obviously felt that crappy dialogue from movies where the dialogue didn't matter was important for whatever fantasy he was envisioning as they had sex. But he wasn't going to use cop expressions as he rammed him; he drew the line at that, despite José's fantasy pleas. He would have started laughing, and it would've been all over.

Sean had always lost interest in José's little contemporary art history lessons, and after a few sessions of furtive coupling and discombobulated conversation José would, Sean thought, mask his adulterous guilt with litanies of his and Nestor's buying sprees and obsessive redecorating, interspersed with stray comments on Nestor's stifling compulsions and emotional inadequacy due to his tortured family life. From where Sean had stood, or kneeled, the problem in the relationship was more likely José's relentless and exhausting self-infatuation disguised as the false modesty of personal deprecation—he had a feeble habit of calling himself stupid in a way that he didn't expect anyone to believe. But it was evident he smeared himself with so much self-loathing he could have been a self-basting turkey. Every so often in their odd hour or two together, José's longing for personal contact beyond his existing relationship that had been crippled by the mutual selfishness of its participants, he would ask a question of Sean, to learn something of his work, but he'd lose interest before Sean could even begin to form a sentence. José had been as curious about the nature of Sean's career as Sean had been in the particulars of José's art collection. Yet on occasion he heard José refer to him as a friend, and José probably considered him to be one, much as he did what's-his-name the potter, for whatever reason in Sean's case, he couldn't figure it out. Maybe it was to know an actual detective, someone on the police force, someone in the fantasyland of erotic daydreams. But Sean didn't consider José a friend as much as an acquaintance now with whom he'd had a few liaisons. For him a friend was someone whose lies you chose to believe. José believed his own lies, and had a relationship founded on keeping them.

And yet, as he glanced over at them sitting there, the two of them, José and Nestor, in this chi-chi restaurant, Sean felt that they were as much outsiders here as he, and to be fair to them, he felt that deep down José knew it. Actually, most people in this artificial world of hypocrisy wrapped in a package of pretensions were outsiders, if that meant anything. It was all connections. But when money was exchanged with such showmanship and calculation as he'd just seen, when reputations were affected by innuendo to a degree unheard of since high school, the social precipice was steeper, the stakes higher. These weren't his own insights entirely, since Peter had, to an extent, prepped him, but he was a quick study. And the goals of the people on display, the plumage, the preening, the power-brokering, were evident to anyone who cared to sit back and look, as Sean did. Yet Sean found that he had actually liked what he'd seen, through Peter—another outsider whose charm and genuine knowledge, as far as Sean could judge, helped propel him into an arena where basically being an informed salesman or a pawnbroker with a pedigree made it seem as if you had a higher social standing, as if it mattered. And it did, in a way that Sean had become aware of only recently. He wasn't sure if he wanted to or could circulate in such a scene, but he certainly enjoyed being on its periphery. He wasn't sure, either, about Peter's ultimate goals, whether this all really meant something deeply to him, or if his love for the whole nature of being among art and money gave him genuine satisfaction. Those were the kinds of questions, he felt, he shouldn't ask until he knew the answers.

From what Sean could tell of him, that is as much as he was able to read through his desperate glibness, José wanted to be considered a connoisseur, a manly aesthete. José was very well educated—Stanford and Stanford Law—and was proud of having escaped from his hardscrabble childhood, the son of Mexican immigrants. Yet he made a point of belittling Sean's own middle-class upbringing, calling it bland compared to the earthy sensuality of a Latin culture, even one that José only dipped into now and then either to embrace a now-fashionable and growing minority of Americans, or to ascribe a pecking order to ethnicity. José's parents had refused to speak Spanish in front of their children, so he had grown up with only a passing acquaintance with the language. He was a better listener than speaker of Spanish, when he did actually bother to listen to what someone else was saying, usually waitresses, from whom he tried ordering in the lingua franca, though anyone with a Taco Bell tutoring could order a tortilla salad. So he teased Sean about his education from the John Jay College of Criminal Justice, as if it mattered when you were getting sucked off, as if an Ivy League–equivalent degree were necessary to have the kinds of discussions José had favored, which were generally one-sided, emotionally guarded, materially proud, and ultimately pathetic. Sean was confident enough in his own intelligence, fairly sure of his own limitations, and had little college envy. He liked what he did, up to a point, was good at it, and usually felt at ease in most situations. Granted, he was usually in situations that didn't call for intricacies of etiquette, but they had their own rules. Any awkwardness he felt was usually offset by his friendliness—the reticent friendliness of a detective, but still a friendliness that most people reacted warmly to, even if Sean made sure that it was surface friendliness. Until Sean hooked up with Peter, he had never communed, so to speak, with whatever constituted the upper crust nowadays. This crowd seemed more like ridiculous posers than anything he would call high society, as far as he could tell. Peter had treated him as an equal, which for Sean meant that his opinion mattered, which was a courtesy most people didn't afford anyone other than their superiors in the workplace.

"What do you think of them, as a couple?" Sean asked Peter.

"I can't say I know them well," he said. "They were always more Toby's friends than mine, though we used to see them at parties and had dinner a few times. Nestor's uptight, José's proud of his own opinions, and there's always a bit of tension when they're together. I never really cared for spending time with them, but José and Toby have a sort of California connection that probably accounts for their being closer than I cared to be. What about you?"

"Well, I had several dates with José while Nestor was out of town, and I didn't learn about *him* until our second or third time together. It was only a little while later that I actually saw them together. At a party they threw for some friends of José's and some gym buddies of Nestor's. I was happy to be called away on some work thing."

"I think Nestor would be horrified that José considers it an open relationship when he's not around. Yet to hear him tell it, their longevity is the greatest thing in the world."

"When the whole Nestor thing came up, he said they'd been together a total of twelve years or something like that, except for a brief time when Nestor left town to escape José."

"But he didn't have the balls to stay away."

"Well, that's what I thought," Sean said. "He talked a lot about what things meant for him and Nestor—and this was as he was trolling for skank online. But, for José, I got the feeling that as far as their relationship went, it was more about quantity than quality—he wanted to stay with someone until he was old, just so he could say that he had stayed with someone until he was old."

"I wonder how Toby's doing with them. Though I probably can guess."

"Why don't you ask?"

"Why don't I?" Peter said. "It's all so civilized. Well, we don't have to do anything, since José's coming here."

"Well! I had no idea," José said to Sean, and to Peter. "Small world, amigos! How are you doing? Toby's fine, thanks, no need to worry, he wouldn't come tonight, he's at home pining, but we've been cheering him up, so don't you worry your little head about it," he said in a rush. "Sean, it's been *too* long. Who would have thought that you'd end up with Peter? This is how it's ending up, isn't it? This isn't just a one-night thing, right?"

"José," Peter said.

"This is true love, isn't it, Sean?" Jose went on. "Have you met Toby? No, I guess not, too painful, but you must, he won't be able to resist you, either. I wish I'd known before we left that I'd run into the two of you, or that I even knew! I thought as much, well, I thought maybe, since Toby said you were dating a detective, and then I thought, detective? Maybe Sean, but no, not in the open, not our old friend Sean. And who do I see! The two of you! Together! Wow. I can't wait to let Toby know. He'd be thrilled to hear I'd guessed. I can tell him all about you. Our old friend, Sean, with Peter, Toby's old boyfriend. Small world. Small world. So, Sean, how are you?"

"How much coffee did you have today?" Peter asked.

"Just high on life, as always," José said. Sean knew he'd had a history of substance abuse—poppers and Vicodin, mainly, with a rum chaser—though he didn't seem anything other than flush with obnoxious cheer at the moment, usually leaving the imbibing and snorting to the times when he was unsupervised. Nestor had remained at the table, but was looking over at them. Sean waved at him to join them. Perhaps his stiff-backed presence would slow down the runaway train of José's monologue.

Sean liked Nestor. He actually found him more attractive than his partner, who looked like he'd put on some weight (not that he should talk). José was handsome, certainly, in a classic Mexican way, with full lips, broad nose, black eyes. And Sean often thought he saw his double among the Mexican delivery boys dropping off food at apartment buildings throughout town. José had a dazzling smile that was at its most appealing when unexpected, usually when he'd laughed at something or, even now, when he was filled with his odd amused bravado. Nestor was blond with the thick physique of a bantamweight bodybuilder, almost one of the clone queens, though Sean suspected Nestor didn't use steroids; he was too fussy about what he put in his body. He was rather obsessively neat in the way of some gay men. He called himself an architect, though José had made a point of telling Sean that Nestor didn't have a degree but had been able to get by on sheer ability—thus managing to praise his partner's skills while underscoring his educational want.

But Nestor did have the irksome exactitude of someone who liked arranging things. Still, he was talented and had an appealing sweetness, made more apparent by its contrast with José's fundraiser ferocity. Their apartment was quite a nice space, with everything just so, the Mexican paintings arranged just so, the phallic pottery just so, the photos of José in South Africa or Nestor in the Yucatán just so. All of it just so and absolutely inert. During one of the pre-sex tours José had given Sean of the apartment when José was nattering on about each item, uttering words whose meaning never reached Sean's cerebral cortex he was so uninterested in the look-at-me nature of it all, Sean had wanted just to say, "Don't you two ever make a mess?" But that was apparently all swept away. Anyway, he couldn't even guess what it would be like to live with Peter. Sean had always lived on his own or, more recently, with his mother (that was going to have to change), and he could hardly point fingers at how others lived their domestic lives.

"Hi," Nestor said, stooping to give Peter and then Sean a little peck on the cheek. "What a surprise." His smile was shy, his manner tentative, but the contrast with his long-term boyfriend helped prevent Sean from reaching over to throttle José. "Sorry to barge in on you like this, but we just had to say hello." José had already seated himself, and Nestor slipped into the other empty chair.

"We were going to stop by anyway," Sean said. "After we'd finished."

"But José beat us to it," Peter said. "So! How is Toby doing? Nestor, it's a question for you," he added as José inhaled and looked about to launch into another breathless soliloquy.

"As well as you can expect," Nestor said. "He's thinking of visiting his parents."

"So he's worse than I thought," Peter said.

"He's coping."

"If you can call listening to Björk all day coping," José said. "You should meet him, Sean."

"I'm sure I will, someday," he said.

"So tell me all," José said. "I want the dirt, the dish, the scandal, the first meeting, the first kiss, the first you-know-what."

"Another time," Sean said. He bristled at this girly talk, this nelliness. He hated this public prissy act.

"Tell us what's new with you," Peter said. "Meet anyone interesting?"

"We never meet anyone new," José said, ignoring Peter's meaning. "You're our first new couple in ages."

"Well, later," Sean said.

"We should let them get back to their dinner, Joseph," Nestor said. Sean remembered he always called José by an American name whenever he began to grow impatient with him.

"If you see Toby tonight, let him know I'll call him," Peter said.

"Maybe you should just call him," José said.

"Maybe he will," Sean said.

"Maybe he will, then," José said. "Peter, you must know by now that Sean's such a girl behind closed doors!"

"Joseph," Nestor said.

"I know it's always awkward to have two friends who know each other who have split up, it's like a divorce," José said, "and hard on both parties, and frankly I don't know how you and Claire did it, Peter, staying friendly, and Claire with Toby and all, but it's hard on Toby right now, and I don't know how hard it is on you, but I'll be sure to let him know. Nice seeing you again, Sean, I hope we can catch up."

"Later," Sean said, getting up, and shaking Nestor's hand. José leaned over and kissed him. Sean resolved never to call him ever again. Girl behind doors, indeed. Motherfucker.

"Well," Peter said, as they left the restaurant. They'd eaten their dinner in a bit of a rush, spurred by the whirlwind of José's jokey hostility, which Sean could understand to a degree—José was friendly with Peter's ex and would take his side in any breakup. But the sheer oddity of the encounter, the histories of the four participants, puzzled him, frankly. He hadn't anticipated the dynamics of relationships being so laden with mixed motives, and the theatrical manner of gay men in public embarrassed him. He hadn't signed up for this. As for relationships, certainly he knew that everyone was basically selfish and duplicitous and antagonistic, but add that to a quartet of intermingled couples, all of whom had had sex with each other to some degree, and you had a logarithmic increase in tension. You didn't need the bitch queen crap on top of it all. He wasn't sure he would cotton to many more such encounters. He didn't want to become that in any way.

He also began to be aware of the danger of his own desires. He wasn't afraid of outward risk—or had become less so the more he was faced with it, since you can get used to anything. But the shifting possibilities for emotional harm were something new. He was aware of his own cold appraisals, masking what could be hatred, but he doubted that; but that could be, maybe, ill-feeling toward the motives of others he so coolly assessed for the possibility of physical damage. He needed to understand the history of the relationships that led to flare-ups such as the one he'd witnessed. He needed to read the signs of dissent around him with a different set of rationalizations, if that's what they were, since he had been so surprised at the venom in someone he had been intimate with. His naïveté in interpersonal relationships unsettled him, unexpectedly. He clung to the thought of Peter, who somehow, here, had managed to be of the group and yet apart, but in the sense of being in two places at the same time—

he knew how to keep a conversation afloat and brush off discord, no small feat. And he hadn't gone all too queeny, either.

The types of faces he had become adept at reading, the stresses, the grimaces, the arched eyebrows trying to mask a lie were not as useful here as he had thought, and the types of personalities he had been able to identify through years of practice were perhaps less identifiable in this new milieu, that of the relationship, and that of the social circles the relationship brought him into.

"What just happened," Peter had said, but he knew exactly what had gone on. That was a phrase people used when they saw the explosion of personality and hadn't yet manufactured the words to describe it.

"Angry friends of angry ex-boyfriend and suddenly rediscovered old sex partner all together in one place. Simple, wasn't it?"

"I just realized that Toby is probably in hell at their apartment," Peter said. "That relationship was one he was afraid ours was going to turn into, long-suffering, with edgy conversations and unspoken anger."

"What did it turn into?"

"It ended. He drifted. I found you."

"Simple."

"It is if you don't look for motives everywhere."

"I didn't use to, not in relationships. I didn't have any. Romantic ones, I mean," he added. "I'm not looking for motives. What I'm surprised at is suddenly finding that the way people behave among friends and acquaintances leads me to suspect them. I'm less sure of myself than I thought."

What surprised him too was that, as much as he liked the companionship and the romance, he was beginning to feel something new to him, an almost pleasurable unease at the possibility that his opinions on things were about to change, as if his standards had been somehow wrong up to now. It was as if he wanted to change to please, and this was entirely foreign to him, who had been content in his own skin, up to a point—as long as most people didn't know him well. The possibility that he might show himself as he was, as a lie revealed, perhaps, was actually thrilling, if scary—if, indeed, true. He knew he wanted to proceed further, despite his uneasiness about what he might discover about himself, because of what he had come to like in Peter, even in a world he was not part of, since it didn't matter, as he knew so much less about the world he was familiar with than he thought he did. He knew then that he had entered into a new phase, where his instincts were of less use than his training, his experience, had led him to expect, where he would have to learn again through ignorant mistakes, where the danger lay as much in what he didn't know about the future as in what he had done long ago. You could try to read a face, but you couldn't decipher how people reacted to each other. You could try to look for motive in some potential public act of discord, but you couldn't foretell the repercussions of intimacy. You couldn't be prepared for the possibilities of love.

# THE ADELAIDE LAMENTS

The irises recoiled in their vases behind Adelaide as she opened the door to Claire. She was taller than Claire remembered, a Demoiselle d'Avignon sheathed in leather and swirling in cigarette smoke. Claire had heard her Clydesdale tread, her booted feet clomping on the parquet as she cantered to the door, whinnying, "I'll get it, Rosa." Adelaide stared for a long moment at her, pretending not to recognize Claire, holding her head back, as if her eyes were set on her temples, focusing. "Claire!," she said at last, exhaling smoke.

"Adelaide! Hello," Claire said, managing a smile and extending her hand. She had hoped to see Mrs. Driscoll before her harpy daughter showed up.

"It's been a while," Adelaide said, turning to let her in. Claire entered past the tendrils of smoke and Adelaide's rasping cough. "Mother's expecting you. Did she tell you I'd be here? We haven't seen you since—when?—since you were just out on your own, wasn't it?"

She had met Adelaide at art events. Claire hadn't known Mrs. Driscoll personally until fairly recently, though she was aware of her collection, and had run into Adelaide briefly on several occasions, though they hadn't been anything but the merest acquaintances, knowing enough to be intrigued by what others said about each. That, of course, didn't stop everyone in that world from considering a passing fancy an old friend and shared hors d'oeuvres a relationship. Everyone knew something about everyone else; up to a point, everyone had a provenance. Peter had been better known to Adelaide then, and their divorce and Peter's reasons for it had been the one-day's wonder of the art world, and then Peter had settled into his own rather more anonymous role as just another gay dealer and she had been sent unmoored into the thicket of feral females. She had chosen to be blinkered at that time, not wanting to discuss it much, but that certainly didn't prevent others from speculating and commiserating and bashing and laughing. Adelaide knew enough about her to be unpleasant, as most people do about others whom they meet for a few minutes of introductions and innuendo. Adelaide was a figure; she had long cultivated a stable of artists, and lured them to her paddock out east on Long Island with promises of sunshine and solitary inspiration.

"Your mother mentioned you'd be here," Claire said. "She told me you had wanted to see the Tissots before they left. We've kept them here longer than is usual."

"How kind," Adelaide drawled. "Yes, Mother knows how I feel, but it's beyond my doing." She took a long drag on her cigarette and coughed out bursts of smoke. "You don't mind, do you?" she said, waving it at her. "Mother does, but she's stopped nagging. Nagging does me no good. You'd think she'd know that by now. After all these years. After all these confrontations. You don't smoke, do you? Delightful, filthy habit. I should stop," she exhaled again, watching the wisps float away. "But why?"

Claire didn't think Mrs. Driscoll ever nagged, though her vagueness belied a shrewd interior. Claire got the feeling that Adelaide liked to bait her mother as much as anyone else around her. She had an arrogant opinion of her own intelligence, yet at the same time wariness about her decisions that made her both brash and abashed: a narcissist before a broken mirror. She couldn't get enough of her own fractal impressions, and with the sense of entitlement Claire found common among the rich, Adelaide held on to her character traits, good or bad, as if they were what defined her, for better or worse, like the image of human feelings or foibles embodied in the Greek gods. The rich paraded their faults regardless of what others outside their set thought, rather like the stalking frozen figures in a frieze. Adelaide's love life was unhappy and her career mottled despite her surface of carefree contempt. Divorced twice, dangled here and there by duplicitous dealers she dated, always dropped by them at the last minute. For who would want to harness Adelaide? Hers wasn't exactly a free spirit, but rather one meant to roam the moors near some cursed village. Adelaide was closer to sixty than fifty, yet tried to pass for forty-eight and carried herself with the petulant preoccupied selfishness of a spoiled teenager who couldn't find anything that fit. Claire admired her up to a point for choosing a profession, when she could have lived a life of committees and manicures. She was clearly a woman who liked power but who squandered the strength of her intellect by second-guessing herself. She tried to project a steeliness in her opinions, but she often contradicted herself depending on who spoke to her last. Adelaide could never decide on her own whether someone was an actual up-and-coming—she questioned others to such an extent that whatever consensus was reached was meaningless, for no one knew what she wanted from them. Claire's colleagues were often called upon to opine for Adelaide on some camera-happy East Village swain snapping away at half-dressed parties filled with inebriated hipster losers to gauge the strength of the market for twee Nan Goldins of the trust fund set. Or Adelaide would declare that some fashion photographer whose models had painted-on bruises was the very thing, and then try to force his work on a market that at that moment craved fresh-faced Helden-milkmaids. She had the money to make things happen up to a point, but she was someone who lived less by the reason of her intellectual instinct than the whims of her nagging self-doubt. She had friends among the artist class, and many of them were deadbeats who needed her for free lunches or cast-off fashions. She was also rather ungainly, and more so when she stood beside her put-together mother. Claire sympathized with her unfortunate fashion sense, especially given her own less-than-perfect figure. Despite what must have been a lifetime tutorial, Adelaide had little sense of style but many clothes, which she gave to grateful acquaintances of the artists she was sheltering until she grew restless and changed her mind again and a coterie of new clinging art-world barnacles would adhere themselves to her until she scraped them off with the next week's change of plans. Gifts dropped from her like afterthoughts. She was generous but unsound, so her generosity was essentially meaningless. She was so very different from her mother that Claire could only assume that Adelaide channeled her real energy into a fierce rebellion that carried her as she caromed toward her twilight years. For Mrs. Driscoll had decided opinions, decidedly expressed, that changed only after the wisdom of experience suggested it, while Adelaide's judgments shifted as the light does on a day of passing clouds.

Mrs. Driscoll was standing near the mantel over which hung "A Widow," fussing with a bowl of yellow chrysanthemums. Claire heard music—a recording of Brahms' Third Symphony, which graced the room with the subtle musical urgency of emotional recoil. Mrs. Driscoll gave Claire a wide smile and Claire noticed the flicker of disapproval at Adelaide's still-fuming cigarette which, she saw, Adelaide had moved behind her back. Perhaps she wasn't so very brazen after all.

"I'm so glad you could make it over for tea, my dear," she said, extending her hand and drawing Claire to her for a soft embrace. "I wanted you to be here for the paintings again with me before you whisked them away. Thank you for letting me live with them a little longer. Adelaide is going to miss them so."

"I've moved beyond missing them, Mother," Adelaide said. "I told you that many times." Mrs. Driscoll looked at the cigarette; Adelaide glanced around the room for an ashtray that Claire assumed had never been there—this must be an old routine between them—and said, "I'll be right back." She left, the scent of tobacco smoke trailing her.

"I used to think rebellion was a phase, but phases don't last for forty years, do they?" Mrs. Driscoll said a moment later. "She will be willful," she said. "You look marvelous, Claire. Chanel suits you."

"Thank you. But it can only suit me now and then. I can't afford more than a couple of these suits."

"No matter. You don't need many."

Claire thought she might have been thinking of her leather-clad daughter, who had chosen to age gracelessly, if indeed it was a choice rather than the tragic flaw her mother might have considered it. Claire wondered at the tempered hostility between the two women; Mrs. Driscoll, she thought, could probably be imperious, though she thought that Adelaide brought that out. Adelaide, to Claire, seemed aware in some way of not meeting a maternal expectation. Was Mrs. Driscoll the kind of mother who tried to impose herself on her children in ways alien to their character? Or did she consider that character-shaping? Had she been a taskmistress, instilling what she considered to be good breeding in an unwilling student? Claire's own mother had never really encouraged her; she was preoccupied by the trivial. She had made a point of telling her many phone friends how hard it was raising two girls, though Claire remembered how little she actually did—she was an indifferent housekeeper, at best; her mother accepted responsibility as if it were a bill one kept misplacing and ultimately never paid. It was her older, testy sister who seemed to be the authority figure in her family.

"I don't mean to pry," Claire said, "but Adelaide seems rather put out. Is it the paintings?"

"You're not prying, Claire. Adelaide likes scenes. And like Eleanora Duse, she'll never retire. No, I think she's resigned to my doing what I want with what I own. It's something else. Probably a man. It usually is."

"I see."

"You would, wouldn't you?" She paused for a moment, listening to the music from the other room. "I love Brahms. I wish he had written opera. I used to sing his songs when I was younger; I had one of those parlor voices, and my husband and I would entertain ourselves with Brahms songs, and Schumann. Nothing anyone else would want to hear, of course. But my husband had such a marvelous touch, well, we all loved making music together."

"Is Adelaide musical?"

"No, poor dear. I think she resents that, too. Thom, her brother, has a lovely baritone voice, and sometimes sang with us at the piano, at Christmas or when we had guests who could carry a tune. So old-fashioned. But we loved it. Adelaide just wasn't musical, wasn't interested in learning an instrument, yet still felt left out when we all had our little songfests even though she said she couldn't stand them."

"Perhaps she disliked not having musical talent."

"Of course. She must have thought it was something I chose not to give her."

As she said this, the maid came in with a tray of tea and cakes. "Thank you, Rosa," she said. "I'll take care of it."

"Don't think of me as a monster," Mrs. Driscoll said, "because my daughter and I don't get along. I'm not a world-weary old woman." She considered. "Well, perhaps I am. You know, families. Children do follow their own paths, in life and love. Adelaide's paths have been many. One hopes she will finally choose wisely."

"Are you sure she's not still bothered by your selling the paintings?"

"No more than she is of everything else. Which is very. I know she'll miss them; she grew up with them here. And she professes to be uninterested in them, though we both know, she and I, that she's lying. I think for once Adelaide knows I'm doing the right thing, that she would be unable to deal with them properly, and that she and her brother would fight over them. Still, because she can't control what's going to happen to them, at some level she resents it, and she affects her attitude of blasé contempt. It's Adelaide's way of coping. She finds many outlets for her energy. That is just one."

"She's well known in the art community, as you know," Claire said, as if this were a mark of respect.

"Mildly notorious is more like it, I think," Mrs. Driscoll said.

"You disapprove of her?"

"Not at all," Mrs. Driscoll said. "Well, I've always been concerned about her lack of home life. It's my generation. Every mother wants to see her children settle down. But you have to accept what's given. Even an ungrateful child. Not that we're exactly in Lear territory. But I hate to see her unhappy, even though it seems we can't agree on anything. She's a strong woman, but strength has its limits."

"I didn't mean to pry," Claire said.

"Oh, but you're not," Mrs. Driscoll assured her. "I've told you how much I want you to feel at home with me. In this respect, it means I can pry and you can ask. Well, that is, we can ask things of each other and not consider it prying. How's that? Tell me, are you close to your mother?"

"She died when I was just out of college," Claire said. "Both my parents are dead."

"Oh, I'm so sorry. So young. And your parents would surely have been so proud of your accomplishments."

Claire didn't answer. Her mother surely would have been glad of her hobnobbing with the well-to-do, and her father probably would have resented it. He had lived in a solitude of anger and muddleheaded inebriation. Her mother had never seemed to get much enjoyment out of life, for herself or through others, even her daughters. Her father's need for oblivion, and his disgust with the world filled her with shame, sometimes, when she chose to think of his wasted years, and of her fear of him in his savage unhappiness. Him sitting in the dark kitchen, muttering to himself, as she caught sight only of the outline of a pilsner glass in the glare of the table lamp, his head silhouetted like a stein against the shadows. With the clinking of the glass, the dyspeptic conversations with himself, he was like the half-living tableau of an Edward Hopper painting, a picture of murmured weariness and nighttime ennui. In the meantime, her mother would have slipped away for another endless phone conversation with some parish biddy, or have escaped to one of her good-works groups, less for the good work than for the group and less for the group than for the escape.

"Do you miss them?" Mrs. Driscoll asked.

"I miss the idea of them more, if you can understand that. My mother was not particularly maternal. My father was, well, rather absent in many ways, as well."

"You poor thing. Well—having parents around doesn't always mean life's a bed of roses, either."

"My older sister, Catherine, always acted as a mother to me. Well, she was very bossy. But she helped me in many ways. She lives in Ohio, and has her own family now. But we see each other at Christmas or Thanksgiving. I adore her children, two little girls."

"I guess she's a devoted mother."

"Like a prison matron." Claire paused. "I didn't mean to be unkind."

"No matter, Claire," Mrs. Driscoll said. "It's funny about families. Each one is so different, and you can never predict how children will turn out. You try to guide, but you can't in the end change."

"You can't change anyone."

"I have this feeling that after I die, Adelaide will turn into someone completely different, maybe into Miss Marple. She may become a demure spinster. After all, she's lived the life of a bitter divorcée for years. It must be exhausting for her—not that she tells me, but I can tell. I would like to predict her future somehow."

"Whose future?" Adelaide asked, entering the room. She had changed out of her leather pants and into a gray skirt and an ivory silk blouse. It suited her, as well as anything could suit those shoulders and those hips; Claire could sympathize with problem areas, as her sister would have pointed out. The clothes softened her a bit, like a blanket tossed over a horse. Claire wondered how it must have been for Adelaide, having such a handsome brother as Thom, and a fine-looking, if not, glamorous mother. She should probably consider a fashion coordinator of some sort, Claire thought, and was grateful again for the lessons she herself had learned from her brittle sister. Luckily for Claire she had learned enough to dress with some style, but either Adelaide felt indifferent to clothing, or she was tone-deaf to fashion. She had probably felt herself ridiculed enough by the mirror to ignore it.

"Yours, dear," Mrs. Driscoll said.

"The future is now," Adelaide told her. "Is that tea Assam? You know that's what I prefer."

"I was just telling Claire that you might do something very different with your life after I'm gone. And yes, it's Assam. It's always Assam."

"You're never going to die, Mother," Adelaide said, sniffing the teapot and helping herself to a cup.

"What's your guess on what I'll become, Claire? Did you and mother talk my future over?"

"No, we didn't," Claire said. "And I didn't speculate."

"Too bad. I could use some suggestions."

"All I know is that anybody can change," Claire said. "They just have to want it."

"How sweet. Like a saying on a farmhouse pillow," Adelaide said. "In my book we are who we are at a very early age and that's that. Isn't that right, Mother? Mother will tell you I've always been unconventional. And that's what I'll remain. Not for me the lady-of-leisure act."

"I never thought that, Adelaide," her mother said.

"Tell me," Claire said. "How is your gallery doing? Are you still specializing in photography?"

"Not as much. Less the representational stuff. More photo-graphic abstractions."

"Such as . . ."

"I'm looking for artists who have an Eastern edge—Eastern as in Asian. I've got one who appropriates the concept of the mandala and makes art in nature. In the manner of Andy Goldsworthy. He takes pictures of twigs or leaves he's arranged into circles and patterns as they're blown away by the wind and rain."

"That sounds fascinating," Claire said, actually meaning it.

"I'm not sure if it works, though I think he's good," Adelaide said, gathering steam. She brightened as she began to speak of her client. "I don't know if the market can bear more than one lyrical nature fabulist like that, what do you think? I don't know if his stuff will ever sell well enough to appear at auction, so you may not consider him worthwhile, but he's got something, though I'm not sure if he's just right for me, or if I'm going through a phase. I'll decide sometime."

She began to pace, smoothing her skirt, and her hand moved up to her hair, as if she were expecting to be coming into the view of someone just outside the window. She turned back to Claire. "In the meantime, I'm putting together a show of his stuff, and I've managed to get him a commission to move toward stuff that stands around longer. There's a big market in memorials, as you may be aware, everyone dying, everyone wanting to remember it, everyone loving to think of long-lost whoever taken so cruelly from us, but everyone dies, get over it. But still, I can see the point. What do you think? I'm not sure."

"I'd have to see more of his work," Claire ventured.

"Still, I think he's good, and maybe his sculpture will help break him through to the big time. It's a bit more commercial, and that's the way I see this person evolving, it's the only way, you can't do art projects forever, unless you're an academic and a tenured one and I think this guy's too good, though I can't be sure until I see him work in firmer stuff than twigs and branches. He's an artist who can change, unlike most people, and he sees the market situation, unlike some artists. His name's Rodolfo Jiménez. What do you think? I'm not sure, but he's got talent, that much I know, though others may disagree. What do you think?" She was both authoritative and uncertain, which Claire found oddly exhilarating.

She hadn't been on the receiving end of one of Adelaide's "what-do-you-think" conversations before, though she'd been warned of them by acquaintances.

"I don't know what to think," she admitted. "I have to see his work."

"I think Adelaide may decide to become a Thomas Kinkade dealer when I'm dead, just to spite us all," Mrs. Driscoll said. "Selling little nightlights on television of unsettling little New England cottages in the snow."

"Mother, that isn't even funny." She gnawed on a cookie.

Rosa came in, signaling to Adelaide that she had a phone call. Adelaide left, the memory of her sad face lingering. Claire wondered what drove her to such petulance. Her peculiar world was of no importance to anyone but her mother and those whom Adelaide kept in food and tossed-off clothes. Yet everyone felt her presence to be somehow an unrelenting misfortune, and waited for her to be gone.

Adelaide returned in a minute, looking even more put out. She sat on the sofa opposite Claire and Mrs. Driscoll, freshened her cup, and sipped more tea. She began to feed herself the dainty little butter cookies—they were called cat's tongues, Claire remembered. Adelaide shoveled them into her mouth unthinkingly, to ward off conversation, perhaps, and the quizzical looks of her mother. She leaned back and said nothing, staring ahead. Mrs. Driscoll glanced at Claire with a muted quizzical expression and looked back at her daughter. Adelaide glanced then at Claire, and her long, narrow, impenetrable eyes met Claire's and arrested them, lost in some unknowable memory, and not a happy one. Adelaide appeared less the horsy English heiress now than an ill-natured ruminant, as if Picasso had turned one of his Demoiselles into a bovine study, "Dora Mar with Cowbell."

"Are you all right, Adelaide?" her mother asked.

"Fine, Mother. Just a change of plans."

"So you're not going out, then?"

"No." She looked out the window. Gazing at the leafless sky as if it held the answers to an unasked question. "That damn Beckmeister canceled on me."

"Richard Beckmeister," Mrs. Driscoll said with a sigh, to Claire, with the tone of one who has heard this song before. "Stringing her along," Mrs. Driscoll said. "Do you know him?"

"Richard Beckmeister? You?" Claire asked, looking at Adelaide.

"What do you mean, me?" Adelaide asked.

"I didn't mean, I'm—I'm sorry. I was just surprised," Claire said.

"Why should you be surprised? Why shouldn't I be seeing Richard?"

Because you're a foul-tempered hag, Claire thought, but she said, "He didn't seem like your type, that's all. I thought you liked artists, not dealers," she added, as if that would help. Richard's type was thin, younger, and more pliable than Adelaide. He and she were about the same age, and he favored those twenty-five years younger, a few inches shorter, and fifty pounds lighter. Claire had been one of Richard's squeezes, albeit temporarily, and she hadn't been nearly soignée enough for him. She was frankly shocked that Richard should start to look to the stables for playmates.

"I don't have a type," Adelaide said. "Anyway, we've dated a few times. Does that matter to you? I know he's a roué and I know he's probably looking for something more, but I chose to go out with him. I wanted to see what all the shouting was about. Not much. I can tell you that right now."

"Adelaide, I didn't mean to imply anything. I'm sorry he cancelled on you. He can be very irritating that way."

"Don't tell me *you* dated him."

"A few years ago. Just a couple of times. We decided it wasn't working."

"Who *hasn't* he dated," Adelaide said. "I didn't expect much, I never do"—which Claire did not believe—"but apparently our course has run. What do you think of him? I guess I should be glad I gave him a whirl, but really he's much too old for me. Another loser. The bastard. Sorry, Mother." She looked at her mother briefly and then at Claire, holding her head back, as she had done when she answered the door, as if reassessing Claire, and determining whether she would charge at her or not. But she shook her head and poured herself more tea.

Claire could certainly sympathize with Adelaide's disappointment, her peculiar sense of humiliation. She couldn't say she knew her as anything other than her reputation, her chilly condescension the only contact that until a few moments ago they had had. Hers was a discontent born of continual loss, perhaps. Surely even the unfortunate equine, bossy, and frustrating Adelaide longed for love, or at least a careless interlude to tide her over between bouts of indecision. But as a woman of fifty-something, wasn't she too old to be so angry about so unimportant a person to her, really, as Richard Beckmeister? He was an art dealer, but she was a well-to-do heiress of a certain age with social connections aplenty should she choose to exercise them, and no need to feel the flicker of Richard's inconstancy. But then, she considered, he might have been looking to Adelaide as someone to buy into his business. She knew he had been somewhat overextended, and had more a few paintings he had been trying to unload. Perhaps wooing Adelaide had been the key to her pocketbook. Perhaps standing her up meant he had made a sale elsewhere.

Claire could merely speculate about the course of Adelaide's life, as she knew it only in public pieces and secondhand gossip. She had little sympathy for Adelaide when seeing her as a stubborn daughter of a strong-willed mother whom Claire admired, but more for her at any rate as a woman who was always being told she wasn't good enough to love, let alone have dinner with, which may have been more galling to her. As for herself, Claire was aware that in so many ways she was yet another single woman in her thirties with a failed marriage, a career, and a bleak future if one looked at it romantically, which she tried not to. She kidded herself that she had too much at stake for her livelihood to contemplate too much what romance might exist for her. She knew this was delusional, since she was just short of pining for anyone who might show her interest, but she could without too much effort focus on the work that served her well; it was satisfying in itself, which was a great reward. Adelaide had money, she dabbled with enough talent at a career to be somewhat known at it beyond her eccentricities. Her money allowed her entrée to art circles and artists, and she had some talent for spotting talent, but Adelaide nevertheless could afford to devote more energy to worrying over heartache than making a living, though heartache was not a quality that seemed to be natural to her. Perhaps she had changed in some way that she was unwilling to admit, especially to her mother and to a relative stranger whom her mother was befriending. Adelaide's sullen face awoke in Claire a momentary compassion, even as she knew it would fade away at the first obstinate word that Adelaide spoke. Sudden unforeseen misery, even of the social kind—and Claire was certain that this meant as much to Adelaide as a deeper torment might—led her to forgive, if just for now, Adelaide's unbridled condescension and her exasperating flightiness. Claire, at least, was meeting her own ex–brother-in-law in a little while, and could afford to be the picture of charity and concern for someone her superior in living large, if narrowly, on a more exalted stage than she had been born to. At least her man hadn't canceled, even if that man was only a former relation, and a study in frustrated anger himself.

"I sometimes think I've wasted my time," Adelaide said, with a voice that mingled regret and exasperation, perhaps impatience even to be admitting something aloud.

"Don't be silly, dear," her mother said. "You've accomplished so much, your gallery, your artists."

"They mean so little to me at the moment," she said.

"You can't let this man ruin your evening."

"Oh, he hasn't," Adelaide said. "I am annoyed at myself even for thinking along those lines with someone like him. I'm tired, that's all. I need to clear my head. Claire," she said, turning toward her with a more businesslike tone, "'A Widow' was always part of my girlhood. I used to think it so sweet, but so much like a second-rate Renoir—which means what you think it means. I used to think of it as a cutesy picture of a pretty woman and a child, ruined by an old woman's face. It was so familiar, its prettiness was so comforting and old-fashioned and reliable. It was Mother's art. But now that Mother has decided to part with it, well, perhaps now that I'm older, I suddenly realized that it was one of those paintings whose meanings grew with you as you aged. And I have aged. For most of my life, I've been like that fussy little girl arched over the chair, bored and bored and bored. I then used to think of myself as the alluring young hopeful woman who hopes to conquer death through romance. Fat chance. Frankly—and Mother, forgive my saying this—I'm more like the biddy with the book in that painting than the bimbo with the boyfriend."

"You're never too old for whatever you want, Adelaide," her mother said.

"Oh, but I am, mother. I am. I'm too old to be so young, and I never was. I told you we are who we are, we are what we are. We stay that way. End of story. Anyway, Claire, I'm genuinely going to miss that painting Mother loves so much. But I tell you, and you, too, Mother, that I'll be glad when it's gone. It seems when I look at it as if my life has slipped away there over your mantel. I hope someone pays Mother a lot of money for it. I hope they deserve it. Now I need a cigarette. I've been here too long. I need to get out. Claire, I may see you before the sale," she said, rising to full equine height. Her hauteur returned, her momentary lapse into self-reflection dissipated like an exhalation. "Mother, I'll be leaving tomorrow. Goodbye, Claire."

Adelaide retired, probably to telephone some unfortunate upon whom she'd force herself to spend time with her for the gift of a free meal and odium. How she ever thought of herself as the young woman in that painting was beyond Claire. That was Claire's fantasy, not some horsy harridan's. But Adelaide's imagination had been stirred by "A Widow" to think beyond herself, beyond her appearance, just as anyone who lives with a work of art can succumb to its variable meanings, just as anyone who absorbs the life of a picture can become a part of its imaginative universe. She shouldn't have been surprised at the dream of romance Adelaide had had about a painting she had known since she was an infant. But she was. For Claire, Adelaide's romantic longings just didn't jibe with her plainspoken dismissiveness, though it might have with her notorious tendency to second-guess herself, which, Claire admitted, she did while still managing to come across as strident and opinionated. That was a neat trick. And who was Claire to judge the suitability of someone's romantic follies?

After she left the room, Mrs. Driscoll and Claire were silent for a moment.

"How often do you see your daughter?"

"Actually more often than you'd think, Claire," she said, turning her eyes toward the painting above the mantel, and letting them rest there. "I have always thought of myself as the young woman in that painting, no matter how old I've gotten. I have always believed in possibilities," she said. "My daughter has not."

"But she can recognize talent in artists," Claire said. "That shows perception."

"But she only senses what people can do, or create, I think. She can't sense what they may be, or has little interest in it. Or what she can become."

Claire looked at her watch. "I must be going soon, Mrs. Driscoll, as I have an appointment."

"Business or pleasure, dear?"

"That's a good question," Claire said, with a small laugh. "Actually, I'm meeting my ex–brother-in-law at the Frick. He's in town, as I think I mentioned, and he called me to see if we could meet."

"Why not dinner?"

"I don't think it's that kind of thing," Claire said. "And I suggested the Frick because it's near you." She paused, and looked up again at the Tissot. "Our staff will be here tomorrow morning to retrieve the paintings."

"Thank you for letting me keep them just a little longer," Mrs. Driscoll said. "Now that I'm saying goodbye to them, my life is entering a new phase."

Claire knew how important these family artworks were to people, in some ways more cherished than sepia prints of dead parents, who were, after all, memories. The artworks changed, in some way, as their owners changed toward them. "I know that, or I should say, I can see that," Claire said. "I hope you can come to the pre-sale reception I'm going to be holding. I should love you to see how your paintings will look surrounded by other art of the period, and to see what stars they will be in my sale."

"I'd like that," she said. "Perhaps I can induce Adelaide, or Thom, to come."

"Yes, do," Claire said, not meaning it, yet smilingly bidding Mrs. Driscoll adieu. Adelaide unsettled her a bit, and she wasn't sure how she'd behave if she showed up at the gallery. Not that Adelaide was prone to public displays of peevishness, but Claire wanted Mrs. Driscoll to appear with her painting sans her children. Though she had to admit that Adelaide would add another level of cachet to the proceedings, and probably bring some new and noisy art-world acquaintances to the showing. It could signal a shift in the staid world of nineteenth-century works of art, if the bohemian hipoisie descended, even for an evening, to eyeball the genre paintings and still-lifes they would usually be expected to shun.

Adelaide had always sought out the views of others, more as sounding boards than anything else, yet she attracted a cockeyed following, despite the steely willfulness of her shifting views. She probably made up her mind about someone's talent immediately, and asked what others thought as background noise as her perception of someone solidified in her mind. Yet what she had said about herself indicated she had always been disappointed in what she was. And had no trouble saying this to her mother, which Claire found surprising. Children usually fault their parents, not themselves. And parents were often thwarted by their children, especially if their happiness relied on their children's—and for most parents, it did, didn't it? Even someone such as Mrs. Driscoll, whose composure seemed born of having accepted the follies of the world during a long life, must have been unnerved to some degree by the brusque unhappiness of her daughter. It surely must have rankled that Adelaide was at best a coolly cordial daughter, at worst a hostile and curt one, and her outspoken misery was undoubtedly meant as a rebuke to her mother. Claire herself hadn't undermined her mother in public or tried to assert herself in any way other than quietly, if determinedly. Not that her mother would have noticed anyway. By the time she was old enough to consider college and beyond, she felt her mother thought of her less as a daughter to be guided (what little guidance she had ever offered) than as someone who was a potential threat to her own waning desirability. But Claire had never considered her mother's romantic life. Few do about one's parents. Still, Claire had felt that her mother, always a pretty woman, would have been more attractive if she'd been less preoccupied. She might then have relied less on whatever Claire's father thought of her, and more on how she considered herself. She took care of herself, certainly, with judicious makeup and such. But she didn't carry herself with confidence, but as someone who would rather be somewhere else. During those long, cold mornings of Lenten mass, when twelve-year-old Claire was ravenous enough to regard the unappetizing buttered bread and weak cocoa that awaited her for breakfast with pleasure as she swallowed the dry dissolving communion wafer, her mother's devotion had borne the mark of someone who had chosen to be in church because her other options were even less tenable. She thought her mother believed in her religion, since she ordered her life so much around it—the liturgical year being the social calendar of her set—but she ultimately couldn't be sure, since her mother was always so vague about behavior and even her own belief. "Your teachers will know about all of that much more than I possibly could," she would tell her whenever Claire had a question about services or basic catechism. She realized how much she had to thank her martinet sister for whatever she remembered about the proper way, *any* way, actually, of doing things. In any event, Claire would never have stormed about like Adelaide—she was of course nothing like her—but also since her own mother could be so wily in her passivity. Perhaps it had been an elaborate scheme to prevent adolescent aggression, perhaps nothing more than indolence. Perhaps Catherine's moxie had worn her out. Claire had felt no need to rebel against her mother as any other overgrown schoolgirl might have, since her mother never seemed to care much about anything Claire did as more than a passing subject of temporary conversation easily forgotten. Even when her exasperating indifference finally prompted Claire to demand her mother's attention—it was for her junior prom and she had questions about a dress, so important to her at the time—her mother had responded to Claire's cry of, "You never listen to me! This is important!" by saying, "I'm sorry, dear, there's no need to shout, I was just thinking of something else. I can hear you, you know," which was her answer to everything, and Claire knew that even if she retorted with "You never hear what I'm saying," she knew she was defeated, since her mother's detached manner offered no entry points for the arrows of her outrage. Nothing could shake her mother from her imperturbable apathy regarding anything other than plans for doing something else. Anyway, the actual events of her mother's life mattered little; for her, planning was all, the meetings, the gossip, the triviality, the getting to. Claire's protests were pointless, and her mother would never notice her, for whatever reason. Her mother's was an unhappiness, if she was indeed unhappy, if that preoccupation was a way of coping with a loutish drunken husband who barely noted her except to criticize, that led Claire to believe that she should become self-sufficient, not quite as take-charge as her sister Catherine, but someone who would know enough not need to ask questions that demanded answers. Until Peter had come along, of course, noticing her, positively embracing her with his active optimism and making her feel that what she had to say was worthwhile, an entirely new experience for her, and one that blinded her to anything other than that realization that she might be worthwhile. The imagined freedom she would create for herself in marriage, the deliverance from the dull insignificance of her girl-hood eventually vanished, however. That her divorce left her feeling aimless was a result, in part, of her sense that her self-reliance had been tempered with denial, and she had questioned whether her mother's lack of interest in her children had been a way of distancing herself not only from a hopeless husband but from a child who had not come up to whatever standard she had anticipated she might. Claire had blamed herself, then, for the failure of a marriage she probably might not have entered into had she been a more forth-right young woman, nurtured in her childhood rather than neg-lected, then jumping at the first encouragement of her intellect, followed by her naïve heart, followed by a dissatisfaction that had plagued her for nights and days and months.

Walking to the Frick in the deepening afternoon, Claire could sense that Mrs. Driscoll was bothered by her daughter's predica-ment, even as she also sensed that this was nothing new. But hearing it with Claire at hand must have made Adelaide's de rigueur despondency more poignant, even pitiable to her. What mother—other than Claire's—would not want her daughter somehow set-tled, or barring that, somehow happy? To be confronted with a miserable child was a reproach to a parent that Claire found painful to witness, less for the child here than for the mother, this one in particular. Again, she did not know what kind of mother Mrs. Driscoll was—we can only experience the careless, feeble nurturing of our own—and Claire felt that Mrs. Driscoll was savvy enough to question and maybe rue what she might have done over the years to lead her child to become such as she was. Yet, she also felt that Mrs. Driscoll would not waste time, too much time, regretting what she could no longer control. She did believe in possibilities. But the evidence was in, too, and Adelaide was done, finished, an adult, thus the vague hopeful prediction that Adelaide might change into someone more benign after Mrs. Driscoll's death. Claire did not believe it at all. She thought that Mrs. Driscoll probably felt herself to have done what she could have to raise the child she had brought into her privileged world. Did Mrs. Driscoll realize, *had* she realized, that as a girl Adelaide might have hated being an outsider to some of her mother's love, if that's what had happened? She had to have known she was not a pretty girl; did she sense that in her mother's looks? Did she resent Mrs. Driscoll's evenings of parlor songs, singing *alte Liebe* with her then-besotted husband, hearing her mother's voice enraptured in a language she could not comprehend, an outsider to her parents' love, an outsider to the expressions of desire or longing or intimate whimsy that she could not share? Did she have an inkling of her father's indiscretions as her mother got a bit older, did she see the way these spottily discreet affairs played out between her parents, in discomfiture and compromise? Did she believe in the lasting power of love, or did she only scorn what passed for it when she was a child and maybe too young to realize what became of marriages after the parlor songs were sung and the tattered pages of German lieder put away for good? Did she want what they had at the time, did she feel loved conditionally, had she given up? Had she ever believed in possibilities?

Claire had, and still did. She often wondered what might have been, if she had not married Peter and had begun to realize that, for all of her self-reproach, if she had chosen differently she might now have looked back with a regret as bitter as the loss she had felt at the time. Her world was larger because of what she had lived through—she chose to examine it as a pathway to a fuller life. She certainly had a sort of entrée into gay life that she would likely not have if she hadn't kept herself in touch with Peter and welcomed Tobias into her heart. Yet a fat lot of good that did her. She wasn't likely to meet closeted straight men there. But she had wanted to know how the other half, or really, the majority of those in her profession, lived. She had been forced to allay her peremptory judgments of people, learning that to consider them as fully as human as herself was a step toward a grace she hadn't then been aware of wanting. Yet in other ways, she felt that her own romantic life had been marked by a deliberate tentativeness that narrowed her, somehow, for men she might begin to love. It wasn't anger that drove her, it wasn't quite fear. She felt in danger of losing herself to the preoccupation of a job, much as her mother did in her otherwise-engaged manner, and knew that simply knowing this wasn't enough. The thing is, she thought that her greatest risk had been being in love too young and learning hard lessons too young. What she was beginning to understand was that it was more treacherous to her future happiness, whatever that might be, whatever shape it might take, if she held on to her reluctance too much, like an actress unwilling to commit to a demanding role and finding too late that it could have made her career. She didn't want to become an angry, dry-eyed Adelaide, and she didn't think she would. But she didn't want to become her mother, either, living in a fog of meandering social daydreams.

She didn't want to end up as the wizened old woman reading a romance novel in the Tissot painting, and she had, for far too long, been willing to let herself flutter about like its pretty widow hoping that a handsome stranger might call again and rescue her from her self-absorption. And she would never, she knew, wear leather pants when she was in her fifties. Adelaide had taught her that much.

# THE DOG AND THE VIRGIN QUEEN

**F**rank did not see Claire enter, or if he had, he quickly reassumed his study of Hogarth's "Miss Mary Edwards" in the Frick's dining room and pretended not to have noticed her. But she noticed him, of course, after wandering through the large hall, and the gift shop—she never missed the gift shop—and the Fragonard rooms, and glimpsed him from the doorway just outside the room. Her heart gave a small leap; she had been half dreading this meeting, and she had begun to know why. That is, she had begun to admit to herself why, and she was unnerved by her attraction to him.

He had his arms behind his back and was leaning over a table with silver urns on either side, trying to look at the brushwork on the dog at the bottom of the picture. Claire noticed that his jacket hem was slightly worn away; white piping had begun to show where the fabric had dissolved. He still dressed as if he were a threadbare priest, she thought, which touched her. At least the tweedy jacket didn't clash with the gray flannels. At least he looked like someone to protect, which was not what she had anticipated. And still, casual tweediness became him, she thought.

Claire admired Hogarth, and this portrait, hardly an iconic

work—most people knew him from his scabrous series of lithographs of manners and venality—still bore the artist's confident intelligence and eye for sure, if cruel, detail. Claire had half expected to find Frank in the Octagon Room, poised between admiration and dismissal before the religious works or an annunciation scene there. She recalled that he had been a great fan of annunciation art through the ages, despite his abrogation of much of what he had once believed, or professed to believe, when he had been a priest. Frank had liked he way different artists depicted that moment when the angel Gabriel—although in the gospel of Luke, the angel did not have a name—gave Mary his startling news. What made the whole category of paintings so compelling to him, he said, was that tension between what was being told and how it was received. "It wasn't necessarily good news," Frank had said to her once, when she'd been married and they'd discussed her profession and the art they liked. "But somehow she accepts it; it was an act of faith, the handmaiden of the Lord's wish. I am still stunned by it."

She liked annunciation paintings, too, but for the various representations of iconography there, and the placements of figures, more banal, probably, than his spiritual interest, but more varied, perhaps, within the parameters of the subject matter. She liked to see how the lilies were placed, how Mary's shawl was displayed, where the dove hovered, even how the angel and Mary looked at each other, if they did. She was fascinated by how the faithful interpreted the heartfelt apocryphal. Frank had, she thought, been drawn to how artists imagined the tenets of faith.

Claire's particular fondness for this Hogarth portrait stemmed as much from his intelligent mastery as his subject. You could tell the sitter was a strong personality, a determined woman both forthright and humorous. Hogarth managed to give her eyes a witty gleam, and the arch of her eyebrows displayed both discernment and clear-eyed acceptance: this is what the world is. Her mouth, with its faint smile, also had the possibility of a sneer at the corner of the lips. This you could tell from standing and staring. But when you knew a little of the background, the portrait sang. The "Miss" of the title had been a Mrs. The "Miss" was a fabrication. Mary Edwards had inherited a great fortune when she was twenty-four. She was one of the greatest heiresses of her day, an eighteenth-century Doris Duke. Typically, she was courted by the ne'er-do-wells among the aristocracy, who sought her wealth to ease them in their own profligacy. Her luck in fortune did not make for fortunate love, however, and she ended up marrying a wastrel Scots guardsman with the still amusing name—to Americans—of Lord Anne Hamilton (his godmother had been Queen Anne). He assumed her family name, and tried to assume her fortune, gambling much of it away, and attempting even to transfer stocks from her holdings to his. Mary moved on this, before she lost her fortune to him, and had the records of her marriage destroyed and then had the child she bore him—Gerald Anne Edwards— declared a bastard. It was an extraordinary act of courage for a woman at the time—at any time—but she managed to reclaim her money, even at the expense of her reputation. Wealth, however, counted for more than name in some respects. She died not too long after the date of the painting Hogarth did of her, but in it she still looks healthy, still composed, certain, and gleaming with almost Byzantine raiment: a Theodosia who has triumphed over the court conspiracies surrounding her. She wears a deep red gown, and fabulous jewels grace her throat; she sits, no beauty, no Gainsborough filly, but someone of almost papal magnificence and strength. Here was a woman who had taken control of her life.

"Do you think the dog is smiling or snarling?" Claire said, coming up behind Frank, who probably pretended not to hear her tread on the floor.

"Snarling," he said, turning to her with a smile. He leaned down to kiss her cheek, which he hadn't done the last time they had met, when they'd simply hugged. She felt his arm linger on her back, and was embarrassed at her reluctance to let the moment pass. She felt a tingle at the brush of his five o'clock shadow on her face, and she was tempted to run her finger along his jaw. Was he wearing cologne? No, surely not. Not practical, tattered Frank. Perhaps her banker friend's closet where he'd been staying had potpourri that Frank's homely tweeds had picked up.

"I was just wondering that myself, and leaning toward snarl," he said, releasing her hand and, after giving her an appraising look, turning back to the painting. She still felt him looking at her, though, as if he could see how she had been blushing at his touch. "But I was really trying to read the paper on the desk behind her." The sitter's right elbow rested near a document unfurled and begging to be read. "I was trying to figure out what was on it. You see the dog is looking at the paper, and not exactly at her, which is unusual."

"Yes," she said, turning to the painting and glancing at Frank again. "Dogs are usually so intent on their masters or mistresses. They don't bother with inanimate objects."

"I think I can make it out: 'Do—thou—great—'" he paused and strained to see more. "'Make—lives—or—deaths glorious.'"

"Those are famous lines," Claire said, "about the Armada, from Elizabeth the First. I studied this painting. You can only barely make them out. But people at the time knew them. It was Queen Elizabeth's speech to the fleet before they went to meet the Spanish Armada. So Hogarth is making a rather obvious point about Miss Mary Edwards's independence, comparing her to the Virgin Queen."

"How so?"

"She fought to get her fortune back from her unscrupulous husband, at a time when women were taken advantage of and usually had to turn their money over to their husbands."

"No fool she," Frank said.

"Well, she had been, but managed to get things as right as she could."

"What happened to the husband?"

"You know, I don't know," Claire said. "He wasn't painted by Hogarth—although his little son was—as far as I know he faded into a deserved obscurity."

"She must have been a tough cookie."

"And Hogarth could be flattering her—probably was, since she gave him this commission, and Hogarth wasn't an idiot. I think he respected her. I think the dog in the picture is actually trying to smile but the little grimace at his lip is his way of saying not everything is what it seems. Or maybe that Miss Edwards, not actually a virgin, had become her own sort of Virgin Queen."

"And got out of her marriage."

"At the cost of social shame—but there's a lot of that, you know." She paused for a moment, then turned to him. "Do you know," Claire said, realizing she was changing the subject, but unable to stop herself, "Do you know how hard it was for Peter to come out to *me*, to himself, after being married? He suffered."

"I find that hard to believe."

"You don't give him credit for sensitivity. I didn't used to. But like this heiress, who gave birth to what was legally declared a bastard in order to save her fortune, and really, herself, Peter had to suffer the humiliation of being a married man who announces he's gay. That was one of the things that ultimately made me forgive him, if not myself: he suffered. He lost the prestige of being a straight, married man in a field that attracts a lot of gay men. He became more or less just like so many other men in the field."

"Please. What prestige?"

"The prestige of being a straight man. You're still the top of the heap, you know."

"I find that hard to believe."

"Well, you would, wouldn't you?" she said. "You think only of yourself. You don't put yourself in context."

"Who does?"

"True. But some of us try."

They looked together at the painting, falling into an oddly companionable silence, despite the rather peremptory tone Claire felt she'd assumed. She felt slightly embarrassed at her pleasure in Frank's company, having meant to keep things light—well, as light as Frank could be with her or anyone.

"You don't think leaving the priesthood is a loss of prestige?"

"I didn't say that," she said, in a more gentle tone. "All I meant was that Peter had to feel a shame at how he would be treated, beyond what he felt I would feel."

"I won't compare us, then."

"But you do. I know. Still, you lost your faith."

"I didn't lose my faith," he said. "I lost a vocation. There's a difference. My beliefs are still with me, shifting as they may be. It was my commitment to a life I should never have undertaken that galled me."

They had been alone in the room, except for a guard, who walked behind them, her foot treading noisily on the floor. A couple of chattering young women passed behind them suddenly, heading for the Reynolds portrait of John Burgoyne that hung to the right of the Hogarth. The women were dressed in what Claire thought of as High Junior League, with prim skirts and pearls, outfits that probably disguised Victoria's Secret panties and flimsy black bras.

"So beautiful," said the taller blonde.

"I know. He looks just like Josh," said the other.

"We'd better get a move on," the taller one said after the briefest moment of inspection, "if we want to get to Prada before it closes. I had my eye on those shoes there."

They left as noisily as they'd entered, and to their fading footsteps Claire and Peter looked at each other. She suddenly felt so confined in her little world of art and meaning and appraisals and symbols and icons upon hearing two normal women discuss art as looking just like Josh, whoever that handsome stud might be. Occasionally she felt so preoccupied by her own circle of colleagues that she neglected the larger world, the important world of Prada and panties and less-than-high-minded friends.

"This portrait," Claire said, with a thought about her own place in the world. "Tell me. Do you think less or more of it, knowing something about its subject?"

"More. But it's still a strong painting; I was drawn to the expression on the woman's face. Just as I was to the one on the Reynolds over there. This woman lived a battle every bit as fierce as that soldier did."

"More fierce," Claire said. "She fought a husband. And she won."

"So knowing that makes the portrait richer for you."

"It does, but it's not essential. I think people are interested in stories, they think of stories behind the paintings they see—they make up a past anyway. This one happens to be a particularly rich one for this particular subject."

"I wonder what the story of that dog is," Frank said.

"I think it's sweet, really," Claire said. "Look at how gently she touches its head. Look at how graceful his hands are. Look at those simple rings on her fingers."

"Yet look at her jeweled neck."

"That's just for show. For the portrait. For her."

There was always something of public recognition in the commission of a portrait, a self-conscious awareness of narcissism or just rewards or even faith, in the artist. One's memory becomes linked to his legacy. Even private noncommissioned casual remembrance became public in the most unexpected ways after the September 11th attacks, awkward testaments to lives lost that acquired an artfulness because of the desperation behind their owners' grief, because of the public face of loss shared by so many, because of the way single lives assumed shape out of a mass execution. Claire had heard of the floating photographs and falling snapshots drifting down from obliterated offices and passengers' purses on doomed planes that littered the ground around the sites downtown, had seen the posterized portraits of missing siblings, friends, colleagues. But that was a recognition that was not sought.

She knew that she was, in her small way, part of an industry that gave shape to careers and by implication to the people involved in those careers as subjects or even muses. Hogarth's manipulative control gave us leave to wonder at the mystery of the sitter's thoughts, the sitter's life. She knew that her fondness for genre paintings arose from her imaginative speculation about the lives depicted there, the tableaux of overwrought emotion and kitsch sentiment. She was drawn to the possibilities of what others may have experienced within the same world the artist made. Then, too, with portraits, we wish to know more, because the best portraits give not a mirror into ourselves as much as a doorway into our life we either wish we could enter, or consider from afar. We cannot ever know what people think, but portraits enable us to believe we may hold a clue. Yet if Hogarth had been less of an artist, had been incompetent, this portrait would surely have disappeared like the countless snapshots stored away in boxes, under beds, in landfill, swept away like the posters of the missing by the brutality of life going on without them. Just a face, a life unremarked here, except for an artist's giving it an elusive meaning that kept it alive, in its elusiveness, through the years.

At the same time, Claire loved the luminous quotidian drudgery of the anonymous women in Vermeer's "The Little Street," a portrait not of the powerful, but of the quiet power of everyday tasks, the spiritual breath drawn from private chores unnoticed, but necessary for ordering a life in such a way as to live beyond the ordinary, that is, in the spiritual, knowing one has worked hard and long and with the sureness of fulfillment that only work can bring. Surely that anonymity mattered as much to an artist such as Vermeer as a portrait of the powerful may have to others.

They moved together to the adjacent room, a small space with an austere van Eyck Virgin and Child. "I wanted to show you something," Frank said.

He led her to Fra Filippo Lippi's "Annunciation." It was two panels, the Angel on the left, the Virgin, with a halo-graced dove fluttering at her head, on the right.

"An annunciation? Are you thinking of reenlisting?"

"God, no," he said, and a sudden shy smile broke across his handsome face. "I still like religious art, though. I like images of devotion, if not the devotion itself." He stood before it, a half smile on his lips, even the hint of joy in his expression. Claire had never really seen that look of concentration and wonder in him. "I know nothing of Lippi," Frank said. "But I am fascinated by how he created side by side two worlds. I'm probably not telling you anything you haven't already seen for yourself."

"I'm hardly an expert here," she said, to urge him on.

"This isn't my area, either. But look at how the angel on the left is corporeal, his feet are on the ground, like a dancer's, having just landed. In the other frame, the Virgin, who is mortal, appears to be hovering. You don't see her feet under her robe, which barely skirts the ground. It's as if the Holy Spirit with the little halo and the golden seed of God entering her had lifted her onto another plane. Yet she casts a strong shadow. The light here—" he pointed behind Mary's head—"is much brighter, making her shadow darker. And yet she has just said, or was about to say, 'How shall this be?' And the Angel tells her the Holy Ghost will come to her, and she says, 'Behold the handmaid of the Lord.' It's all about faith."

"And still you love it."

"I can admire what I don't have. Although I have faith. Just not, as I said, vocation."

"You're more like your like brother than you realize," Claire said. "You do have an eye, or at least an appreciation."

"But I can't be like my brother. It's a matter of temperament."

"You don't have to be like your brother. You just might accept him into your life."

Frank considered. "He thrust himself upon me. He came to me the other day. To talk." Frank told Claire about his brother's visit, and the story of their mother's childbirth fatalities.

They walked to the garden court, where a small bar was set up at one end, for the late-closing Friday evening crowd, though the Frick was rarely crowded, which was one of the many reasons Claire liked it, and why she suggested that Frank meet her there when he'd called asking to see her. She didn't know if she was ready yet for another touchy dinner with him. She had decided to keep it for now at drinks, and could plead fatigue after her tea with Mrs. Driscoll and Adelaide should Frank start annoying her with his brutal self-loathing. She liked him and felt drawn to him in a way she didn't care to identify just yet. She was uncertain whether that was because he led her to a past that she was trying still to move beyond, or because he represented a past she had partly idealized, the youthful love without youth's selfishness. Or maybe she was drawn to him because his smoldering anger, so different from the studied neutrality of his brother, intrigued her because of its hint of danger. Danger from an academic ex-priest—woo hoo. But he was unpredictable, she felt, and she didn't know if it was moodiness or the anguished revelations of someone beginning to know himself more who was troubled by what he's discovered.

They sat by the cool shimmering fountain, its gurgle punctuating the string quartet that was playing what sounded like Fauré. It was Fauré. "Après un rêve." They must have done their own arrangement. It was awfully mournful music for cocktail chatter; most people probably didn't know the words. Just as well. "I was dreaming of happiness, that fiery mirage." But the tune was such a longing one, almost despairing of hope. They really should be playing something less impassioned. The music took her out of herself for a moment, and while she couldn't quite recall the other words, the melody's evocative rise and fall gave her pause. *"Hélas, hélas,"* she recalled. She was prevented from saying any word she wanted to say, and remained silent. The constraint seemed to last a long while, neither she nor Frank looking at the other, till the music stopped, and some people applauded; the clink of glasses and the bouncing voices resumed.

Claire smiled at Frank, hoping to encourage him to get to what he had wanted to say, but not wishing to appear too self-involved herself, nor too impatient. She had the feeling she was willing herself away from him—a sure sign that she might like him more than she thought. She tended to recoil at the first flush of attraction, not trusting herself to keep hidden any recess of affection she might reveal under the influence of longing. Frank used to express himself as if he were talking to a student, back when she and Peter had been getting divorced, and she had foolishly approached him for counsel.

She should've stuck to her girlfriends, and not the groom's brother. But the whole priest thing, the daddy thing, the shoulder to cry on thing. Mistakes all. She had listened to him declaim with the certainty of one who either believes in what he is doing or has memorized its tenets well enough for his speech to pass as belief. Claire realized later that he had probably tried to convince himself of his faith in his calling, if not his faith itself, and her marriage and his foundation began to crumble at the same time. Perhaps the ritual of rote recitation, even the chalky homilies of post-Cana counseling, might have been enough to sustain the wavering beliefs of a less rigorous intellect, or one that felt itself duped and angered by belief. Frank had been skilled at the ritual of words; it was probably why he was a good teacher—or so she'd heard—since he could perform in the theater of the classroom. He had always been on the cusp of brusqueness, and students—and sometimes young women—fall for that brusque tone. She had often attributed that to his priestly demeanor, not his human misery. She had begun to realize that his curt doctrinal admonitions, his "this is what the Church says" spiels, were the lines of an old ham going through the performances, in a role he no longer suited but hoped his bravado might help him bluster through one more night, like an O'Neill figure towering and about to topple as the revelations set in. In her few meetings, or encounters, or whatever they were with him since his return to New York, Frank had been both humble and hubristic; he was still charging into certain conversations thinking he could gain an advantage by verbal aggression, yet his blather would quickly disintegrate into fumbled apologies, as if he had acted rashly because that was what he had learned to do, but that he had begun to learn that his witty machete-sharp words had consequences when uttered so carelessly. He didn't get out much, that was too obvious, and between the vexatious yet understandably moralizing Church manner and the autocracy he acquired for the classroom he hadn't learned the give and take of social conversation. Certainly not the come hither and go yon of the date. She often didn't know how to go about dating rituals herself, but she knew this was more from a deliberate scaling back rather than cluelessness. But who could tell the difference on the other side?

She looked over at a couple, heads bowed together like conferring linemen, smiling as they spoke. Frank, beside her, leaned slightly away from her, aware perhaps of her thoughts in the way she held her head. How different he actually was from his affable younger brother, despite what she'd said to Frank earlier. Peter had worn his confusion as preoccupation. Frank seemed to want to will her to know what was inside. She suspected he had reserves of reluctant kindness, though, and was at a loss to explain himself to himself. She wondered if she were attracted to him because he was like his brother in some ways but not gay—and she wondered too if that made her a hopeless case of living denial. Let him go. But she remembered his almost tentative caress on her arm, and felt herself blush with a pleasure she had told herself she was forbidden.

"I think it was tragic for my mother," Frank said, finally. "The graves. I don't know how much one should ever really know about one's parents. Only enough to try to understand and then, well, maybe only enough to think you might have an understanding and lose interest. Enough to humanize them, perhaps. Beyond the disappointment every child feels when he recognizes that his parents are not gods upon the earth. I don't know that I wanted to know this so much except that it told me two things."

He paused and turned to look at her, after having spoken until now with his head facing straight ahead. The music had become more along the lines of what she'd wished for earlier. It sounded Mozartean. It was probably Haydn. When she couldn't quite recognize a Mozart melody in a string quartet, it usually turned out to be Haydn. Claire heard a lot of string quartet music in museums. She spent so much time in them, Claire felt they were her rendezvous points throughout the city. Even when she traveled she tried to find a local museum, large or small, to establish herself there, almost psychically, as some people stop in a homely church to pause for momentary spiritual refreshment, acknowledging with a genuflection or a brush of holy water on the forehead, a glance at the parish bulletin, a brief prayer at a votive candle, announcing quietly, I am here now, among you. I am safe. She had privileges at so many museums around town that for her it was as easy to duck into the Whitney to breathe the contemplative energy of an Agnes Martin hanging there as to pop into Starbucks for a decaf, or into St. Patrick's for a brush with God. Yet she always felt the grace, as it were, of her position, that allowed her to flit amid exalted art almost without thought, yet never without succor.

"What two things?"

"That for my mother, her marriage had been a failure to her even before my father walked out, and that when they were still together she blamed herself. When they were no longer together, she blamed him. Until he died. Then she blamed herself again, and then, I think, me. The other thing was that I was as much a party to their concealment of what had happened as they were. I would not see, I refused to be curious, I did not want change. Remarkable."

"What?"

"That a child could will himself not to know. And yet elsewhere, I devoured books and learning. I lived for a different sort of knowledge. Maybe my father took my solitude as a sign that I was destined for monastic life."

"And you haven't yet proved him wrong."

He looked at her with a trace of wonder. "I haven't spoken so freely in I don't know how long. You have a knack"

"It helps me in my work."

She wondered, what had he thought those many years ago when he, away from home, had heard that their father had left? She had not known Peter and Frank's mother, had nothing but speculation based on her own experience to guide her here, but she felt their mother would have been beyond devastated. She had seen a son into the seminary. She had lost two children, she had another son she had to have known was different. She had no hope of grandchildren—that great desire among mothers that the line continue. She had no one. Even if her marriage had dried into a husk, even if her husband had been carrying on—could she have known? could she have been as stoically ignorant as her son had seemed to be?—still he had remained her husband, and her home still welcomed him at night. She may have been miserable with longing and suspicion, but at least she had a husband. Then, so callously, did he flaunt his so-called better, richer, never-more-productive life before her as he walked out to the mistress in the car. That must have left her breathless. Claire wished someone could have given her some comfort, such as it might have been. It was a sentimental feeling for someone she did not know. But as her mind recalled her own painful if less tragic awareness of her husband's behavior, she descended, she felt, into cheap scenarios of protective, salubrious embraces, cooings of new beginnings, to a woman she would never know. She really should take her own comfort.

"Have you ever shared anything with anyone?" she asked him. "Even when you made your decision to leave the priesthood. Did you talk it over with anyone? Do you have any friends at school?"

"I was both ashamed and angry," he said. "I wanted no one."

"Tell me." She turned to him. "I hope you don't mind me asking this. What did you think when your father left your mother?"

He didn't answer right away; indeed, he seemed just the least little bit taken aback by her question. She wondered if his sudden flush were anger, whether he was going to close up and resume his professorial contemptuousness, even after their small moments of shared, almost unacknowledged pleasure.

"I felt betrayed," he said.

"Did you think about your mother?"

"I felt betrayed. I felt that he had duped me into living his dream. Which was a lie, of course. He didn't know what he wanted. Well, he wanted out. I felt betrayed, and I felt, too, that he escaped. And, for my mother, I felt pity. At the same time, I felt heartless. I couldn't help myself."

"Experience is different for different people," Claire said.

"At that moment, when Peter called to tell me, because my mother didn't," Frank said, "when Peter called to tell me, I felt anger at him. I remember asking him what he'd done to make that happen. I remember feeling he deserved it. I remember feeling, as I said, betrayed. So, no, I didn't share it with anyone. I didn't even pray. I sat, if I remember right, in my little room in the parish house, knowing I had to say Mass, give thanks, enact sacraments I didn't want to be a part of, I didn't want to believe in. I didn't want anything to do with communication, with service. You probably hate me for speaking like this."

"No," she said, looking at him, touching his arm, daring to leave it, sensing the flesh beneath the tweed. "It was excusable. Maybe not compassionate, but understandable."

"You think I'm shut out from understanding," he said, with a slight tremor in his voice, which he was trying to conquer. "Have I been such a monster?" His eyes held her, and she felt, for the first time, something beyond his critical gaze, his appraising look.

"No," she said.

"I feel things and I'm not able to do anything better with myself. I have begun to think that I can't do this alone, that I need the prodding and suggestions of people around me who are sensitive to nuance, to people themselves, people with faith in something beyond themselves. I don't know if it's too late for me to change. I don't know how to be someone who would not think only of betrayal, but maybe of trust."

"Don't say that," Claire said.

"Help me, Claire," Frank said, with urgency and even passion. "Help me. I can't go on being selfish and ignorant and willful. Help me look as you do, who can appreciate what I scorn. I spend my days in books, in regrets, in fantasy. I don't even know how to live." He had not been looking at her as he spoke, but at the rim of the glass he held. With his last words, he turned and looked first quietly at her, then back again to the glass, then the fountain, anywhere but at her face.

She didn't know how to live either, she thought. She had not expected this, certainly. Who expects to be asked for such a thing; such help as she could give would be false, she who had blundered through trust and had lived through betrayal, and had only inch by inch begun to think herself capable of letting down her guard, but fearful of it at the same time. She felt like the Virgin in an annunciation painting herself, as if saying as Mary did, "But I have never known a man," and then being expected to follow blindly the path of faith regardless of such ultimately feeble but true protestations. She had no holy spirit to guide her, no angel of the Lord, but this lonely, sad man. Was his a family of such misfits that they couldn't have relationships with anyone? Had the entire family from father and mother to sons been destroyed by some malaise of self-destructive denial and misplaced longing? No, Peter was as happy as anyone could probably be—he searched for a connection, he really wanted that communing of minds that relationships can foster. But Frank? He was looking to her for guidance, she who had been really only looking to herself for five years, or even more. He had such serious flaws, his anger, his impatience among them, but she found herself aware of how much, really, she kept finding herself wanting to tell him what she knew, about her day, about Adelaide, even, about what she saw and felt and wanted. But how much of this was a mark of her own desperation for a connection, how much her own longing to reconnect to a past through a man related to her former husband? Could she ever escape her past?

"I think," she said, "we've had too much art for one day. I know a restaurant nearby. Let's eat."

# A Hot, Uncertain Breeze

One night was more than enough. Toby had been glad, of
course, to see his parents doing so well. Still overcaffeinated.
Rather more edgy and alert than he'd ever known them, which was
a little disquieting, but oddly entertaining still. For one night. He'd
felt oddly happy being back in L.A., had welcomed again the sun in
his eyes; he'd become too used to the gray and shifting New York
light, which he loved, but he needed this, this brilliant sunshine
muffled by the haze as the day drew on.

He turned onto La Cienega. Thank God he'd rented a convertible. "What led me to this town," he sang to the CD, an old Jayhawks record. Thank God, too, for pop music. He'd begun to chafe
at the higher yearning of the art set he'd surrounded himself with.
So much meaning. Relax, relax. He knew that he was just as likely
to begin tearing up, though, should the song shift into remorse. He
was safe for now, happy in the moment, for now, far away.

And out again of his parents' house.

They had had a little get-together among their A.A. friends for
him. Their A.A. friends were all that they had left—the attrition of
age and the alienating effects of Celia and Bill's years of alcohol
abuse had diminished their circle of pre-recovery buddies. Most of

them weren't part of Toby's life as the old friends had been; he hadn't seen them in his youth, hadn't heard about all but a few—the ones who'd survived and gotten sober—in those long evenings of guffaws and sudden arguments when their parents gave endless cocktail parties that ended like Buñuel movies, chaotic and, to an observer who wasn't a son, bleakly funny. But this new crop of acquaintances, these fellowshippers, as they termed it, were new to him, and ranged, to Toby's surprise, from the breezily decrepit survivors his parents' age to twenty-something actors and studio types who'd blown through trust funds or squandered early promise through drinking and drugging and DUIing. Toby didn't know them, but they certainly knew him. Bill and Celia shared about him, as they said, at meetings, something Toby would probably have found stiflingly mortifying if he thought about it too long, but his parents had assured him they spoke about how they had neglected him, not about his own character flaws. These terms of recovery-speak were often beyond him—character flaws, sharing, faking it till you make it, easy does it, feelings aren't facts, step work—and his parents provided quick glossary definitions, but he hadn't cared to dwell too deeply on the argot that tumbled from their coffee-scented mouths. As in his youth, he tuned them out until they homed in on him and demanded his attention. And unlike the years of his youth, they didn't embarrass him with their behavior. They now embarrassed him in absentia with talk of him, and probably his sister, during the baring of souls in their endless meetings. But they were so happy now, so giving, so unlike who they had been, that he was both charmed and a little frightened by their selfless transparency. He was beginning to learn about them anew, and, in some ways, this unsettled him. He, to an extent, preferred the colorful selfish wastrels of long ago to the motley proponents of sobriety who looked him in the eye and really, really wanted to know how he was.

Bill and Celia had arranged this get-together for Toby, to introduce him to a gaggle of their groupies and, he suspected, to make him feel better about the happy lunatics they spent their days with. They had so wanted Toby to meet Pete H. and Jane S. and Lorrie M. and every other acquaintance with an initial and a 30-day chip. His parents' home had become its own sort of A.A. club, where the gregarious couple could entertain as of old—only without the cocktails and consequences. After meetings, a group of five or six or seven would descend on the homestead, sit around the now-clean pool, and chatter on about their lives, their pasts, their hopes, their struggles. Toby could picture it all, and shuddered inwardly as he shook hands with everyone. They made him claustrophobic, these hopeful losers.

But he really couldn't even think of them that way; they mocked themselves as much or more than he did in his mind. Bill and Celia, more observant than in the past, noticed his hollow smile and rolling eyes and urged him, here and there during the evening and the next morning, to go to Al-Anon, to learn how to cope with the alcoholics in his life. "But there are only two," he had told them. "I don't want to know these other bozos you drag home. It's bad enough I have to translate whatever gibberish you're spouting at each other around me as it is."

"That's not the point, sweetheart," his mother had chirped. "It's really more about you. And it's also about understanding how we alcoholics think."

"I understand how you think," he had said. "And you're both nuts." At which Bill and Celia smiled, which was galling to him. The sympathetic concern of his parents, so new and equally irritating as their forgetful dipsomania, was a new shiv in the prison arsenal of his tortured home life. It had been three years and they had changed wonderfully—the whole program of A.A. was so beneficial to them, he couldn't argue with its success—yet he couldn't help himself dismissing aspects of it as just another product of the stupid self-infatuation of his parents' generation. And besides, his feelings were a fact. What the hell did that mean, anyway? Was what he'd been feeling for the past couple of months anything other than a fact? In any event, with all of this mumbo jumbo floating around, these were arguments he couldn't win. The tautological language of recovery could never be parsed.

"Just try it once," his father had urged, in his role as avuncular paterfamilias, a role Toby hadn't been familiar with when he was growing up. Usually at home Bill had played the teetering professor or the bumbling plumber (or those were the roles that Toby in his youth had assigned to his father whenever he had seen him reeling; he'd pretended they were rehearsing for parts they would never get). "You don't have to stay. It's more about what makes you tick, and how we affected you, and how you cope with it and how we've changed."

"Maybe if we'd gotten sober earlier, you might have been different," his mother had chimed in. "Maybe if you had learned more about yourself, you'd still be with Peter."

"Mom, he left *me*."

"Exactly."

To shut them up, he agreed to try one out. So here he was, heading to a meeting at the base of the Hollywood Hills. It even had a name: As Lois Sees It, for the long-suffering wife of the philandering Bill Wilson, one of the founders of A.A. Why did they have to name these things? A simple address would suffice. But he knew that along with the mania among recovery groups for hortatory sayings was a passion for naming things in cutesy ways. Everything was a joke with these people.

His cell phone whirred. He gave it a quick glance; it was Claire.

"Hello, beautiful," he said brightly.

"I have this feeling you're somewhere that's not here. Are you in a car?" she asked.

"L.A., and you betcha," he said, oddly cheerful.

"Since when?"

"Sorry not to call. Since yesterday. I needed to get away. José and Nestor were driving me crazy."

"But . . ." She paused. "To your parents'?"

He laughed. "I know. But they've been great," he said, a bit ashamed of his inner condemnation.

"That doesn't sound like you," she said.

"I know. I hardly know myself out here again. But it's true. Guess where I'm heading."

"Surprise me."

"An Al-Anon meeting. For people who love alcoholics. Or hate them. I haven't decided. I never thought, never *believed* I'd be going to a self-help meeting voluntarily. That was for Bill and Celia. But they asked. I'm the perfect son and said yes. You still there?"

"Yes," she said. "I just—well, great! I hope it does you good, whatever else."

"If I start speaking about self-empowerment, shoot me."

"That's more like it."

"So," he said, pulling to a stop at a red light. Another convertible pulled up, a middle-aged man in a baseball cap and beard behind the wheel. He was barking into his cell phone, too. Their eyes met without recognition. "How's the sale?" he asked, looking back ahead of him.

"Closing in. I wanted . . . the reason I'm calling, besides seeing how you are, is to ask if you can come to a cocktail party for the sale. We don't usually have them, at least not for most sales, but my bosses have budgeted one in for me, since it might cast some more light on the department. Anyway, I was hoping you could show up, and bring some of your cool friends."

"I don't have any cool friends, Claire."

"Of course you do. Every time I've run into you, except at the Met a few months ago, you were with a gaggle of buddies, you and Peter."

"They're all Peter's friends," he said. "I'm the loner type, I've decided."

"You are not," she said. "See if you can round up some new friends, then. I think you'll have fun."

"Will Peter be there?"

"Probably. I asked him. I hope you don't mind."

"Of course not. It's a big party." They lapsed into a pause.

"Have you spoken with Peter?" Claire asked.

"Not in a week or so. I will, though. I have to," he said.

"He seems happy," Claire said. "He came to the Impressionist sale, with Sean."

"I knew that. From friends who ran into him at a restaurant afterward."

"See? You do have friends."

"I guess. We'll see."

"I liked him," Claire said.

"I'm glad."

"How long are you going to be out there?" Claire asked, after another pause.

"I'm not sure. I just got here. I actually needed to get away from everybody. From friends. The friends I have. Had. No, have. From the sympathy, too. Of course, my parents' new A.A. friends are all sympathy, which also drives me crazy. So there's no escaping sympathy for the boyfriend. Ex-boyfriend."

"Where are you now?"

"La Cienega."

"I mean tonight."

"My friend Jason's. I could only last a night with my folks, as much as I love them. And their terrific, supportive, giving, loving friends. Jason's out here from New York. He was pre-Peter. Friend. Not boyf. He's trying to become a documentary maker. You know, what you do when you can't get a real movie career going. He hasn't done much documentary work but has found some in television. He's got a nice place in the Hills."

"And you'll be there for a week or so? Not prying, just wondering. I hope you can be here next month, that's all."

"Oh, I'll be back. Maybe. I think. A couple of weeks? I really don't know."

"Well," Claire said, "I hope you can get back to New York in time for the party. Even if you don't bring friends, your presence would make it all hipper."

"I'll try," he said. "Really. Even though I'm not feeling that hip these days."

He had felt increasingly unsure of his opinions, and he knew this was because of his own willful disassociation. He existed so much in a contemplative reverie, worrying about where things might lead, what he might do, how he might maintain a certain distance from a depth of emotional commitment, that he had in some ways become an outsider to his own life. He had mocked Claire for what he considered her stasis, living in a past of carefully edited mementos while avoiding the probable chaos of romantic entanglements. Yet he continued to keep himself apart, afraid that were he to allow himself to surrender to the inevitable cozy tedium of a relationship—not that any was on the horizon—he would lose a part of himself that he would be unable to recover. But what part was that, exactly? What he had had with Peter was not, looking back a continent and only months away, so bad. Compared to José and Nestor, he and Peter had been paragons of enlightened commitment. José and Nestor lived a life of fear—fear of losing control over each other. For José it was fear of Nestor's walking out on him again—this had happened twice before and both times unannounced; for Nestor it meant fear of José's furtive philandering and thin-skinned selfishness. When Toby had stayed with them, it was as if his presence heightened the bickering they usually kept in check in public. They had become puppet characters, bashing each other over the head with recriminations as well as that effective long-term relationship tool, silence. They would spend evenings walking around Toby, speaking to each other through him, while he would squirm and long for the comfort of the pullout sofa for an evening of fitful sleep when they finally retired to their bedroom, reluctantly out of sight of a third-party endorsement of their suffering. José's desperate sardonic banter, his unpleasant groping when Nestor seemed safely away, Nestor's mute hostility at the temptation that Toby's presence seemed to create for José, coupled with Nestor's wish to appear the supportive friend through it all, while trying to appear more compassionate in his consideration than José, all made Toby's lingering anxiety over his breakup and his future unbearable. Their hell was just the relationship, or just one of its possible iterations, that he had feared his and Peter's would become, though he and Peter were nothing like José and Nestor.

Yet he marveled again at the renewal of his parents' lives and their lengthy, once bitter, marriage. He had long ago decided that during their drinking days they had stayed together to ensure their mutual torment. Their sullen, sloppy alcoholic prison had informed his own fear of falling into a similar pattern of subjugation and reproach, one not fueled by substance abuse. Yet that had not happened with Peter. What had happened was that Toby's fear had become palpable; he saw little of what he actually lived through and began to live what he had foretold for himself as if it were real. He saw what he might become, like Scrooge with the Ghost of Christmas Yet to Come, rather than what he was. His parents, once they had put booze aside, began to slowly feel their way toward understanding each other better, as they grew, they said, to understand themselves. This he could see. Their self-knowledge Toby didn't care to discover. But Toby also found that his parents had discovered an outlet for their individuality; they had separate friends. They had friends in common, such as their agent, and Bill and Celia each had a group to call one's own. They would talk about their marriage separately in different A.A. meetings, they told him and, it seemed to Toby, they actually liked each other now. He didn't know if it was love as Stockholm Syndrome or a love returned to life after a decades-long dormancy. He found it somewhat dismaying on the phone, and especially in person, to hear them discuss their feelings so matter-of-factly, as if feelings, too, were now palpable objects to be assessed in a world marked by self-acceptance. But feelings aren't facts, he wanted to tell them. What are you two talking about?

So, he wondered, what was he escaping, now that he'd fled to L.A.? New York was certainly big enough to get lost in, as was L.A., and here people didn't expect to bump into you around every street corner. He certainly knew enough people beyond the exasperating José and Nestor, and he did have, he admitted, his own small circle of acquaintances beyond Peter. But, as he'd done with Peter, he realized, he'd retreated, withdrawn, given up.

But he'd promised Celia and Bill he'd attend this stupid meeting. He glanced at the dashboard clock. Half an hour, and he didn't intend to show up early. How did his parents manage to get along, knowing so much about each other? We all need secrets, and they probably still had theirs. And still, despite their new openness with each other and even with him—they'd asked for his forgiveness for their previous behavior—he felt he hardly knew them any more. Their transparency held something back from him—he mistrusted it. Or perhaps he mistrusted his own reaction to it. Peter had a similar quality, Toby realized, only in him it was guilelessness. It could also have been a calculated way of getting what he wanted, a feint of manipulative politeness. He missed him. It hurt to acknowledge that. Peter had moved on to someone he hoped might offer more, and Toby resented that promise of happiness for him. How many times had he wished that Peter would just go away, leave him alone, stop trying to be so, whatever it was, comfortable. How many scenarios had Toby run in his mind that involved a breakthrough of sorts, an actual shouting argument with Peter the conciliator? But Toby had known that the shouting would never come; he hated the drama of it all, though he longed for its release, and Peter would not, refused to, provoke him. Tobias knew, too, that he needed to be aware of any growing annoyance, his carefully controlled temper. He felt that even raising his voice in anger could lead to a loss of control, and wasn't that what he feared most? He couldn't bear to seem at a loss; he feared the specter of cataclysmic rage. So he imagined himself exquisitely outraged with calibrated decibels of venom, detailing his emotional position with logic, cunning disdain, and withering triumph. He knew, though, that were he ever to have confronted his lover with what he believed wrong in their relationship, should he ever have provoked himself to such a state that he might speak unguardedly from the heart, he would not be able to utter a word that wasn't drenched in selfish justification. And yet, Toby only said what he truly thought when he had lost control of himself, and no one wants to hear screams of outrage, however seemingly justified. It was so much easier to say I love you and mean

it, he thought, than to explain the meanings of how that love had
changed or why it needed to. For him, clarification so often mingled with contempt because people couldn't read his mind. No
wonder Peter gave up.

He'd been driving the local streets to the meeting house, like a
tourist, reacquainting himself with the city. It had rained the day
before, a rare thing in an arid year, and the streets were, for now,
clean in the sparkling sun, the air held a momentary freshness, as
L.A. might have done in the early years of the last century. The haze
would likely descend again on the rim of the mountain, but for
now, the sunny clarity gave him, as he scanned the near horizon, the
odd sense of hope he always felt at certain combinations of time and
weather. The breeze had begun to warm, but the sky still burned a
cold blue. "I'm gonna make you love me, I'm gonna dry your
tears," he sang to the Jayhawks, still playing on the CD. As if.

The meeting house was on Lockwood Drive, just outside the
gates to Hollywoodland Realty, with the famous looming mountain sign perched above, comfortably precarious. The house looked
like any number of cheaply constructed pricey apartment com-
plexes that clustered here and there on the soft streets at the base
of the hills, carrying an air of desuetude and cautious hope. Low-
rent recovery in a high-cost city. Did he really want to do this?
He'd promised his parents. They would ask. It would be easier than
dissembling.

An earnest-looking woman wearing her hair too long greeted
him as he reached the top of the open steps to the meeting house,
which was shaded by a rather large eucalyptus tree in the back, its
piney scent wafting around the entrance.

"Welcome," she said, extending her bony hand. "First time?"
She looked as if she'd been mandated into recovery, with pale,
soupy eyes that tried hard to focus on him.

He nodded, she smiled with a wan and knowing look—fellow addicts, aren't we?—and pointed to an open door just to the left of the entry. About twenty people were in the meeting room, their chairs arranged in a large oval. Toby found an empty seat; he'd have preferred sitting somewhere unnoticed, but this layout prevented that. He'd accompanied his parents to a few meetings when they had first gone to A.A., and he remembered how welcome people had made them all. He had been uncomfortable, wanting to tell greeters that he wasn't an alcoholic, although his parents definitely were, but he couldn't bring himself to be so obsessively forthright. Here, alone, amid people he were sure where whiners—like himself, he admitted—he didn't quite know what to feel. This experience, this process, was a disquieting one to him. He rarely discussed anything, really; he and Peter had talked, certainly, and Peter was never at a loss for something to say. But even when he was in a crisis—when his parents had hit bottom and he had flown home to help push them along the road to recovery—he didn't so much talk about what he was doing as say where he could be reached. Peter must have learned his tact from dealing with his own parents—or his glaring, self-absorbed brother. For himself, Toby knew he had acquired a sullen reticence as a defense against his parents' querulous or gushing inebriation. Peter had learned to accommodate as he grew up; Toby had learned to withdraw, while maintaining a semblance of social skills. Peter's brother Frank had withdrawn both intimately and socially. And Claire, who made up this odd quartet of theirs, she herself with her drunken father and scattered, hostile mother, she had become—what? A seeker of truth. He smiled at his cliché.

"First time?" his neighbor asked him. What is it with these people?

He had revealed too much already. No smiling! But he decided to plunge in regardless of the consequences. "Yes," he said, feeling brave, and turned toward the woman who had spoken. She looked about thirty, his age. She wore her hair long, too, again rather too long, compared to what had become fashionable back home, in New York.

"Yes," he said. "My parents are in recovery, and they thought I should check this place out. To help me deal with them," he added, which she probably already knew; she had the look of a regular. "My name is Toby," he added.

"Heather," she said. "Do you live nearby?"

"I'm visiting my folks. Studio City. I live in New York."

"Wow. Great," she said. "Welcome." And their conversation died.

He noticed that most of the people here were women. He should have figured that; most men don't bother to learn to deal with their alcoholic girlfriends or wives. They suffer or leave. He saw a couple of guys who might be gay. Gay men he could understand. So many of them feel they can fix each other. But that wasn't what this was about, his mother had said. This was for understanding alcoholic behavior and one's own reactions to alcoholics. In this way, the Al-Anon reasoning went, one could also perhaps learn aspects of one's own behavior. Snore, snore. Toby wasn't sure what he wanted to learn. He had promised his parents, he kept repeating to himself, as a mantra, like Natalie Wood in "Miracle on 34th Street" repeating "I believe, I believe," to talk herself into the reality of Kris Kringle. And despite the enormous change in their lives, he still hesitated to credit them with any particular insight. They were still somehow like they were in their drinking days, to him, minus the arguments and shards. And yet, like Claire with her selective memory of life with Peter before he came out, with Claire keeping alive a false past through the refraction of an idealized snapshot, he had a picture of Celia and Bill as who they used to be, not who they were now. He hadn't even granted them the dignity, in his mind, of personal growth. He thought his job was done by getting them sober. He hadn't realized that he had in some way to change with them, if he wanted to appreciate them. According to them. People—some people, anyway—kept moving on, becoming more or less, and a person had to adjust. He realized that with Peter he had wanted both to keep a certain status quo—though he would have been hard-pressed to try to define exactly what that consisted of—and to avoid being trapped in a relationship that was, in his words during one silent spat, "going nowhere."

"My name is Aimee," said a woman with a kabuki pallor. "Welcome to this twelve-fifteen meeting of Al-Anon. I just want to talk a little bit today about acceptance."

He had been so lost in thought he'd missed the beginning of the meeting, the reading of this and that that he'd remembered from meetings with his parents. Or maybe these meetings just started, like automatic nightlights. Again his mind had begun to drift— maybe these meetings led to self-examination through daydreams— and he missed part of her talk. He forced himself to pick up her conversational thread and vowed to himself to pay attention.

". . . so it's like, I know maybe he does too much crystal, and I know I can't make him change. He's a tweaker. I know that. But I don't know how to put up with him any more. The sex is great, but then I feel he's just doing it to kill time, he's so stoked . . . then Roger disappears and two days later I get the same old phone call, he's somewhere in the desert, holed up and wasted, and he wants me to come drive him home 'cause some other tweaker bitch he scored with ran off with his bike. . . ." Heads nodded in appreciation. Toby was suddenly fascinated.

Aimee didn't look as if she turned down the chance to tweak, herself—or turn down anything, really—but she had a kind of hard vulnerability that touched him. What did she hope to get out of this little talk? Affirmation that she was a doormat? Or did speaking her story aloud help her see how absurd her situation was? Compared to her life of desperation and car trips, he himself had nothing to complain about.

He wondered what Aimee did, how she managed to go on in a life of such desperate drama—scoring, not scoring, getting clean, hoping her sex fiend Roger would stay calm enough to keep it together. He knew he wanted a sort of drama in his life, but one that didn't involve his actually doing anything. And he had begun to squirm with discomfort in his own comfortable relationship because he thought it had been so static. He'd been looking for drama, instead of actually paying attention to what was going on. Not that he and Peter hadn't lived; theirs was a glamorous existence of sorts, with parties, art openings, travel. He still couldn't isolate his dissatisfaction and name it. Its elusiveness was as frustrating as the feeling itself. And he had been told in the past day that feelings weren't facts. Whatever.

And what was Aimee here looking for? She was still going on about her tweaker boyfriend with the apologetic defiance of someone who knows she's wrong and feels that a brave face will help her see otherwise. She looked about fifty, and her skin had a glossy sheen, as if she'd been lubricated with a mineral oil mist, though Toby thought he heard her say she was thirty-five or something like that. She'd done a lot of hard living.

"Thank you, Aimee," said a speaker whose name Toby didn't catch. This speaker handed a basket around for contributions for rent and such, and asked if any newcomers were present. Heather looked at Toby. "Toby," Toby said, raising his hand a little. "Visiting from New York."

"Welcome!" said several voices.

"We'll start our round-robin. Toby," the speaker said. "Let's begin with you."

He looked at the speaker in a panic. "We'll talk about acceptance, as Aimee outlined," the speaker said.

Is that what she did? He thought she'd talked about how hopeless her life was.

He sighed. "Well," he said. "Acceptance," he said, buying time to gather his thoughts. He had no idea he'd be compelled to speak. He'd brain his parents. "I'm actually here, I mean, this is my first Al-Anon meeting."

"Welcome!" said several other people.

"And I'm here because my parents . . . they live here . . . I'm from here . . . and they've been sober about three years. I'm visiting, and they thought I should maybe take in a meeting." He paused. They expected him to go on, were looking at him with mute encouragement. He looked around the circle, just above the eyes of the people sitting there, not wanting to meet their gazes. Trapped. "Anyway," he said. "I just came in from New York. My boyfriend left me," heads nodded in sympathy, "and I was at loose ends and flew back to see how my folks were doing. I helped them get sober, and their lives have completely turned around. They're actors"—more nods—"and last night, well, anyway, they had a party of all their A.A. friends, and they said I should take in a meeting to see what it was like. My boyfriend wasn't an alcoholic— I mean, isn't—my ex-boyfriend, I mean—so I'm not here for him, but I don't really know, frankly, what I'm supposed to get out of this, but I promised, so here I am. As for acceptance, well, I guess I'm going to have to live with what happened with me and Peter. My boyfriend. Ex. Boyfriend. We were together for about five years and, well, it wasn't working out, so he found someone else. History." Toby realized he had been painting Peter as a cad of sorts, when he knew that wasn't what he wanted to convey. He also realized he was talking about Peter to a bunch of strangers, which shocked him. He became aware of himself. "So—acceptance. I'm working on it."

"Thank you," several people murmured.

"I agree with what Toby was saying," said one woman, who sat on the other side of him from Heather and whose name was Janelle. "When my husband picked up someone at a bar, and I found her number, I thought my world was ending." Her voice faded as he stopped listening, horrified that he'd set in motion a chain of recollections about drunken infidelities, which was different from his own experience, and not what he had hoped to do at all. He had come off as an injured party, and had before this admitted to himself that he couldn't do that, either to himself or to Peter, as sorry as he had felt for himself a couple of months earlier. Well. This would be the testing-the-waters meeting. Maybe he'd try one back in New York. He was already thinking of getting back. That was something.

When the meeting ended about a half-hour later, several people came over to him to offer phone numbers and consolation. "Call anytime," said one rather cute man named Cal who appeared to be about his age. "I know what you're going through," he said, looking at him with dreamy pale blue eyes.

He couldn't know, but that didn't matter. People usually spoke about what they wanted to hear themselves, no matter what another person said. Toby's rambling about Peter had been on his mind, and he'd said just enough to give the wrong impression, if indeed it was the wrong impression. He wasn't sure any longer. And just enough to trigger everyone else's relationship troubles. But that's what this stuff was all about, wasn't it? Botched relationships. Self-awareness, maybe. There was a bit too much of that going around.

How easy it would be to fall into an attitude of patronizing weariness about the meeting and the earnest, helpful, rather too egocentric people who populated it. But he, too, was as self-absorbed as any of them, if less aware than they of what it was that made him tick. Maybe he'd learn, if not about himself, at least something about his parents, who now seemed so different. They were sharper in outline yet softer in touch. It was as if an absence of rancor had forced them to live on other emotions, whatever they were, and discover new ways of expressing themselves.

Maybe, too, he'd find out something about himself, although he also had to admit he wasn't eager to uncover the roots of either his rage or his reluctance to express himself. He knew how foolish he was; on the hunt for the new in his profession, yet conflicted elsewhere. People were a mix of regret and futility and frustration and longing. How little he knew Peter. He had hardly thought of him as a person between those electric moments when they had first been attracted to each other and were inflamed by desire that was both furtive and pent up, and when he had learned from Peter himself that their lives together were over. In between he had come to think of him as simply another body, a hindrance to whatever his idea of contented happiness might be, and whoever knows that. Their lives had become living together, the décor, the restaurants, the vacations, but it was less an exploration of each other, at least on his part, than a commodification of a relationship. And so often he had let himself stew with unspoken resentments, because he couldn't or wouldn't articulate whatever it was he wanted. Part of that was because he honestly did not know. Another, bigger, part was his inability, his refusal, to express himself except by omission. How frustrating it must have been for Peter. Still, it took two to louse up a relationship. He did regret how he had couched his remarks earlier, his first impression among these people would be the guy whose boyfriend had left him. But hadn't that been his characterization of himself these past few months? Hadn't that been why he'd fled to L.A.? Hadn't that possibly been a reason for his parents insisting that he take even this action, this 12-step whatever to get him outside himself?

He had toyed, briefly, with the idea of relocating out here again, to be near his parents, aging as they were. The art scene was certainly lively enough. In terms of contemporary art, California was often given too little credit, considered merely an entertainment market, with art tacked on, and the Industry sapping the creative energy out of the other arts. He didn't necessarily agree, and he didn't think it was a bad thing in any event. For himself, though, he felt he belonged in a living world, one where people visited, in which there was an interchange. Movies were fine, but not really for him. The gallery life excited him. Like his parents, he guessed, who were theatrical beings, thriving on the give-and-take of live performance, he liked the theater of the gallery installation. He loved this city, but still found its fine-art scene a little wan, a diaspora of tired, sun-bleached talent. He needed to find his center again—was this a lapse into recovery-speak?—but it couldn't be through escape.

"So?" his mother greeted him on his return home to pick up his things. As usual, she was making a fresh pot of coffee. His father was in the basement, rehearsing lines for a walk-on he'd won in a television crime drama. He was reluctant witness number two.

"It was interesting," Toby said, lapsing into the noncommittal tone he always used to assume around his parents.

"Did you meet anyone nice?"

"Mom, it wasn't a date meeting."

"You know what I mean."

"I said hello, got some numbers."

"Did you share?"

"I did," he said, after a few seconds. They were quiet for a moment.

His mother nodded at him, approving. "Coffee?" He took a cup. "It's a start," she said.

"It was."

His mother poured some milk into his mug and added more coffee to top it off. "I'm glad you went. Thank you." She kissed his cheek.

He suddenly felt as if he wanted to cry. He wasn't ready yet for genuine emotion, even from his mother. She'd barely said anything, had, in fact, been tactful, for her, and her reticence had made him realize how his own guardedness had defined their relationship, all his relationships, for so long. It had been so essential to him, this reserve, that its preservation mattered more than whatever he was protecting underneath, a torment of feeling he had chosen to suppress. He was afraid to speak right now, as if, like his occasional outbursts of rage, he would regret saying too much, showing too much, and so, indeed, becoming open to interpretation, becoming, even fleetingly, known.

"I'm glad I went too," he said, softly, and left the kitchen to seek a temporary refuge amid the dusty banners and flotsam of his childhood bedroom. To pretend, for just a moment longer, that he was still alone in the world.

# KINDERTOTENLIEDER

H e had made her defensive and, as always, his first thoughts were regret, followed by annoyance. His third, inexplicably, was longing. He knew with the certainty of someone who'd been much more a part of the world than he had that if he could have examined his actions in a book, if he could have been a probing, searching Deronda, he might have assessed his hero's motivation with detachment. But his experience lay with discarded dogma and old literature; and his own life, only now seriously examined beyond his frustrating years of vocation and its rejection, was so deliberately circumscribed that he could not trust his own instincts. People as they aged knew the social signals, could read, or at least thought they could, the conflicting emotions that drove the actions of friends, lovers, associates. Or ex–brothers-in-law. But he had been as sheltered in some ways as the most cosseted athlete or pop star; in his case, he hadn't mistaken the fawning of fans or yes-men as a true indication of feeling, kept from reality by a carapace of meretricious idolatry. He had no circle of friends; but life amid the seminarians and parishioners seemed to exist in an adjacent universe, as did the academic shuffle of class, students, and colleagues. But he still was unsure of the reality of his perceptions. He hadn't, come to think of it, mistaken academia for the real world, either—not that he could ever, not with the campus life as one alternatively flickering neon sign of air quotes and earnestness. His life was as real as anyone's, yet his relation to it had been almost tangential; he had yet to grasp both what it was he wanted and what it was he had experienced. He couldn't fathom the meanings of his past, though he replayed scenes from it often, and looked over and again at what he had lived through without fully absorbing it, as one does housework to the muted babble of a television documentary, picking up the odd fact here and there, but losing sight of the argument. Frank saw, in the weeks since he had blurted out his plea for help—and he still winced at the thought of it—that because he could never articulate his unhappiness, no, it wasn't just that, because he had never fully recognized his sense of intellectual, even emotional purpose, he had mistaken his shapeless general resentments for a life of missed opportunities. Yet he had been so impatient with his own curiosity, had, in fact, tamped it down so continuously, that he had never nurtured a part of himself that could lead to understanding and growth. Even during those interminable years of religious study, he had brushed away doubts as unworthy; he had learned or become accustomed to ignoring any flicker of inner conflict to the point where he assumed a demeanor of disdain. No wonder Claire was so guarded with him.

And yet this whole exercise in opportunistic corporate strategizing through the shrewd devotion of St. Teresa had been his way in, he thought, to a greater understanding of himself—using her genuine and canny work ethic and mystical nature to create a guidebook for the businessperson who liked to look to religion, or to religious leaders, for ways to strengthen their executive paths and for him not to renew his faith, but for a glimmer of how her determined pursuit of a higher good could lead to a sense of ease with oneself. He hoped that writing what was essentially a glib examination of corporate structuring and employee motivation through the example of a sainted mystic would lead to his own earthly exaltation, perhaps. What it did, too, was give him a concrete reason for a sabbatical and a chance to be in New York and to be nearer to Claire. Admitting that was surely progress, was it not? Mixed motives were a mark of intellect.

For the past couple of weeks, with Claire increasingly occupied in finalizing her sale, Frank had devoted himself to finishing his admittedly not very long manuscript for his book. He was driven to complete it to allow himself more time to think about what to do next. He had several months to decide whether to return to school, whether to look for some other position, whether anything with Claire might actually work out. A lot depended on her. And he hadn't even told her how important she had become. He beat around the bush, embarrassed by his longing, never having truly sought the comfort of someone else, preferring usually to brood about what might be. He and she had spoken briefly since their meeting at the Frick and dinner afterward, but he didn't want to impose on her again when her professional life consumed so much of her time right now.

At that fraught dinner after their walk through the galleries, with him paralyzed with uncertainty about whether he should have asked her for her thoughts on how he should proceed—what he should do, essentially, for her to want him—they had—or he had—loosened up after a while, and they had managed to talk of other things, of his school work, of his academic colleagues, of the rewards of her job. They spoke of her sister, of their adult rivalry. Her parents. And they spoke, too, of Peter. Frank had, with typical insularity, assumed that since their divorce, Claire and Peter had been less friendly than they turned out to be. Frank thought that because he had chosen to ignore his brother for so long, she, with more justification, had acted similarly and had expunged Peter and those memories. That hadn't been so, obviously, but Frank had not realized how much Peter still mattered to Claire; he was no longer her husband, but she still loved him. Most divorced couples rarely even spoke to each other, and Frank had assumed that when the husband was gay, a different kind of acrimony entered into the split and its aftermath. He knew of one man whose wife was so bitter about their divorce, about her husband's coming out, that a sympathetic judge had granted her alimony for life, no matter that the children were grown, that she had a job and enough money to survive. She wanted revenge. What Frank hadn't counted on here was Claire's capacity for forgiveness, even if she tended, too, to dwell a bit in the past. Neither had he considered his brother's ability to smooth things over. Because Frank was so abrupt, when he wasn't feeling apologetic about his abruptness he assumed others were as likely as he to burn bridges.

"I think you've got to deal with Peter," Claire had finally said, over coffee.

He'd stirred his milk into the cup and hadn't answered at first. "We're so different," he finally said. "How am I supposed to approach him?"

"You're brothers. He's a part of your life. You don't have to be friends. I'm never going to be my sister Catherine's best buddy, but I respect that she's my sister, even if she drives me crazy."

"I respect that Peter's my brother. That doesn't mean we have to be in each other's face."  .

"You know nothing about Peter except what you've assumed up in your mountain home. If you end up hating each other, fine."

So he had, after a week of dithering, called Peter to meet him at his apartment. He had hoped to make it a quick visit for coffee, but

Peter had insisted on an actual evening together, with dinner. Frank hoped the new boyfriend wouldn't show up.

"You made it!" his brother said with his usual cheer when he opened the door; Frank smelled something cooking. Peter held the door for Frank, letting him in, and touching him on the arm with a little pressure as he passed, following their handshake. They had never been particularly physical with each other, and Frank noticed the contact. "Thanks for coming."

Peter's hall was lined with bookshelves that held more volumes than Frank had expected; he didn't remember Peter being a reader. As he went by, he saw books of literature, a guide to Shakespeare, a biography of Proust, auction catalogs, furniture books, cookbooks. He was tempted to say, "Have you read all these?," something non-academics often asked of him, but he stopped himself. Instead he said, "Nice collection," with a touch of envy. Peter's tastes were wider than his own.

"I think it's coming together," Peter said.

"I didn't think you'd had so many books."

"Just for show," Peter said. "The porn's hidden behind them. Just kidding. Anyway, come on in, I'll show you around."

The hall opened onto a large living room to the right, with enormous windows looking out onto Ninety-ninth Street. The bedroom was farther along the hall, with another room next to it, a study. The décor was kind of English—lots of wood—which was about as much as Frank's untutored eye could detect.

"We kept it simple," Peter said, as Frank looked around. "Toby and I. Our tastes were different, but since I was, well, am, the furniture person, we kind of went my way a little more. I would sell the good stuff," he added, seeing Frank run his finger along a sideboard. "Are you interested in any of this?"

"Not really," Frank said, and managed a half smile.

"I didn't think so. No problem. But it's comfortable here. Make yourself at home."

Frank had gone to an upright piano that faced a wall that abutted the den. He picked up a framed photo next to a small vase that held three fragrant white hyacinths. "I had totally forgotten about this," he said, looking at himself years before.

"Bring back memories?"

"Well, yes. But more. It was so long ago." He paused. "Another life."

They both eyed the photo, which showed Frank at about twenty, wearing a shy grin and a surplice. He was in seminary. Upstate. Two decades past.

"I'm surprised you still have it, or even that you found it."

"Call me sentimental. The thing is, though, that I don't have any recent photos. And anyway, that was how I remembered you. I could have chosen one from the wedding, but, you know how it is."

"Of course." He picked up another photo, a color shot of his parents, in a silver frame. "How long ago was this taken?" The tones were still bright, though faded, like a dream. His father had the laughter of a careless moment; this didn't seem a staged grin and grip photo, but one taken at random, at just that instant when joy isn't self-conscious and the face assumes a mask of pleasure for the camera. His mother had the half-annoyed expression he remembered so well, irritated at the suggestion of some frivolity beyond her ken. "They look so different than I remember," Frank said.

"We all do."

"I mean from each other," Frank said. "Looking at this, you could probably predict their marriage was troubled."

"I know," Peter said. "It's easy to read into. In a way, that's why I like it—I'd much rather have this, as prophetic as it turned out, than a posed wedding portrait. They're all in a box some-

where. Even though they're at odds and ends, and their tempera-
ments so different, visibly, they're alive. And there's something a
little poignant, too. As if Mom suspected something and didn't
want to spill."

Frank looked up from the photo and around the sunny room
which, he noticed, was filled with photographs displayed in bijou-
like frames, important mementos, chosen artifacts of life. He recognized very few people, no one, really, except Toby, whom he
remembered from years past, and Claire, in what looked like a
recent shot. "No wedding photo of you, either," Frank said, dryly.

"Well, you know, Frank, I do have them somewhere. Claire does,
too, I'm sure. But even she doesn't have hers up. We're still part of
each other's lives, though, as you probably figured. Don't you have
any pictures of Mom and Dad, or anyone?"

"No," he said. "I never thought about it."

"That sounds cold."

"It wasn't deliberate," he said. "I just didn't bother." Peter
didn't say anything, but something in his expression urged Frank
on. "I don't know why I never wanted any. It's not that I don't
remember. I never take photos. I don't own a camera. It's as if the
past lives in little snapshots somewhere in my mind, and I don't
need anything to prompt me. But then, seeing these, I don't know
what to think. Really, it never occurred to me. I've got some post-
cards up."

"Then you do have friends," Peter said.

"A few."

"Anyone you can share your thoughts with? Or just people you
talk about work to?"

He didn't answer. He felt it better not to reveal, although by this
time it was obvious that he really couldn't name anyone as a friend,
a true friend, a confidant. He had hidden too much and, during the

years of his vocation, kept so much at bay that opening up was not an option among the people he knew. Someone might have found out his doubts. Someone might have discovered his failings. Someone might have, with casual, unsuspecting friendliness, seen into his heart even though his unhappiness was manifest in every stilted gesture, every stifled snarl, every tortured pause.

"What does your place look like?"

"Well," he said, after considering for a moment. "Not decorated, anyway. Not like this. When you lived like I used to, things were arranged for you, or you moved into furnished rooms. Now, it's comfortable. Secondhand odds and ends. Books. It's home, I guess."

He knew this sounded odd, and yet he wasn't deliberately ascetic. Or maybe it was just privacy, his eschewing personal items that might tell of himself to visitors, the very few he had. Here he was, on the far side of forty, feeling again at a disadvantage regarding his younger brother. Peter had such an ease about him, was so adult, in ways Frank hadn't even begun to consider, concerning how he lived his life.

His brother seated himself on one of two sofas that formed an **L** at the other side of the room, taking advantage of the light that washed in, Frank thought, and realized he never thought about his own rooms this way. An ideal spot for reading, even for letting the afternoon fade behind one's head. He'd have to reassess his apartment. Though he probably would change nothing.

Peter had one arm thrown on the back of the couch, and his legs crossed, comfortably casual. Frank stood at the piano, picture in hand. He felt himself scrutinized, not unkindly, and felt, too, that he could see himself here, oddly waifish amid the muted sophistication of his brother's home. Frank had never thought about creating a home, beyond calling it so because it was where he slept. Here, his brother lived amid the cozy acquisitions of someone who knew the value of things, and for once Frank didn't mentally sneer at Peter's profession as typical for gay ne'er-do-wells with an artistic eye. It seemed his brother lived as someone who thought about objects, value, their place in one's life, the physicality of things, their dimensions, their personal meanings. Frank wondered if his own lack of thought about such things was in some way a squandering of what might be important in life. But these were just things. Still, Frank didn't even have things. To ignore the physical effects of life had been to him a cause, a martyrdom of resentment and vouchsafed hostility; his calling, such as it had been, had allowed him to ignore the world. Later, his abrogation of this vocation had given him leave to resent the world because he had been wronged by it. He had denied himself the idea of comfort with all the smug self-laceration of a deluded penitent. What rewards lay in his own stark deluded simplicity? His longing now for a chance caress, his heightened awareness of his brother's casual half embrace, shamed him. Not for the desire of contact, but for the knowledge of his ignorant denial. Oh, what he refused to see in his life!

Frank knew his was a nature that was alternatively reserved and admonitory. And yet he was cowardly, in that he usually only voiced opinions when he was sure of not being contradicted. No; that wasn't entirely true. He had a defiant streak—why else abandon his vocation—and he could argue his field among colleagues. Outside of that rather narrow area, he grew hesitant, felt uninformed. He had been the person dispensing advice in the past, too, by rote, by the book, without too much worldly knowledge, rather than being the person seeking counsel—until very recently. He had not considered how much he had wanted the sort of friend to whom he might possibly unfold himself, open himself, someone else who would know what it was to have sustained private regrets and could understand or sympathize with another person's emotional byways, who could regard the qualms another felt in his self-worth. His brother, whom he barely knew yet had begun to appreciate, if not yet admire, would not likely be one with whom he might share his heart's desires. Yet he was someone he might be able to trust.

Because Frank had so often thought in absolutes, he had mis-represented his brother's past actions, or had thought of them as misguided moral choices rather than what they most likely had been, a grappling toward understanding. He had considered Peter's mar-riage a moral failure rather than a lapse in judgment or even just a mistake. Or even a phase of his life that was valid in itself for a while. Frank had come to know that Claire had needed no help from Frank those years ago, hadn't needed Frank to side with her against Peter, as he had tried to have her do. Their marriage, its dissolution, their feelings toward each other were not his business. He had been jealous of their intimacy, he realized, and angry at Peter for squandering what he himself so yearned for at the time, and did now.

"Did Claire ask you, by the way, to see me?" Peter said from the couch. Frank realized he'd been lost in thought, holding the photograph.

"Have you spoken with her?"

"Not today. She's pretty swamped. By the way, are you going to the party next week? I'll be there."

"I haven't told her. But probably."

"She always liked you, you know, Frank," Peter said.

"I like her too." He made as if to sit near his brother, thought better of it, and remained standing. "Do you have anything to drink? Water?"

"How rude of me," Peter said, jumping up. "We'll eat in a little while, too."

"I don't know how to talk about Claire," Frank said, after

drinking from the tumbler Peter handed him. "Up to a point. Well, any point. Especially with you." Peter walked back to where he'd been sitting. He indicated the facing couch with his hand, but Frank shook his head. He couldn't sit just yet. As in a classroom, he needed to stand to think. He hardly knew what he was about to say, but standing somehow made it safer.

"Claire means a lot to me," Peter said.

"I know."

"Still. Despite how things worked out. We're better off, of course, though your old Church wouldn't have believed that. I know you judged me back then, back in your vestal priestly days, and you probably still do," Peter said. "But you could never know what it was like for me. For us. Whatever you may have thought at the time was nothing compared to what I thought myself, about myself. About what I was doing to someone I loved." Peter rose to get some water for himself; Frank pulled back as he passed, as if avoiding his touch. He had merely stepped to get out of the way, but moved too quickly. "Don't worry," Peter said, noticing his movement. "I won't get too close."

Frank turned toward the kitchen. "That's not it—"

"I said don't worry," Peter said. "You know, when you left the priesthood, I didn't judge you. At all. I'm not a saint. Believe me. But I'd learned to appreciate that how others go through life is their business. It was your life. And it meant nothing to me—I mean, I didn't want you to be unhappy, but it was your decision. Just as my marriage had been mine. Ours. Claire's and mine." Returning to the couch, he said, "Tell me. Did you learn from what you'd done, from your decision to leave?"

Frank looked at his brother's face, searching for a meaning he couldn't discern. Finally, he said, "Just that I'd wasted a lot of time. That I'd done what Dad had wanted. Not what I had wanted. I didn't know what I wanted. Only in bits in pieces, but nothing whole. Only in negative capabilities, so to speak, only in what I didn't want. I've only ever known what I didn't want. Not what I did or even do." He leaned against the frame of the arch separating the living room from the hall. "What did you learn from your marriage, from leaving?"

"That I couldn't be, speaking of negative capability, what I'd married to be." He paused. "And you still judge me, don't you? I shouldn't care. I'd gotten used to it. But there you have it."

"Every time I've seen you, you've been antagonistic," Frank said.

"No," Peter said. "Every time I've seen you, you've retreated from me. That's different."

"What do you want from me?"

"The question is what do you want, Frank? Is this about us, you and me, brothers, or is it about Claire?"

"Claire has nothing to do with it."

"Claire has everything to do it. You don't suddenly show fraternal affection because you've been here for three months and decided to call me."

"I can't say what made me decide. So Claire suggested it. What's wrong with that? I've been wrong before. Don't you think I'm capable of trying to put things right?"

"I don't know," Peter said. "I don't know you, after all. Except that maybe this is the easiest way to prove to Claire that you're really not a loser." He shook his head. "Sorry."

"Don't be. Nothing is easy," Frank said, in an irritated manner. "Nothing has ever been handed to me. I did what I thought was the right thing to do. I did what I had been told. I did what I was supposed to until I couldn't any longer. That's what I learned when I left. That I couldn't live that life. It was wrong to keep plodding away at something I hated so much, and I hated it not because I didn't believe—everyone always thinks that—but because I didn't believe myself worthy to be what I was. Do you know what it's like to hate yourself?"

"Do you know what it's like to be hated?" Peter said.

"I do," Frank said, after a pause.

"You couldn't," Peter said. Peter had moved closer to his brother, but seated himself again on the sofa by the window. "But that's not something I want to go into," he said, looking to his right, to a small watercolor on a dainty little easel, beside yet another photograph of friends unknown to Frank. The watercolor showed a spare beach scene and was, Frank thought, probably more expensive than anything he had ever owned in his life. Even his car. As if that mattered. Peter turned his eyes away from the seascape and looked up at his brother across the room.

"I did come here for you," Frank said, finally. "Even though Claire said I should try. It was something I knew I needed to do."

"Or else?"

"Or else nothing. I had to do it." He walked to the sofa, and sat, across from his brother. "It was time for a change. Before anything else."

"Anything being—"

"Before anything else. That's all." He didn't want to tell Peter about asking for Claire's help. Help for something he couldn't quite articulate. The asking, the desperation that had driven him to do it, had been so monumental a change for him, this letting down of his guard, even so briefly, to ask for guidance. He sensed that Claire had understood, even though she had been discomfited by his questions, she had understood that his asking itself was a leap forward. His actual request implied more than the question of help did itself. For them, the two of them. He also wondered how much of his life had been motivated by what he'd only half articulated. Frank had felt in the past a certain sense about himself that something wasn't quite right, that his choices, if such they had been, were an aim to please. Even that was a choice, he knew. What he felt was that his choices had been his means of keeping an equilibrium, avoiding any confrontation with his father about what he might actually like to explore in life. Frank suddenly recalled one clear hot summer afternoon, at that hour when the light and shadow seemed equal. It had been a Friday, and his father had come home early. Frank had been eight, perhaps, and now, thinking back, he realized that it had been two years before Peter had been born and probably around the time of the death of one of his two unknown barely born sisters. Frank had been reading on the front porch, *A Separate Peace,* he recalled, that tract for precocious, sensitive boys. He had probably been a little too young for it, yet he had known this book was cherished by certain other children he admired, who were a little older, and had known to seek it out in the telepathic manner of adolescents.

"You have such gifts," his father had said. He'd been watching Frank from behind, in the doorway, a glistening highball in his hand. "You can do anything."

Frank had been pleased but embarrassed. He appreciated the recognition but hadn't ever believed the praise, especially since it had come at odd fulsome moments, often around cocktail time and usually interrupting something Frank would rather have been doing. He had hoped his father wouldn't ask what he was reading, another unwelcome intrusion on his precious solitude. Frank looked at his father, then his book, then closed it and put it away. His father sat opposite him, placing his sweating glass on the tile floor next to the wicker rocker he'd chosen. "Come here," his father had said, extending his arms. Frank reluctantly rose and approached his father, who pulled him toward him and hugged him. "You have so much, Frank," he whispered. "You're so special." His father embraced him tightly, breathing down the back of Frank's head; Frank could feel his words down the neck of his T-shirt. "Do you know what you can do? Do you? Frank? Do you?" Frank had said a muffled "no," under the grasp of his father's forearms, but his father hadn't heard, or ignored him. "You could work for the government. With your gift for languages, you could work for the CIA. You could teach. You could be a leader of men. You could go far. Your mother and I want what's best for you. We want you to be happy. We—" and he choked back a sob. "You're our special boy," his father had said to him, softly, to Frank's intense discomfort. After another length of silence, he said, "Your mother hasn't been herself lately." Frank had thought she had been visiting her sister, as she'd done a couple of years earlier, to let Frank and his father have some "guy time" for themselves. At least that had been the story.

"Is Mom okay?" Frank managed to ask, panicked, through the clench.

"She'll be fine, she'll be fine," he had said. "She'll be home soon." His father held him for endless minutes. "You're our special boy," he said again, finally releasing him, and picking up his cocktail glass.

"I don't want to be special," Frank had said.

"Think about what you want to do, Frank. Life is hard."

"When?"

"When you're older." He hadn't said anything further at that point, merely looked sorrowfully into Frank's uncomfortable eyes. Frank had thought, as children often do, that he'd done something wrong that he'd been unaware of, had been forgiven and brought back to the fold with this little scene. His father occasionally afterward would drop little hints about future career paths, and had begun to add priesthood to professor or CIA analyst or whatever it was that they had been called in those days. A couple of years later, after Peter had been born, his father had begun to speak of Frank's entering the priesthood with a little more directness, rather than hints. Now, knowing that his mother's visits to her sister were most likely a cover-up and maybe a recuperation from the deaths of his newborn never-known sisters, Frank considered these scenes differently. Had his father's urging of a vocation that Frank would ultimately prove unsuited for been driven by a wish, then, to prevent him from being a disappointed father? As if celibacy were a cure for anything. Had his father's cryptic comfort been a result of his mother's miscarriages? Or had his father at that point, even with another addition to the family, begun to think of, to wish for, another life? Maybe he thought that if he could get a son into the priesthood, his chances were better than average of being forgiven for future transgressions. He was someone who believed in his religion but had chosen to ignore its tenets, and hoped for salvation through some other means.

Frank had known unhappily married men who were proud parents. One colleague in his department at college, with a newborn girl, still made ominous remarks, when kept at planning meetings, about his wife's irritability when he was late. That old ball-and-chain routine never spelled sweet home life. Even Frank, clueless as he was about those around him, could sense that. Had his father been like that? Had the misery of living with his increasingly distant, disappointed mother outweighed even the possible joy of reborn fatherhood? Our parents' secrets are ones we shouldn't really know, he thought; but that was beside the point here. Theirs had been a family not of secrets, so much, as of recesses; no one looked beyond the surface. Frank certainly hadn't. He had never learned to question, in ways that might have befitted himself; that is, he had never sought to understand the nature of casual deception, nor to separate calculated secrecy from self-denial, from not only how we deal with each other, but ourselves. His family, his parents, kept so much from each other that Frank had become used to withholding information from himself. Peter's own path to self-discovery must have opened in him an appreciation of the same in others. Had Frank dismissed his brother's coming out and divorce with scorn because of offhand belittlement, or because he had envied his brother's grasp of self-awareness? Likely both.

He and Peter had lapsed into a silence that was not exactly companionable, but neither was it antagonistic. "You know," Frank finally said, "I came down here to the city for a few things. I needed a break. I wanted to try to write this book. I wanted to see, maybe, if I could connect with Claire. I hadn't thought of you. Let me put it this way, I tried not to think of you."

"But I wouldn't let you," Peter said.

"The thing is," Frank said, getting up and going back to the piano where the photo of their parents stood, "I still would have avoided you, if it weren't for Claire. I have to admit, I hated my past. You reminded me of it. Claire reminded me of it in a way that was less painful, or equally painful, or maybe one more tie to whatever it was I think I want in life. I really have no clue." He considered the photo. "There's so much about our lives I don't know, and didn't know even when I was there."

"You mean the miscarriages. The *'Kindertotenlieder.'*"

"Don't think that hasn't occurred to me," Frank said, surprised again at his brother, what he knew, or sensed. People looked for instances in their lives when they could absolve themselves of responsibility, such as he had done, perhaps. "You know that song where she sings, 'this misfortune has happened only to me.' That was Mom, I think." He remembered those bleak visits to her while Peter was at college. "And Dad was the father who still sees his kids in the sunshine despite their being dead."

"But that doesn't have to be you," Peter said. "You don't have to live in loss, or in a dreamland."

Frank ran his finger along the top of the photo of his younger self. "I never looked happy, did I? I'm surprised you found this one shot of me smiling."

Peter didn't say anything.

Frank turned to him. "We have a lot to talk about."

# THE TRIUMPH OF BACCHUS

I t was going to be cheese straws. She had to live with them. Claire had hoped to get the catering department to offer actual canapés, but the head of specialists nixed that. "Be happy you're getting a reception for a day sale," he had told her. "And no one ever eats at these things anyway." She was grateful for the party but knew that cheap food signaled cheap works—many in the art world thought with their palates. The glamorous evening sales were really only for Impressionist, modern, and contemporary works, the newsmakers with the big-ticket prices. Hers was important enough for her, for the auction house up to a point, for the consigners, but merely a blip in the annual budget, and this reception was her department's nod to her having put together a selection of works likely to keep the black ink black and the prospective clients interested in the nineteenth century, in representational art of another era, in middling works that had charm if not depth and a few pieces of actual worthwhile art.

This sale might realize $20 to $24 million, at her best estimate. Her stars were Tissot, the Courbets, a Bouguereau, a few others. Her lesser lights were still likely to be snatched up by newcomers with a taste for the near-old, designers with foyers to fill and dealers with a client list. She'd put together an intelligent sale, she thought, with a broad selection, but, at one hundred and five lots, perhaps a little too big. She couldn't help herself. She wanted to include so many items, even the profusion of sweet but really minor works showing peasant girls selling flowers, even that numbing procession of bland limpid longing looks of a sitter at the painter who would rescue her from milkmaid obscurity, even that excess of banality had not been enough for her to trim back her sale. It didn't matter; in a way, the auction-going public expected to see them. One mustn't disappoint those with a taste for the simpleminded.

With these hundred-plus works to sell, the sale might last almost two hours, though she hoped not. Most lots sold at the rate of one a minute. An auctioneer could keep things going smoothly, and her sale, if things sold, would maybe be just over an hour and a half. Longer than that, and people got antsy, dealers drifted away, the curious began to clutter around the elevators, and the sale's energy sagged like dripping leaves. It could be hard to build momentum and keep it if works lay there unclaimed. She thought she'd structured the sale well to keep a pace, with some big stuff at the beginning, the Tissots in the middle, the large Courbet mill scene toward the end, and enough paintings that were valued at around $150,000 to keep interest up to the end. One had to sprinkle a few masterworks amid the fluff, for anticipation and payoff. She wouldn't know of the duds until the sale actually got under way in a couple of days. The pace of a sale depended on the pace of the individual sales, and if an auctioneer had to coax a reluctant buyer to show a little mercy for an unclaimed Gérôme, it could prove deadly. Some of the works might have done for a Part Two sale, but only the big evening auctions had part twos, where the lesser lights found buyers, and it was all business, no glamour, few headlines, fewer stars. But nineteenth-century auctions didn't have the cachet to be split among leading and supporting roles—how dreary an evening Impressionist sale would be if it included everything the house had to sell over two days in just two hours. Even the diehard Impressionist sale groupies—and there were a lot of them—would be likely to fade away after the fortieth Degas sketch of a ballerina's ankle.

For Claire, the excitement had been in finally successfully completing a sale of her own, on her own, by her own judgment. She hoped it would do well enough to keep her momentum going at Sotheby's. It wouldn't likely lead to a sudden realization that nineteenth-century art deserved a place in the evening sales; it was likely, if all went well, to help maintain or cement the reputations of some fine artists and, in particular for Claire, help find a home for "A Widow."

Her thoughts flew between a muted satisfaction at her work and a trepidation at the possibility of failure. She didn't want her buyers going into the late afternoon wrung out from exhaustion. She'd been to a few evening contemporary auctions where people had sat on their hands for an hour, and it was awful, like being forced to attend the funeral of a stranger.

She mustn't think that way. She already had some interest in her big pieces. And she knew the midrange five-figure works usually walked out without too much prodding; the economy had been picking up, the decorating tastes were again accommodating recherché looks. It wouldn't be a total bust. A small museum in Georgia had eyed the big Tissot, and Claire had spent some time with the curator there, who was advising the largest benefactor on a possible acquisition. The benefactor, a manufacturing tycoon named Lew Kling, was an alumnus of the university where the museum was based and liked nineteenth-century American and European art. He'd already bought a few Bierstadts and Hudson

River School paintings at the American sale the month before. Her curator here, Tom Dunkel, said that the Tissot would make up for what he couldn't get in Impressionists. Kling had come late to the Impressionists, and the good stuff was safely displayed in museums. Kling was putting together a solid, nicely idiosyncratic collection, and to the delight of small communities around the country, local-boys-made-good had begun to bequeath their collections to their almas mater and not to the dusty big-city monoliths whose vaults were overstuffed with minor masterpieces that never saw the light of day. For Kling, the $3 million it might take to procure the painting would be nothing, especially compared to the $20 million a Monet water lily could cost him, if one turned up. This would make a little gem for his collection, would be among the glories of this out-of-the-way museum, would delight the academics and provincials in the college towns around, and spark community pride and so on and so forth. Claire was getting ahead of herself. Still, the painting was likely to be displayed quietly, proudly somewhere safe, somewhere it was going to be loved.

She would let Mrs. Driscoll know of the museum's interest. She wasn't sure she'd let her know about another potential buyer. Two days earlier, Claire and her colleagues had taken "A Widow" to a townhouse on East Eighty-eighth Street, just off Fifth Avenue, to see how it might look among the other works on display there. Claire didn't think it quite fit with the owners' collection of antique telescopes and astrolabes displayed like limbs along the shelves near the house's grand salon on the second floor. She didn't know the owners of the house, although she'd heard of them—Gerard Blunt and his wife, Effie, who had a reputation for endowing little chamber music festivals for American musicians in Europe, so the Blunts could be assured of something to listen to while they traveled in Italy or Aix-en-Provence in the summer, and could write off their vacations through a circuitous system of philanthropy and ulterior motive. The Blunts had expressed their interest in the Tissot through their art adviser, a pinched little woman named Madeline Apley with severe bangs, ugly German glasses, and the air of a Balthus governess dominatrix, with whom Claire had worked before when arranging art sales with other culturally inclined but socially autistic businesspeople who had acquired wealth and were looking to acquire its trappings. Claire had not expected to meet the Blunts personally—she knew that they were more interested in music than visual art, and that they were still more generous with their pocketbooks than gracious with their time. She had heard from Peter, who had gone to some of the musical evenings they hosted for good causes, that they would place themselves in a room on the other side of the salon from where the audience gathered to hear the musicians. They sat in a separate room, isolated from the hoi polloi like the king and queen in Velázquez's "Las Meninas" looking from the doorway onto the artist and his subject. So she didn't expect to see them when she brought the Tissot to the townhouse.

Claire had leaned the painting against a wall that might have claimed it, if it were the kind of home that welcomed art. But this really was a myopic place, she felt. It had the personality of a solitary mathematician. She thought an antique map might work better here, rather than a study in human longing and the passing of time. She hadn't said anything, but she and the art adviser's eyes had met—at least Claire thought their eyes met, though she couldn't quite see the pupils through Madeline Apley's Coke-bottle lenses. Madeline had shaken her bangs and they had both stood in silence, imagining the painting mounted near the competing instruments of interplanetary detection of an earlier age. Madeline would probably tell the Blunts to bid on something from the scientific instruments and maps sale coming up in a few weeks, rather than on this work, whose discovery lay more in uncovering an inner universe.

This was why Claire and other specialists took paintings for visits. Some collectors were genuine connoisseurs, with whom one could discuss the work in depth, even down to the brushwork, the paint used, the models, the original frame. Others had a wall to fill. This couple was looking to expand their decorative style, and perhaps in a moment of out-of-character frivolity had asked Madeline to find them something fun. This hadn't seemed to be a townhouse of fun. It was one where Bartók string quartets probably accompanied every deliberate move from coffee making to teeth brushing. Claire couldn't fault them their taste or the dour atmosphere of their home. They simply weren't right for this work, and their adviser knew it.

Claire had given herself some moments this afternoon to look over what she'd done. She had spent a few hours hanging her sale—most of the works, anyway—her mind mulling over individual paintings and the odd sculpture or two she'd got. There were four large galleries opening onto each other, on the tenth-floor exhibition space. The largest one, which the public first fell into as they turned off the elevator, had a partition facing the archway, so that upon entering, a person would see displayed the prized painting of a sale.

Claire's heart beat rapidly as she inspected her galleries—hers for now, until the night before the sale, when the works would be removed to a holding area behind the main sales room, to be taken out one by one for viewing as the auction proceeded. The galleries looked magnificent and would look better if enough people came to fill the space. Larger galleries were at their best when filled with people admiring the art, eyeing each other, and speculating on the commercial outcome of it all.

Claire had invited just about everyone she knew for the reception that evening—it was only minutes away, would run from six to eight—and had also extended invitations to the press, most of whom wouldn't bother to come, except for the usual underpaid art-world freeloaders.

Auction houses took far less time than museums did to mount exhibitions, understandably. Claire and her staff didn't have to worry about what the wall cards would say, other than the price estimate, and they didn't have to write concise little explications of the art beyond what was in the catalog, and for that, they had help from scholars. They were free from having to agonize over the placement of objects in relation to each other or having to provide a narrative of a career or a chronology of an era or to try to show off a painting in the best scholarly light. The exhibition space had the look of a museum hall, but there was also a whisper of commerce in the air. It wasn't necessary to create a hushed atmosphere of contemplation; it was important to show off the goods, brightly. Because auction houses tended to operate on volume as well as quality, a public showing of the paintings and such lasted for only a few days rather than the months a museum would give to a show. Claire was sometimes surprised that so little of the public actually came to see the paintings that Sotheby's and Christie's had for sale; the exhibitions were free, and a person could see a lot of marvelous art that often ended up in private hands and out of sight. But many were still intimidated by auction houses, feeling that perhaps they'd be accosted by a salesclerk and trapped into spending thousands, or sensing they'd be recognized as being art-illiterate, neither of which would be true. Most people didn't really know about auction houses, and were barely aware of when sales took place, anyway. Her reception, then, to which the public could surely come if anyone knew of it, would be like a big congratulatory party for herself, and her art.

She had called Mrs. Driscoll to let her know "A Widow" had the most visible spot for the show, and was seen in part on the back cover of the catalog. Another work had served as the front cover art—it was less desirable, and less costly, than the Tissot, but it had a kind of oomph (read: naked nymphs) that caught the eye. On the back cover, she'd used a detail, the figure of the little girl draped moodily but with a self-possessed charm, over her chair. It showed Tissot's wit and had a Renoir-like freshness that might appeal to that set, and there were a lot of them, still. So "A Widow" was the first painting a visitor or buyer would see upon entering the galleries on the tenth floor. The large Courbet mill scene was in a similar spot in an adjacent gallery, and the other cover lot, "The Triumph of Bacchus," a delectable example of nineteenth-century academic art at its most self-consciously mythic and unabashedly, quaintly, hedonistic, was on the far wall near the bar and snacks, where it belonged.

"You've got pride of place," Claire had told her.

"I'll be prepared," she'd said. "I've been prepared for a while."

Claire knew what she meant. Seeing her beloved painting would have a poignancy (albeit one that a few million dollars might ease), though Mrs. Driscoll still felt strongly about selling it, and surely appreciated her treasure occupying such a spot. Claire's sale had been made up mainly of odds and ends, as it were, that is, much of it had come from very many estates and the holdings of very many far-flung homes and storerooms. Certain collectors who purchased art as an investment usually tried to turn over their acquisitions after about seven years, curiously enough the length of the statute of limitations for most crimes.

Mrs. Driscoll, of course, had not been that kind of collector, or investor. She had loved art differently, had grown up with it differently; its investment for her, while now worth money, had been of a meditative, emotional kind. For "A Widow" had been, to Mrs. Driscoll, the recipient of the kind of intense gazing one has in a relationship. Only with people, it lasts for just a short while. With objects that somehow adumbrate one's spiritual path, the relationship is even more oddly personal. She had learned the language of her cherished painting and had, perhaps, understood it, or tried to, even more so than her marriage. They had been a couple.

Claire knew she was guilty of thinking too much about a painting, entering too much into its fraught tableau like a reckless heroine in a horror story who can penetrate the two dimensions of the canvas and become enmeshed in a tragedy of unwanted knowledge. But the familiarity that we feel for fine art that we've known for so long brings with it its own grammar, as if a shorthand for moods and states of mind had developed between the art and its viewer. In some ways, it was as a couple grows. Even her low-rent Greuze knew how each of her days ended, Claire thought, as she'd sit and stare at it as if it were a meditative stone that she rubbed while chanting. Imagine how a finer work, such as the Tissot, might feel for the viewer when gazed upon for so long, so often, so intently. She and Peter, Claire thought, despite their ultimate differences, had developed a similar unspoken dialogue so that they rarely, at one point, needed to communicate to each other their preferences with more than a look or the hint of a facial gesture. She missed that sense of communication in her life, those shared semaphores of intent, even amid the growing resentments in the last year or so of her marriage. Even when she knew that something had gone wrong, she had taken comfort in the knowledge that someone still knew her somehow. You can understand much of what a person might want without knowing exactly what it is he needs.

So Claire had taken these few moments alone, before the friends, acquaintances, consigners, and buyers made their way among the art, the gewgaw renderings of lavish interiors, the sun-dappled softness of comely maidens plucking fruit, the steely landscapes of raw soil and gouging water, the delicacy of quiet sentiment of family scenes, the turmoil of historical recreations. She walked, her heels click-clacking on the shiny parquet, around the galleries, savoring her moment of accomplishment, before the terror of the sale and the reality of the results set in.

No one was here yet but the guards and the staff setting up the bar. She stopped before one of her favorite little paintings, a portrait of a young man by, most likely, the Italian painter Giovanni Boldini, who worked in the nineteenth and early twentieth centuries, in a frankly realistic manner. This portrait had a photographic directness but also harked back, modestly, to the great Renaissance portraits of ambitious and ruthless courtiers, churchmen, and aristocrats. This showed a man of about thirty, who looked at the viewer, or slightly below the viewer's gaze. It reminded her a little of Parmigianino, and then, of one in particular, which reminded her always of Frank. This picture had come to her only fairly recently, at about the time that Frank had reentered her life, with his own particular and attractive gloom.

Frank had the brooding intensity of Parmigianino's "Portrait of a Man with a Book," and like the figure in that great painting, Frank's dark eyes seemed to seize upon some unseen quandary in the middle distance, angry for its not revealing itself to him, who should know, who should know better, who should already have known all about what it was that was demanded of him. He had been rarely out of her mind, despite the pressing and occasionally overwhelming demands of putting this sale together. They hadn't met after their dinner together; she had traveled, she had been consumed by work, she had, frankly, avoided him. He frightened her—and she frightened herself. She felt like the quandary the man in the book wanted to get to the bottom of.

"Every time I see you, you're lost in thought."

She turned around quickly. "Toby!" she said. "You came! You're the first one here. Sorry—I, well, you know I was somewhere else." She felt as if she'd been caught in something untoward. Toby looked far more relaxed than he had those few months ago. Had it been that long?

"You asked," he said, smiling. "And I came. This is impressive. Our little Claire, all grown up."

"Well, nothing's sold yet. So hold your congratulations until Friday night. Or maybe your condolences. Whatever."

"What do you mean? You'll be great. You put this together. And that Tissot is as fabulous as you promised."

"Isn't it? Wait'll you meet its owner, if you can." She took his arm, and they began to walk slowly through the gallery. "How was L.A.?"

"Mom, Dad, sunshine. Great, actually. I could live there."

"You did."

"But I could again. Even with Mom and Dad and eternal sunshine. You get used to gray sky and blinding blue-white clouds and cold light and it all being mixed together in New York. But I could live there. Not yet. Someday."

"So you came back. Did you miss it here?"

"You know, I did. Despite everything."

"Well, I missed you. Really."

"So what's up with Peter's brother?"

"What do you mean?" she said, a little loudly.

"Oh, Peter mentioned you'd had dinner a few times with him."

"Twice. And you're talking to Peter?"

"Why not? You did."

Well, she thought she'd been gracious. She had no idea what went on in other people's relationships—after they ended, even.

"What did Peter tell you?"

"That friendly Frank was in town, that he's been writing some bogus business book, that he'd looked you up and down and that he was, well, why don't you ask Peter?"

"I will, but I want to know what—"

"Oh, Claire, don't get all defensive. It's not like you're everyone's topic A. Well, you *are* a little bit, in this circle, but still, he just mentioned it. I think he'd be good for you."

"Thanks. I—"

"And don't say if you need my advice you'll ask for it. I know, I know. I haven't seen him yet. Maybe we'll actually have a conversation one of these days, now that he isn't all angry because I stole his brother away from you. Still, you've been on the market for a while. What took him so long?"

"Cut it out," she said. "There's nothing going on." Yet she couldn't resist a small smile, which Toby noticed. "Did you come alone?" she asked him.

"No, I brought a crowd, as promised, who straggled in after me. They're over there," he said, indicating a group of young men who were standing by "The Triumph of Bacchus," the painting by Charles-Émile-Auguste Carolus-Duran, a multihyphenate who had an important atelier in Paris that had attracted American artists.

"They're laughing at my painting," Claire noted.

"Just a little. And can you blame them? But really, they're laughing with it."

The "Triumph of Bacchus" was certainly over the top, with its procession of nude Baccahantes who had a definite Belle Époque beauty. They accompanied a sullen, louche, limpid Dionysus on a traveling throne being pulled by studs who wouldn't have looked out of place hoisting Jane Russell around during the shipboard swimming pool number in *Gentlemen Prefer Blondes.*

Ludicrous, yes, but it had a panache that made its academic vulgarity rather sweet.

"Well, they'll just love the Frederick Leighton painting in the back gallery."

"You mean 'Music,'" Toby intoned. "I know, that's the kind of painting that aesthetic pansies used to drool over." He leaned in to her ear and whispered, "He wears it to the left." That picture showed a long, lithe youth in white tights with a subdued but noticeable bulge, attired in a Renaissance-era black frock jacket, carrying a mandolin, and enrobed in a red cape. It was so very, very earnest.

"They should take a look at 'Morning Splendor.' Lots of nude guys in that one, too," she said. "Morning Splendor" was a sunny scene of innocent homoeroticism in a Thomas Eakins mode painted by a British artist, Henry Scott Tuke, showing mainly unclothed young men on the beach of a solitary cove.

"Don't think I didn't notice."

"See," Claire said. "Something for everyone."

"We could pool our money and buy it as a kind of timeshare," Toby said.

"Actually, this one has a few interested parties."

"Do I know any?"

"I can't say."

"Well, give me a hint when it's sold, so I can introduce myself. Let me go looking for my friends. I'll bide my time until Peter comes."

"You're waiting for him?"

"We haven't declared war, Claire," he said, turning back to her. "Of course we speak. It's different now, but we do. Did you think we wouldn't?"

She didn't actually know. Although she had kept in touch with

Peter, most women she knew barely spoke to, or of, their ex-hus-
bands or -boyfriends, unless children were involved.

"I still love him, Claire," Toby said. People were arriving now in
shoals, and she knew she couldn't devote more time to speaking
with only him. "Didn't you?"

"Yes," she said, quietly. "I did. I do. But—"

"I know. It changes. All I can say is, keep trying."

"But what about—"

"The new guy? We've got to meet sooner or later. I can't go
through life burning bridges. And, you know, I have to learn to live
a bit with the past. I know I snapped at you when I came over, that
snowy night so long ago, it seems now. I mistook your mementos
for crutches. Rather than what they were—mementos."

"They were crutches, too," Claire said.

"Only if you live with them as if they were still real. As if they
were still now. As if your life were in the same place."

"It was. For a while. "

"We know. So was mine; actually, mine wasn't, but I didn't want
it to change. I learned a few things in the past few months."

"All this from L.A.?"

"No." He laughed. "Well, just a little. Some of it here. Let me
rejoin my friends." He kissed her cheek. "Ciao for now."

That's got to hurt, she thought. But she remembered how much she
had longed to meet Toby after Peter first told her about him. That was
different. That was a series of unwanted discoveries. That was then.

Now, she saw Mrs. Driscoll entering. She was with her son,
Thom, and Thom's wife, Jocelyn. They hadn't seen Claire yet, but
all three stopped to look at "A Widow" from the entrance to the
gallery where it was displayed. Her friend Bernice had arrived, too,
and walked quickly up around the trio, to Claire. Bernice was alone,
and chic, and in a hurry.

"Darling, I haven't seen this many gay men since the Jackie O sale," she said, kissing her. Claire sniffed. Bernice was wearing Fracas.

"Don't you usually wear Arpège?" Claire asked.

"An eye *and* a nose," Bernice said. "I decided it was time for a change. But I still had to choose one of the approved scents for our set of lunch ladies, you know. Anyway, Philip thought it was my perfume, and I didn't want to disappoint him when he bought it for me." Philip was Bernice's current squire.

"You'll confuse everyone. It would be as if you had abandoned Chanel."

"Never. Philip doesn't dare buy me clothes. Anyway, I wanted to catch you before the Driscoll woman descended upon you."

"She's nice," Claire said.

"I know she is, in her way," Bernice said. "But I want to avoid her daughter-in-law."

"I think she does, too," Claire said.

"Still, I like her son," Bernice said. "He isn't as dumb as he marries."

"Shh," Claire said. "Here they are." She held out her hands as Mrs. Driscoll neared. Bernice had found an acquaintance and slipped away.

"Claire, this is so lovely," Mrs. Driscoll said, kissing her on both cheeks. "You remember my son, Thom, and Jocelyn, his wife." She didn't say daughter-in-law.

"I don't know how you did it, but Mother parted with her prize," Thom said. He was tall, like his sister, but instead of Adelaide's faux-bohemian animus, Thom was all confident corporate bonhomie. She wondered if he rated Claire a buy or a sell. She realized that Mrs. Driscoll, rather than thinking her painting would be squabbled over by Adelaide with Thom's intercession, wanted to prevent her rapacious son from trading it in for a more current model of society art, like his wife. Mrs. Driscoll wanted to control her legacy by taking the sale out of her children's hands. If they really wanted it, they could buy it. They had the money. And she probably knew they wouldn't. She knew her children.

Thom was sophisticated in terms of business, knowing but indifferent in terms of the visual arts, Claire thought. She assumed, though she didn't really know, that he had art interests only insofar as they applied to general conversation at moneyed events such as museum benefits. He was like a person who didn't care for football, yet was aware of the leading teams, the scores, and the players without caring who won or lost. He wasn't craven, and he supported the causes of his crowd. His wife, Jocelyn—his second wife, that is—with whom Claire had never exchanged more than a few uneasy sentences, had her sights set on making a name as a patron in the visual arts, banking on her sister-in-law's cachet, her own past as a gallery employee, and her mother-in-law's reluctant guidance. Jocelyn had the expression of someone who felt she was missing out on something happening in the next room, her eyes darting around one's face during conversations as she looked for people who might prove more useful to her than whatever person she might be talking at. She'd gone the full princess tonight, Claire thought, with her hair pulled back from her head in a severe chignon, as if it were being punished, a jeweled band holding strays in check close to her elliptical Mannerist head. Softening the severity of her hair was a gleaming necklace of small diamonds in a platinum setting that flowed down her front like a brook.

"That's a beautiful necklace," Claire remarked, as Jocelyn said hello. "You don't see patterns like that any more. Is it an antique?"

"Oh," Jocelyn said, as if relieved to speak of something she actually knew. "It's a gift from Thom's mother. A family piece." She was both confident and uncertain—a woman who knew how to mingle but apparently didn't know how to offset the perceived disapproval of her mother-in-law. Claire thought that Mrs. Driscoll probably had accommodated herself to her new daughter-in-law, but that she rather liked being just a trifle cool to her, to throw Jocelyn off. Little games of power.

"My mother's, actually," Mrs. Driscoll said, looking at Claire pointedly. "A gift from my father on their twentieth anniversary." The necklace might have been a peace offering to Thom's second wife and, maybe, a reproof about the dissolution of his first marriage. Whatever the family dynamic, something was always being brokered. Claire hadn't known the first wife, who lived, apparently, in Los Angeles now. Perhaps the necklace had also been a consolation prize for the Tissot's being withdrawn from the family.

Claire knew that Jocelyn was active in social affairs—she was a woman who liked to dress up and lunch and go out, the very model of a successful middle-aged businessman's second wife. She liked being on committees. Planning things. Good things. Worthy things. Her friends probably told her she did too much, she was always running around. But how could one give up the luncheons, the teas, the fittings, the manicures, the Pilates, the benefits, the maddening whirl? Really, there just wasn't time. Claire figured that tonight they were just making a token appearance here for Mrs. Driscoll's sake. There might be more jewels some day, if they pretended to care.

Sure enough, they took a quick walk around the painting and made as if to leave. They'd been there for about five minutes. "Mother, we'll talk tomorrow," Thom said to Mrs. Driscoll, bending to kiss his mother's cheek. Mrs. Driscoll let herself be pecked by Jocelyn, who then offered Claire a quick little smile, as if to apologize for having nothing to say. Thom shook her hand with a touch more pressure than she would have liked, and ushered his wife out, stopping briefly by the bar to say a word to an acquaintance.

Jocelyn turned and gave a little wave to her mother-in-law, and they disappeared to grace another event.

"Second wives have to work harder," Mrs. Driscoll said to Claire after they'd left. She looked at Claire's quizzical expression. "Don't underestimate her."

"I won't," she said. "And I don't. I was just thinking how much like my own mother she is, in some respects." She was like her mother not in social conquest but in ambition, in her own sphere. Her mother had been more at ease, or what passed for ease in her mind, being among friends outside the home.

"A social being?" Mrs. Driscoll said. "Well, I'm sure you realize that even the Jocelyns of this world make things run for the better." She gave Claire's arm a little squeeze. "Now, I must take a look at your sale. Can you spare me a few more minutes in this throng?" The galleries had filled, much to Claire's delight, almost imperceptibly while she was engaged with Mrs. Driscoll.

"What do you think, then?" Claire asked her. "Is 'A Widow' in good company?"

"I never doubted it," she said. She took Claire's arm, and they ambled through the galleries, Claire saying quick hellos here and there to some of the many people she recognized.

"Oh, my," Mrs. Driscoll said, as they passed a Ricci painting, "The Courtière," that Claire had acquired from the collection of another society matron. It showed the broker-woman receiving people, at morning—at least it seemed morning, to judge by her outfit. Ricci was less interested on the surface with the characters, and more with the surface of their lives.

As with the other, finer, Ricci in her sale, this one showed the artist's great skill in creating the look, even the feel, of different fabrics, from the delicate embroidered rose of the day dress the courtière wore to the pale satin of a young attendant standing behind her, to the gleaming folds of ivory silk of the women standing far-ther back, chatting animatedly like a brood of elegant hens. Claire had estimated its worth on the market at about $60,000, and it would likely sell, if her sale had momentum. This was at the top end of the low end, so to speak—many works priced at under $100,000 needed a certain élan to convince buyers that in some ways the pic-ture was the equal of those priced much higher; sometimes buyers felt a work wasn't worth $60,000, but would be convinced they had a steal at $120,000.

"So Lillian is selling," Mrs. Driscoll said. "I had no idea."

"You know Lillian Clack, then," Claire said.

"We haven't seen each other much these last few years, since Lil-lian spends so much time in Palm Beach. I should have examined your catalog a little more closely beyond my own interests. I was too concerned about the little essay on my Tissot."

"That wasn't entirely my work," Claire said. "I had help from a specialist up at Columbia." Auction houses occasionally farmed out catalog work to scholars, who not only assisted in authenticating some questionable works but whose help on the catalog sometimes prevented questions of worth and provenance later on, if a work's history or even ancient ownership were questioned. It paid to have academics on one's side.

"But if I'd been less fascinated by my own possessions, I'd at least have noticed Lillian's painting. I remember seeing it over the sideboard in her dining room. It had been in her family for years, one of those paintings that seems so comforting because of where it was placed, familiar at dinner or gatherings year after year."

"Her children weren't interested in it, so she's cleaning house."

"Serves them right." She paused, considered. "Maybe it skips a generation."

"Cheese straws," said a voice behind Claire. It was Peter, with Sean.

"I'm so glad you could make it," Claire said, giving her ex-husband a kiss on either cheek and taking Sean's hand in both of hers. "You remember Mrs. Driscoll, don't you?"

"Elizabeth, you look marvelous, as usual," Peter said, shaking her hand. "Your painting is the star of the sale."

He *would* address her by her first name, thought Claire. Sean looked more at ease than he had at the sale a month ago, but wore the same probing expression as when she'd met him; he tried to appear neutral but couldn't help sizing her up. He had a different kind of appraisal than Thom Driscoll's, who made her feel like a speculative commodity. Sean seemed to want to get to the bottom of her, so to speak.

"Have you seen anything else?" Claire asked.

"Not yet," Peter said. "We just got here. You couldn't persuade them to spring for more than chips, huh?"

"I was lucky to get the cheese straws," she said. "You know what it's like."

"Food is an economic indicator at auction houses," Peter told Sean. "The message is, if they splurge on snacks then you're in for a big sale."

"So what do they think of this one?" Sean asked her.

"Well, surprisingly, my colleagues all think it will do well. The thing is, we don't usually have cocktail parties for day sales. So they did me a favor."

"Claire's been a good girl," Peter said with a grin. "Listen," he said, in an undertone to her, "can we talk, just for a second?"

She nodded.

"I'll mingle elsewhere, Claire—and see who else I know might have unloaded art for you," and Mrs. Driscoll drifted off.

"Don't mind me," Sean said to Claire.

They walked into one of the back galleries, where she'd grouped some of the minor landscapes by late nineteenth-century German and Italian artists. En route, they passed a small Tissot study she'd liked, a preparatory ink and oil sketch of a hand and a draped figure, for a late work, "The Ruins of Inner Voices," which had been lost. It showed a rough-hewn yet graceful hand clutching a wooden stick, and a supplicant of some sort in an ocher cape. It had a spiritual energy that Tissot aimed for in many of his later, biblical theme paintings, which, to Claire's mind, weren't as successful as his social tableaux, being somewhat overthought. But because it was only a study, he had, she thought, recorded only the sinew or gesture, and not had time to rationalize the milieu in which to place them. She would have liked this study for herself, but knew better than to think too hard about longing for it.

"Frank's been to see me," he said to her when they were away from the crowd. "You sent him, didn't you?"

"No," she said. "I mentioned, I'm sure he told you, that he should try to set things right with you. I meant that if he wanted us to be friends. Anyway, does it matter how he got there? I thought you wanted to reconnect with him."

"Well. I did. No, it isn't that. I'm glad he came over. I think we may have a future, he and I. Not that we'll ever be close, but we have some sort of shared past. At least shared parents."

"I'm happy for you, then. Very."

"The thing is—he'd have come to New York and never returned a call or seen me after I burst in on him if it hadn't been for you. You have power over him, you know."

"I like him," she said.

"He likes you. Frank doesn't say much, but he can't help revealing everything. He's not used to the ways of the world. I think that his book and you are the only two reasons he came to New York. And I think you came first."

She didn't respond. But what she had been thinking about for the past month was what to make of all of this. She'd been able to put thoughts of Frank out of her mind while she was putting this sale together. He wasn't just another man whom she could date and dump. He was part of her life in a way that meant she held back further from any sort of commitment.

"You know, Claire," Peter said, sensing her mood, "when we were married, at the end, when you broke down, in one of your rare outbursts, and said you never really knew me—do you remember?"

"Yes."

"Do you know I sometimes thought the same about you? I sometimes felt you analyzing, felt you questioning, felt you looking at the world around you, but I rarely felt you allowing me in. Perhaps we might have ended up differently."

"You mean still married?"

"No, I mean I might not have been married to you for so long. Something had nagged at me. Our . . . reluctance, I guess . . . to probe too deeply into ourselves probably allowed us to overlook something in each other."

"But I tried to understand. I was all about understanding."

"You did. You were. Of me. Not you. We were wrong."

"You make it sound easy."

"It isn't easy. It hasn't been easy for me, certainly."

And Peter had been a person who committed. Three times so far, but he'd made the effort. He had the gift of easy intimacy, even if that had involved, during their marriage, a kind of self-delusion, that awaited discovery, some part of him that he chose to withdraw from her for his own continued happiness. One can never understand fully the nature of desire, either in oneself or others. For Peter, he later had told her, it involved an emotional transparency that he couldn't find with a woman; for him it ultimately had been a matter of a person with whom he could fully be himself.

For Claire, she wasn't sure. Had Peter's inability to reach a kind of oneness with her been there all along, or was it a gradual discovery of misplaced romantic love? Or had she sensed his and withheld a part of herself, or had she been, was she still, someone who was reluctant to let herself fall freely into the heart of another? She had always, just perceptibly, but enough, held back. Whatever shape it had taken, she had, perhaps, never given fully of herself—had always had some trace of being otherwise occupied. Like her mother, perhaps, though in a far less self-loathing way. Claire's intimacy with Peter, or what she had understood as intimacy, though it might have been something different, was predicated by what, exactly? Had she believed herself fully engaged, or were her lingering doubts about where to proceed with Frank clouding her judgment about the life she had lived with his brother? What had she withheld?

What was it about her that she didn't know he wanted to know? Where she thought that she and Peter had devised a common language of likes and dislikes and tempers and moods, it might just have been the equivalent of guidebook phrases without an underlying sense of nuance. Words without idiom. She had deluded herself into believing she could understand others. She looked at a world of others, felt sharply through a life of gazing, but had not so very much allowed another man that quality in herself that she prized; she hadn't allowed him to see her doubt herself, or beyond that, to see what she truly wanted in the smallest inconsequential moments. That was understanding, that was transparency, that was falling in love truthfully, for real knowledge bred truer love, she believed. And she had withheld that knowledge and, thus, a part of her, and, so, deep affection. In any event, she questioned now her own continuing inability to connect in any strong way with anyone, after what she had learned of marriage to Peter, until her feeling for Frank began to trouble her because it would not go away—that is, she couldn't will it into the longings of someone merely a stepping-stone to truer love, as someone merely with whom to connect for however brief and casual an interlude. Now, after what Peter had said, she wondered how much that failure of hers had been formed not only by her breakup but by the marriage itself. And she had had the temerity to advise Frank to reach out to his brother, as if she knew about connecting.

But she did—she believed she did—or she believed herself capable of it still.

"I'm not saying you should make a decision now, right here, or that you should make a decision at all," Peter said, touching her arm. "I'm just saying consider."

"Consider?"

"Think about what you want."

"Like you?" she said, not unkindly.

"I always do," he said. "It doesn't always work out. Look at you. Look at me and Toby. But I try, I really do. That's all. I'm just suggesting, not telling, nothing more than offering up a little suggestion, that maybe you might try. If not with Frank, since, God knows, I can't recommend him—I certainly wouldn't have chosen him as the ideal brother—then anybody, well, somebody. I don't want to see you alone, that's all."

"Speaking of Toby," she said, "isn't that him over there with Sean?"

Peter turned to where Claire had been looking. "It looks like things got ahead of me," he said. "I'll go over and finish the introductions."

"I have a feeling Sean can handle it," Claire said.

"Oh, I do, too," Peter said. "I don't know about Toby. But it's too late for that."

She thought Toby would be all right. She saw Peter join his ex-lover and his current beau. They were all grouped in front of "Bacchus" as if they'd stepped clothed from that monumental canvas and assumed roles in the everyday world. Peter and Toby embraced, then Peter, his arm on Sean, said something that made Toby laugh. How quickly he'd recovered, she thought. Or maybe he'd realized something about himself, or had found the strength to look beyond what he'd lost.

She hesitated to join them, and felt a little wistful, even, as they chatted, an outsider to their world. Then Peter, looking toward her, caught her eye and beckoned her over, just as she saw his brother, Frank, entering the gallery near them. Something on her face must have registered an odd surprise, because Peter turned to what she might have seen, and saw Frank. Frank shook his brother's hand, then Toby's, then was introduced to Sean, all quickly, it seemed to Claire. He looked at her just as she neared the group.

"You two know each other, of course," Peter said, as Claire joined them.

"Claire," Frank said. "Sorry I'm late." It was nearing the end of the cocktail hour.

"I'm glad you could make it," she said, letting him kiss her cheek. She felt flustered, as if she were on a prom date. She detected that scent again, from the Frick. Maybe he *was* using cologne. For her?

"Why don't you show Frank around," Peter said to her. "Maybe you can join us afterward, if you have time. Sean and Toby and I are having dinner. That includes you, too, Frank," he added. "Of course."

They moved away from her. Claire noticed the "of course." Things had changed, it seemed. Frank said, "Why don't you show me your big work? I think I passed it coming in." He touched her, and she felt herself tingle, like the woman in the painting at the thought of a letter from her beloved. What was wrong with her?

She led him to "A Widow," not quite knowing where to begin, but feeling, all of a sudden, a need to tell him more about the sale than she had done before, more of the specifics of her working life beyond what she'd said before—how much it meant to her, how the pictures worked together here, her reactions to certain artists, her relation to patrons, clients, buyers. Before, she had spoken of her work fervently but a bit abstractedly with Frank. Before, it had really been about him. It had really been about her avoiding him. It had been about her, but not quite. Before, well, there had only been a few befores, in any event. Her passions, her career, her passions for it, and for more, had not existed between them.

"Which one are you?" Frank asked, as they stood before the painting. "I know, I think." He was less dark than he'd been, less uncertain, though he had about him some funny little eagerness. Claire had told him of the buyer interest, of Mrs. Driscoll, of the family dynamic, briefly. Of Adelaide. Of Thom and his trophy wife.

"You saw that in the painting, didn't you?" she said. "The lives of these women, and the girl."

"I saw you," he said. "You identify."

"Well," she said, pausing—not knowing if she would answer in the way he had hoped, for she now wanted to.

"I think you're the little girl sometimes," he said.

"Why?"

"Looking for something other than what you have."

"Really? To tell you the truth, I had thought, most of the time, that I identified with the widow herself."

"Oh," Frank said. "I figured that, too. But then, you'd have to have a suitor, or a possible suitor, in the language of the time of the painting."

"Oh, not necessarily," she said. "One can dream of one."

"The little girl is dreaming of something. The young woman is hoping for someone. The old one is remembering and dreaming and longing."

"Now," she said, with a laugh, "you sound like me."

"I'd like to think of you as, not the widow," Frank said, coming closer to her, "but as someone who thinks of someone else."

"Who?" she said, looking away from him. She saw a crowd of acquaintances she suddenly needed to join.

"Me, of course. It's been too obvious, hasn't it? Haven't I avoided this until now? I can't any longer. You know what I'm talking about. Can you think of me?" he said. "Can you think of me?"

"I think I'll be going now, Claire," came a sudden voice beside her. "Thank you so much for a lovely reception."

"Oh," said Claire, turning to her, flushed. "Frank," she said. "I want you to meet someone. This is Mrs. Driscoll. She owns the 'Widow.'"

# WHAT THE MARKET WILL BEAR

T he first five lots had sold within four minutes, at or near their estimates, showing a solid but cautious crowd. The sixth-floor sales space had been reconfigured so that the room, now about half the dimensions it could be during the big evening auctions, looked full, and a full house was more liable to generate the heat needed to propel a sale.

George Balfour was leading the proceedings. His pallor and tonsure gave him the air of a padre from a Spanish Renaissance painting, but he was more Voltaire than Zarbaran, more at home among the moneyed set than at the friary. George was often called upon to preside over charity auctions, among the older and the young-collector types. George was the kind of man husbands didn't mind their wives flirting with, gay but not flighty, someone to occupy the little women while the providers devoted themselves to hedge funds and golf handicaps.

Claire liked him; he had shown her the bureaucratic ropes of the office, and had never made unfortunate "just between us girls" remarks to her about Peter's and her divorce, and his life, such as she'd been subjected to from a few of the other specialists. He respected her reticence, and she warmed to his unforced been-there, done-that savvy. He began the sale by adding to the usual remarks that "interested parties" might be bidding, a sign that some buyers in the room might be vested in some way in the lots up for bidding.

"Teatime," he said to the room, as the turntable spun to reveal the first major work of Claire's sale, a painting by the Hungarian artist Mikhaly Munkácsy. Claire had given the work an estimate of $300,000 to $500,000, and she expected that it might sell for a little above that.

Munkácsy painted domestic interiors, bourgeois parlors, women at genteel leisure. He created, through layers of color, remarkable depths in a scene that seemed both spatial and psychological. These interiors were really about nothing other than themselves—a woman pouring tea, a woman perusing a letter, a woman in seated profile lost in quiet—but because of the refulgent chiaroscuro and the heft of the objects that emerged from the inky morass of canvas, they seemed to elevate the everyday into the contemplative; sewing as a path to spiritual enlightenment.

In this painting, four women were engaged in their own thoughts, in an afternoon of mottled light. At the right, a figure in a bright white dress calmly prepared tea, standing behind a table draped in a rich embroidered cloth, rather like the oriental carpets that shrouded tables in Vermeer. The fronds of a large fern plant isolated the figure of the woman dispensing tea from the triangle of her acquaintances by the window on the other side of the canvas. That trio of two seated and one standing had a quiet intensity. The standing woman, her arm resting on a case before which a vase of pink flowers glowed, wore a faraway gaze and had the sunken eyes of a Max Beckmann self-portrait. She seemed to be peering into the light out the window. Turned three-quarters to the viewer, a woman in deep black, her brown hair dappled by sunshine through the mums and gladioli of the bouquet on the table to her right, read a letter, which glowed with a muted translucence against the velvet sobriety of her dress. Opposite her, with a face shadowed to the viewer, her body in the halo of light seeping in around her, a woman sat neither looking nor appearing to be engaged in anything other than stillness, a marker against the lengthening afternoon. The casual clutter of the space, just lived-in enough to seem real, added to its faint melancholy. It was not a bleak picture by any means, but one of unspoken companionship that, by the grouping of the figures, the drooping shadows seeping into the folds of the dresses, and the carpet creases, carried the solitude of thought and its essential separateness. The women, one pouring, one reading, one peering, one immobile, belonged together, but who could tell what tender, mundane, or high-flying thoughts were in their minds? Who could tell what kept them apart? The painting showed both the confinement of leisured domestic life and the freedom of longing, and it spoke to Claire's dreamy nature, especially in its evocation of the inability to connect. She saw something of herself in so many works of art: the passionate widow, the hopeful bride in other paintings, the pensive woman looking toward the light here, but she had begun to feel that she could no longer go on visiting herself through what she saw in art. She needed to do more. And to think less.

She loved this painting, though, and it, like so many in her sale, could provide long hours of pleasure to the buyer, as would many works from the nineteenth century, costly and not so, household names or unknowns.

"Bidding starts at two hundred seventy thousand," George said. A hand raised. "Number one-seven-oh. Thank you. Do I have two ninety?"

Another hand went up, then several more quickly. She saw Peter arrive. He had told her he'd be bidding on several works on behalf of a growing number of clients whom he had begun to advise. She was glad to see him move in this direction. The role of art adviser suited him more, she thought, than being a dealer in furniture. Somehow, still, despite his success in the field, Peter didn't seem a natural for retail. Though dealers would cringe at the term "retail" in connection with their profession.

The bidding went quickly for the Munkácsy, and it had gone up to $480,000 already.

"Five hundred thousand," George urged with the placid demeanor of a baccarat dealer. "Number two-one-three. Thank you." It continued in this vein for about half a minute, and the work finally sold at $600,000, above the estimate. It seemed the market was eager for her paintings. So far.

The room had begun to fill. Unlike evening sales, day sales were looser, with people moving in and out more freely. For one thing, day sales usually didn't have assigned seating, and dealers, art advisers, consigners, and the curious stayed for a few lots generally, waiting to bid or buy or discover prices, then drifted out, dropping off, if they won, the necessary documents with Client Accounting. The sale, while serious, still had a casual air that seemed old-fashioned, befitting the artifacts of another age. More so than the Impressionist or modern art, which traded in the currency of great wealth, or contemporary art, which often meant new fortunes, nineteenth-century and, to a degree, the remaining Old Masters on the market outside the big names, spoke of old money. Even if it were acquired recently. Something about this area spoke to a respect for the significance of art that didn't make a statement of one's power, but told of one's taste.

For this sale, Claire was handling a few absentee bids, along with her colleagues, through which potential buyers who could not attend in person had authorized the house—in this case, Claire or her coworkers—to bid up to a set maximum, with the understanding that they would make every effort to purchase the item for as little as possible and never exceed the limit that the absentee bidder had set. She had been standing at first near George, up at the front of the room, and had handed him an absentee bid on one item already. Others wouldn't be coming up for a while, so she was free to move about the auction room as needed.

"Sold to one thirty-six for five hundred fifty thousand dollars," George said, rapping his auctioneer's block onto the lectern. This was a lovely Courbet field scene. Claire recognized the buyer, an art consultant named Tamara Wilson, who advised clients around the country. She had a good eye and was skilled at matching the art to the client. Peter and Claire had known her when they had been married, but in the past few years Peter had kept up the friendship more than Claire, though Claire and Tamara had discussed business amicably enough. Tamara was one of those people whom couples split, unofficially, during and after a marriage. Peter, with his gregarious charm, had walked away with the bulk of their marriage friends. She didn't resent this. Claire realized how few of their friends were hers—she hadn't really thought about it in the past, but seeing the Munkácsy painting of the women together in solitude brought home for her just how much she had isolated herself. In that regard she had more in common with Peter's brother— name him, she told herself: Frank—than she had acknowledged. For what had she done but focus on her career, at the expense of other areas of her life? Surely her imaginative empathy blossomed or overran itself, in these last years, as she lived more in a world of paintings than not. Just as Frank had lived among his books and his teaching after his move to a lay life.

Three midprice lots had just gone by unsold, and Claire felt a blip as momentum slowed. It might turn out to be an auction where only a certain kind of painting at a certain price point would sell. Still, too early to panic.

A Bouguereau was coming up; she had six in this sale, having sensed a growing taste for his polished and, to her mind, cloying fetishistic paintings of women and children. This one up for sale showed a mother, an Italian peasant, perhaps, kissing her standing, naked child, who was clutching an orange and nuzzling her mother with a far too knowing expression for someone so young. It was a highly skilled, beautifully finished interpretation of a Renaissance mother-and-child—Raphael of the Bois de Boulogne—but to Claire's eye it had an unsettling hollowness. And that child. Surely she would grow up to be Swann's Odette, scheming and duplicitous and charming.

Claire knew it would sell, and probably for about $600,000. George started bidding fairly high, at $400,000, at the bottom estimate rather than just below it. To her surprise, several paddles went up instantly; Bouguereau's two-dimensional porcelain portraits had more admirers than she had anticipated, and the price started rising quickly. She saw Tamara raise her paddle at $450,000, and keep it raised. She saw Peter raise his, too.

"Do I have five hundred thousand?" George said. "Anne, on the phone. Thank you. Next bid will be five-fifty. Do I have five-fifty?" Tamara raised her paddle, as did a man standing in the back, whom Claire pointed toward to bring to George's attention. "Yes, thank you. Standing in the rear. I can't make out your paddle. Six-fifty. Thank you." He looked over at the phone, where Anne nodded. "Seven hundred," said George. He looked around. "Going once. Going twice. Thank you, Anne. Number? Two-four-oh. Thank you."

The market was bullish for Bouguereau, and she hoped it would hold for Tissot, coming up.

She saw Frank enter, scan the room, see her, smile, and take a seat near Peter. Just in time for her Tissot sale. Just in time for her big painting. Just in time for her to be brought back with an awful surge to what she felt in the crowd, at her picture, Mrs. Driscoll's picture, and Frank's earnest proposition. Mrs. Driscoll's departure the night before had prevented Claire from answering him directly, and the rest of the evening she was cowardly, she knew, as she used the opportunity of escorting her out to greet other groups and avoid Frank. She had needed time to think. No. She had needed time to avoid thinking. And she couldn't not think. The ridiculous possibilities of a future she hesitated really to contemplate—the absurdity of at any point becoming the sister-in-law of her former husband. But little pictures of coziness, little scenes of domestic life, little ruminations on happiness, on seduction, on sex, flickered in her mind.

"Tissot's 'Widow,'" George said. The turntable spun slowly and the painting she'd worked so hard to acquire, the beloved possession of a woman she admired and had come to regard as a kind of mentor, came into view. Her sale would live or die on this one work, this touchstone, this reminder of what love might mean, what it might signify to those who yearned for it, to those who lost it and remembered, those who read about it in books, those who had only an inkling of what it could be in an unforeseen future. Those, like her, who sometimes confused its flesh-and-blood presence with its representation.

"We will start the bidding at seven hundred and fifty thousand," George said. Claire looked around the room. Peter had raised his paddle. He hadn't told her he was bidding. But she should have become used to his not telling her things by now. Frank, sitting next to him, caught her eye again, and gave her the biggest smile she'd ever seen on his handsome face.

And so what? And so what, she thought, of her girlish inhibitions, when a smile like that could make her momentarily ignore the hard work ahead, drawing him out, helping him grow, and everything one would endure to socialize such a wild child; when a smile like that seemed to indicate he had already begun to change, when a smile like his showed he might act upon his hopes and, she knew now, hers, too—and to connect.

"Thank you, number two-oh-three. Do I hear eight hundred thousand? Anne, at the phones, you have a bidder? Eight hundred thousand, yes? Thank you."

The picture needed to make about $1.25 million in bids before it could be sold. Mrs. Driscoll wouldn't accept less, and had told her frankly that she would like $2 million. Peter raised his paddle again, at $850,000. A third buyer raised a paddle, a woman Claire recognized. She saw Bernice enter, notebook in hand, lending latecomer support. A minute longer and she might have missed it. Frank, she saw, turned when Bernice walked up the aisle to find an empty seat two-thirds of the way up. He then looked again at Claire, who could not move from her spot, right now, although she longed to greet him. More movement in the back. Thom Driscoll had come in. She didn't believe he wanted to bid on this painting—he must have wanted to see how much it brought, for his mother. And Adelaide, unhappy Adelaide, at his side. Were these the interested parties George had mentioned at the beginning of the sale?

"One million," George said, and the crowd, such as it was, oohed, as always happens when a painting hits that magic number. It was Peter's paddle. She wondered who his client was. Thom Driscoll raised his hand, at $1.25 million. He *was* bidding, too! What could he want with this? Did he wish to possess it, did his sylphlike wife want it? Did his mother ask him? "In the back. Ah," said George, recognizing him. "Thank you. Do I hear one-point-five?"

Peter raised his paddle. Frank whispered in his ear. Frank. Whispering. She was astonished at Thom Driscoll, however, whom she had written off as a businessman whose interests in art lay only in possessing it to appear cultured, despite the genuine culture of his mother, and Adelaide as the sullen let-it-all-go daughter. Claire was shocked at her continuing naïveté. She should have considered the possibility of this. Thom may have been ruthless and callous in business. But he was also a son who loved his mother. We can be both. We can be stern and solitary and still aching for love. Again, she must have judged wrong. Again, her instincts were unsound. He raised his paddle again, at $1.75 million. Her eyes met his, and he gave her a nod of amused recognition. He, like so many men in her life, had been keeping something from her. He had probably never even told his mother.

We so rarely know what others think, and we think we can read the minds of those we love, those we have grown up with, those we wish to become close to. She had spent her career studying not only the images on canvas, but the faces of colleagues, friends, and had been wrong so often she wanted to laugh at her folly. Thank God she could laugh—and now that she had seen the smile on the face of the man she had come to regard as maybe, perhaps, a lover, she wanted to throw her head back and cry, "I was wrong!" She was right about this picture, she was right about a lot of art, she was wholly in the dark about other people.

"Two million," George said, and the crowd murmured approval as the number increased. "Sold!" No matter how this sale went off, she had sold this painting. And it looked like Thom Driscoll was the buyer. She wondered what his mother would say. She wondered what he'd do with it. Claire had managed to sell the painting, back to the family that had consigned it, an odd journey for it. An odd way for a son to show—what? Love for his mother? Love for art.

Love for his wife. Love for secret transactions. She barely understood her own motives, let alone anyone else's. Was she herself coming back home, a widow of the heart returning to a family that had been rent by sorrowful misgivings?

She wondered how Frank would react when she spoke with him, when she told him what she would do. She would speak with him. Very soon. She couldn't wait. The sale seemed suddenly slower. Oh, sell, she thought, wishing the works whisked away so she could turn her attention from the work she loved to a man she might. She had been so afraid of losing whatever it was she thought she'd kept for herself all these years after being with Peter that she had deceived herself about what made people tick. She just didn't know. Art did not teach her that. She learned to reappraise, perhaps, what life taught her through the refraction of artists' meanings. She could only know other people by beginning to trust more, fear less, move on. She couldn't live in the works she admired, she couldn't be as one of those solitary women whiling away a forlorn afternoon of feeble hope or extinguished dreams. She needed to move beyond the canvas. Life wasn't art, but then, so what? Its symbols were harder to decipher, but surely the rewards greater. Yes, she thought, of course I can think of Frank. Of course. Haven't I been? She smiled again. She sought his eyes looking for her—had they ever really left her? She had heard his words gush out at her when they'd been together. How could she not have known someone so bursting with life wouldn't want to share it with her, was trying desperately not to keep it in any longer? "A Widow" had gone home. And so would she. Of course. It seemed right, it seemed odd, it seemed scary. It didn't matter. She would see what happened. Frank. Oh, Frank. Oh, the time ahead for us. Oh, well. Who knew? It certainly wouldn't hurt, especially now, to try. She'd been wrong before.